Killing Pit

John Kelly

New Generation Publishing

Dad suffered with Parkinson's disease. This book is dedicated to him.

"I saw that, of the natures that contended in the field of my consciousness, even I could rightly be said to be either, it was only because I was radically both."

The Strange Case of Dr Jekyll and Mr Hyde

By Robert Louis Stephenson (1886)

Prologue

Epping Forest
September 2005

Martin Pope suddenly pulled over. Jason Cameron saw his chance. He overtook the surveillance convoy, screeched to a halt behind Pope's car and dragged the bastard out.

The surveillance convoy converged like angry dogs. Everyone involved aghast. Trevor Mason, the surveillance commander went berserk.

'You bloody idiot, Cameron. This isn't a game. Arresting Pope won't help us find the boy.'

Cameron snarled, 'The little shit is giving you the run around.'

Martin Pope got bail after four hours. Insufficient evidence to hold him they said. Somehow Pope spotted the surveillance team, commenced a game of cat and mouse, making obscene gestures at the surveillance officers.

Without warning Mason lunged at Cameron, forcing a beefy sergeant from Liverpool to separate them. 'Cool down you two. Let's try and co-operate.'

Cameron spat on the ground. 'Co-operate, I don't need your co-operation. I'll find the boy.'

He marched Pope toward a green surveillance van, keys still in the ignition, pushed Pope into the back and locked the doors. Like rabbits in headlight beams, no one moved.

Martin Pope, spectacles perched on his beak nose sat in the rear of the van peering out of the back window, amused by the scene unfolding before him. Oh yes, he'd given them the run around all right, his smug look said it. Pope knew without the boy they had no evidence and he wouldn't cough anything. They tried to interrogate him with their tricky questions and false rancour. The little bastard had the best brief in London.

Mason rounded on Cameron again. 'Let him go Cameron, this isn't helping the boy.'

Cameron grinned, walked toward the driver's door of the van, daring Mason to try something. He climbed in the driver's seat, slammed the door and drove off. He could see them in the rear view mirror scuttling about, running for their cars like confused rats. Jason Cameron knew the forest; they didn't. Within five minutes of driving without lights along the narrow forest roads he'd lost them.

The last place the police would look would be the scout hut. Confident, he made his way there. Parking up near the hut he opened the van doors to see a grinning Pope, arrogant expression illuminated by the interior light.

'Doesn't matter what you do to me, I won't say anything'

Cameron shoved him backwards.

'Shut up Martin.'

He rummaged through the little wooden drawers in the back of the van to discover a treasure trove of sticking tape, tiebacks and tools. He noticed a portable CD player and thought about taking it, wincing at the thought of Pope screaming under the pressure of Blake's attention.

Cameron's alter ego, Blake, whispered inside his head. 'Tie him up and take him to the scout hut. Then leave it to me.' Adding for good measure, 'He will talk, trust me. And bring the CD player.'

Cameron thought about the missing boy. Scared, hungry; getting weaker by the minute. If they had any chance of getting the boy back alive they needed to act quickly. Blake was eager to get on with it; Cameron still not totally convinced knowing the consequences if they failed to find the boy.

Cameron covered the hut's four small windows with black bin liners whilst Blake remained passive inside his subconscious. Cameron ripped electricians tape with his teeth, stealing the odd glance at the surrounding woodland.

A half hour later a dog-tired Cameron allowed Blake to take an active role. It was Blake who hauled Pope out by his hair, heaved him like a deer carcass through the door of the scout hut; his head clouting the doorframe.

With one final peek at the surrounding woodland, ensuring they were alone, Blake quietly closed the door to the outside world and with it any doubts he may have harboured about the course of action about to be undertaken.

Blake knew that for Cameron it wouldn't be that simple. Cameron would have doubts. It was his nature.

Cameron didn't agree with torturing Martin Pope. Blake certainly did. It was Blake's idea to snatch Pope under the nose of Cameron's police colleagues and drive him to the scout hut. With good reason since Blake believed this was the most expedient way of finding the boy. After five minutes of intense persuasion, Cameron acquiesced.

With his terrified captive manhandled to his feet, Blake removed Martin Pope's spectacles. With pure spite he crushed them under his boot. He forced Pope onto a wooden chair, took off Pope's shoes and socks; peeled away his piss wet trousers and underpants and secured his hands behind his back with electrician's tape. Blake's final *coup de grace* was fastening Pope's stumpy lower limbs to the chair legs using black plastic tiebacks.

Satisfied with his trussing, Blake savagely ripped

the tape from Pope's mouth.

'Children are precious,' he snarled, 'and shouldn't be used to satisfy your disgusting perversion.'

Pope pleaded, 'Please, stop it. I don't know anything about the missing boy.'

'Yes you do Martin.'

Blake took the hammer from the pocket of Cameron's black leather jacket, rolling it around in his hands, admiring its simplicity.

'Martin, I know you took the boy; witnesses saw your car. Tell me where he is otherwise...'

Taking the hammer firmly by the wooden stem, he swung it in the direction of Pope's genitals. Pope winced and twisted, his party sausage penis flopping about between his legs.

Blake smiled, amused.

Sliding behind Pope, Blake switched on the portable CD player and popped the disc. He examined the play list, grinning. Returning the disc he pressed the play button. The first track, a Trini Lopez classic, boomed from the speakers: *If I had a hammer*. DS Mason had good taste.

Grabbing Pope's face, Blake squeezed. 'Where is the boy?'

Pope's eyeballs the size of marbles, roved the oblong room, the hut empty except for a wheelchair parked in the corner.

'Please... don't hurt me.'

Blake lowered the hammer. Pope blew a relieved sigh, sweat bubbling across his forehead.

Cameron couldn't allow this to happen. It went against his moral code. He returned, forcing Blake back.

Cameron realised he was close to allowing Blake to take over the integration. If that happened, he would be submitting to the will of Blake. That would have dire consequences for Martin Pope.

In his late teens, Cameron found a fox in a field; peppered with shotgun pellets, the fox emitted a pitiful scream, doll eyes pleading to be put out of its misery. Cameron couldn't do it; he walked away. Moments later, Blake returned. Like a twig, he snapped its neck.

With tremendous effort and willpower Cameron kept Blake at bay, knowing that without strong medication Blake could return without warning. The ordeal of holding on drained him of energy. Shattered, Cameron flopped into the wheelchair. It rolled into the wall with a clunk. Trying his best to remain focused, desperate to remain in control; he slowed his pulse, regulated his breathing, his body wracked with tension, Blake eager to take command.

If Cameron did allow Blake to take over, would Pope divulge the whereabouts of the boy? Was torturing him the best way of getting Pope to talk?

In truth, Cameron didn't know. This doubt, according to Blake is the enemy of good coppers engaged in crime detection. And Cameron truly believed he was a good copper. He believed the constraints upon policemen favoured the criminal. Blake knew this. He depended on it.

Cameron glared at his sweating palms: Blake muttered inside his head, desperate to return again.

In disbelief, Martin Pope's eyes widened. 'I know **you**,' he insisted, twisting his head from side to side, seeking a better view of Cameron's face. 'I've seen you before, when you were younger. It is you; you're the boy from the pit.'

Cameron felt light-headed; the memory of the killing pit washed over him, made him weak, confused.

Blake saw all of it from deep inside Cameron's brain. He sensed Cameron faltering, the doubts rising. Cameron fought to hold on. Unfortunately for Martin

Pope, Cameron was failing, miserably.

Suddenly, Blake burst from Cameron's subconscious.

Eyes filled with blood rage, leaping from the wheelchair Blake took the hammer and pirouetted like a demented dancer. With Cameron no longer in control, his alter ego firmly in command Cameron would be unable to remember anything.

'I'm Blake,' he hissed into Pope's face. 'I exist, believe me, I really do. I must confess though, much of my existence has been piecemeal.' He grinned. It looked like hell. 'Here one minute, gone the next!'

Pope's mouth gaped, his bottom lip quivered.

'I'm telling you this because from this point on you're not dealing with Jason Cameron. He is resting. Cameron the cop, living by the rules. So: no good cop bad cop routine, just little ole me.'

Blake raised the hammer and smashed it hard onto Pope's big toe splattering it like a raspberry just as Trini sang the words, *hammer in the morning.* Fragments of skin stuck to the metal head. Pope squealed like a wounded piglet, pleas drowned by the booming music, blood dripping onto the linoleum floor, Blake singing along to the tune.

Blake loved rhythm in police work. He brought the hammer down a second time making an awful mess of Pope's other big toe.

Blake, eyes wide, face contorted, flicked his tongue, snakelike. 'Where is the boy, you filthy pervert?'

Through horrendous pain, Pope nodded with some enthusiasm, tears and snot mixed with phlegm, making him gag, heart rate hammering faster than the beat of the music, his feet exploding in pain.

'Promise you won't hurt me again, please. I'm begging you.'

Blake made a show of lowering the hammer. 'The

pain ends when you tell me where to find the boy.'

'I buried him in a pit. I'll take you, I promise.'

'For your sake Martin,' Blake snarled, 'I hope he's alive.'

Chapter 1

Haughton Village, North Yorkshire,
18 months later.

Thursday morning. The rain finally stopped.

Jason Cameron's stomach tightened. He looked skyward through the grubby windshield at the canopy of dark green. Droplets of rainwater leaked through fingers of foliage. The forest swallowed them.

Doctor Kumar's words flashed into his head:

'The subconscious mind is like a forest. Blake is in there somewhere, hiding.

'Is it much further?' Cameron asked.

'About another five minutes,' Lukas Meek shouted above the noise of the diesel engine, the jeep's wheels spinning, fighting to gain purchase on slippery rocks.

'What killed it?'

Lukas shook his head; black locks flicking the side of his rugged face, a gold earring swaying back and forth. His black beard stained brown near his mouth by cigarette smoke.

'Could have been a wild dog,' he said. 'Badger baiting, can't really tell. The head is the only thing intact. Say, Harry Mullen wasn't happy about the forestry dragging you up here. Mullen said it was bugger all to do with the CID, so what's your interest?'

Cameron thought about this. In two weeks it was the only time he'd been allowed to stray from his desk, Detective Inspector Mullen having buried him in paperwork, Cameron immersed in examining uniform arrest files, checking evidence, ensuring continuity. Boring, bloody boring. He thought he was here to help.

Eventually he said, 'Maybe I fancied a ride in the forest, you know to get me out of the office.'

An indignant Lukas said, 'So long as you realise it

isn't a playground mate, there's at least fifteen square mile of trees. And it's bloody dangerous.'

Cameron shuffled in his seat, his next question superfluous. He asked it anyway: 'Have people been lost in here?'

Lukas sniggered, explaining, 'Too true, once or twice I've helped coppers look for hikers who stray off the public footpaths. They walk in circles because everywhere looks the same, unless of course you know where you're going.' He laughed again. Stifling his rancour he looked sideways at Cameron for longer than necessary given the treacherous route.

'Sometimes when they have mountain bike races in here, we paint the trees with green arrows, keeps them on the outside edge of the forest, safer that way.'

Once or twice Cameron noticed yellow dots about the size of tennis balls painted at waist height.

'And the yellow dots painted on the trees? What's their significance?'

Lukas shrugged. Cameron noticed his cheeks turning pink.

Lukas was unsettled, nervous, finding it difficult to navigate the forest despite his supposed local knowledge.

Cameron said, 'I get the distinct feeling you don't like the police?'

Lukas gripped the steering wheel, the tendons on his arms like taut leather straps.

'If the police don't bother me, I don't bother them.'

It didn't answer Cameron's question although it did offer an indication of the indignation he could feel emanating from Lukas. There was something else Cameron recognised. It felt like a distant echo, an intangible memory trace. There was something about Lukas Meek. Something peculiar about his voice; his irritating manner.

'The forest is like a massive bowl,' Lukas said. 'The land round here was pummelled by big rocks from outer space.' He poked his face close to the windscreen, looked skyward.

Cameron said, 'You mean meteorites?'

'Yeah, meteorites.' Then he muttered something under his breath.

Suddenly, Lukas braked; Cameron forced to grab the dashboard with both hands, the track ending in a sentry-like wall of looming pine trees dark and forbidding.

'Damn, I think I took a wrong turn.'

The battered jeep smelled of engine oil and dogs adding to the nausea Cameron already felt.

'Only joking.' Lukas sniggered, a sound that wore at Cameron's nerves.

They veered left down a rutted path and deeper into the forest, Cameron thought about the film *Deliverance* when Burt Reynolds ploughs through undergrowth heading for the river. No rivers in Winston forest. His childhood memories held images of small streams, bubbling to life after heavy rain feeding a green spongy carpet of moss and lichen.

After a mile of driving in silence interrupted only by sinewy branches thwacking the bodywork the jeep finally crunched to a halt. Without a word Lukas got out, paused for a second and then disappeared into the forest. Cameron lost sight of him for a couple of minutes. What's he doing now, the idiot?

Bugger it.

Finally deciding he should show willing, Cameron looped his camera strap around his neck, tucked his trousers into his socks and climbed out of the cab, stepping into a muddy puddle that turned his foot into a wet sponge. Lukas reappeared on the track, gave Cameron an odd look, head tilted to one side.

'Harry Mullen told me you were Mrs Moon's son.'

Cameron nodded expecting an inquisition.

Instead, Lukas smiled and said, 'Sad about your mother.'

Cameron refused to dwell on the concept of sadness; he'd been described once by a colleague as melancholic. The colleague had been unaware that Cameron's mother had recently been murdered after an intruder broke into Gatekeeper Cottage where his mother, Heather Moon, had been sleeping.

She'd disturbed the intruder and felled by a fatal blow to the head with a hammer. A local criminal, Frank Slack had been arrested and charged with her murder. Regrettably the case against him had proved weak and worse, vital evidence had been misplaced causing the whole case to collapse.

'So you knew Heather?'

Lukas picked up a stick, throwing it into the undergrowth. Cameron half expected a dog to appear since he'd noticed an abundance of dog hairs clinging to the greasy upholstery. A chunky silver dog chain sat on the back seat.

'Yeah, I used to see Mrs Moon in the forest.'

'She enjoyed it here.' Cameron looked off into the trees thinking of Heather.

Lukas also looked toward the tree line. When he eventually spoke his tone was sombre, reflective.

'Yeah, I like it in here.'

Cameron wasn't eager to move from the track into what seemed like a daunting canopy of conifers. Entering the forest thirty minutes earlier his anxiety had been on red alert. His concerns had settled, the snake writhing in his gut, dormant. Any expectation of discomfort had morphed into excitement; similar to the feeling experienced when you haven't driven a car for a while after a road accident; scared at first, then eager to get on with it.

'I know about you, Sergeant Cameron.' Lukas glared at him. 'Mrs Moon told me you got lost in here when you were a kid.'

Cameron wasn't surprised Meek knew about his ordeal. Someone was bound to mention it. His mother though? Now that was strange.

'What else did she tell you?'

Lukas's gormless smile revealed broken stumps of teeth. 'Told me she had a son who was a cop in London.'

'I probably won't be a cop much longer.' Cameron shrugged. 'And I no longer live in London.'

Lukas spat, rubbing the mucus into the soil with the heel of his boot.

'That's a disgusting habit.'

Lukas spat again, this time not bothering to rub it in.

'He got away with it you know,' Lukas said. 'Frank Slack.'

He evidently wanted to talk about the case, so Cameron humoured him.

'The CPS wouldn't pursue the case,' Cameron offered, 'due to lack of evidence. If new evidence is uncovered he could be rearrested.'

Lukas found another stick and snapped it in half, the resounding crack reverberating through the trees, its echo lingering. Birds set up a cacophony of startled calls.

Quieter now Lukas said, 'Doesn't it bother you, the fact he got off?'

Cameron shrugged again. He didn't commit, moving away from Lukas who was edging closer each time he spoke, invading Cameron's personal space.

Cameron said, 'I've asked for the case to be reviewed.'

Lukas raised his voice an octave, interested. 'What

16

does that mean?'

'It means the Chief Constable can re-open the case against Frank Slack, have a fresh look at the evidence.'

'Can they do that, have a fresh look?'

'Lukas can we get on with this before I change my mind?'

Cameron insistent as frantic anticipation replaced his original anxiety.

They set off into the trees, Cameron a few feet behind Lukas, the smell of decay and mould fuelling his memories.

'How long were you lost?' Lukas called over his shoulder.

'Three days.'

'What did it feel like?'

'Hey, I was just a kid, eight years old, my memory has faded.'

'How did you get out?'

'A man found me wandering and took me to the police.'

Lukas stopped. Raising his hand like a soldier he sniffed the air.

'What a bloody stink, can you smell it?'

The stench of death, human or animal is easily recognisable and never forgotten; it clings to your nostrils, crawling inside you, sticking to your clothes for days.

'Down there.' Lukas gestured to a natural pit six feet deep, roughly twelve yards across, about ten wide stretching into the forest.

Cameron stepped closer and peered over the edge. In the pit lay the corpse of a badger, ripped to pieces; the head the only thing intact, its glassy eyes staring up into the trees.

Crouched on his haunches Lukas plucked tobacco from a small tin. Casually rolling a cigarette in his

17

fingers he lit up inhaling deeply. 'Could have been a dog; you know, a stray.'

Cameron was thankful for the purging aroma of smoke.

Fat black flies smothered the animal's body, busy laying offspring in the little that remained of the flesh.

'The carrion been busy,' ventured Lukas.

With a handkerchief held to his nose Cameron clambered down the crumbling soil of the embankment. The smell increased, disgusting and ripe. He'd seen his fair share of post mortems but this clawed at his gut, made him wretch.

'Any animal tracks?' Cameron managed to ask.

Lukas scratched his shaggy black beard; exhaled smoke.

'Loads of tracks mate. My guess is it's been here a couple of days and every predator for miles around has stopped by for a takeaway.'

Cameron used his Polaroid camera to take a few snaps, trying to take his mind off the smell.

'Who reported it?' He looked towards Lukas, forced to narrow his eyes as a shaft of sunlight pierced the canopy. Cameron shifted his position, careful not to step in the bloody mess around him.

'A couple of hikers came across it.' Lukas removed his cap, scratched his greasy hair. 'Guess they followed the stink.'

'Is it badger baiting?' asked Cameron.

Lukas took another drag on his cigarette. Let it penetrate his lungs.

'If it's not badger baiting, what else could it be?'

Cameron wasn't sure what to make of the mess or indeed the vile individual who guided him to it.

Cameron stared at Lukas for a couple of seconds before answering. 'I haven't a clue. At a guess, I would say this is the remains of several animals, not just a

18

badger.'

Lukas scowled, 'Dead animals are dead animals. Can't see what all the fuss is about.'

Cameron caught a glimpse of something in the trees, no more than slight movement. Something or someone circled them.

'What's that over there?' He pointed to a pile of cut logs.

Lukas absently looked into the forest, shrugged.

'Probably a deer, there are loads in here.'

'Are you sure? It looked more like a big dog.'

Lukas shook his head mumbling 'city dwellers.'

Cameron didn't believe him. A large dog had been stalking them, he was sure of it. Satisfied it had disappeared back into the thickest part of the forest he relaxed a little and took a few shots of the scene. After five minutes they walked back to the jeep returning to Winston, mostly in silence, Lukas occasionally muttering.

Chapter 2

Sitting in his black Jaguar in the small car park at the back of Winston police station, Detective Chief Inspector Victor LaSalle thought about "Operation Bifurcate." He decided he detested it.

Impeccably dressed, he was a precise and deliberate man whose stoic manner hid any hint of passion. His intolerance of bull-shitters had earned him respect and admiration.

Looking up at the two story building, Victor felt a pang of nostalgia. The building meant more to him than simply bricks and mortar. Lately Police stations like Winston have come up for sale. Sometimes they are converted into expensive apartments. Victor read the plaque embossed into the mortar above the rear entrance and reflected on the station's history.

Winston police station had been built in the 1930s using sandstone. It stood like a bastion on the edge of town, a reminder of distant days when policing was Dixon of Dock Green and Z Cars style; a style Victor relished. The ground floor with its snooker room, small kitchen and enough office space for a single desk each, housed ten uniform police officers, working in shifts until its recent scale down. Despite his protestations to the Chief Constable, only a Detective Inspector and a Detective Sergeant now remained and one custody sergeant posted on a temporary basis until it closed for good and sold off. Victor knew that whoever is lucky enough to buy a former police station can make a tidy profit. Victor knew the new owner very well. He didn't need the money.

The station had been sold three months ago by the Chief Constable. In her briefing document to her senior officers Christine Krill outlined how she believed it had outlived its usefulness. *Her police officers* would be better deployed from the more modern station at Scarborough over fifty miles away.

Victor had witnessed the Chief persuade the local Parish Council it was the best thing, promising the money raised would go toward recruiting more officers to patrol the streets of Winston. She'd been aided in her machinations to the council by a very influential local landowner and Chair of the Parish Council, one Walter Slack; Victors surrogate grandfather, now the proud owner of Winston police station.

Before it could undergo the transformation into swish apartments, it had one last swansong.

Victor flicked through the briefing documents given to him by the Chief Constable.

Jesus, he thought, this kid Jason Cameron is one sorry mess. And here sat Victor LaSalle, deceiving him, pushing him into a corner, for what? To satisfy a weird concept dreamt up by a mad doctor and an ambitious Chief Constable.

Victor had been persuaded by the Chief to participate in the operation, placating him with promises of promotion, something she knew Victor craved. He understood the requirement for flamboyance in the police service but the operation stretched the boundaries of modernity.

The briefing document read like a medical case study. Cameron had the symptoms of a man in disarray, his life unfolding like the thread on a worn out tapestry.

Cameron's mother had allowed his father custody, ignoring the boy for most of his formative years. A drunken, self-pitying individual, Cameron's dad killed himself, never fully recovering from the breakdown of his relationship with Heather, Cameron's mother.

The document outlined his role in the traumatic undercover operation in London involving a paedophile ring and the accusation of manslaughter following the

21

death of a paedophile in Cameron's custody.

It was all there, laid out like an epitaph. The Chief Constable had said, *'take on some of the characteristics of his father; it will speed up the operation.'*

Victor, at first reluctant, now rose to the challenge, believing it would convince the higher ranks that he could be flexible, flamboyant even.

Victor stopped reading. He contemplated how he should play his part in the custody suite. Vodka might help.

Hang on a minute. He never drank during the day, never.

Victor rationalised his behaviour. He was up for promotion therefore his participation in the operation is necessary. It was a little over the top though asking him to pretend to be a heavy drinker, *and a philanderer.* OK, let's face it, the latter wasn't difficult.

Victor took a swig from his hip flask.

He read the final page of the "Operation Bifurcate" briefing sheet again, marked, 'Police Eyes Only' written in red:

"Detective Sergeant Jason Cameron suffers from Dissociated Identity Disorder. It's a rare condition stemming from psychological causes. It can result in the manifestation of two or more distinct and separate personalities existing in the same person.

Cameron's diagnosed condition was instrumental in his acquittal of the killing of Martin Pope, a known paedophile who died in Cameron's custody.

During the interrogation of Cameron by the Metropolitan Police, his other personality, using the name Blake, stated he had vital information which would identify the killer of Heather Moon, Cameron's mother who was brutally murdered at Gatekeeper Cottage in the village of Haughton close to Winston,

North Yorkshire, six months ago.

Additionally, Blake says he will assist in the identification of abductors who, twenty years ago snatched a boy named Brian Mullen the son of Detective Inspector Harry Mullen. Brian is still missing.

Detective Sergeant Cameron is effectively pending medical retirement. The Chief Constable of North Yorkshire Police, Christine Krill has made the decision, following medical advice, to allow Cameron to operate in Winston. **Cameron still believes he is a serving officer**, *posted to Winston to assist North Yorkshire police as a recuperative gesture.*

The Commissioner of the Metropolitan police has sanctioned the operation, deeming the risk necessary in the pursuit of dangerous criminals who have so far avoided capture using conventional means.

A tap on the car window revealed DI Harry Mullen, shuffling his feet, waiting for Victor to either get out of the car or wind the window down. Victor slid the portfolio under his seat, got out and stretched his legs.

'What is it, Harry?'

'What's going on Victor?' Harry, on the road to retirement, looking dishevelled, worn out.

Victor twitched a smile. 'I've told you, it's on a need to know basis and you don't need to know.' Victor noticed the hurt etched on Harry's face and felt a twinge of regret; he wanted to divulge the depth of the operation to Harry, after all Harry had to deal with Cameron on a daily basis. The chief though, had been unequivocal:

'On no account must anyone outside of the agreed participants be made aware of the operation.'

Harry wasn't in the loop, simple as that.

Mullen said, first looking skyward and then at

Victor, 'There's no way Lonnie Slack is involved in drugs. It's not his style.'

Lonnie Slack, Walter Slack's grandson, had been arrested, by arrangement as it happened, as part of the operation.

'Sleep with dogs and you get fleas, Harry.'

Victor realised the remark had been a stupid thing to say. No wonder Harry looked bemused.

'What's that supposed to mean?'

Victor couldn't think of anything to add. He'd persuaded Lonnie to assist in the operation by offering him a chance to get on the good side of his grandfather Walter Slack who believed the boy was a loser.

'Deal with DS Cameron like I told you last week. Just roll with it, Harry, and then you can retire in a couple of months, pension intact and a wife who still wants you in her bed.'

Harry stiffened. Victor made himself ready for a physical attack. It didn't materialise. Harry spat on the ground then stormed off toward his house next door to the police station. Victor felt awful. With a bit of luck though, Harry might vent some of his anger on DS Cameron. That could enhance the chances of the operation arriving to a swifter and hopefully successful conclusion.

Then again, what would constitute a successful conclusion? Victor didn't know. Since this began he'd felt like bloody Oliver Reed; even began to look like him.

Victor got back into his car and read the final paragraphs of the briefing document:

"The alter ego calling himself Blake, has agreed to assist in the operation providing Cameron has no knowledge of the said operation. His rationale for this request is one of safety for his existence. He feels

24

Cameron will resent his involvement and hamper his chances of identifying the criminals.

Doctor Ashram Kumar, a qualified psychologist and adviser to the National Crime faculty, will monitor the operation. He has communicated with Blake, agreeing a set of emotional triggers, which will allow Blake to manifest himself through Jason Cameron, and so enable him to identify those responsible for the said abduction and the murder of Heather Moon.

Victor blew air through his lips. What a weird way to manage a police operation.

**

Metropolitan police stations were hustle and bustle. Sweating bodies crowding into small waiting areas; cell walls adorned with graffiti; lewd comments etched in plaster walls. Shouts could be heard from prisoners in cells, detectives walking the corridors grumbling about working overtime. And traffic, human and vehicular, seemed to be never ending.

In comparison Cameron thought Winston police station was quiet, eerie almost, with old-fashioned sash windows, carefully laid out notice boards: a clinical atmosphere, no mess, no ambience.

The first floor CID office was unusually spacious. A computer terminal lounged in the corner, giving access to the Police National Computer and the criminal intelligence systems. The room had the perfect layout for a forward command post.

Sitting at his desk, Cameron wondered if this was where they held briefings about his mother's murder?

During the murder enquiry Cameron regularly visited Winston police station. The Chief Constable, sympathetic, yet determined to keep him away from the case, agreed he could speak to Harry Mullen, the senior investigator, at force headquarters thirty miles away. Harry awkward in his dealings with Cameron deflected him away from the enquiry teams in an indignant fashion. Cameron understood why. Harry believed it would be unhelpful to involve him. After all, he'd only recently signed off sick leave following mental exhaustion, the result of a protracted undercover commitment and a harrowing court case.

Throughout his career, Cameron had been aloof, a loner with few friends. Often colleagues made representations to superiors, not wanting to work with him. *'He's off his head,' 'bloody dangerous,' 'can't trust him.'* Cameron's unpopularity made him a recluse until they discovered his flair for undercover work

No one doubted his ability in undercover operations. Cameron had been surprised by how many came forward to provide character evidence in his favour during the internal enquiry and his subsequent trial for manslaughter.

Cameron had unusual talents and the police service had utilised them to good effect. The toll on Cameron's mental health was massive. He insisted there was no way he was going back undercover until the Martin Pope operation came along. By then Cameron no longer believing he could detach himself from the disturbing and despicable subject matter of the operations. The Pope assignment overwhelmed him, Cameron becoming detached from reality, and worse still, he ceased to function as a policeman.

Two weeks since he'd walked through the front doors of Winston police station. In that time he'd managed to read through the boxes of witness statements in Harry Mullen's office, examining the forensic evidence from the scene of his mother's murder at Gatekeeper Cottage. The Chief Constable had agreed; poke around if he must, as long as he didn't interfere with the ongoing enquiry into the death of his mother.

Cameron satisfied Harry Mullen's team had done a reasonable job. The detectives had conducted themselves professionally by following the evidence trail, which pointed definitively at Frank Slack. His hammer, his fingerprints on the metal stem. Case closed.

Slack, a known house burglar, had been seen by witnesses talking to Heather Moon outside the cottage the day she died. When the hammer went missing, the CPS dithered, dropped the charges; the enquiry team becoming disillusioned, simply going through the motions. The euphoria of catching Slack dampened like water on hot coals.

DI Mullen shouted Cameron from his glass fronted office, 'Lonnie Slack is in the cells. He's been caught with a bag of cannabis in his car. Paperwork's on your desk.'

Mullen adding: 'Remember Jason; treat Lonnie like any other suspect.'

Cameron intended chatting informally with Lonnie after the official interview, aware the opportunity to grill Lonnie Slack was too good to miss. Lonnie was the alibi witness for his uncle Frank, the murder suspect. Cameron grabbed his worn leather briefcase, gulped the last of his tea then headed to the custody office.

Outside the cell area, Cameron pressed the entry button. The Sergeant, perched on a high stool behind the charge counter, was tall, stick thin with a waxy complexion. Cameron hadn't seen him before. He wouldn't have looked out of place showing tourists around a museum. A white handkerchief poked from his shirtsleeve with expensive looking black cufflinks

27

replacing buttons. A gold watch hung loosely from the sergeant's skinny wrist.

Introducing himself, Cameron asked if he could take fingerprints before Lonnie's brief arrived.

'He's with someone. Can you come back later?' The sergeant sounded dispassionate, disinterested.

'I'm sorry; did you say there was someone with Lonnie Slack?' Cameron tried to stay calm, afraid of increasing his stress levels.

The sergeant slammed the desk hatch.

'You'll have to wait.'

Cameron heard laughter echoing up the green tiled corridor from the interview room. He marched past the sergeant's desk and found the door to the tiny room closed. Pushing it open he found Lonnie Slack, feet on the table, amiably chatting with DCI Victor LaSalle.

Cameron couldn't believe his luck. He'd tried each day to bump into LaSalle and now here sat the great man himself, lolling about in an interview room with his bloody prisoner.

LaSalle's rosy complexion indicated he might have recently returned from the gym. His shoes were pebbled with sandy mud rather letting down his otherwise immaculate appearance. Dressed in a pristine grey suit, white shirt, his bright red tie almost matched his ruddy face.

Lonnie Slack in contrast, wore baggy denims and a dinner stained tee shirt, boasting a pock-marked face and runny nose, clear indications of his poor lifestyle.

'What's going on?' Cameron said calmly.

LaSalle avoided looking at Cameron, instead he smiled, said to Lonnie, 'let me know if you hear anything about the burglaries Lonnie.'

Cameron pulled Lonnie's feet to the floor.

'DCI LaSalle, you are contravening the rules of evidence.'

Lonnie made a move to stand up; LaSalle held up a hand. The gesture subtle, enough for Cameron to realise LaSalle was used to being in control.

LaSalle winked at Lonnie, stood up and placed his hands behind his back. His suit jacket slipped aside, revealing flamboyant blue braces.

'Lonnie asked to see me on a personal matter,' LaSalle explained. 'Nothing to do with the case, we're related, you know family.' *Family* was said with teeth clenched.

DCI LaSalle had an aura, little to do with his status; more intrinsic than his rank.

'Sir, I think we should talk out of earshot of the prisoner,' suggested Cameron.

'I agree.' LaSalle pushed past him, Cameron noticed the sickly smell of mints and booze on his breath.

The sergeant hovered in the corridor, ringing his hands like Ebenezer Scrooge.

'Sorry about this Vic, I tried to tell him but he wouldn't have it, he's new.' Visibly dithering, the sergeant taller than LaSalle, yet clear who had the edge.

'Lonnie Slack has been arrested on a drugs charge and I haven't interviewed him yet,' protested Cameron.

LaSalle tilted his head backwards, giving the impression he was insulted.

'Lonnie, as I've already said, is a member of my family DS Cameron and family is what we are made of; wouldn't you agree that without family we are nothing, a blank page. They are the cement that binds us together.' LaSalle waited, watching Cameron, who stood motionless, looking defiantly at LaSalle, trying to find a chink in his armour.

LaSalle continued, 'I'm sorry I've upset you, Cameron, but rest assured I am not here to interfere.' He turned away, and out of the blue added: 'I'm sorry about your mother, it coming so soon after your problems in London.'

Not about to be put on the spot despite the menace in LaSalle's demeanour and the fact LaSalle outranked him, Cameron said firmly but politely, 'I'm not used to being judged from a distance, Mr LaSalle. In the Met it was good practice to have a face-to-face meeting with new colleagues. We can learn a lot from personnel records but I believe in assessing a person's ability by direct contact and interaction.'

Cameron guessed his file would be sitting on LaSalle's desk.

LaSalle shook his head, obviously not too pleased.

'I read your record with interest, DS Cameron.'

His feathers were ruffled, Cameron could tell. LaSalle said, 'In my case, you assume I'm breaking the rules and you also assume I am trying to usurp your authority. You should be grateful, Lonnie will admit on tape, without a solicitor present, possessing the cannabis for his own use. Feel free to ring me later to thank me.'

Cameron, about to speak when LaSalle raised his hand saying between gritted teeth, 'Say another word, DS Cameron, and you and I will fall out.' An asinine grin appeared briefly. 'I really would prefer our first meeting to end amiably.'

LaSalle let himself out of the custody suite without looking back.

Chapter 3

Cameron waited a couple of minutes. Made sure LaSalle had left.

'Why did you allow DCI LaSalle visit Lonnie?'

Ron Stark busied himself typing on the desktop computer, his armpits boiling beneath his crisp white shirt. Beads of perspiration bubbled on his brow like sweating dynamite. Cameron realised he made Stark uncomfortable although he had no idea why. He'd only just met him for crying out loud.

'DCI LaSalle asked to see the prisoner and I had no reason to refuse, especially when Lonnie agreed,' protested Stark

'I don't believe you.'

Stark stopped tapping the keyboard, the room silent apart from the whirring of an overhead fan.

'How long have you been here detective? A couple of weeks? If you're going to survive in the sticks you'll need to be a little more appreciative of the way things work.'

A futile argument; Cameron knew about the town. How everyone seemed related or connected. His father had rented Gatekeeper Cottage in the nearby village of Haughton. Five years for the villagers to eventually accept Michael Cameron. It seemed strange though how those same locals had no problem with Heather, his mother.

Cameron had a thought. Aware custody sergeants were the same countrywide; loquacious kings of their castles, a wealth of information, he ventured, 'Sergeant, what do you know about badger baiting?'

Stark paused in his typing for a second, then continued at a faster pace; hitting the keys hard, annoyed.

'It's a disgusting thing, is badger baiting.' Stark said

above the clatter of his typing. 'Folks round here say it doesn't happen, but I know different. It's the same buggers the local cops bring in for poaching who plunder the bloody sets.'

Cameron recognised insincerity when he heard it. He decided to encourage the dialogue in the hope of learning more.

'Like who?' Cameron leaned on the desk, trying to look relaxed.

'For example, take Lonnie. He's the grandson of Walter Slack who is probably the most well known inhabitant of Winston, and that includes Victor LaSalle.' Stark tugged his handkerchief from his sleeve and blew his nose.

'Walter is the Leader of the Parish Council and a local landowner. He's the man who insists Winston embraces its cultural history including all dubious country pursuits, except for fox hunting which he leaves to the snobs.' He tapped his nose with his finger.

Cameron decided to stroke his ego.

'What do they call you round here?'

Stark stopped tapping the keyboard, thinking about the question.

'*Awkward* mostly.'

A tiny smile twitched the corner of his mouth.

'If they want something they call me Ron.'

Cameron forced a grin and held out his hand. Ron Stark gave it a limp shake.

'Ron, would you mind looking at some photographs?'

Cameron pulled the photographs from his suit jacket and handed them like a pack of cards to Stark, who pushed his spectacles to the end of his nose.

'I didn't realise detectives still used Polaroid cameras. Where were these taken?' He failed to hide the surprise in his voice.

Cameron explained the location. If necessary he could easily find his way back there. During his time as a young patrol officer in London he got into the habit of remembering street names and permanent fixtures, hating the thought of getting lost, realising he could use the same skill in any situation including darkened alleyways, and if necessary, forests.

Stark flicked through the pack again, this time stopping on the close-up shot of the pit. He studied the photograph, Cameron thinking the sergeant looked a little shaken.

Cameron had no idea what the scene represented, he'd guessed something hadn't been quite right.

'What do you make of it?'

Stark laid the photos individually on his desk and passed a hand over them.

'For a start, the injuries to the badger may not the work of terriers, too much...' He searched for the right word.

Cameron said it for him, 'Carnage?'

'That's it, carnage. The dogs don't take long to kill it once it's cornered and tired.' Stark stopped on one particular photograph; he stared at it. 'The amount of footprints say to me they were at it for a long time, the dogs I mean. It doesn't happen that way.'

Stark couldn't hide the excitement in his voice. 'The badger is sometimes shackled; it's normally over in minutes. More importantly, look at the blood and guts, there's more than one dead animal in there.'

'You seem knowledgeable?'

He ignored Cameron's question, began tapping the keyboard again. Finally he said, 'Anyway, there are no sets in that part of the forest.'

'How do you know?'

Stark smiled, showing a perfect set of white teeth.

'I know because I am the wildlife officer for

33

Winston, a volunteer position of course, expenses only.' He added conspiratorially, 'It gets me out of the house and away from my missus.'

Cameron, unimpressed and not warming to the man asked, 'If it is badger baiting, what kind of individual would be involved?'

'That's easy. The kind of individual you're about to interview for drugs possession.' He paused, 'By the way, who reported this?'

'Seems a couple of hikers followed the smell and reported it to the Forestry Commission. They in turn sent a volunteer named Lukas Meek.'

Ron pushed his computer back a couple of inches to emphasise his point.

'No chance. Those tracks up there aren't open to hikers, they're fire roads. The public footpath is miles to the north. The so-called hikers were probably poachers after deer.' Stark appeared genuinely annoyed.

'What do you think did it?'

Ron Stark undid his top button; studied the photos again.

'I have absolutely no idea. I could ask around if you like.'

'That would be helpful.' Cameron collected the photos, signed the paperwork on Lonnie.

'I'll speak to you again when I have a better idea of what's going on.'

Stark nodded.

'By the way,' asked Cameron, 'what's the story with Victor LaSalle?'

The sergeant considered his reply.

'I'll just say this, Vic is an enigma; he must be connected to half the bloody population of Winston. Then again, everyone round here is related somehow, it's bloody incestuous, is what it is.'

'I get the impression Vic likes to throw his weight about?'

Sergeant Stark used his handkerchief on his nose again, harder this time, making a theatrical special effect of it. Cameron stepped back a couple of feet.

'Aw Vic's OK, just don't upset him; he has friends everywhere, and relatives.' He laughed. 'Anyway, more to the point, what's your story?'

Cameron knew that it would be unusual if the police in Winston didn't know he was a burn out. Stark probably wanted to know the inside story to fuel canteen gossip.

'My story goes like this; the Met suspended me after I was investigated for assaulting a prisoner. Following my acquittal, North Yorkshire police offered me the chance of a short term posting here in Winston.' Cameron examined the skeletal face of Sergeant Stark.

'I'm guessing you already knew that. It seems everyone around here knows about me.'

For the first time since their encounter, Ron Stark relaxed.

'Yeah, to be fair I did know. I also know the Chief Constable thought it might be a good idea to put you here because the local hacks will like it, you know keep the station open for a bit longer even though its been sold. You know how it goes. A reporter asks the Chief what she is doing about burglaries in Winston. The Chief informs them very smugly that a newly appointed flash detective from London has been sent to Winston, he'll sort it.'

Cameron raised his eyebrows. It seemed there was more than one story about his posting. He asked Stark,

'What do you know about Lukas Meek?'

Ron pulled a face, avoiding eye contact. 'That scruffy individual is the Billy Liar of Winston. I wouldn't tell him the site of a blackbird's nest.

35

Honestly, the lad is simple, take nothing he says for granted.'

Cameron had been surprised when he'd first met Lukas at the south entrance to the forest. The Forestry Commission said they were busy with seasonal fires and would send a local volunteer who had keys for the forest gates. When Lukas Meek arrived wearing a scruffy green pullover, Cameron had been disappointed. Meek's filthy habit of spitting every couple of minutes together with his shiftiness certainly didn't make him the type of person the Forestry Commission should trust.

'Does Lukas Meek know about the badger sets?'

'He knows they exist, doesn't know were they are though.'

Cameron dropped the photos into his leather briefcase.

He recognised he might need Stark later. 'You haven't asked about my spotted bow tie, everyone asks about the bow tie.' He said nonchalantly.

Ron Stark folded his spectacles, gently returning them to their case.

'Listen, for all I know, all London detectives look like biology professors who wear tatty suits and bow ties.'

Cameron laughed; his rancour false.

'By the way, I'm sorry about your mother.' Stark sounded like a priest, saying it like an afterthought. Cameron felt uneasy.

'Thanks Ron. Please put Lonnie back in his cell, don't want him doing a runner. I'll interview him in a jiffy. I just have a quick call to make.'

Stark about to press the gate release button paused.

'A few of us were a bit surprised when the Chief sold the station. Then out of the blue they sent you here, you know, with your mother being killed and this lot dealing with it.'

Cameron shrugged. 'I do as I'm told.'

Ron Stark hit the release button.

There was something distinctly peculiar about the sergeant. Cameron couldn't put his finger on it.

Chapter 4

The cell reeked of stale piss. Lonnie sat on the bed edge like a smug child, dangling his skinny legs over the rail, giggling.

'Never done that before Uncle Vic.' Lonnie rubbed his hands together. 'You know totally conned a copper. Scary shit this acting business.'

Victor LaSalle shook his head in disbelief.

'Knock it off Lonnie, you enjoyed every second.'

Lonnie screwed his face up, 'Don't like him much do you, Vic?'

'It's not about disliking DS Cameron; it's about not trusting him and everything else about his presence in Winston.'

'Shouldn't you be off, Uncle Vic, he'll be back soon?'

'How many times have I told you Lonnie, I'm not your bloody uncle!'

Victor LaSalle looked after Lonnie Slack, cared for him as one would a younger brother. Not because Lonnie had an inimitable charm, reminding Victor of a useless car salesman, telling the truth about an old banger he was about to sell to an elderly couple; it was more than that, more akin to having a halfwit brother, someone to look after. Since Lonnie had become a teenager, Victor had taken him under his wing, protecting him, watching over him, keeping him safe.

Safe from what though, Victor wasn't sure. Often Victor had feelings of immense dread when he thought about Lonnie. The same feeling you get when you know someone is about to impart bad news. And so, Victor took care of Lonnie, kept an eye on him, always.

'Cameron's got paperwork to attend to. Anyway, I got the feeling he felt very uncomfortable in the interview room, more claustrophobic than a normal

38

person.'

Lonnie picked his nose. He wiped the residue on the bedclothes.

'Why drugs, Uncle Vic, everyone knows I don't do drugs?'

Victor admired Lonnie's inability to spot the obvious.

'The stuff they found in the car was dried leaves. If I'd have used stolen property it's more difficult to explain later when we drop the charges. This way, we can just drop the charges when the stuff is analysed.'

Lonnie made a knowing face and nodded his head, appearing to comprehend the cleverness of the ruse. Victor knew Lonnie had no idea what he was talking about.

'That dog's foot thing is a bit weird, why did you want it?'

Victor didn't answer straight away, preoccupied, thinking about the fall-out the operation might have.

'Apparently,' he answered eventually, 'according to his doctor, Cameron has a dislike of cruelty to animals, particularly dogs. Shortly before Heather Moon was murdered, her pet terrier went missing. The thing you gave me might…' Oh what am talking about, thought Victor. 'Lonnie it's too complicated, just do as you're told, please.'

'What the hell is going on Uncle Vic?

Victor thought about Lonnie's question. How could he realistically answer it when he hadn't the full picture himself? Instead he shrugged. 'Just keep your powder dry Lonnie, I'm going to need you later when things get really weird.'

Victor dragged himself up from the metal chair leaving Lonnie in the cell whistling.

Victor thanked Ron Stark for his co-operation. Debated letting him know a little about what was going on and decided against it. The least Stark knew the better.

Outside the temperature had dropped. It always became colder in this part of Yorkshire at night, even in the summer. He realised he felt the cold a lot more recently. Victor pulled his overcoat tighter, fumbled for his car keys; opened the car door. He slid behind the wheel, the warmth welcoming.

Chapter 5

Deep inside Winston forest Lukas Meek edged closer to the creature locked in the compound.

Meek carried raw meat supplied by the local butcher. A fat smelly man; he took the odd deer carcass from Lukas in exchange for the raw beef preferred by the creature.

Blood from the meat stained his boots, drying brown like mud from a building site. Lukas cautious, head bowed, avoided low hung conifer branches, the trees towering above like massive Christmas trees without baubles.

Leaves rustling to his left startled him. After a quick scan of the trees to satisfy himself no one was about, Lukas moved further into the trees, the plastic bag he carried plump and wet.

The compound languished in a deep gully with natural soundproofing. The miners who built the compound years ago had chosen well. No one ever came to this part of the forest, except to visit the compound; a mere handful knowing its exact location.

Lukas approached the compound gate and slid the key into the massive padlock. The animal, sensing his presence crashed excitedly into the mesh of the metal cage. Lukas undaunted, confident the lupine's presence could not be detected.

God the beast was huge, only a month and at least a stone heavier. In the beginning, when it was a pup, he'd fed it cooked meat. Now he gave it raw meat. As he got closer the lupine howled.

**

Jason Cameron returned to the CID office. He rang the Forestry Commission in Pickering, eventually tracking down a supervisor who worked the Winston area. Cameron introduced himself. He asked about Lukas Meek to learn that Ron Stark had recommended Meek as suitable for the position of volunteer warden. It didn't surprise Cameron. Stark had been a shifty bastard.

He made a note of the two hikers who found the badger set; a husband and wife who lived in Winston. He rang them. The husband explained what they'd found. He described a compound containing metal cages, a long narrow pit and dead animal carcasses scattered about. It wasn't where Lukas Meek had taken Cameron. So why had he lied?

Cameron collected the arresting officer's report on Lonnie Slack; headed back to the custody suite. Since his posting to Winston this was his first prisoner. He blamed Harry Mullen who'd kept him occupied with file checking and telephone enquiries.

Stark was still in the custody suite moaning about working overtime because of Lonnie Slack. Cameron promised Stark he would be 'out, asap'. He grabbed a portable tape recorder from the metal shelf.

Cameron unlocked the cell door to find Lonnie sitting on a metal chair reading a tatty comic. Cameron decided to interview him casually, in the cell, the door open, not wishing to risk bringing on a panic attack. Doctor Kumar had reassured him that Blake, his alter ego was firmly under control. The suppressing medication was strong enough to withstand any of Blake's attempts to invade Cameron's consciousness.

Since accepting the diagnosis of his condition, Cameron had grown less tense concerning the dilemma of his other self. It had been Kumar and the Chief Constable who eventually persuaded him to participate in an operation involving Blake's becoming more dominant. Cameron had first resisted.

Slowly, and with patience they'd instilled into him the importance of Blake being able to assist in tracking down those responsible for his mother's murder. Yes, Cameron would go along. In the beginning he was fully in the picture until Kumar hypnotised him, effectively glossing over the true nature of Blake's involvement.

'It will ensure the operations success,' the Chief said. In other words, like Harry Mullen, Cameron was out of the loop, thus allowing his conscious self to firmly believe he had been genuinely posted to Winston as a recuperative gesture and to give an independent opinion on Victor LaSalle, a man under investigation.

Cameron sat on the only chair. Lonnie had one of those faces made from spare parts. This arrogant, disgusting little man had admitted to possessing cannabis, as DCI LaSalle had promised, probably knowing his grandfather Walter Slack would somehow get him off. After ten minutes of questioning, Cameron switched off the portable tape recorder. He scrutinized Lonnie's feral features.

'I want to have a word about Frank Slack.'

Lonnie smirked. 'You can't talk to me about Frank's court case, I know my rights.'

Cameron's pulse quickened.

'It took you two weeks to come forward with an alibi for Frank, why take so long?'

Lonnie's bottom lip quivered.

'What if it did? I was scared. The cops don't like it when they lose.'

Cameron crossed his legs, the movement necessary, something different in an effort to stop his brain misfiring. He squeezed his thighs together, made fists, hands tightly clenched. All to force Blake back into his hiding place.

He thought about his medication. Cameron wondered if he should increase the dosage.

As calmly as he could, he asked Lonnie, 'Frank Slack's your uncle?'

'So what, it doesn't mean I wasn't telling the truth.'

'The arresting officer's report states Walter Slack is your grandfather and guardian. What happened to your parents, Lonnie?'

Lonnie didn't like the question.

'They went off when I was a kid,' he moaned.

'Granddad wouldn't like it if you verbal me.'

'Is that what you think is going on?'

'Why else do you want to talk off tape? It's not right.' Lonnie's eyelids flickered, his brain searching for the right phrase. 'It's contravening the law.' Lonnie smiled, impressed with himself.

'Badger baiting seems popular round here,' said Cameron nonchalantly

Lonnie fidgeted, 'If you say so.'

'Are you involved in badger baiting?'

'Nope, are you?'

Cameron gripped the tabletop, the veins expanding on his arms. Lonnie noticed the intrinsic change in Cameron's demeanour. His eyes widened, unease locked behind them.

Cameron continued, trying desperately to remain in control.

'Answer the question Lonnie or so help me I'll damn well...'

Lonnie terrified, shouted, 'Ron, get in here, this lunatics threatening me.'

Cameron shook his head violently, slowed his breathing, back in control again.

'That's all for now, Lonnie.'

Once out of the cellblock Cameron relaxed a little. He sure as hell needed a consultation with Doctor Kumar about his medication.

Chapter 6

Cameron poked his head into Harry's office. Harry Mullen had cleared his desk. Harry was such a miserable bloke, forever pouting and rarely cracking a smile. He used to be a charmer and a joker according to his colleagues.

Cameron decided to visit him at home, let him know about Lonnie Slack. Maybe cheer him up a bit.

Time enough though to fire up the office computer. Using an antiseptic wipe from a plastic container in his drawer, Cameron wiped the keyboard and screen, a stickler for cleanliness. Typing in his police temporary identification number and password, he logged onto the Criminal Intelligence System. He searched for the name 'Lukas Meek'.

The computer responded immediately. Nothing. No trace. He wasn't surprised. What did surprise him had been Meek's disclosures about Heather. Unusual, he thought. Bizarre his mother would choose to discuss Cameron with Lukas Meek, a comparative stranger.

He'd noticed Meek's tobacco tin covered in used match stalks. Delicately varnished with lacquer; a tin lovingly made by an inmate incarcerated at Her Majesty's pleasure.

Cameron logged off and tidied his desk. Leaving by the back door he walked through the car park towards the police house next door. The evening was fresh, better than the stuffy confines of the office. The lingering smell of diesel fumes filled the air. Two cars stood in the car park, Cameron's old blue BMW and an expensive looking black Mercedes sports. The number plate on the sports car included the letters RON.

Cameron wondered how the hell could Ron Stark afford expensive cufflinks, gold watches and a sports car?

45

Passing through the gate at the end of the car park Cameron courted the distinct feeling he was being watched. Instinctively he turned around to spot Stark peeping through the barred custody window. Cameron gave him a polite wave. Stark ignored him, continuing to stare beyond Cameron toward the forest, which covered the gently sloping hills surrounding Winston. The conifers watched over the market town like a wooden sentries.

Mullen's wife, Janice, answered his knock. She was a sullen and melancholic woman who hardly ever spoke. Much younger than Harry, she had the bone structure of a stunner, yet preferred to dress down in dark dismal shades, like someone in mourning. On the odd occasion Cameron had spoken to her she'd seemed reluctant to engage in conversation, eyes forever flicking to the floor, anywhere but at him.

'He's round the back,' she told him, gesturing the way.

Cameron found Harry Mullen tending his vegetable garden. The station didn't warrant a full time D.I. and when Mullen retired Cameron knew from the Chief Constable there were no plans to replace him. Barely two months away from retirement and rarely in the office. Not a bad job.

Mullen still wore his grey pinstriped suit; a green pair of Wellingtons protected his trousers. Harry looked his fifty-five years, breathing laboured as he bent over and tugged at weeds loath to let go of their grip in the soil. He doubted Harry would be this reluctant to let go in two months time.

Checking, he discovered Harry had a decent enough record; Cameron knowing from station tittle-tattle that it had been Heather's murder which had finally whittled him down.

He had no axe to grind with Harry. He couldn't

understand why Mullen resenting his raking about in the ashes of his mother's case. But then, Cameron felt he had little to lose by poking about in the muddy waters of an incestuous police force controlled it would seem by Victor LaSalle, informant handler of Frank Slack, the main suspect in his mother's murder; someone who'd been in and out of gaol most of his adult life.

'Need a hand with the weeds, Harry?'

With barely an acknowledgement, Harry said, 'I've spoken to DCI LaSalle about Lonnie Slack.' He kept his head bowed.

Was it Harry Mullen and not Ron Stark who had notified LaSalle when Lonnie had been arrested?

'And?' snapped Cameron

'Victor said you accused him of breaking the rules. He told me you were disrespectful to him in front of a prisoner.' Mullen straightened, eased his back. 'I advised you to put aside your personal feelings, Jason. It's a fact that most people who are dragged through the doors of Winston nick will be somehow connected to the Slack family and Victor LaSalle. Don't push it, lad, just do your job.' Under his breath Harry said, 'Whatever that is.'

Cameron felt his colour rise.

'Harry, La Salle waltzed into the nick and started interviewing Lonnie Slack without permission. Who does he think he is?'

'He, my young colleague, is DCI Victor LaSalle, *your* boss and Lonnie Slack's uncle.' Harry's pause was profound. He met Cameron's eye. 'There's something going on round here and unfortunately, just like you, I'm in the bloody dark.'

Mullen's wife appeared at the kitchen window, gave her husband a wave.

'My tea is on the table,' said Harry, a touch sullenly.

47

His spade plonked against the wooden fence he set off towards the large ivy covered police house. The greenery hid its rotting window frames and broken roof tiles.

'It's OK Harry,' Cameron said to his back. 'Very few people understand my style of police work. Most colleagues don't even like me. You're just another one in a long line.'

Mullen stopped in his tracks, turned to Cameron, and forced a smile.

'That's the first sensible thing you've said since arriving here.' He made to go toward the back door of the house and changed his mind. Arms folded, he said: 'OK, I admit I dislike your familiarity with senior rank and your taste in clothes is odd. Your bloody Cockney accent grates on me. You are an annoying little sod. To be honest I don't care much for you, but for Christ's sake please don't upset the apple cart. We've had enough upset round here to last years. God knows why you are here in Winston. It baffles me. But while you're here I want you to do as you're told.' A little louder he added, 'Do I make myself clear?'

At least now, Cameron knew where he stood. He decided it was a waste of time mentioning the badger baiting. He began to walk away when Mullen said to the back of his head, 'Hand the badger baiting over to the RSPCA, its bugger all to do with the police.'

'I thought it might have some bearing on the stories about the creature stalking the wood.' Cameron said.

Mullen peeled off his Wellingtons, banged them individually on the concrete step leading to the kitchen, appetising aromas of home cooking wafting into the air. Cameron noticed fresh sandy brown mud attached to the heels of the Wellingtons. The soil in Harry's garden was dark brown, peaty.

'Stick to everyday police work. Forget about stories

and tittle tattle.' said Mullen.

About to leave by the garden gate Cameron experienced a subtle change in Harry's demeanour, almost as if a wave of melancholy had descended over the man. Were his eyes moist with the onset of tears?

'I did my best for your mother you know.' He said solemnly. 'Not an easy case. When the hammer went missing and the case collapsed, there was nobody more shocked than me. We all took it badly and yet I still get the feeling you're unhappy about how I handled it.'

Cameron felt some sympathy for Mullen. He'd done his best; unfortunately it hadn't been good enough. Somehow the evidence trail to the main suspect Frank Slack had been broken. That shouldn't happen. Harry Mullen was the senior investigating officer, therefore his responsibility. After six months they'd streamlined the murder team. The witness statements were now stacked in boxes in Harry's office.

'Harry, you're probably the oldest DI in the force. No offence, but you're close to retirement. To be honest you are...' Cameron hesitated, choosing his words carefully. 'Shall we say, lacking in flare and motivation?'

Harry Mullen raised a fist in the air, changed his mind. Instead he said, 'You smug little prick.'

He then slammed the kitchen door.

Janice Mullen, like a jealous lover, watched from behind the kitchen curtains. She'd shared Harry with the job for more than twenty years still resenting its hold over him. It had been Janice who'd persuaded him to finally take the plunge and retire, acutely aware he would forever hold it against her.

Janice couldn't wait to move into their new house on Winston Grange. She was glad to be leaving the crumbling police house. The house was a bit like Harry.

She hoped the move to a different house would cheer Harry up, knowing he would retire grudgingly. Unfortunately the move had been delayed . . . Yes, by Harry's excuses. For some reason she couldn't explain, Janice suspected the cancellation had to do with the arrival of Jason Cameron.

Harry Mullen adored being a policeman. Janice wanted him out of it. She cared about his feelings for the job, although she maybe didn't show it too much. Everyone knew he had high blood pressure, the doctors warning him to be careful. Despite this, Victor had persuaded Harry to take on the murder of Heather Moon knowing full well it would be bad for Harry. But that was Victor LaSalle; get someone else to do it. He'd then take the accolades.

About to turn away, Janice took a little more time to spy on Heather Moon's son. Jason had a way of looking straight through her, reading her thoughts, poking around in her subconscious. Despite his manner, she liked him well enough, handsome in a boyish way, intelligent, exciting, unlike Harry. Janice suspected Cameron had a penchant for poking and prying until he got at the truth.

She whirled as Harry stomped into the kitchen, slamming the door. She noticed his socks had holes in them near his big toe. Like Harry, and the house, the socks were worn out.

'What did he want?' she inquired.

'He's poking about in the hope he might find out who killed his mother.'

Janice started to bite her nails. Hadn't she guessed that already?

'Have you asked him?'

Harry stared at her. 'Asked him what exactly?'

Janice Mullen poked her head through the curtains again. She watched Cameron walk to his car.

Arms folded, she rounded on her husband.
'Have you asked him to help find our son?'

Chapter 7

Cameron leaned back in his metal chair. Tapping his pen on the wooden desk top he thought about Detective Chief Inspector Victor LaSalle.

At his mother's funeral, La Salle stood at the back of the church, head bowed. Cameron had the impression he was one of the undertaker's assistants.

During a meeting with Harry Mullen at the canteen in police headquarters shortly after the funeral, he'd asked Harry about LaSalle. Like a father proudly describing the talents of his offspring, Harry was endearing in his account.

He remembered Harry's words: 'Victor's mother had connections with the travelling community. One day she vanished leaving Victor on the doorstep of the police station wrapped in a blanket. Walter Slack volunteered to raise him.'

Cameron, interest piqued, said, 'It's strange the social services allowing a man like Slack to raise Victor?'

Harry was indignant. 'What do you mean *like* Slack? Social Services agreed Walter Slack could adopt the child because of his standing in the community. Not least because it would be difficult to find parents with Walter's financial backing.'

Cameron let it go.

'How come LaSalle joined the police?'

Harry had been only too pleased to talk.

'Victor joined when he was twenty, after working for Walter on the estate where the new houses are now built. There were rumours that Victor couldn't write when he joined. Some folk believed they 'de fiddled his entry exam because he was a top class hooker, the police being rugby mad.'

Quite a bit about Victor LaSalle intrigued Cameron.

Rising in the ranks like a whirlwind, LaSalle's tactics for dealing with criminals had earned him national recognition. He got massive coverage in the national press. They loved his direct if somewhat draconian attitude to crime and criminals. Two successive Chief Constables of North Yorkshire had ridden on his coat tails. LaSalle's success attributed to his local knowledge; the intelligence supplied to him by his numerous informants, and of course the influence of Walter Slack. For certain, Victor LaSalle was a recognised figure in the local community. Someone you didn't upset.

Right now though, LaSalle didn't seem to be that man.

Making a couple of entries in his official diary he checked in with the control room. The female operator thanked him for this, and assured him there were no messages. 'You can retire from duty now,' she said adding a chirpy 'Mind how you go.'

Thursday, six in the evening. Cameron was tired and hungry.

Grabbing his jacket from the back of his chair, he headed for the door, pausing when he noticed a large envelope in the office in-tray.

The envelope had a brown stain on its front the size of a beer mat; likely soiled by something wet. Since it was addressed to him, he opened it, emptying the contents onto his desk.

Jesus, what the hell is that! Cameron gawked. Shocked and surprised to be looking at the severed paw of what he presumed was a dog. A paw placed inside an envelope after it had been freshly cut.

Cameron searched his drawer, found his flick knife – something he'd hate to be without, just in case – and with the blade he delicately probed and prodded the paw.

He drifted: began to think about Blake. He looked at the knife. Not something he would hate to be without. The white bone handled knife belonged to Blake; his only tangible link with him. Cameron jolted. Why in holy shit would he keep the knife in a drawer in the police station of all places?

The knife held significant memories in his struggle with his condition. Sometime ago whilst working undercover he'd been rumbled by a black drug dealer who recognised him. Cameron had tried to talk his way out of the situation.

The encounter happened inside a filthy toilet block at the back of a pub in Hammersmith. The man gripped Cameron by the throat, threatening to expose him. The next thing Cameron remembered was the man's muffled cries as he pressed his palm onto his bleeding eye socket, blood dripping from the bone handled knife held in Cameron's hand.

The doctors described these episodes as "fugue states" when Cameron lost time and became Blake. The fear of these episodes forever haunted him. They could happen at any time without the control of medication.

Back in the present and shivering, he retracted the blade. He placed the knife in his jacket pocket. Deep breathing exercises helped calm his memory of Blake, enabling him to turn his attention to the appendage.

No note. Neither did the envelope bear any postmark or stamp. So: it must have originated via the internal system.

The corridor was empty; no one had come into the CID office before or after him.

Was it a message or a threat of some kind? Neither prospect alarmed or upset him, but honest-to-God intrigued him.

Carefully placing the appendage on a piece of white paper he took a couple of photos. Unclipping a small leather wallet from his briefcase, Cameron used tweezers to pluck several hairs from the paw. Gingerly, he dropped the hairs into a plastic evidence wallet. Wrapping the paw in a plastic bag, he made his way to the outside waste bins and made a show of depositing the bag there, a clear message of defiance to anyone watching. He washed his hands in the gent's toilet.

Cameron decided keeping the appendage would not be necessary. It had clearly been severed from the limb of a small dog, possibly a terrier.

Pointless making any assumptions about the identity of the sender; a waste of time and energy: Better to let things rumble on until he could piece everything together.

After his arrival in Winston two weeks ago, Samantha Moon, stepdaughter to his mother Heather, had invited him to stay in one of the spare bedrooms at Gatekeeper Cottage. Damned if he could remember if Sam said she would be working late. He'd drop off in town and grab a sandwich before heading home.

Cameron left by back door of the CID office to drive the half-mile to the High Street. Parking his black ten-year-old BMW on the cobbles outside the butchers, he went inside and bought a pork roll.

The High street offered a variety of shops. Good since market towns countrywide were in decline, shuttered shop fronts a grim reminder of what used to be; FOR SALE signs like graffiti emphasising it.

Maybe the new housing on the edge of the forest helped Winston to avoid such decline?

Prior to his transfer, Cameron had read about the protests from locals who believed the housing developments were encroaching on the woodland. In time this would destroy the natural habitat of the wildlife. Not his business, he decided. The sandwich was, since Cameron was starving.

About to attack the sandwich he noticed a small boy standing alone outside the supermarket's front doors.

He looked confused. Cameron bent down; about to ask if the boy was lost when a coarse looking woman dressed in denims grabbed the child. She dragged him unceremoniously away from Cameron, and shot him an accusing look. Before Cameron could explain, she walked briskly away, looking back every so often until she turned a corner. What the hell? Cameron asked himself, three weeks in town and they treat me like a pervert. The woman's reaction had been over the top.

An elderly woman waiting at a nearby bus stop added insult to injury when she shook her head at him in obvious disgust.

Cameron, miffed yet curious at these reactions, continued along the street. At the newsagents he idly examined the books and magazines on the racks. He selected a local magazine entitled "Yorkshire Gateway," its front cover indicating lead stories, one of which definitely piqued his interest since the author was Heather Moon, his mother.

**

The shrilling telephone made Lukas jump. He grabbed the handset uttering a lazy hello.

'It's me,' whispered the caller.

Lukas felt his colour drain. Automatically he stood to attention.

'I didn't say anything, honest,' he bleated.

The tone of his brother Ron Stark sank a lance of terror into his heart.

'Tell me exactly what happened, Lukas. And don't think about lying to me, you moron.'

Lukas nervously rolled a cigarette holding the phone between chin and shoulder.

'The forestry rang me; told me some hikers had found dead animals in a pit. From their description it was bloody obvious they'd stumbled into the compound.'

He paused, lit his cigarette, taking a deep lungful. He hoped for some praise. It didn't come. Lukas continued. 'The forestry sent this copper. Turns out he's Heather Moon's son. Man, I tell you I nearly died.'

'Did he recognise you?'

Lukas laughed.

'No he didn't- incredible right?' Lukas inhaled again, continued excitedly.

'I'd dumped Monday's leftovers into an old badger set thinking I would cover them over later. I took him there and pretended it was what the hikers found.' Lukas cackled. 'The dozy bugger won't have a clue it's a different place.'

'I wouldn't be so sure.'

Lukas sensed annoyance in his brother's tone.

'What should I do?'

Lukas could feel his brother's breath, like a sibilant hiss of disdain vibrating down the mouthpiece.

'Is the lupine ready to fight?'

Lukas relaxed a little. He sat down.

'Stronger than an ox and angry as hell.'

'Have you found the other one?'

Lukas paused, thought about lying.

'He's still roaming the forest.'

'Keep looking.' he hissed. 'For your sake, I hope Jason Cameron is as bonkers as they say and this weird plan of Walter's isn't going to cost us.'

'What weird plan?'

'Oh forget it. Just don't do anything stupid otherwise…'

The line went dead

57

Chapter 8

Cameron parked on the road. He paused to admire Gatekeeper Cottage. Roughly three miles from Winston town centre, the cottage had to be the smallest property in Haughton Village and probably the oldest. Surrounded by forest on three sides its half-acre garden stretched toward the trees.

Overlooking a babbling stream, lush birch trees towered high above the garden. This compensated for the lack of space at the front. The rear section ended abruptly below a hundred foot escarpment; a chunk of overhanging rock like a peaked cap maintained a permanent shade.

Rounding the corner, he felt heartened to see Samantha Moon reclining in a deck chair enjoying her favourite herbal tea. Samantha, or Sam, as she preferred, reminded him of newspaper photographs of young women getting back to normal after anorexia; no bust to speak of, legs thin, sinewy.

'The kettle's boiled.' She said without looking round.

Cameron sat on the lawn, crossed his legs and hoped she was pleased to see him.

'No thanks,' he said, 'I hate that muck you drink, it tastes like nettle juice.'

Cradling the mug with both hands she continued to sip the steaming fluid.

'It is nettle juice, you idiot.' She fired an amused grin. 'It must be on your father's side, Mum loved herbal tea.'

He lolled on the grass, hands beneath his head.

'She wasn't your mum, she was mine. You came as part of a package, remember?'

A short time after his arrival in Winston two weeks ago, Sam contacted him to suggest he move in. There

58

is three bedrooms so you're welcome.' She'd made that very clear.

Sam got to her feet. Se smoothed her cotton skirt, Cameron noticing the light brown tan of her calves and wondered if she was the same colour everywhere? Initially, appalled for the way his mind sloped, it had taken several days of soul searching to convince himself it was perfectly normal. After all, she wasn't his blood sister.

He'd found out about Sam when his parent's divorced.

Cameron would never forget hearing his own father moan about the divorce and his miserable life without the beautiful Heather, Cameron's mother.

Determined never to be compared to his father under any circumstances, he would endeavour to stay on the positive side of life. Self-pity is a crutch for the weak-minded and counterproductive. And, it makes you miserable.

Cameron said to Sam, 'I was thinking about Nigel and Heather the other day, you know just musing.'

'And what pray were you musing? Were you perhaps annoyed at their ungodly liaison?'

Cameron squirmed, hating her mocking tone. And yet, at the same time she excited him. In a sense it felt abhorrent to poke around in his mother's past but a nagging thought repeatedly nibbled at his subconscious.

He was confident Heather wasn't consciously seeking another partner when she met Nigel. This was more or less proved when Cameron's parents' relationship disintegrated gradually. Heather citing the fact she wanted to be a free spirit. Nigel had simply happened, their affair somehow bizarre, crass almost.

'Just wondered how they met?'

Sam answered absently, 'Dad fell in love with

Gatekeeper Cottage. He popped by to see your dad. Found out he only rented it.' She fell quiet.

'What are you staring?'

She aimed a finger toward the brick folly way down near the bottom of the garden. 'That,' she said. 'When I was little, Dad told stories about how the folly was a secret gateway to another world.'

'And is it a gateway?'

Dismissively, Sam said, 'Dad enjoyed telling stories.'

Cameron smiled. Yes, he decided he looked forward to his conversations with Sam. Good company. In his mind he compared them to lovers sitting on the grass.

Sam said, 'You never go near the folly do you?'

He shook his head.

'I was playing in there when I was about four years old. An adder bit me. They rushed me to hospital. Apparently I had a really bad reaction to the bite.'

Sam nodded thoughtfully.

'Heather often spoke about your little adventures.'

Cameron sat up.

'What did she say?'

Sam gave him her favourite raised eyebrow; very sexy.

'For example, how you got lost in the forest and came out a different boy.'

Cameron's neck glowed; anxiety mounted like a bushfire re-igniting after rainfall.

'It was a scary time.'

How he hated discussing his time in the forest. He wore it like a scar. Why were people more interested in his childhood than the person he had become?

Sam took another sip of tea. Licked her lips, the movement innocently sexy.

Sam never wore lipstick, in fact, come to think of it, she never used make-up either. Cameron didn't believe she needed it with her flawless complexion.

'Tell me, Sam, if you didn't live here at Gatekeeper cottage, were would you live, London maybe?'

She screwed her face up.

'London, God no. If I had to choose anywhere it would be Edinburgh. I fell in love with the place during my first conference there.' She took another sip of tea. 'Thank goodness they still hold the conferences there every year. I never miss.'

Cameron sighed, 'I agree, Edinburgh is awesome; full of life and culture. We went there once with Mum and Dad.'

Sam asked, 'Do you resent my life with your mother? It must hurt, deep down.' Sam gently placed the mug of tea on the grass, expecting him to be angry.

Cameron acknowledged that he could have played a bigger part in his mother's life and this saddened him.

When his parents' divorced, he'd moved to London with his father. Heather did keep in touch, even visiting him a couple of times during those formative years.

A moody child, Cameron failed to give her the response she'd hoped for. Aged eighteen, his father killed himself, the incident traumatic without doubt. To see one's father hanging from the stairs in their terraced house in London had a disturbing effect, then and now.

After she died, Cameron realised too late that he needed his mother, Heather being the only remaining link to his past. An only child, both parents from small families, her funeral managed to attract one distant cousin and an aging aunt. He'd thought it unusual at the time for several locals from Winston to attend. Even Sam admitted she didn't realise Heather knew them.

Really he should cite more of his thoughts to Sam, mainly those concerning Heather. How cold and detached she could be. On the rare occasions they met, he would discuss his police career. Acrimonious daggers had been drawn, similarities between Cameron and his father dissected. They would argue. Cameron once accused her of abandoning him.

After a while, Heather was insistent he let her know in advance of any intended visit, mainly because Nigel and Sam could make themselves scarce, and not have to bear the brunt of possible arguments between Jason and Heather.

Early memories of Sam were of her face in the back window of Nigel's car as he drove away from the cottage.

Cameron dragged himself back to the here and now. Deciding to leave out the post-mortem of his mum and dad he brought the conversation to the near past.

'When they investigated me I was in a bad place. For the first time in my life I felt sorry for myself. I'd worked hard for my career.'

Cameron glanced at Sam to ensure she was listening. Satisfied he went on.

'Once the trial was over and they decided to charge me with discipline offences, I contemplated leaving the force. To be honest I was thinking did I give a damn about returning here? I admit it was hard at the time, but then I thought that maybe it was time for me to come home.'

She smirked. 'I like you when you're vulnerable. When I first met you, I thought, "He's an arrogant bastard." His pained look hurt her, 'Don't worry, I've changed my opinion.'

Cameron felt comfortable in her presence.

'I met Victor LaSalle today,' he said, changing the subject. 'He told me we are the sum parts of our family, that without it we're an empty shell. He's right. I have been ignoring my past.' He noticed her smile, pull up her knees and wrap her arms about them, forced to admit: 'Sam, the only family I seem to have is you.'

Ignoring this she asked, 'Did LaSalle mention anything about Mum's case or about Frank Slack?'

'Why should he? The case against Frank Slack was weak and anyway, LaSalle only played a small part in the investigation.'

Jumping up, startling him by her action, she folded her arms and paced the tiny garden like a barrister.

'I disagree. According to local coppers, LaSalle used Frank Slack as an informant. I think somehow LaSalle knew Slack would get off. He said as much in the newspapers.'

Cameron knew more; well he believed he did. His decision to keep the Chief Constable's suspicions concerning LaSalle to himself, knowing they would upset Sam. He would keep her in the dark for now. That way she wouldn't accidentally tip his hand to those hoping the Chief's misgivings about LaSalle would be buried along with his mother.

Ignoring any of this he said: 'Those butterflies over near the folly. There seems to be an awful lot considering butterflies are in decline?'

Sam made a shade with her hand.

'They're Gatekeepers, very common around here. If you look closely, they have an eye on each wing. Each eye has two pupils. Lovely aren't they?'

Cameron arched his brow.

'Don't you find things round here a bit bizarre? The local rag is called Gateway, the name of this cottage is Gatekeeper, and your dad said the folly was a gateway.'

Cameron looked again at the folly, 'And now the damn butterflies rejoice in the name!'

Sam shivered, tugged her cardigan tight.

'It never crossed my mind until now.'

After a brief smoothing of her crinkled skirt she walked purposefully toward the cottage. Cameron heaved himself up and followed.

**

Inside, the house felt warm, the air infused with the scent of roses, Heather's favourite flower.

The living room sported a nice clutter, ornamental pot animals of every shape and size dotted on shelves and spare surfaces, from wild birds to large dogs. Cameron leaned back in his mother's leather armchair and looked out onto the side garden and the dark forest beyond, aged leather protesting under his weight.

'Why did LaSalle attend Mum's funeral?' Cameron said, 'I didn't know he knew her?'

Sam had her back to him, busy rearranging a couple of the animals.

'There,' she said. 'I always felt the lion looked odd placed with that hideous looking dog.' She studied it. 'At least I think it's a dog.'

Cameron peered around her, seeing what she meant yet daring to think that maybe the dogs round here are more dangerous than normal.

Cameron didn't know if she'd heard the question about LaSalle and asked her again.

Sam ignored him, looked out of the window in a reflective mood. Six months since Heather's funeral and still she hadn't grieved, nor ever cried in public. At times like now, it was easy to guess her imagining her step-mother in the garden, or seeing her dad and Heather together, drinking tea.

Cameron said it louder, 'Why did...'

Without looking round she said, 'I heard you the first time.' Turning to him she went on, 'I suppose he was the senior officer and wanted to pay his respects. Why?'

Cameron had selected a recent copy of *Yorkshire Gateway* from the coffee table by the chair. He casually flicked through it, surprised at the number of articles about the forest and the new housing development. He found a quote from Walter Slack, Lonnie's grandfather:

"I sold the land to the developers because I believe it will help the economy of Winston grow by attracting more people to the area."

Sam folded her arms defensively for some reason, or Cameron saw it that way.

'Jason, what's your interest in Victor LaSalle? When I mentioned his association with Frank Slack, you closed ranks, told me I was being paranoid. Now you seem to be conducting your own enquiry.' She pointed an accusing finger. 'I know you're not telling me everything.'

He didn't answer it directly, instead he asked: 'Sam, do you miss Nigel?'

She fired her answer at him, her words slamming him into the armchair.

'Of course I miss him you idiot, who wouldn't, he was a kind, wonderful father.'

Cameron pulled himself up and leaned forward.

'The same man had an affair with a married woman.'

Her indignant stare made him feel small again. Damn it, Cameron disliked upsetting her; he wanted her on his side. So many times he'd been alone with just Blake rattling around in his head. Now he needed her to be his confidant, assist him in his quest.

Cameron remembered the package left for him at the police station.

'Sam, what happened to that vicious little terrier, the one Nigel bought for Heather?'

'Molly wasn't vicious.' She paused eying him. 'She was misunderstood.'

She flopped down onto the leather sofa and let her legs dangle over the arm.

'Why do you want to know?'

He shrugged, thinking about the severed paw. 'I'm just interested.'

'If you are genuinely interested then it won't hurt to tell you that Molly went missing the day before Heather was killed.'

Chapter 9

Friday morning. Gatekeeper cottage harboured peace. Sam had left for work at the Veterinary Surgery in Winston where she was a junior partner. Given time alone, Cameron took the opportunity of looking through some of his mother's paperwork left in her bureau. An old copy of *Yorkshire Gateway* intrigued him. It contained one of her articles; one a mere 'filler' tucked away at the bottom of the fourth page:

"Over the past twelve months, more than twenty sightings have been reported of a strange creature stalking the woodland near the town of Winston, North Yorkshire.

Dubbed by locals as 'The Beast of Winston,' the mysterious creature has been spotted roaming in thick woodland near to the new housing developments on the town's outskirts.

About as tall as a man with shaggy fur and a lolloping gait, the peculiar creature has caused a frenzy of chatter, and not least an element of unease, in our normally sedate market town.

According to witnesses, it is seen mainly in the largely wooded area of Haughton Village, approximately two miles from the new housing development of Winston Grange, where lush green undergrowth conceals any proper sighting."

Cameron made a mental note. He decided he would speak to the people who professed to have seen the creature, in case the article had any remote connection to Heather's death.

There was a "Next Week's Stories" page where Cameron's mother again featured in another article about dog fighting in the area. The phrase "dog fighting" bounced off the page, making him nauseas.

Cameron knew that dog fighting attracted individuals who also enjoyed other forms of distasteful entertainment, no matter how debased or disgusting. A few years back Cameron had been tasked with infiltrating a dog fighting racket. A prominent businessman called Angus Goodman had been clubbed to death after an evening of dog fights in a run-down warehouse in the Kent countryside. The local police asked for the Met's assistance. They seconded Cameron. It took him weeks of undercover work before he ascertained the truth behind the man's demise.

It transpired that a local policeman called Eric Moy had been organising the bouts. Goodman had lost a fair bit of money over a couple of weeks. When he asked for credit and it was refused, he threatened to expose PC Moy. An argument ensued. PC Moy hit Goodman over the head with his police baton.

For several weeks Cameron immersed himself with the clientele of the dog fights, boozing with them, shagging with them. He eventually found someone who had footage on his mobile of the attack by PC Moy. When he submitted the evidence to Kent police they refused to believe it was Moy on the footage. Two days later Blake dragged Moy through the front door of Kent Police HQ. He confessed everything. Sometimes it was better to let Blake take over.

The Kent coppers allocated to his debrief didn't know about Blake. They only knew about Cameron. They failed to hide their disgust of a policeman who could so dispassionately ruin a colleague's life even if he was a cold blooded killer who enjoyed a disgusting pastime.

He sincerely hoped Heather had restricted her investigations to the periphery of this very dangerous group of people.

He considered the article on the dog fighting. Did this article have anything to do with his mother's death? No reason it should. Heather's murder was more likely an opportunist affair with little planning. DI Mullen had also embraced this opinion.

The evidence definitely pointed to Frank Slack, the one-time handyman employed by Nigel Moon. For pities sake, the guy had been seen chatting to Heather before her murder.

Cameron had read Frank Slack's police file. Slack's modus operandi stood out. First he'd get to know the property; the habits of its occupants. Happy with this he'd wait until the owners vacated the property and then break in, usually during daylight hours. One drawback though: The police had no indication that Slack was prone to violence.

In his mother's case, the burglar, after killing her, apparently left empty handed. A strange way to behave for a thief? Plus the recent spate of break-ins had been concentrated in Winston, not its surrounding villages. Fact: Heather owned numerous paintings and pieces of pottery, none of which, as far as he knew were of any rare value. Nor did she appear to have any enemies. And why were there no signs of forced entry?

The lack of motive in the case against Frank Slack had been influential on the C.P.S's decision to eventually drop the charges. With the hammer gone missing and Lonnie Slack coming up with a credible alibi, Frank had been released from remand prison.

Cameron considered Sam's concerns regarding DCI LaSalle. He thought about her infatuation with the theory that LaSalle tampered with evidence to protect Frank Slack since he was a useful informant. Cameron didn't like LaSalle. On the other hand he sensed that for all his faults LaSalle wasn't involved in any cover up.

'*Harry Mullen.*' Cameron whispered the name. Each

time he'd raised the question of the murder, Mullen had become defensive.

Cameron was convinced the answer to the murder would be found in the background of those people known to Heather. It was unusual in his experience for the killer to be a stranger.

Immersed in thought he stared vacantly out of the side window towards the forest.

He jerked upright. A slight movement caught his eye; something or someone in the trees, watching. There! Yes, faint movement some six feet into the tree line. And again, this time higher up.

Ragged with thoughts of his mother's murder, he grabbed his miniature binoculars from his briefcase and scanned the trees. *There again!* About twenty yards distant, beyond the garden fence, he saw what he took to be the vague outline of a head partly masked by a large branch of a conifer.

Whatever, or whoever it was, he got the feeling it was watching the cottage. The surrounding fence was six feet high meaning the thing had to be clinging to the tree trunk. Too large to be a cat and dogs don't climb. It must be a man then. In a second the shape disappeared.

Cameron placed his binoculars on the table, flopped back into the armchair, his neck bristling, palms wet.

He glanced at the article again. He decided to ring Sam at work.

'It's me. You busy?'

She sounded like she was eating something. Cameron glanced at the ancient wooden wall clock. Suddenly it chimed. Bloody hell, he realised, lunchtime already. He'd been at Heather's bureau for over three hours.

'Sorry, I have a backlog, just grabbing a sandwich between patients.'

Cameron couldn't think of animals as patients.

'I've been reading Heather' articles in *Yorkshire Gateway*.'

Sam breathed heavily, sounding frustrated.

'She wrote freelance for a local magazine, so what?'

Cameron paused, longer than necessary. Sam could destabilize him without actually trying hard.

'What do you know about strange creatures in the forest?'

Sam laughed.

'Jason, there are dozens of local stories about weird creatures in the forest. Heather did a bit of research and made up a piece for the magazine. Honestly, I can't see where you're going with this.'

'Myth is often based on reality.'

'Heather told the police about her findings and they dismissed them.'

'What findings?'

Sam spoke slowly. 'She thought Lukas Meek was organising dog fights in the forest.'

Lukas Meek again.

'What if and just humour me Sam, what if Heather blundered into something when she was doing her research for an article?'

'Like what?'

'Like for example, something which made a burglar hit her over the head with a hammer. Remember nothing was stolen.'

She munched on her sandwich; disinterested, speaking between mouthfuls. 'Pick something up from the supermarket for supper. I'll be finished about six. We can talk then.'

Not to be deterred he insisted, 'Indulge me Sam. Please find out what you can about dogs treated for serious injuries at the surgery going back twelve months.'

There was an indignant huff .The line went dead.

He replaced the receiver.

Almost straight away the phone rang. Quickly he snatched it from its cradle.

'Hello.'

'You busy?' queried Victor LaSalle.

Cameron sighed.

'Just enjoying my day off; trying to relax.'

'We should meet, say half an hour at Winston Grange housing development.'

'Make it an hour.'

Chapter 10

When Victor sold his house in Winston town centre, Walter Slack persuaded him to put a deposit down on one of the new houses at Winston Grange. Until then, Victor had moved in with Walter believing it a short-term solution. Unfortunately, the builders had proved unreliable, houses being erected at a slower pace then expected.

Then rumours about strange creatures roaming the forest stunted take up. Naturally this worried potential buyers, take up slowing to a trickle. That, together with the abduction twenty years ago being linked to a recent spate of young boys being stalked, had taken its toll.

Victor lent against the ornate stone fireplace being careful not to dislodge the numerous photographs adorning the mantelpiece. The majority showed Walter posing with Lonnie and Frank. A few others were of Walter and Victor taken years ago.

Victor often wondered why Walter never married after his wife Isobel died over thirty years ago. During his own childhood Victor couldn't remember ever seeing Walter with a woman. Content with his lot, Victor decided. Apart from this bloody daft police operation which Walter agreed to help fund.

The operation clearly bothered Walter. Forever on the telephone to the Chief Constable demanding updates. It appeared Walter had become infatuated with Jason Cameron. Heaven knows why, thought Victor. Cameron was like a bumbling idiot.

'Cameron agreed to meet me,' Victor said. 'He's like a little lost boy blundering about the place. God only knows how the little shit ever got into the police service. We must have been hard up at the time.'

He glanced at Walter seated in his favourite chair of rich leather, apparently looking out of the wide window

73

toward the road bordered with wooden flowerbeds, lovingly crafted by Lonnie and Frank.

Victor noticed Walter grab his shaking hand, grappling to keep it still.

'Are you alright Walter?'

Walter Slack winced, the pain in his arms and legs troubling him though still he refused to complain.

'I'm all right Victor. I just wish this bloody thing we're doing wasn't necessary. Don't like airing my dirty washing in public.'

Victor admired the old man. Since his acquittal Walter wanted one thing; to clear his name. If some cockamamie police operation helped do that then it would be worthwhile.

'Do you think it will work?'

Victor watched Walter heave himself up and cross to the fireplace to poke the open fire with the metal tip of his walking stick.

Walter rubbed his brow. 'I have one worry Victor.'

'I'm not surprised Walter. The whole idea gives me a headache'

Walter nodded in agreement. 'I'm not confident that Doctor Kumar will be able to control this character Blake once we force him out into the open. We may have to take drastic action to ensure he doesn't cause unnecessary harm.'

**

Janice Mullen blew her nose. In five minutes she would unlock the door to the property office wearing a brave face. Janice had never lost a piece of evidence in twenty years. She remembered the fuss the morning of the remand hearing. She'd told the exhibits officer, the hammer wasn't in the evidence drawer. It had vanished.

She felt terrible; especially knowing the case against

Frank Slack would collapse. Apart from Slack's criminal convictions the only tangible evidence was the hammer. LaSalle had been inconsolable, blaming Harry. Would Harry ever get over the stress of it all? Janice didn't think so.

When the court case collapsed, Harry appeared to shrink. Janice didn't recognise the hunched figure forever scowling, losing his temper. Perhaps this is why she fell for Victor LaSalle. Of course Janice regretted her past misdemeanours. Even considered coming clean about her affair with LaSalle. It wouldn't help, not now. The damage had been done.

She glanced at the silver wristwatch Harry had bought her for their twenty-fifth wedding anniversary. In forty-five minutes the investigation team from headquarters would arrive. Questions would be asked. She could hear their resonance even before they arrived:

Had she mistakenly put the hammer elsewhere? Is there anyone else who could have entered the property office without her knowing and removed the hammer? Question after bloody question.

Not so much the investigation bothering her, more the thought of Harry jumping through hoops. Two months left of his service. Still they pestered him. Not fair.

One positive thing to emerge from all this: the internal enquiry into Victor LaSalle. If nothing else, this gave her comfort.

Startled, she heard a light tap on the massive oak door of the property office. Crossing from her desk to open it she was surprised to see Jason Cameron standing in the corridor.

**

'Hello Mrs Mullen, can I come in?'

Janice's face glowed ruby red.

'It's not convenient I'm afraid, the Internal Enquiry Team from HQ is due any minute.'

Cameron gently pushed the door inward, 'I won't be long, promise.'

He slid by her into the cavernous room. What struck him straight away was its incredible tidiness. Police property offices were notorious for mislaying stuff. Mostly, they were haphazard affairs, boxes stacked to the ceiling, paperwork mounting in trays. Janice was evidently a fastidious clerk, this one fact making it all the more unusual for anything to go missing.

Cameron knew the team from HQ were arriving that afternoon. He'd also decided it was an appropriate time to confront Janice about the hammer. Today, she would be on edge; concerned. Today Janice would be vulnerable.

'Did Harry mention I might pop in?'

Janice closed the cumbersome leather bound property register with a thud, and looked edgily at the door.

'No he didn't mention it. Is it about the hammer?'

He tried not to make it obvious. The hammer being lost bothered him the most about the case.

A great deal about the enquiry was troublesome. Fingerprints were only useful if the suspect had a record, otherwise the prints could belong to anyone. Surely though, Janice would have at least been interrogated before now? She was after all the custodian of the evidence therefore quite logically the first port of call for the investigation team.

Many things about the enquiry and the general set up in Winston appeared dysfunctional. Like a poorly written play about police work, the reality kicked well and truly into touch, the players merely acting.

Cameron put his neurosis down to medication. A good enough excuse, he figured.

'There doesn't appear to be much going on in Winston yet your property office is full to the gunnels?'

Janice visibly wilted. About to speak, the office door opened. Harry Mullen walked in carrying a tray with two coffees and a plate of digestives.

'Didn't know you were here otherwise...' He nodded his head at the tray.

Cameron wondered if Harry had deliberately interrupted.

'I was about to ask Janice about the disappearance of the hammer.'

Harry put the tray on the counter and folded his arms. 'Janice is being interviewed this afternoon about it,' he said. 'It's taken care of.'

'Seems to have taken a while for anyone to actually try and ascertain what happened to it?'

Harry put an arm around Cameron's shoulders and guided him to the door. 'It's like that in the sticks, you'll get used to it.'

Janice Mullen raised her voice. Harry winced.

'He's still out there, in the forest somewhere.'

Cameron pushed Harry's arm away. 'Who's out there, Janice?'

Harry moved toward his wife, she shrugged him off.

'I've seen him. Tell him Harry, *please*.'

Harry eyes grew sad, moist with the onset of tears.

'She's been under a lot of stress.'

'I understand Harry.'

Cameron did understand. He left them alone. Despite the thick door he could hear Janice whimpering.

Cameron guessed it wouldn't be the last time Janice Mullen would approach him.

Chapter 11

The wipers on the BMW groaned. Not far now. He spotted Victor LaSalle waiting at the entrance to the sprawling housing development wearing his customary grey Italian suit under a black overcoat. As usual, looking like an undertaker.

Cameron guessed the meeting was something to do with his Mother's murder. LaSalle wanted to confide in him about something. How Cameron knew this he wasn't sure. Just a feeling he had.

The raindrops got bigger, Cameron admiring the tiny eruptions in the sandy mud. Yes, and Harry's Wellington's had been coated in the same sandy mud.

Where had he seen that colour of mud before?

LaSalle leaned against the wooden fence looking out across the fields toward the forest

Cameron parked, killed the engine, climbed out and closed the car door with a soft click. Ambling over to LaSalle he stood alongside him. He placed a foot on the bottom rung of the fence. Apart from a quick sideways glance LaSalle didn't at first acknowledge him. Cameron noticed the faraway look in his eyes. To all intents, had it not been for the absence of proper attire, they could be taken for a couple of hikers about to set off for a journey into the forest.

In some ways Cameron felt like he was on a journey, destination unknown; like he was in mist and every so often it cleared offering glimpses of his path. Strange too, that he was seeing Blake more regularly in his mind's eye. How could that be possible? Doctor Kumar assured him Blake was under control.

LaSalle flicked Cameron another quick glance then continued to look at the forest.

'Cameron's a Scottish name, isn't it?' LaSalle eventually said.

'My father was Scottish. Where did your surname originate, the label on a can of peaches?'

LaSalle ignored the quip.

'Dad was French, he worked on the fairgrounds, or so I was told. I was given name Slack after Walter took me in, changed it when I was nineteen when I found out about my father's identity. I never traced him though, despite trying very hard.'

Cameron saw despondency in Victor's eyes. He said sincerely. 'Sorry, I was being defensive.'

LaSalle acknowledged Cameron's apology with a nod.

'It's amazing isn't it, DS Cameron, the housing development I mean.' Suddenly LaSalle was animated, pointing toward the houses. 'They build the roads first then allocate the plots later. 'Some get corner gardens, others larger ones backing onto the forest.' He pointed with a leather-gloved finger. 'See the one over there, the one near the junction? That's Harry Mullen's new house; when he eventually moves in. Mine will be up there, five bedrooms and a double garage.' LaSalle indicated the tree line. 'Planners stopped short of the original forest, wanted to protect the wildlife.'

He stopped talking for a couple of seconds, peering harder at the tree line. 'Some funny goings on in the forest lately, pet dogs missing and strange sightings; little kids being stalked by a weirdo. Some buyers have pulled out, scared, worried about the safety of their kids. Who can blame them?'

Cameron wiped his glasses with his handkerchief, annoyed he hadn't worn a raincoat.

'Why you do you want to see me?'

LaSalle pinched his nose with his thumb and forefinger. Without looking at Cameron he said, 'When you lost your mother did it help when the funeral was over?'

Cameron hated answering personal questions. Nevertheless he said, 'You mean as in closure?'

LaSalle rounded on Cameron, his look serious and a little unyielding.

'No, I mean the intense feeling of regret when someone dies. You know when you begin reflecting on how you treated them, how much you loved them.' He glanced back at the forest then at Cameron again.

'You look a lot like Heather.'

'This meeting can't be simply sentiment for my Mother.'

LaSalle sighed, changed tack.

'Lonnie told me you asked about Frank Slack.'

Cameron pushed himself off the fence. Cameron had a sudden urge to frisk LaSalle for a tape recorder. Why he wasn't sure. Perhaps it was just copper instinct? Hell, they were both coppers and what did Cameron have to hide? It *was* LaSalle they were after. Christ, he hoped so otherwise...

Finally Cameron said: 'Lonnie gave Frank his alibi. I asked him why he took so long to come forward.'

LaSalle popped a peppermint into his mouth and chewed.

'Why didn't you ask me, I'm the senior officer?'

'I asked to see the case papers from the outset. Harry said you wouldn't allow it. When the hammer went missing and the case collapsed I thought you might have something to do with it.'

Their eyes met; a light flickered in LaSalle's as if he intended saying something. It died, Cameron adding, 'Slack being your informant.'

LaSalle placed a finger across his lips. Gently he patted Cameron's chest, frisking him. LaSalle stood back, satisfied.

'The Chief Constable has instigated an internal enquiry into my dealings with informants.'

He regarded Cameron with an icy stare.

'Did you know about it?'

Cameron considered lying then changed his mind. There was something in LaSalle's demeanour, an indication of sincerity. No one had mentioned LaSalle was a heavy drinker. Cameron suspected the guy was tipsy. Also, he looked melancholic. Could it be LaSalle is grieving?

'The Chief told me about the investigation,' Cameron offered.

'You know the Chief well, don't you?'

Cameron didn't reply.

LaSalle waved a hand in the air. A silver grey CID car appeared from behind a nearby machinery compound.

'Someone is keen to meet you.'

After negotiating the concrete road to the top of High Cliff nab, the CID car stopped in a small car park near to the viewpoint. A man in his seventies sat on a wooden bench admiring the view. His white hair buffeted by the wind whistling across the rocky outcrop. Cameron recognised him immediately.

He wouldn't forget the Chief Constable's brief about Walter Slack, recognising him from photographs he'd been shown when the top brass explained Cameron's role in Winston.

Cameron knew about Walter's relationship with LaSalle, everyone did. Slack adopted Victor when he was a child. The pair had formed a tight bond and not something that Cameron believed he should underestimate.

The Chief had warned Cameron to be careful around Victor and Walter, very careful since Victor LaSalle's career was on the line. 'To be honest,' the Chief had said, 'if La Salle could wriggle free of corruption charges, he would and that would put him in a position to continue to control the snake pit they call Winston.'

A couple more things the Chief had made clear from the outset: One. Cameron would be allowed to poke around until it became evident his enquiries were encroaching on the work of the internal enquiry, and Two, that the investigation into his mother's murder would be reviewed by an outside team of detectives. Cameron recognised the well-intentioned carrot and bit. The driver of the CID car, a young policewoman, parked, remaining behind the wheel like a loyal chauffer. LaSalle and Cameron approached the bench. LaSalle selected a place farthest away from the old man leaving enough space for Cameron to squeeze in between the two of them.

As he settled, Cameron noticed an orange butterfly tattoo on Slack's neck, its colours as faded and ancient as its wearer. He recognised the butterfly, a gatekeeper, its living counterpart in abundance near Gatekeeper Cottage.

'Thank you for coming to see me Mr Cameron, rarely do I get the opportunity to engage in intelligent conversation.' Slack gave LaSalle a sideways glance. 'It's the Parkinson's disease. Because I shake a bit they think my mind has gone.

'Unfortunately, like all engines the brain needs oil which in my case is dopamine, or lack of it.' Walter Slack patted Cameron's hand. 'Do you know about Parkinson's, Mr Cameron?'

Slack had struck a nerve. According to the doctors, Cameron's brain used too much dopamine. It's why he sometimes did the things that landed him in trouble. Apparently he'd been informed the drug caused his brain to misfire like an engine with dodgy spark plugs.

Cameron spoke without looking at Slack.

'The brain's wires get crossed and the messages

transmitted cause tremors and similar side effects.'

Cameron glanced at Walter Slack, unsure what to make of him.

'Mr Slack why am I here? Is it to discuss your medical predicament or is there some other point to this...' Cameron waved a wayward hand, 'rendezvous?'

'Please be patient Mr Cameron. I like to feel my way around a person.' Slack flexed his left hand a couple of times.

'I knew your mother, a nice lady.'

'Is that why you wanted to see me, because you knew Heather?'

LaSalle leaned over the cliff edge, looking out over the expanse of dwellings in the valley as though he was contemplating jumping off the cliff.

'I asked Victor to bring you so we could have a chat.' Slack studied him.

'You are indeed a strange man and that interests me.'

The old man shuffled, tying to get more comfortable.

'Tell me Mr Cameron, what did it feel like to be accused?'

'What do you mean what was it like?' Cameron asked.

Walter Slack winced, altering his position on the bench, affording a better view of Cameron's reaction to his next question.

'You were accused of torturing and killing a suspect, how did you feel?'

'The Old Bailey acquitted me.'

'Ah ha, then tell me Mr Cameron what did it feel like to be accused of something you didn't do?"

Cameron flushed, took a deep breath and said slowly, 'I felt abandoned, let down.' He paused, adjusted his bow tie, adding, 'Then angry.'

Slack nodded thoughtfully.

Twenty seconds ticked by. Slack broke the silence.

'I have a great deal invested in Winston Mr Cameron. Because of this I'm going to ask for your co-operation in a matter which requires careful handling.'

'Is this about your grandson?'

'It's not about Lonnie, Mr Cameron, it's about me.'

Cameron sensed animosity in Walter Slack, directed like a laser straight at him.

**

Detective Sergeant Trevor Mason, some thirty yards away watched the three men from the safety of the trees. He cursed the wind whistling off High Cliff, killing their conversation. Damn it, even nature was against him.

Trevor felt the cold these days. Surveillance, particularly rural operations, made his bones ache. He was here on the Chief's orders, specifically requested, Trevor not having the heart to refuse. Oh well, at least the overtime was just amazing.

Mason hated Cameron with a passion. Should this game of cat and mouse finally bring Cameron down, then great, he wanted to be part of it.

Shit! Suddenly, Cameron turned. He looked toward him, tilting his head, scanning, rather than glancing. For the second time Cameron instinctively stared at him or more specifically his location. Surely Cameron couldn't see him; his camouflage coat and trousers more than enough to disguise his whereabouts.

Chapter 12

'How much do you remember about being lost in the forest?

Cameron, now positive everyone had a copy of his personal psyche evaluation. He shuffled his feet; looked at his surroundings, noticed a wheelchair resting under a small tree.

Blake muttered something about being careful around Walter Slack.

In the beginning, after his ordeal in the forest Cameron initially refused to listen to the voices in his head. His teachers accused him of talking to himself. His fellow school children ridiculed him to such an extent he frequently played truant.

As the years past he began to answer the voices. This allowed Blake to grow inside his head; share his mind; help him overcome his fears. More importantly Blake had a skill for sensing deceit, often warning Cameron who in turn learned to trust Blake's instincts.

Composing himself Cameron asked, 'Why are you interested in my childhood, Mr Slack?'

The old man twisted his feeble frame, achieving a sideways view of Cameron. LaSalle sat head bowed like a playground sulk. Something Cameron hadn't expected and more sure now that something had penetrated La Salle's Teflon coating. It couldn't be the internal enquiry? LaSalle had been investigated before and surfaced smelling of roses. This was different, more sinister and unnerving. Otherwise why would this normally brusque man become a cooling ember on a fire stacked high and hot?

A blur of movement caught Cameron's eye in the trees to the right of where they sat, subtle and yet a touch out of context with the foliage. They were being watched, by what or whom he didn't know.

Slack broke Cameron's concentration.

'I admit I'm interested in your recollection of what happened when you were lost in the forest, Mr Cameron. And yes, it is a strange request but please humour me.'

A strange request indeed. One Cameron had been asked many times before by those sent to evaluate his sanity following his experience in the forest. How many times must he tell it before they believed him?

The police at the time were convinced he'd been snatched and harboured against his will somewhere else other than the forest.

Next they accused him of romancing, making it all up; covering for someone. He told them about how he was found by the man in camouflage. They made him look at some men behind a glass screen, asked him to pick the man out. Things had grown fuzzy; he remembered feeling sick, passing out. When he came round, they were taking the man away. The man stared at him, his eyes piercing.

His mother had cried. Later behind screens in the hospital, other men in green poked and prodded him in vulnerable places. Still he would not detract from his story.

Deciding to humour the old man he looked away from the forest.

'It goes like this Mr Slack: I was in the kitchen of Gatekeeper Cottage. My parents were arguing in the living room . . . something to do with holidays because they kept ranting about France. I hated it when they shouted. Heather always had the upper hand because she was eloquent, Dad, never good at putting his point across.'

Cameron paused for a second bemused, yet

fascinated that Slack wanted to hear his version of events. His listeners were silent, Victor engrossed in his far off place, old man Slack flapping his hand, bidding Cameron to continue.

'My parents must have suspected the neighbours could hear the commotion because the front door slammed. They continued quarrelling in hushed tones, growing louder when the holiday was mentioned.

'I heard a plate smash. Heather was shouting, telling Dad how much she hated him. Scared by it I ran out of the kitchen into the forest at the back of the cottage. I kept running until I thought my lungs would explode.'

Cameron stood up, stretched, the memory relived like a poor quality video recording.

'Before I knew it, I was hopelessly lost. I sat and cried, and eventually fell asleep. Dark when I woke. I was utterly terrified.'

Cameron paused, the memory uncomfortable. He flopped back onto the bench.

Walter Slack said, 'Please, DS Cameron, I'm still listening.'

It felt peculiar but Cameron continued, hoping there'd be some relevance to the disclosure on Slack's part.

'Imagine me stumbling about in the dark, shouting for help; sounds of the forest the only replies. Can you imagine it?'

Slack shook his head.'

'I drank water from a stream the only light coming from the Moon. I sobbed not knowing what to do for the best. I rested on the soft moss; lay my head back and looked beyond the trees to the stars, dread replaced by a weird lethargy.'

Slack interrupted, 'What came over you?'

'Silly as it may sound I felt the forest calming me, soothing my fears. The night didn't seem so scary. I

87

covered myself with leaves, curled up and fell asleep again.'

Cameron looked at Slack who still insisted: 'More, DS Cameron, please I beg you.'

Cameron shrugged, continued his story.

'Daylight woke me. No idea of time, but early. I was bloody hungry. Bit further along a track, I found a bigger, deeper stream. I risked another drink then picked red berries. For all I knew they could have poisoned me.

'"Robinson Crusoe" had been on the telly and I remembered how he'd built a shelter on his island. Dad told me the forest was like an island. If I ever get lost, stay in one place; let people eventually find me. So I built a shelter from twigs and sods of soil. It took me a long time. Afterwards I played games, you know, pretending to be Robinson Crusoe.

'I thought about how my hero would get out of fix like this.'

'Robinson Crusoe?' offered Slack.

'No, I liked Crusoe. My favourite though was Sexton Blake, the detective. My dad watched him on the telly as a kid and told me stories about him. He was better than Sherlock Holmes apparently.'

Right then images of Blake, his other self swung by, Cameron mentally sidestepping them, effectively hiding Blake in a far corner of his brain.

Each time he recounted the story he always felt the account belonged to someone else.

'A couple of deer appeared, tentative at first, then bolder. They drank from the stream. They didn't seem to mind me being there.'

Cameron regarded his audience. Walter Slack had been nodding thoughtfully throughout the account. LaSalle, standing now, still clung to his vision of the diminishing skyline.

'There's more,' the old man hinted, more or less demanding the finale.

Cameron obliged.

'I was sitting by the stream when I heard twigs snapping, the sound of heavy breathing. A giant of a man approached the clearing. He wore strange clothes, and I'm thinking the forest's come alive. The man smiled. I was terrified. He had a gold tooth and a hairy face. I should have been overjoyed at being found. But I wasn't. I was horrified and ran.

'He quickly caught me. I remember screaming and hitting out. His hands grabbed my hands to prevent me scratching him. I screamed again and again until he dropped me onto the wet ground. I rolled down a hill and fell into a deep pit.

'I remember standing and then slipping over, unable to get a foothold. The bottom of the pit was sopping wet, greasy and it stank. Out of nowhere came a massive dog, bigger than any dog I had ever seen before. It mauled me, biting my arms, sharp teeth piercing my skin. I must have fainted. The next thing I remember was being in hospital surrounded by nurses and policemen.'

Cameron breathed a lungful of air.

He felt weird. He'd told the story countless times as a child, and more recently to Doctor Kumar, the psychologist. Yet today had been the first time he'd told a stranger. Why then did it feel like a lie? With patchy recollection and bits missing, it always seemed like someone else's memory.

'Did the police tell you anything about how you looked?' asked the old man.

'Yes they did. Because my clothes were fairly clean they didn't believe I'd been lost, not at first.'

The old man slapped both his hands on his knees, like an excited child. 'That's very good Mr Cameron, very good indeed.'

He paused, mulling over what he'd been told, eventually he said: 'What have the doctors told you about your recollection of events in the forest?'

Cameron washed his face with his hands. 'That my story is fragmented, disjointed, in the wrong order. That my brain has mixed things up.'

Cameron had no idea why Walter Slack needed to hear about his childhood ordeal. Eyeing the old man he somehow appeared relieved, happy to have shared a memory by reliving it. Slack returned the look with a broad smile and a glimpse of a gold tooth.

The realisation dawned on him. Cameron said quietly, 'It was you wasn't it Mr Slack. You found me in the forest?'

Walter Slack clutched Cameron's hand, gave it a squeeze.

'The forest was used by evil men watching dogs fighting in a pit designed for such things.' Slack's left hand trembled; he grabbed it with his right to quell what amounted to slight embarrassment.

'Victor hates the old ways, the dog fighting, the badger baiting. Won't go anywhere near the forest, will you Victor?'

Victor shook his head.

'After I brought you home,' Slack said, 'the police arrested me. They were convinced I was the one who abducted you. Because I believed in the old ways, they thought I was mixed up in other more unsavoury practices. The newspapers were relentless in their pursuit of the story. As a result I served ten years for a crime I didn't commit.' He shuddered. 'I felt dirty.'

Cameron's recollection of his own ordeal had been fragmented into indistinct images, connected yet interrupted, like poor wiring. He'd tried many times to piece the memory together and failed. Did Walter Slack have vital information which might help unravel his childhood trauma?

Questions buzzed, demanding to be out. 'How did you find me?'

Slack said, 'The police searched for three days, initially concentrating in the town and then the forest.' White spittle congealed in the corner of his mouth stretching like elastic. Slack licked cracked, dry lips.

'At first your parents presumed you were with friends, unaware you'd been listening to them argue. The police searched the forest, but it's so vast. Nor had they any evidence you were in there. Not top of their agenda either; something else was going on.' Slack lowered his voice. 'Another boy had gone missing a couple of days earlier. Naturally the police put two and two together and made a connection.'

'Did my parents know it was you who found me?'

Slack looked at LaSalle for a second and back at Cameron.

'Heather asked me to look for you.'

'You knew my mother?'

Slack looked into the distance, left hand all of a tremble again, his bottom lip twitching.

LaSalle spoke this time, his voice barely audible.

'Your mother was the daughter of Harry Slack, Walter's younger brother." He caught Cameron's disgusted glance. "I know, I know, shocking isn't it, finding out like this. Pity Heather decided to conceal her family ties.'

LaSalle popped a peppermint into his mouth, savouring it for a second or so before saying: 'Heather had a relationship with a man from the travelling community, fairground folk. She got herself pregnant. Fifteen she was, and deemed too young to care for the child.'

He glanced at Slack for approval adding, 'When

91

Heather couldn't cope, Walter offered to take care of the boy. Four years later, Heather met your father and you were born.'

Cameron couldn't help himself and blurted: 'What are the Slack family, a bloody adoption agency?'

A flippant remark, meant to disguise his surprise. Some surprise! The news felt like a lump of lead had been dropped onto his stomach. His breathing grew laboured; emotions wavered between disbelief and morbid excitement.

Breathing regulated, Cameron took stock of what he'd been told.

'Did my father know?' he asked.

Slack answered. Struggling with his speech, he cleared his throat.

'Your dad found out when Heather attempted to change her will in favour of the boy. They were arguing about it the day you ran into the forest.' He raised his voice an octave to drive the next point home. 'It wasn't France they were arguing about; it was your brother *Frank*.'

A thunderbolt hit Cameron; Frank Slack, his brother? What a god-awful thought.

He asked, 'How did you know about the argument?'

Slack hesitated. 'When Heather asked for my help she told me.'

Rapid heartbeat controlled by several deep breaths, perspiration bubbled on his face and to him he sweated dynamite.

'You still haven't told me why you brought me here.'

Cameron wiped his brow with his handkerchief. 'There's obviously something else on your mind, a favour perhaps from your newest family member? Or is it that you enjoy amateur impersonations of Stephen Hawking?'

LaSalle couldn't help laughing out loud. Slack's scathing look stifled it.

'You are correct Mr Cameron.' Slack sought Cameron from an angle, effectively shutting LaSalle out, giving the impression of two confidants discussing secret plans.

'I would like your assistance with two things. One: I want you to discover the truth behind the original abduction; Victor will assist you. Two: I would like you to find those responsible for the despicable and cruel dog fights which are taking place somewhere in there.' He wafted a defiant left hand toward the forest.

Cameron had already guessed LaSalle had read sections of his personal file containing details of operations to which he'd been assigned. Why else would Slack be asking for his assistance in the murky world of dog fighting?

Cameron raised himself from the bench and stood next to LaSalle.

'What's your interest in me?'

LaSalle wasn't expecting the question. He said nothing.

'Tell him Victor.'

Victor's face sagged like a melting plastic mask. His shoulders drooped.

'Okay, here it is for what it's worth. Heather came to see me a couple of months before she was murdered. She told me she was being stalked.'

Cameron glanced at predatory clouds stalking sky, and engulfing the sun, the sensation underlining his dread.

He managed to ask, 'what did you do?'

LaSalle, hands deep in his pockets, looked uncomfortable, harassed.

'Heather was writing weird stuff in magazines about creatures in the forest. I initially believed she was away with the fairies.' He saw disappointment on Cameron's face.

'Oh come off it, Cameron, you know the score. A lonely widow reckons she's being stalked. We check with the neighbours and they tell us she's a weirdo. Because of her articles, suddenly rumours are rife about dog fighting and strange creatures stalking the woodland.' His glance was a dare. 'What would you have done?'

Cameron didn't hesitate.

'My job, DCI LaSalle, I would have done my job.'

Slack interrupted, 'He feels guilty Mr Cameron. He liked Heather, isn't that correct Victor?'

Cameron realised someone, probably LaSalle had doctored Heather's case file. Absolutely no way Frank Slack should have been their only avenue of enquiry.

'I still don't get it,' Cameron admitted. 'Why was Frank Slack considered a suspect when there are so many loose ends?'

The whole charade felt like Cameron was walking through mud; every step an effort.

Victor spoke slowly addressing his comments to the town of Winston nestling peacefully below.

'I knew Frank was visiting Heather. To be honest we had little else to go on. When we found the hammer and identified Frank's prints what else could we do?'

LaSalle sat on his haunches, picked up a blade of grass, let it go and watched it float away in the wind.

'A good, honest woman is viciously murdered.' LaSalle said. 'I knew it would be someone she knew. Frank fitted the bill.'

LaSalle smoothed creases from his trousers. 'I know everyone in Winston, Cameron. I live, breathe and eat the town of Winston and still I can't seem to find out who killed her.'

'What do you want from me?'

94

'I want your help DS Cameron.'

Cameron looked on as LaSalle fetched the wheelchair and helped Slack climb into it. Once at the police car, Slack dragged himself from the chair and with the assistance of the policewoman, squirmed into the back.

LaSalle shouted above the wind.

'Walk back to your car Cameron, you look like you could use the exercise.' About to get into the car he called: 'Frank, your brother will be in the Fox and Hounds at seven. Meet him, it's important.'

Cameron shouted back, 'What happened to my grandfather, Mr Slack, your brother?'

LaSalle answered, 'Died years ago in a fairground accident.'

They drove off.

Thirty minutes later, after scrambling down the rocky shortcut below High Cliff avoiding the concrete road, Cameron finally got to his car. Cameron climbed into his vehicle. It wouldn't start. Bonnet up, and several tries later, he still had no joy. He was stranded.

Hidden in the trees, Trevor Mason tried keeping a straight face; 'Let the bastard walk.'

Smirking, he left via the track behind High Cliff, keeping to the trees. His own four wheel drive half a mile distant and well hidden.

Cameron pulled his collar up. The walk would do him good; give him time to mull over what had been said. He made his way along the forest track skirting the housing development toward Gatekeeper Cottage. Picking up a stick, he tossed it into the undergrowth.

Some yards on a terrier bounded onto the path, stick in its mouth and tail wagging.

'Good boy, now give it here,' Cameron shouted thinking to prolong the game, seeking diversion from the thoughts, which smothered straight thinking.

Cameron bent down and tugged at the stick and began a tug o' war. The dog was winning, growling playfully; enjoying the battle.

A slim middle-aged woman in jeans, green Wellington boots and a thick woolly cardigan appeared out of the bushes.

'Poppy, let go honey, give the nice man his stick.'

Cameron gave up, straightened and said, 'Just having fun. Nice dog, Lakeland terrier?

The woman smiled. 'Yeah, with all the traits.'

Cameron produced his warrant card. 'Detective Sergeant Cameron.'

He held out his hand, the woman took it gingerly, letting go after only a second. 'Mrs Lombard. Sylvia Lombard.'

'Mrs Lombard, have you got time to answer a couple of questions?'

Sylvia Lombard shrugged.

'Have you ever seen anything strange, here in the forest?'

She plucked a dog lead from her pocket and looped it round Poppy's neck.

'I know who you are. Your mother had a dog from the same litter as Poppy. She'd walk it along this path.'

'Have you seen anything out of the ordinary when you've been walking Poppy?'

Poppy began to yap, the woman shushed him.

'It was me who first saw it and gave your mother a first hand account. She interviewed the dog walkers. It would seem the story took on a life of it's own after that. Has to be said though, many people had seen the man before I did.'

'What man?'

'The scruffy man dressed in filthy sheepskins.'

'I thought the sightings were of a dog-like creature?'

'No. When your mother handed the story into the local magazine, the editor said it would sound more convincing if it related to a creature, you know have more impact.'

The woman fell quiet, then: 'Well, must get on. Good to have met you. Come along, Poppy; let the gentleman enjoy his walk.'

Cameron thanked Mrs Lombard. What she'd told him had given a nasty twist to any articles Heather had published.

Later, around four, Cameron arrived back at the cottage, feet swollen from the walk. The dank smell of rain on concrete mixed unpleasantly with the decaying undergrowth of the forest.

Front door unlocked, he threw his keys on the wooden table in the hallway, shrugged out of his shoes – no sense muddying the floor – and went upstairs to his bedroom.

The bed felt comfortable after that hard bench at High Cliff. Socks off, he began to massage his feet, and boy it felt good.

For sure Walter Slack and Victor LaSalle's alarming disclosures fascinated and disturbed him. If true then the searchlight of suspicion was well and truly deflected from Frank Slack.

Normally patient man, although under the circumstances it would be understandable for him to become anxious, maybe overreact, Cameron had no intention of doing either.

He heard the front door open. Through the pokey bedroom window he saw Sam's car. *She's home early.* Shit, he'd forgotten to pick up something for supper, what with the car breaking down. Cameron wondered whether to call down to her, but didn't. Doubtless she'd have spotted his keys. He quickly changed from his casual clothes into a grey suit and red spotted bow tie

97

and went downstairs. Sam sat at the bureau, cushions propping her slender torso against the hard rails of the chair.

'You're home early, Sam.'

She kept her back to him, pulled down the concertina drawer of the bureau.

'Couple of cancellations meant I could get a flyer. Where's your car, didn't see it on the lane?'

He paced the room.

'I met Walter Slack earlier. LaSalle fixed it up. Car wouldn't start so I had to walk; got back half an hour ago, which reminds me, I should phone the garage, get a mechanic out there.'

She swivelled the chair to face him. 'Sounds like some walk. Where's 'there'?

He wondered how much he should divulge?

'We met out by High Cliff, above the new housing on the edge of the forest. Slack asked me about the time I got lost.' He watched her carefully for a reaction.

'Why on earth would Walter Slack be interested in your childhood adventures?'

Her muted interest showed little evidence of being concerned about the meeting. But that was Sam, pragmatic to a fault. She rarely answered a question without first analysing its meaning. Her nonchalant interest in his disclosure accompanied by a throwaway smile indicated she found the episode amusing.

'Apparently,' he went on, 'when the police couldn't find me after three days, Heather asked Walter Slack to search the forest.'

Sam screwed up her face as if she'd smelled something disgusting.

'I didn't know Heather knew him.'

Cameron couldn't help himself and jibed, 'I thought you knew everything that went on in Winston.'

Sam threw a cushion.

Chapter 13

Victor LaSalle nursed his pint of beer. Frank would be here soon. How much should he tell him? The whole truth might scare him; make him nervous.

Not one of his favourite haunts, the Fox and Hounds. A dull, dour place. Victor looked at his Rolex then shot a glance toward the pub door. Frank Slack waltzed into the bar dressed like a spiv.

'Another pint Vic?'

Victor, already bloated with beer, said, 'Get me a large whiskey. And better get yourself another drink, you'll need it.'

Frank jauntily strode to the bar and came back with the drinks.

'You look worried.'

Victor stiffened.

'This might be funny for you Frank, but I can't see the joy in drinking with a psycho, albeit a cop psycho, can you?'

Frank ran his finger around rim of his beer glass.

'Look at it from my perspective; I lost my natural mother to some murdering bastard then I get accused of killing her. Then suddenly, wham, I'm about to meet my brother. It has to be a good thing Vic, don't you think?'

Victor couldn't help it and chuckled. Frank had a way about him. Always managing to sooth Victor, calm him down; make him smile. Frank was a bloody charmer all right.

'You don't know everything about this police operation Frank. It's about to get tricky and I don't want you or me getting hung out by our balls.'

'We won't Vic. This bloke Cameron will be chuffed to bits he's got a brother. Cameron doesn't have anyone left. He'll be fine, trust me.'

Victor knew how persuasive Frank could be.

'A couple of years ago,' Victor said, 'I attended a course on serial killers and met a psychologist called Kumar who lectured us on the mindset of a killer. He said we all have a beast inside us like a sleeping dog waiting to come out under the right circumstances.' He paused to make sure Frank was listening.

'I met the same doctor a few weeks ago at Hendon Police College in London. He's advising on the operation involving Cameron. When I asked him about Cameron he said that Cameron had a vicious alter ego. If that's true then be cautious Frank. The bloke might look like an insignificant imbecile, but these guys at Hendon know what they're talking about so tread bloody carefully.'

Frank nodded thoughtfully.

'Vic, what's all this rubbish about dog fighting in the forest? Lonnie and the others gave that shit up years ago.'

Victor had to agree with Frank; dog fighting appeared to be a thing of the past until Heather began poking around.

'Don't really know, Frank. Everyone, including Cameron believes someone is organising fights again.'

Frank rubbed his hands together. 'Fights yes, not dog fights though Vic, something else entirely.'

Victor squinted in bewilderment. 'What then?'

Frank leaned closer to Victor, 'Dogs fighting men.' Adding, whilst raising his hands in supplication to emphasise innocence, 'Just a rumour Vic, I'm not involved honest.'

Victor found the concept of men being attacked by dogs for sport revolting.

'Do you know this for sure?'

Frank sucked air in through his teeth. 'No not

entirely, it's just a rumour floating around. Whatever is going on though, Lukas Meek has something to do with it, I'm sure of it. I've tried asking him about it. He won't have it. Meek knows we're close.'

A fat man in greasy jeans and grubby grey pullover came into the bar, clearly worse the wear from drink. Victor kept an eye on him as the man approached the barman.

Frank said, 'There's something else, Vic. Chinese whispers say that Lukas has trained a massive dog that can take on anything and chew it to bits. He's trying to arrange a fight for money involving this dog and someone they call Bull.'

Victor had heard the name before, just couldn't recall where.

Frank read his mind. 'It's the name I heard shouted when Nigel Moon keeled over at the back of the cottage; weird or what?'

'Yes it's weird. When you meet Cameron, make sure he knows about this.'

Victor noted Frank's frown.

'Just tell him about it, okay? I want to know how he reacts.'

The fat drunk looked aimlessly around the bar, settling his gaze on Frank.

Victor noticed the attention.

'Do you know the bloke at the bar?'

Frank lit up like a beacon. 'Shagged his missus a couple of times, I think she told him'.

Victor shook his head. 'Is he likely to cause trouble?'

Frank whispered, 'Oh yes, most definitely.'

Suddenly the fat bloke wandered over to their table, his enormous fist wrapped around a pint of beer, spilling as he walked, face flushed red, eyes rheumy with alcohol.

He plonked his pint on the table.

'Got your minder with you Frank, scared to be out on your own without Mister Big Shot copper in tow?'

Victor slowly stood. He gave the drunk a steely glare. He then smiled warmly. 'You know who I am, yet you are a stranger to me. They say a stranger is a friend you haven't met.'

Victor stuck out his hand. At first the drunk hesitated then grabbed Victor's hand, shaking it tentatively.

'I'm Victor LaSalle, pleased to meet you.'

The drunk looked puzzled, eventually saying, 'Bill Groves.' One rheumy eye roved over Frank. 'Your mate here has been shagging my Irene. Dirty bastard needs a good kicking.'

Victor looked at Frank disappointingly, shook his shaven head and turned his attention to Bill.

'I'm sure he deserves a good kicking. But you and I both know this is the wrong time and the wrong place.'

Victor sensed the man calming.

'Why don't you go over the road to the Miners Arms and let me handle Frank. Trust me I know how you feel. Leave this alone for now, as a favour to me. I really would appreciate it.'

Bill shrugged, 'I've heard about you Mr LaSalle, you could have me locked up for being drunk, so why so charitable all of a sudden?'

Victor smiled, pinched his nose and said, 'Lets just say I'm sick and tired of violence. You look like a decent bloke and I don't want to get you in trouble.'

Bill raised his hands, bent down, picked up his pint, swigged it and left the bar.

Frank astonished said, 'what's with you Vic, I've seen the day you would have pummelled his face inside out.'

Victor said, 'I've got things on my mind, troubling

things. For the first time in my life I feel out of my depth.'

Victor kept his eye on big Bill Groves, watched him stagger to the Miners Arms opposite, relaxed his shoulders; sighed.

He gave Frank a serious stare.

'Someone once said we have three faces; the face we think we are; the face others see and the face we really are.'

Frank frowned again. Victor continued, tapping the table with his index finger to reinforce his point.

'What if there is another one; a face we don't want anyone to see but we know it's there, lurking like an unwelcome ogre, desperate to come out?'

To Victor's amazement, Frank said, 'Like the Incredible Hulk?'

Victor, mid drink, spurted whiskey onto the table.

Chapter 14

At six-fifteen, Cameron left the cottage and drove into town in Sam's car. Feeling benevolent for once since she wasn't going anywhere, she'd condescended, 'Just so long as you deliver it back safely,' her parting shot.

At least he'd contacted the garage who'd been more than accommodating. Being a copper still had clout apparently. He dropped off the keys and the foreman said they'd get it sorted out this evening and told him to contact them in the morning.

Cameron thought about recent developments. If it were true about Frank Slack, where did it leave him? One minute the suspect in his mother's murder, the next...

The 'Fox and Hounds' pub stood on the high street butted up to a Chinese takeaway. Cameron parked on the cobbles. A quick check in the driving mirror told him he'd pass muster even though he hadn't shaved. Strolling up the slight incline to the pub entrance, he stepped around a small Chinese man busy collecting polystyrene food cartons and shoving them into a black bin liner. The man bowed his head when Cameron walked past.

Cameron couldn't resist, 'No respect for tidiness some people.' He received another nod, in fact two; he assumed the Chinaman agreed.

About to enter the pub he paused, conscious of his hands trembling. Right now Cameron felt lonely, abandoned almost. Yet his inner turmoil wasn't about being alone, more about lost opportunities, empty rooms never filled with the bosom of a family. Plus he wanted to believe Frank Slack was innocent, only then could he embrace him as his half brother.

The desire to be part of a family gnawed at him; even if it meant being related to the Slack clan. A loner by choice, he'd immersed himself in work; an acceptable diversion, it compensated some. When his father killed himself, his mother had grown ambivalent toward him. During his visits to Heather, he began to think of her as a ghost from a former life, never the woman he had gone to when he'd grazed a knee, or been bullied at school.

It had been the bullying incident with Stanley Watson which introduced Blake to the outside world. For weeks after his ordeal in the forest, Cameron had been hearing strange voices. His young mind thought they were the voices of a guardian angel, always soothing him when he felt a headache coming on or advising him to stay calm when his parents argued. Then came the incident with Stanley and he knew it was someone else entirely occupying his mind.

It had become customary on Wednesday after sports afternoon for Stanley to wait by the front gates for the younger boys to come out. Stanley would randomly select a boy and begin his ritual. First he would goad the boy about his appearance and then push and shove him around. Then after reducing his hapless victim to tears he would spit in their faces. Of course some parents had reported Stanley's behaviour but it didn't appear to deter Stanley no matter how many times he got himself suspended; until Blake happened.

Cameron couldn't remember it. Apparently witnesses said Cameron went berserk. Stanley needed six stitches. The police put it down to self-defence. Even the self-righteous head of the school Mr Gates had been initially sympathetic, stating conspiratorially that Stanley deserved his comeuppance and Cameron had merely reacted in self-defence. Until Blake blurted out, 'He got what he deserved the fat bastard.'

The noise of a Jeep interrupted his thoughts. It pulled down the side street opposite the pub, similar to

105

the vehicle tailing him since he'd left Haughton village.

Not about to get paranoid, he pushed the swing door and stepped into a room that reeked of smoke and mouldy carpets. The barman, a young man with a pock marked face, had his head buried in the sports pages of a newspaper. He glanced up for a second, then back at his paper.

Three customers only, two elderly men sitting together heads bobbing in conversation, ignored him. Another man sat alone at the table in the far corner by the window. The television above the bar was switched on, volume low. A tarnished metal clock on the wall said six fifty-five.

Leaning on the bar counter Cameron stared at the barman without speaking. Eventually, with a huff, the man folded his newspaper.

'What can I get you?'

'Half of bitter please.'

The barman pulled the beer, plonking it in front of Cameron.

'Eighty pence mate.'

Cameron paid him. The barman chucked the money in the till like it was a major chore, slammed the drawer and went back to his newspaper. Cameron scanned the room. The two pensioners stared relentlessly at the television's boring early evening chat show. The third man, head bowed, looked up. Cameron recognised him from photographs in the case papers.

A nod exchanged, he went over to the small round table, pulled up a stool, sat down and placed his glass on a beer mat.

He peered at the man opposite. Could this be the man responsible for his mother's murder?

Frank Slack appeared relaxed, not fidgety, or avoiding eye contact. He said, straight to the point, 'I didn't do it, DS Cameron, I didn't murder your

106

mother.'

Cameron took a sip of beer, removed his spectacles, gave them a wipe with his crumpled handkerchief. 'Convince me.'

'I'll try.'

Frank Slack was wearing a suit and tie, projecting an impression he'd worn the suit like one would for a wedding or funeral. Out of respect perhaps?

Should Cameron throttle him, choke a confession out of him? No, that was not his way, not since the Martin Pope incident. He'd be patient, exercise control. Blake wasn't going to spoil this meeting, no way.

Frank said, 'Vic told you about our family connection?'

He sounded eloquent enough, hardly a man who burgled houses for a living. Cameron studied him, noted Slack's eyes were dark blue like his own. He had curly black hair, a fresh complexion, his whole demeanour hinting at a man with nothing to hide.

Frank sucked in a lungful of air. It gushed out. He laughed. 'Sorry, got the hiccups must be nerves. They say holding your breath helps.'

He relaxed, took a swig of beer.

'Yes, LaSalle did inform me of our connections,' Cameron confirmed.

Slack wiped froth from his lips.

'Do you believe him?'

'Yes, I believe him.'

'It's good to finally meet you brother.'

Frank stuck out his hand. Cameron shook it.

**

Like its owner, Lukas Meek, the jeep stank of dogs and sweat. Ron Stark regretted borrowing the damn thing. Unfortunately, it had been necessary. His sports car

107

would stand out.

He'd thought long and hard about his conversation with his brother Lukas.

This Cameron bloke was doing a good job of putting people on edge, giving everyone the impression he was eccentric, fragmented in manner both with people and police work; a neat way of effectively disarming everyone by making people believe he was inept, disjointed, incapable of rationality.

Stark convinced himself he knew different. Cameron, he had decided, was a threat.

Fortunately, Cameron drove cautiously, easy to follow without getting too close. Parking the jeep out of sight, Stark approached the pub from the side, slid along the wall, and took a peek through the window. Oh yeah, there they were, Cameron and Frank Slack, having a cosy chat in the corner.

Chapter 15

Victor tucked the Jaguar nicely out of sight down an alley next to the Chinese takeaway. Being black the car melted into the darkness, its front sufficiently enough forward to give Victor a decent view of the cobbled parking area next to the pub and most of the high street.

No need to actually baby sit Frank. La Salle being confident Frank was capable of handling Cameron. Not that Cameron bothered him so much as the nagging doubts about the police operation incessantly burrowing his brain. Weird shit this operation, he thought. Victor needed to be on top of it in case the Chief had held back relevant information which might save her career if the operation went tits up. Of course the other thing concerning dog fighting nibbled at the back of his mind.

Frank's earlier disclosure also concerned him. Could it be that Christine knew about the fights? He'd asked HQ to check the hospitals, and bugger me the information they fed back supported what Frank had told him. In the past couple of months, numerous men in their twenties and thirties, most from the travelling community, had been admitted to Accident and Emergency departments across the county with severe dog bites.

Scanning the street with his night vision goggles, borrowed from Headquarters, he gave some thought about the additional cameras dotted around the high street, invaluable when it came to evidence gathering on drunken Saturday nights. A pity it took this operation and Walter's cash to purchase the damn things. Another unsettling thought; were the Chief Constable and Doctor Kumar staking the place? Watching him, watching them? Victor shivered.

Kumar bothered Victor. The man appeared to have

unlimited access to police information. This didn't sit well with Victor. Yes, worth keeping an eye on Kumar; perhaps ask around, check if there was anything untoward about the doctor. After all, Victor's ability to assess people was renowned, apparently.

Topping this, he'd felt like a chastised kid when the Chief warned him not to jeopardise the operation by poking around. 'Everything is being controlled and monitored,' she'd informed him, 'so give Cameron plenty of rope.'

What on earth was Ron Stark doing creeping about outside the pub? Victor eased himself farther down in the leather seat to watch Stark edge along the wall and peek into the bar. The guy bothered him, gave him the creeps.

He'd recently read Ron Stark's report regarding the original abduction of Brian Mullen twenty years ago. Stark had been taken off the enquiry when he refused to believe Walter had anything to do with it. At least he had that in his favour. Uneasiness maintained its hold. He thought about the original abduction. How everything appeared to point to Walter Slack being the abductor. Why in God's name had no other lines of enquiry been followed? And why did Ron suddenly ditch his CID career and become a wooden top for the past twenty years?

Stark shuffled away from the pub wall and skulked back to a dark green tatty jeep. Sure Victor knew the jeep, just couldn't remember where he'd seen it before?

He felt peculiar, sitting in his car, night vision goggles sticking out from his face like some grotesque extension of his eyes. One thing, they had proved it had been Stark skulking about, green, clear and unequivocal.

**

Cameron believed he could trust the man opposite.

'The evidence against you . . . it was . . .' Cameron searched for an appropriate word. He settled for, 'credible'.

'Mostly it was circumstantial.'

Cameron incredulous; 'You were seen talking to Heather on the day of her murder.'

'She invited me to the cottage, we got on well.'

Cameron insisted, 'For Christ's sake your hammer was used to club her to death.'

Frank shook his head vigorously. 'I left it there after fixing the roof, someone else took it.'

They sat in silence until Cameron said, 'How well did you know Nigel Moon?'

Frank paused, glanced a way for a second.

'Quite well; it was me who found Nigel in the garden the day he died.'

Cameron raised his eyebrows. '*You* found him?'

'I called the ambulance.' Frank pleased with himself.

Cameron couldn't contain his surprise. No one, not even Sam had mentioned this.

'Did Harry Mullen know?'

Frank shrugged. 'They all knew. They asked me about it when they arrested me.'

Cameron had read the transcripts of the tape-recorded interviews with Frank Slack. He couldn't recollect seeing anything about his finding Nigel Moon. Made him think how much more could be missing from the case papers.

Movement in the window; Cameron thought he saw someone looking in but was slow turning his head, his full attention on Frank; hard not to stare.

'When did you first meet Nigel?'

111

Frank undid his tie, took another long pull at his beer.

'I did a couple of jobs for him at the cottage; you know replacing roof tiles and such. It gave me opportunities to see Heather.'

'What happened the day you found him?' Cameron rocked back in his chair, hands behind his head, fingers interlaced.

'I was halfway up a ladder at the front of the place when I heard shouting.'

Cameron swayed forward hating to miss anything.

'I ran around the back. There was Nigel clutching his chest. He went red, like he was burning up, then white. He suddenly stopped breathing.'

Slack paused. 'Man, he had such a horrible expression on his face.' He glanced both ways, whispered, 'You know like he'd seen something that scared the shit out of him.'

Nigel Moon, successful developer, a man who risked thousands on land deals, not the sort to scare easily.

'Did you see what might have startled him?'

Frank lowered his voice.

'I heard someone or something run into the forest.' Frank gave Cameron a long hard stare and beamed, shaking his head.

Cameron glanced over his shoulder.

'What are you grinning about?'

Frank, still smiling said, 'When she told me I was her son, I was angry, upset because you'd lived all those years with her. I never imagined I would like you, especially you being a copper.'

Cameron thought about Samantha.

'Believe me, Frank, I know the feeling.'

Frank tapped the table. 'There's something else.' He leaned closer. 'As I ran round the back of the house I heard a man's voice shout a name.' He gripped his pint glass about to drain his beer, 'I think he shouted "Let's get out of here Bull, something like that.'

Cameron recognised the name Bull from somewhere deep in his past.

To enable the bond of trust to be tightly forged, Cameron would ask Frank a straightforward question; one that would test Frank's honesty to the limit.

'The burglaries in Winston, the ones targeted against the large house. Are you responsible?'

Frank remained impassive.

Cameron added, 'If you are, I want you to stop. I don't intend to arrest you, merely wish to establish more trust between us.'

Frank finally said, 'Funny, Victor's already given me the same warning.'

Chapter 16

Cameron had his car back by one on Saturday afternoon. The mechanic said damp had gotten into the wiring. The bloody rain in Winston never seemed to stop. They didn't charge him much.

Sam had driven him; dropped him outside the garage and gone off shopping. Little had been said between them to mean anything. She appeared distracted. Doubtless they would catch up later. Knowing Sam, she'd want to hear of any developments.

It had been twenty-four hours since meeting Walter Slack and Victor LaSalle. Cameron knew his Chief Constable would ask a plenty of questions. For the first time in their relationship, he decided to be less than candid.

He'd known Christine Krill for ten years. She'd been his Commander during his undercover operations in London, proving a valuable ally when the internal enquiry began. Remarkably astute and very professional, she was without doubt his favourite supervisor. Except that lately she'd developed an edge. Cameron couldn't fathom why.

Her chosen rendezvous turned out to be thirty miles from Winston. It overlooked the Hole of Horcum, a colossal crater on the Whitby to Pickering road, which gave the impression of a miniature Grand Canyon. She'd chosen it to suit herself as apparently she was attending a Rotary dinner in Pickering as guest speaker, this car park on her way.

A hot dog van in the car park enjoyed a roaring trade, one customer sure to have been Christine who never hid her love of junk food. In fact she'd use her size to intimidate and conquer the non-believers in her talent.

Cameron spotted her black Volvo; her ample bosom

114

nestling against the steering wheel. He tapped on the window and caught a benevolent smile as she dabbed tomato ketchup from her mouth with a paper napkin, at the same time activating the electronic window.

'Hello Cameron my love, still wearing the silly bow tie?'

Cameron stood back allowing Christine to slide laboriously from behind the wheel and empty her bulk onto the car park.

'Hello Chief.'

Placing an arm around his shoulder, which she could just about reach in comfort, her wax jacket opened slightly, police uniform evident beneath it. Very typical of Christine; she loved the pomp of being Chief Constable, always eager to talk to television reporters, never found wanting when it came to wit and repartee with local politicians; reluctant to remove her uniform even for social events.

'Let's take a walk,' she invited.

For about five minutes they strolled along a footpath, without a word, crossing the main road before following the track around the Hole. Cameron enjoyed the view. Christine remained impartial to it, town and city life more her style.

A couple of hikers toting heavy rucksacks wended there way up the path toward them smiling and nodding in passing.

Christine stopped abruptly. Satisfied they were far enough away from potential eavesdroppers.

'It's been two weeks, Jason; anything to tell me?'

He took in her piercing, don't-mess-me-about glance. 'Phew, where do I start?'

She tugged a blade of grass from between the heather and chewed on it.

'Let's begin with my esteemed colleague Victor LaSalle.'

He aired his encounter with LaSalle in the custody suite. Then he told her about the meeting at High Cliff with LaSalle and Walter Slack. This she listened to attentively, nodding occasionally, even inspecting the damp ground at the mention of Walter Slack. One thing he didn't divulge was Walter Slack's disclosure about Frank and how he, Cameron, had inherited a half brother. Not that he totally distrusted her, just that it had little bearing on her quest to dissect and disrupt LaSalle.

'Is LaSalle sweating about the enquiry?' Those eyes again, questing for truth.

'I don't think so. He's more concerned about the existence of a conspiracy against him.' Cameron kicked a loose stick in the grass, and immediately thought of his encounter with the dog and its owner. 'To be frank, Vic believes someone deliberately misplaced the hammer to discredit him because of his connections to Frank Slack.'

'What do you think?'

'I believe him.'

'Is he manipulating you as well as the rest of the force?'

Cameron bristled at her comment. Throwaway, yet it took him off guard. 'The man is on the edge; it's nothing to do with the enquiry. There's something else going on.'

'Did you know Cameron, that the Hole of Horcum is one of the few places in England were you are most likely to come across snakes?'

Like a shot out of the blue, this threw him. He instinctively kicked the heather and wished he'd hung onto the stick.

'Speaking of snakes,' Cameron said using the analogy, 'I do think LaSalle is involved in something unsavoury. Nothing to do with informant handling

though, he's too sharp and dedicated to be that stupid.'
He sought her face for a reaction. She was impassive
and waved him to continue.

'Who made the allegations in the first place,
ma'am?'

Christine Krill smirked at the use of her title,
immediately followed up with a hard stare, as if she
were assessing his non-verbal ticks and gulps. After a
couple of seconds she said, 'Harry Mullen.'

Cameron didn't hide his surprise.

'That's weird, because Harry is almost affectionate
when he talks about Victor LaSalle.' It was the Chief's
turn to raise an eyebrow.

Cameron went on: 'What's the gist of his
allegation?'

The Chief Constable hesitated, evidently debating
whether to answer. When she spoke, she sounded
nervous.

'He insists that Vic had something to do with the
hammer going missing because of his link with Frank
Slack. He also believes Victor is taking kickbacks from
insurance payouts. It turns out that six of his informants
have been paid substantial amounts by insurance
companies.'

Cameron shook his head. 'I'm not convinced.'

A kestrel hovered above the heather about thirty
yards away. Suddenly it swooped, seconds later
shooting into the sky empty-handed.

'What do you believe is going on Cameron?'

He took a few paces, came back. 'I'm thinking
someone has it in big style for Victor. I believe that
someone is probably an ex-lover. Victor's problem I'm
afraid, the bugger's a bit of a philanderer.'

'Keep digging, my sweet. I'm sure you'll unravel
the mystery.'

With that she turned and headed back to the car

park.

It took him a few quick steps to catch up.

'Chief, why not simply bring Victor in for an official interview, ask him about his dealings with his informants?'

'Because, my dear, he is up for Superintendent soon and if he is innocent I will be viewed as trying to put the boot in to frustrate his promotion

'I know this is very difficult for you Jason, I really do, but something is going on in Winston and Mister - bloody- LaSalle is involved. Of that I am sure.'

At the roadside she held him back with her hand looking both ways like a mother and child.

Satisfied the road was clear, she placed her hand in the small of his back and almost guided him to the car park.

Christine breathed in, enjoying the fresh air. 'You know despite my love of bricks and mortar it is good to get out of the office.'

Frustrated at her apparent lack in understanding his predicament, Cameron gazed out over the cliff top.

Sensing his irritation she said, 'I know what you're thinking. You believe I have an ulterior motive for slotting you into Winston, notwithstanding your mother's unfortunate demise.'

Cameron confirmed her suspicions by looking at his shoes, shrugging his shoulders.

'Tut, tut Jason, cheer up.'

'What am I doing there Chief? OK you said it's all right to have a peek at the murder file and therefore rattle a few cages. It's just that I still don't see what this has to do with DCI LaSalle. You and I know my medical retirement is waiting in the wings. It's just a matter of time before I'm recalled before the Met medical board.'

She cupped his face in her hands. 'Jason my dear;

118

with your apparent lack of charisma, your unnerving clinical demeanour, you possess an ability to irritate and anger people you encounter. I'm hoping these qualities will flush out enough muck in Winston to enable me to have a good old spring clean.'

He looked directly into her eyes.

'I know you're closing the police station. Guessed there was something weird about the place, its lack of industry and space to move around. It's because you've trimmed it back with the intention of shutting the damn place altogether.' He flicked a quick glance. 'I am right? You had a buyer for the place and couldn't sell it immediately because you're under pressure from the local council about lack of policing. Heather's murder just made things worse.' He gave her another quick look to confirm his suspicions.

He knew she'd already sold it to Walter Slack so why try to manipulate him?

She took hold of his hand and squeezed. 'Perhaps you're right.' She fastened her coat, preparing to leave. 'Please think of Winston for now as an extension of your recuperation.' She flashed him her winning smile. 'Twelve months undercover with the detritus of society and then a court case, is enough to take its toll on anyone.'

Images flashed into his mind. Those of grubby little men discussing their disgusting passions and desires like they were normal and respectable members of society. Fortunately, a great deal of his time undercover was now a complete blank. They said it was his natural defence to trauma, his brain shutting out the horror. They were wrong. Blake, and Blake alone, experienced the trauma.

It had been Blake all along who had ensured Cameron's success as an undercover policeman. The first time they debriefed him he had difficulty

119

answering the questions. Realising he had no option he purposefully became aggressive with the debrief team. This allowed Blake to return. Later when he watched the recording of the debrief he came to fully realise the extent of Blake's occupation of his mind and body.

Blake's cold calculating disclosures about the undercover operation involving a drug cartel made for fascinating viewing. No wonder fellow officers gave him a wide birth. He swallowed hard. She had dampened his fire.

'Chief, you're using me and it feels uncomfortable.'

'We all get used in one way or another. You owe me, remember.'

Cameron looked away knowing Christine would expect him to continue. She had supported him throughout his illness and now she wanted payback.

The Chief Constable changed the subject. 'By the way, last week a car containing two men was stopped by traffic patrol in the early hours, just outside Winston. The cop had the sense to search it and found two bloody badger carcasses in the boot. Imagine that, bloody dead badgers.'

Cameron told her about the pit in the forest. Christine listened and tapped her teeth, another habit when concentrating. It drove Cameron mad.

'What were their names?'

She frowned. 'Oh I see the men in the car; Lonnie and Frank Slack.'

Cameron would speak with Frank Slack again.

'Why doesn't that surprise me?'

'Does anyone from Winston know you spent time investigating the links with dog fighting and the disappearance of the boy in London?'

Cameron went quiet, his voice barely a whisper. 'I doubt it.'

'Good.' She took another lungful of fresh country

air.

'Help Walter Slack if you can, he's the one with the murky connections. Hopefully it will keep him off my back.'

Cameron saw the kestrel hovering. It had returned to try a second swoop into the heather.

This time an unsuspecting rodent wriggled violently in its efforts to escape. For some reason the scene reminded him of Blake; his pulse quickened.

'There's something else, Chief.' He searched her plump face for any sign of deceit. 'Someone is watching the cottage.'

Chapter 17

Sunday morning. Once again the rain hammered the slate roof tiles. He could hear Sam up and about, busy in the kitchen.

Cameron knew he should let her know about the meeting with Frank Slack and the fact he was related to half the bloody population of Winston. The associations and family links were giving him a headache. Years spent worrying about being alone lacking family to rely upon, it now seemed he was part of an expansive family network. And it gladdened him.

He wanted to share his hopes for the future with Sam; let her know what his life had been like and what he was now becoming. He guessed though it would be impossible for her to understand. She would form part of the conundrum, become an unlikely, reluctant link in the chain.

Opening the kitchen door he leaned against the frame, listening. Sam quietly sang *"Yesterday"* that good old Beatles standard. He loved her long black hair, tumbling over her shoulders. He imagined the touch of it.

'I was up early, went to the supermarket and bought some flowers for Heather. I'm off to the cemetery. Do you want to come?' He waved the bunch of flowers.

Sam placed the last of the washing up on the draining board and dried her hands.

'I don't like visiting the cemetery, it's morbid.'

He didn't hide his disappointment. 'It's not morbid.'

Out of the blue she asked, 'Jason where did you get to last night?'

He'd known she'd ask; saw it in her face the moment she'd dropped him at the garage yesterday. He put the flowers on the kitchen table, sat down in what might be seen as a huff.

'It's a long story.'

'I'm listening.'

Reluctant, to say, sure she would be offended, even hurt and why shouldn't she? The main suspect in Heather's murder was his half-brother; a relative willing to assist him in finding the true killer. How ridiculous that sounded.

He dived straight in. Better to be open rather than furtive. 'I met Frank Slack. LaSalle fixed it up.'

She dragged a kitchen chair from the table, plonked herself down, chin in her hands.

She eventually responded, her voice cracked, emotional.

'You met Frank Slack, Just like that! Are you bloody insane?'

Cameron sat opposite her fiddling with a spoon in the sugar bowl.

'If you met him you would understand.'

Standing suddenly, Sam grabbed the back of the chair with both hands. Her knuckles bled white such was her grip.

'You're weird, you know. One minute you sound rational, the next you're like some deluded mentalist.'

Cameron couldn't think of a smart reply. He shrugged.

'Come on out with it, what else happened Jason?'

'Do you know who Heather was before she met Dad?'

'What do you mean, *who she was*?' She screwed her face up. 'She was a bloody freelance writer.'

'I'm talking about her family history.'

'You're annoying me, get on with it.'

'Heather's mother and father died young. Her dad was Walter Slack's brother.'

She held a hand on her brow. 'Jesus, I'm half related to that crowd.'

'Heather had a son when she was sixteen.' He paused to check her reaction before continuing. 'The father was a man she met when she worked in Orchards café. He left Winston when he found out about her pregnancy. Walter Slack raised the boy.' He lowered his head.

'It's Frank Slack, Sam. Frank Slack is my brother.'

**

The rain tapped gently on the brolly. It felt good to share its sheltering canopy, standing beside Heather's grave holding hands. The cemetery close to the police station covered an area about the size of a football pitch. Buried alongside Nigel Moon in a modest plot, Heather Moon had an oval shaped concrete headstone, overshadowed by towering monuments either side.

Earlier at the cottage, Sam's reaction to Cameron's disclosures were at first irrational; at one point she'd erupted in tears accusing him of interfering in Heather's past, besmirching her character. He did his best to convince her he loved his mother, and how determined he was to find out who had taken her life in such brutal fashion.

He told her about Frank's disclosures concerning the death of her father, Sam surprised, taken aback. He asked her about her father's heart attack.

'I knew it was Frank Slack who found Dad, the police told me.' She dabbed her eyes with a tissue. 'No mention about anyone else being there, scaring the shit out of him. It was put down to natural causes.'

'In a way it was,' he'd answered. 'Except it might have been accelerated by what he witnessed in the garden'

He'd shuffled his chair closer, enjoying the interaction. 'Don't worry; I will be digging out the

124

Coroners report.'

'What I said, earlier, about visiting Heather's grave.' She'd regarded him with one eyebrow raised. 'It was crass and I apologise. It was thoughtful of you to buy flowers.'

Sam suddenly brightened, grabbed her coat from the hall and ushered him out of the door.

'Let's go together'.

In the car, Sam had become animated, insisting he dig deeper, even if it meant interviewing the Coroner.

Despite this, Cameron had a feeling she was holding out on him: hiding information about her father's death perhaps? Just a passing sensation similar to the one experienced at the meeting with Christine Krill.

It had taken them five minutes to arrive at the cemetery. A couple of fellow mourners walked past, Cameron surprised to see Janice and Harry Mullen, arm in arm, dressed smartly in overcoats, Janice carrying an umbrella.

Harry nodded; both paused momentarily beside Heather's grave. Janice indicated with a flick of her eyes that Harry should continue. He pursed his lips, hesitated briefly before changing his mind and walked on alone. Harry stopped at the cemetery gates, looking like an uncertain spectre in the rain.

Janice Mullen tilted her umbrella, enabling her to look directly at Cameron.

'They found Brian's blood stained clothes in the forest and gave us permission to bury them in a coffin.' She said like she was announcing an important occasion. 'It took ten years for Harry to persuade them Brian was gone for good.' She sounded proud, pleased with herself. 'I never lost hope.'

Sam and Cameron stood, motionless, uncertain how to respond.

Cameron's eyes widened, slight shock hearing what she'd said. He'd known for a while that Janice had something to disclose and that he'd feel uncomfortable. Right then he wanted to scurry away, hide. Pennies began to drop, memories surged.

'What is it you want to tell me Janice?' he managed through a dry mouth.

She hugged herself with her free hand. 'Two days before you went missing in the forest, my son Brian was abducted, they never found him.'

Harry Mullen began walking towards them. Janice held up her hand for him to stop. He shook his head, advancing no further.

Janice turned slowly toward Cameron. 'You know about missing kids don't you?' Cameron nodded. 'You found that boy who went missing in London.' Her eyes were pleading. 'Please, Sergeant Cameron, help me find Brian.'

Never had Cameron heard anything so plaintive, so . . . appealing.

Chapter 18

Situated on Winston high street, Orchards Café overlooked the War Memorial.

Cameron suggested it would be better if he and Janice went there, and over coffee discuss her missing son. Harry sloped off, giving his wife a tired headshake.

Sam drove to the café, Cameron in front with her, Janice in the rear. She parked on the cobbles outside Orchards, thankful there was a space.

Orchards: a funny little place, the café long, narrow and sparsely decorated.

Cameron went to the green Formica counter. He ordered three coffees from a smiling brunette, twenty-something behind a counter cluttered with packs of biscuits, cream cakes in glass cases, and umpteen pies and sausage rolls. A handwritten sign indicated you could order to eat in, or as a take-out. The pies looked appetising. Cameron settled for just coffee; collected packets of sugar and plastic pots of milk and walked back to the table nearest the window.

Cameron sat down; the cheap chair scraped the linoleum floor, its aluminium, uncomfortable and cold. Several prints for sale offered slight solace from the walls, all depicting scenes from Winston. A couple included views of the forest. The nearest print, a watercolour, showed the town in summer, horse drawn carriages and old-fashioned cars dotted along the high street. Behind the town were lush green hills, the odd clump of woodland, conifers yet to be planted.

Well, well, Cameron was surprised by a photograph of Walter Slack, unveiling the new war memorial. The crowd in the background was thin, sparse, mostly children.

The coffees arrived served by the waitress, a stick of

a girl with a permanent smile on her face. It added to the weirdness Cameron felt since he'd recognised something in Janice Mullen's manner. A long forgotten shadow of pain etched on her face.

Janice Mullen poured several packets of sugar into her cup, absently stirring. Sam crossed her legs, giving Cameron a quizzical frown that more or less acted as a prompt.

Cameron said quietly, 'Janice?' and waited for the woman to speak.

She did, and abruptly: 'I know Brian is not dead Mr Cameron, otherwise I would feel something.'

Cameron placed his hand on hers. 'What do you think happened to Brian?'

She flicked her head back, stuck out her chin, an adamant pose that dared anyone to contradict her. 'Brian was abducted Mr Cameron, outside the school gates, *by someone in this town.*'

'You know this for sure?'

A tear trickled, hastily dried by a serviette.

'Trust me Janice, all you say here is in confidence.'

Her eyes flicked toward Sam who smiled. 'You can trust me too.'

'A man was seen outside the school gates, lurking.'

'Who saw the man Janice?'

She raised her head slowly, 'Well you did DS Cameron. You saw him and told your mother.'

Cameron twisted uncomfortably. 'I did? Are you sure Janice?'

She sniffed. 'Of course I am.' Janice sounded offended. 'Your mother confronted him when the police didn't believe her.'

'Why didn't the police believe her?'

'Heather complained in the past about a man following you. The police set up an operation. When nothing happened they convinced your mother you'd made it up.'

Cameron felt hot, embarrassed, more since he was unable to remember, yet knowing Janice spoke the truth.

Janice slid the chair backwards, determined to look less browbeaten. She slowly raised herself.

'It was because of you they didn't react quickly enough.' Her eyes widened, not accusing exactly, but certainly truthful. 'They thought you and Brian were in it together, somehow.'

Cameron asked, 'Why would they think that?'

'You were like brothers.' A smile flickered.

'Sometimes when I saw you from a distance I thought you were Brian. You even swapped clothes. Surely you can't have forgotten?'

'I'm sorry Janice but my childhood memories aren't very clear.' Apart from nightmarish visions, Cameron had mere snatches of memory to convince him his childhood actually happened.

Janice gave Sam a sorrowful look. 'I'd better go; Harry will be waiting.'

Without further preamble Janice Mullen walked elegantly to the door of the café. The bell tinkled. Half turning she said, 'Brian has been seen in the forest, I know it's him, even your mother saw him; *out there*.' Janice jabbed a finger at the forest.

'Speak to Victor, DS Cameron.' She gently closed the café door.

Cameron let out a whoosh of air.

Sam said, 'If she is to be believed, then it might have been you the abductor was after.'

'What do you mean?'

'Heather confronted the man and then Brian goes missing. I wonder if Brian Mullen was wearing your clothes?'

129

Chapter 19

Christine Krill's personal assistant showed Victor LaSalle into her opulent office. The Chief Constable, slightly hung over from red wine, didn't intend making it a long meeting. The gaseous explosions in her tummy were threatening to make an unwelcome exit. Glancing from her paperwork, she smiled at Victor. He looked immaculate in a grey Italian suit and red silk tie. It would be an awkward meeting.

Victor seated himself at the conference table facing Christine.

Christine noticed his glance at an office wall festooned with photographs and certificates highlighting her career; very like sitting in photographer's studio. How she relished it when colleagues noticed her 'ego wall'. And rightly so; she was proud of her achievements including her supervision of the undercover unit at Scotland Yard. Ironically its most successful officer in the past twenty years was Jason Cameron, a ragged, awkward individual who'd initially regarded her with suspicion. Strangely, Christine admired his forthright manner, his funny turn of phrase.

Eager to exploit Cameron, who stood apart from his colleagues; just how different Christine hadn't truly understood until she'd dispatched him into the filthy world of paedophiles. She'd noted with some displeasure that most accepted Cameron as a kindred spirit. He had thrived until the Martin Pope affair. From then on she'd realised the young officer could be more than just an undercover operative: he could be a chameleon.

With Cameron on board, she'd convinced herself Operation Bifurcate would identify a murderer. If it didn't work, then Cameron would simply be put back into the treatment programme as before. If successful, it would allow Walter Slack to have his chance to finally clear his name. And of course she would have Walter Slack's eternal gratitude and the chance of a lucrative post at the National Crime Faculty, thanks to Doctor Kumar. That was the plan, hopefully.

Christine asked Victor, 'Is it working?'

Victor crossed his legs. 'I'm not convinced.' He loosened his tie. 'Wouldn't it be simpler to ask Cameron to bring Blake into the open, let him identify the killer?'

Christine made a steeple with her fingers and regarded her colleague. She knew he would be reluctant to resort to such an audacious plan and that's why doubts surfaced when Doctor Kumar, her advisor and in her opinion an eminent psychologist, insisted LaSalle be involved. Victor for all his shortcomings, believed in old-fashioned police work. Unfortunately innovation and modernity were concepts out of his reach. The man preferred policing to be grounded in hunches, local knowledge, informant handling.

She said: 'You're upset because I decided to have you formally investigated.'

Victor replied quickly. 'No Chief, I understand the politics.' He examined his hands, paused before adding: 'A senior officer makes an allegation and it has to be followed through.' He wasn't convincing her. 'I know why Harry made those allegations. It had nothing to do with his code of ethics.'

Oh yes, Victor, your greatest flaw is your infatuation with married women. Janice Mullen is no exception. Of course she didn't say this.

She rubbed her podgy hands together. 'Let's hope one day you will settle down with a good woman.' Adding quickly, 'And I sincerely hope sooner rather than later.'

131

Victor stood up, paced the room, finally settling for the comfort of an easy chair in the corner, farthest away from the Chief Constable whose efforts to withhold the previous night's garlic infusions failed miserably.

'It was ill-advised to pretend to Harry Mullen that Cameron was here to poke around in my affairs.' Victor rubbed his forehead. 'Face it, Harry is no fool.'

'You know why I chose subterfuge over honesty, Victor. The advice of Doctor Kumar dictated it and I truly believe it will work. Until recently Winston had one major undetected crime occurring twenty bloody years ago. Cameron's mother goes poking around in the murky world of dog fighting and suddenly she's a murder victim. You can't ignore it.' Christine rubbed her face. 'There's a connection with dog fighting and the murder, thus it would prove counter productive involving too many people in the truth.'

She signed paperwork, then with a certain grace placed her ornate Schaeffer pen in its slim case and added, 'Cameron is the tethered goat.' She paused. 'My little white lie was a good ruse to divert others from the true nature of his presence in Winston.'

Victor looked sullen.

With a twinkle in her eye she asked, 'How did it go with Walter?'

Victor fidgeted with a loose thread on his trousers.

'Walter has his own agenda. Daresay it's possible he convinced Cameron he was genuine, who knows.'

Christine smirked.

'Walter is a human catalyst and has an uncanny ability to get under people's skin. If anyone can get this operation going, it's Walter.' She tapped the table.

'If it's true that Cameron hides another personality, an alter ego, then we want it to emerge.' She thought on what Doctor Kumar had told her about Blake being Cameron's invisible friend.

Is it possible this thing could hide away so successfully and only come out when triggered by outside influence brought on by Cameron's circumstances? Like playing with a ghost; it seemed so bloody weird, and yet Christine half accepted it, which in a way was counterproductive because deep down she believed Cameron a charlatan. Her co-operation in hosting the operation had been based on her need for absolution from the blame emanating from the Pope affair, and to keep on the good side of Doctor Kumar and Walter Slack, both of whom believed Cameron to be genuine.

'Don't fret Victor, Walter will get Cameron interested enough to take the bait and get this Blake personality thing come out into the open.' Christine stifled a burp.

'That, together with your co-operation is how we will lure and capture our fly in the web.' She smirked at her colourful metaphors.

Victor, still on edge, uncrossed his legs and shot her a hard stare.

'I've seen little evidence of a beast. Cameron is more like your petulant lamb.'

Christine grinned.

'Cameron is the link to Blake. If all goes well, our efforts will encourage Blake to come out of hiding and we'll finally find Harry's boy.' Or his body she thought. 'Just imagine it as a play, an orchestrated scenario, on a par with a crime scene reconstruction.'

Victor checked the carpet's intricate weave, before he looked at Christine. 'Chief, this plan of Doctor Kumar's is like something from a movie. No one really knows how this Blake character will react, except Cameron of course.' He looked into her blue eyes alive with anticipation, and knowing she wouldn't budge.

He tried anyway. 'What if Blake refuses to help?

133

It's a dangerous thing you're attempting and if it goes wrong, we could be in for a rough ride, particularly if Samantha Moon gets hurt.'

'You worry too much Victor, just run with it for the moment.'

Victor couldn't mask his doubts about the operation.

'If it's true, that Cameron has an alter ego, a split personality, shouldn't he be in a treatment programme, locked away somewhere?'

Christine huffed. 'The doctors prefer to call it *Dissociated Identity Disorder*. Victor if you're going to complain, then do get the phraseology correct my dear.'

Victor grunted.

'There's something else bothering you.' She came from behind her desk to stand next to Victor, her arms folded. 'What is it Victor, what's bugging you? Is it the internal investigation?'

Victor sighed. 'Look, the other day, when Cameron met with Frank, I saw someone else creeping about outside the pub.'

Christine shrugged.

'I saw Ron Stark, driving a green jeep belonging to that weirdo Lukas Meek; the man everyone knows is organising dog fights.'

Christine sat on the edge of her desk, pretended to make notes. Tapping a pencil against her teeth, she finally said, 'Let's see how it pans out. If Ron Stark is in this up to his armpits, he's exactly where we want him . . . Don't you think?'

Victor had lost. Christine smiled. She knew he would eventually accede. He desired promotion; after all, everyone had a price.

Shoulders hunched, Victor climbed to his feet and went to the door. Without turning he said, ' Chief, I presume you realise that because Jason Cameron is pending medical retirement,' he half turned to watch

134

her face, 'you realise that if anything goes wrong, we could be sued and you will lose your job.'

Christine flushed. Victor always wanted the last word.

She answered without looking up from her paperwork. 'It goes with the job Victor, nothing to worry about.'

Chapter 20

Cameron had decided to overturn the rocks that hid the wickedness of Winston's underbelly.

The scam about his posting to Winston to investigate a spate of burglaries and LaSalle's activities was now unlikely to benefit anyone. LaSalle was involved in something and it wasn't cover-ups or taking bribes.

Cameron intended speaking to the editor of the *Yorkshire Gateway*. Heather may have upset her attacker in one of her submitted articles, even though the investigation by Harry Mullen's team had discounted any clandestine connections to Heather's writing.

Hunger pains made his belly rumble. Sam had left early for work so breakfast was a non-starter. He didn't fancy toast or cereal. He thought about scrabbling in the cupboards for the suitable pan to fry some eggs, and couldn't be bothered; cooking wasn't his finest attribute. Best then to drive back into town. He'd take the short cut around the edge of the forest using the track that wound its way towards the village, the same one that passed the Winston Grange housing development.

Driving through the trees, he considered Brian Mullen. Fractured images niggled at the edge of his brain, echoes of something evil, despicable; connected to the original abduction twenty years ago.

Cameron sat next to Brian at school. Stupid not to realise until now that Brian had gone missing all those years ago. Following his experience in the forest, Cameron had never returned to Winston Primary School. The doctors decided that to have done so would be unwise, for at least a number of weeks. His next school had been in London. During the couple of day's

136

he was missing, Heather had disclosed everything to his father, including her affair with a local land developer named Nigel Moon who also had a twelve-year-old daughter, Samantha.

This on his mind he meandered along the track at a steady ten miles an hour, avoiding ruts and potholes. Rounding a bend, he came across Lukas Meek's green jeep parked at a peculiar angle, its driver's door open, the vehicle looking abandoned. Cameron stopped nearby and approached cautiously on foot.

A torch had been thrown on the passenger seat. A leather harness, of the type used on dogs by owners who dislike choke chains dropped in the passenger well. A pair of worn leather gloves was splayed in the foot-well beneath the steering wheel.

Cameron didn't see anything indicating a struggle. Further out he found what looked like spots of blood on bracken leaves beside the track. Calling Meek's name, he ventured into the forest. Some hundred yards in he reached a clearing with a stream trickling through it. The stream offered a respite from problems, albeit momentary. Cameron rested on his haunches enjoying the tranquillity, watching the woodland. To any onlooker he would appear nonchalant as he scanned his surroundings.

He sensed someone stalking amidst nearby trees, skulking behind trunks, deft darting manoeuvres much like a trained commando. Positive he'd seen the figure soon after he entered the tree line, as light greens and browns of a camouflage jacket and trousers weren't so difficult to spot amidst wind burned timber.

Rustling behind him! Then a low growl; Cameron stood up and turned to face Lukas Meek restraining the strangest looking dog Cameron had ever seen. A big boned beast with the sleek face of a wolf, white rings around its pupils; the spiked grey fur on its back adding

137

to a mighty fearsome vision. Cameron removed his spectacles, gave them a wipe with his handkerchief.

'Looking for me DS Cameron?' Cameron sensed the menace there plus a hint of sarcasm.

The dog growled again, top lip curling to reveal evil looking teeth.

'Found your jeep with the door open,' said Cameron. 'Didn't want to think something had happened to you.'

Meek smiled. 'You're a nosy bastard, DS Cameron, just like your mother.'

Any conviviality spawned at their initial encounter disappeared like smoke, now replaced with an aura of menace and silly childish taunting.

'Careful now Lukas, don't want you saying something you'll regret.'

Meek slipped the leash allowing the dog a couple of feet of freedom. It relished the brief lack of restriction and lurched toward Cameron, barking furiously.

'It's a mighty beast this one, bred for fighting,' shouted Meek.

Cameron remained impassive. He prayed Meek was bluffing.

Meek's voice rose above the noise of the dog's barking. 'They say if you feed a dog raw meat it will become ferocious and mean.' He yanked the chain and pulled the dog to heel. 'This brute's been fed on raw meat since a pup and he's angry as hell. So angry, if I let him go he'll tear you to pieces.'

With his free hand Meek produced a lump of raw meat from his wax jacket, and waved it in front of the dog's nose. The dog went wild, pulling and tugging at the leather leash. Meek put the meat to his lips, bit off a large chunk and chewed, all the while grinning like a maniac.

Discreetly Cameron slipped the flick knife from his

138

jacket pocket into the palm of his hand, the weight of the knife comforting. Would the knife be sufficient enough to halt the dog?

Blake stirred, worried, ready to take over if necessary.

'Let the dog go Lukas, see what happens.'

Meek, suddenly off guard, momentarily changed demeanour, smile fading into a twitch at the corner of his mouth.

'Stay away from the forest Cameron it isn't safe; not for you anyway.'

Meek backed off into the trees and disappeared. Cameron breathed a sigh of relief. He searched around just beyond the clearing for the man in camouflaged clothing. At the place the man had been standing he examined the ground, the footprint in the mud at least a size twelve, the tread like that of a boot print; the type used by the police, he was sure of it. Cameron walked casually back to his car, reasonably confident Meek had gone. When he reached the track, his headlights had been smashed and mud splattered on his windscreen.

Chapter 21

Samantha Moon walked up the cracked path to Gatekeeper Cottage.

Ignoring the front door, she went round the back hoping Cameron might be in the garden. She fancied a long chat with him. The garden a place that seemed to placate and relax him. She had to admit there was something about Jason Cameron beyond his boyish looks. He was intelligent and thoughtful, qualities she hadn't previously associated with policeman.

He wasn't in the garden. She entered the unlocked kitchen.

Cameron was inside talking to someone on the telephone. Sam didn't catch a great deal of what was said.

When he finished she shouted through the open door of the living room, 'Who was on the phone?'

Cameron jumped, obviously not realising she'd arrived home. She smiled.

He stammered, 'I was . . . talking to . . . a friend.'

She dropped her handbag and a sheaf of papers onto the kitchen table.

'I heard you say the name Blake, is that your friend's name?'

Sam had the strangest feeling that someone else was in the house.

Cameron moved towards her. Absently he said, 'Blake is someone I met a while ago.'

Sam glanced at her papers, on them information about injured dogs, yet she felt hesitant about sharing her findings. She blamed him for her reticence.

Since his arrival he'd been bloody moody and petulant, preferring to sulk in his room most of the time or fool around in the forest like some latter-day Sherlock. She wondered how on earth this strange little man had made such a successful a career in the police. And gain the trust of the Chief Constable.

'Who is Blake, someone from the Met?' Sam asked, taking off her coat, consigning it to a chair back.

Cameron grinned. 'He's just the opposite.' He said. 'Blake has an inherent disregard for the law; he is unduly suspicious of the police and very mistrusting of lawyers.' Cameron locked his fingers behind his head and stared up at the ceiling. 'Let's say he's someone who can go places where you and I would stand out.'

'What do you mean; go places. You don't half come out with some weird stuff.'

She noticed a spasm of unease. He said, 'For example, he could infiltrate the dog fighting racket.'

'The police don't believe Heather's death had anything to do with dog fighting.'

Cameron swallowed hard, removing an invisible blockage in his throat.

'North Yorkshire Police haven't exactly impressed me with their investigative skills.' Cameron flopped into a chair, drummed nervously with his fingers on the tabletop.

'Sam,' he said, 'what if there's a link with the articles, they're the only thing in her life which caused her conflict. With conflict you get friction and that can and often does lead to violence.'

Sam knew he said strange things. Sometimes he sounded perfectly rational and others, stark raving bonkers. Didn't his bosses realise he was suffering from stress? Shouldn't he be on sick leave or recuperating in some fancy hospital in the country? They had places like that, for policemen suffering with post-traumatic stress; a bit like they had for priests seeking respite for all manner of things, good and bad. Yes, he should be there and not here messing around with Heather's murder.

141

Sam thought about the tablets he popped and asked straight out, 'Are you still taking your pills?'

'They're just vitamins, I don't always take them.'

She didn't believe they were vitamins. She decided to push her point about the magazine articles. 'If you like, I can speak to Paul Jacobs, the editor of the Gateway magazine. I've met him a couple of times and I'm sure he'll see me.'

He regarded her quizzically. 'Why are you suddenly interested in the case?' Cameron stood, folded his arms and paced back and forth. 'According to you, Frank Slack is the main suspect?'

She noticed how quickly Cameron morphed from a gentle sop into an inquisitorial aggressor. Post-traumatic stress or what? Am I being silly? She wondered. No matter if she was, Sam had decided to contact a friend in London to find out a bit more about Jason Cameron.

Cameron had turned up at her door two weeks ago, Sam felt sorry for him. She'd offered him a short-term solution. It would seem he intended staying longer than originally anticipated. Yes, she liked him; he was interesting and had the hungry look of a man who hadn't been with a woman in a long time.

'Jason, you've convinced me there could be more to this than I first thought.' It was time to stroke his ego, and unashamedly so.

Cameron relaxed, unfolded his arms. 'Alright, interview the editor; let me know how it goes. And by the way ask him about the story regarding the sightings of the weird creature. Apparently, according to a woman I met in the forest the sightings were of a scruffy itinerant, not a dog at all. This Jacobs character decided to alter the story for dramatic effect.'

Sam said, 'This Jacobs fellow has a lot to answer for don't you think?

142

Cameron nodded. 'Indeed he does.'

He moved around her. 'Sorry, Sam, I must dash, I've got an appointment. No doubt we'll talk again later.' He headed for the kitchen door to disappear like a phantom into the garden.

Cameron had gone, just like that. Sam left in the kitchen with her mouth open like a goldfish wondering what the hell it was all about.

Sam shook herself, rushed into the living room, looked down the lane and watched Cameron climb into his car, wanting to make sure he actually drove off. Only then did she come back into the kitchen to look at her notes.

Three dogs had been brought to the surgery in the past twelve months with injuries consistent with dog fighting; Lukas Meek had brought in two dogs on the same day. The other dog belonged to a policeman, Ron Stark. The notes said Stark had been out walking when a larger dog had attacked his German shepherd. Meek's explanation had been vague; claiming the dogs had chased a rabbit through gorse bushes. Yeah, of course it had.

Sam opened the fridge door, pulled out an open bottle of white wine and took a glass from the cupboard. Just the ticket; a healthy measure of chilled wine, help her unwind. She leaned against the kitchen sink looking absently into the forest. A slight movement in the bushes caught her eye. She leaned closer to the window, squinting.

Yes! To the left of the largest conifer; a man clung to a thick branch. Or could it be the light playing tricks? She looked harder, focused on his torso. The figure remained very still. Suddenly, he moved slightly, altered position. *Oh this was hopeless.*

She hunted for Cameron's binoculars. There on the dining table, his battered briefcase. She opened the

143

broken latch to find camera and binoculars. The latter she directed towards where she'd seen the figure. Sam scanned the trees. Nothing; *Bugger it.*

Next she scanned the adjacent trees, slowly moving the binoculars left to right. Bloody hell! There about half way up a conifer a huge man in scruffy clothes watching the cottage. Realising he'd been rumbled, the man shot down the trunk, disappearing into the woodland.

Sam oozed relief. Should I telephone the police? Get Jason to come back perhaps? She picked up the telephone; dropped it back in its cradle.

No, she'd mention the figure when she next saw Cameron. Feeling guilty for holding out on him, she would also let him know about Lukas Meek and his dogs. After all, what could she possibly do with the information?

Quaffing more wine, she flicked through her address book, seeking the number of Clair Cousins. They had attended University together and kept in touch; pen pals taking turns to drop one another an e-mail every couple of months, meeting twice a year in London. Claire worked as a vet in Cricklewood and lived in Collingdale not far from Hendon Police College. If anyone could prise information from the coppers popping into *McGowan's*, her favourite pub in Collingdale, then it was Claire, a bubbly girl who could sell sand to Arabs.

She rang Claire's mobile.

'Hi Claire, its Sam.'

'How are you girl?' The last time they met had been shortly after Heather's funeral. Sam hadn't been good company.

Sam said, 'I'm fine now, honest. How's the new boyfriend?'

'Nine months, not so new.' There was a pause, static

144

replacing conversation. 'You sound spooked Sam, what's wrong?'

Sam breathed heavily into the mouthpiece; she regretted ringing. She knew she was being stupid, but something tugged at the corner of her mind, to do with Cameron. Here was a man, supposedly a professional investigator yet haphazard; someone nonchalantly bungling from one problem to the next. And the circumstances surrounding his posting to Winston; a very odd decision indeed. The local newspaper indicated the Parish Council were in discussion with North Yorkshire Police about the police station closing and the officers moving to Whitby. If so, why post Cameron to Winston a couple of months before?

'I need a favour,' Sam said.

'Anything for you darling.'

She told Claire about Cameron appearing at her door, about her sensation that something was odd about his posting. She made it clear that Cameron was not a threat; but that nagging doubts about his sudden appearance on her doorstep wouldn't go away. 'I'm doing it because I believe Cameron should be resting. Maybe by finding out a bit more about his condition I can help him.'

Claire hummed. 'I do know quite a few coppers who drink in the pub, maybe they know something. You sound like you have a soft spot for this Cameron character.'

Sam thought about it. Conceding that yes, she did fancy Jason Cameron.

Confirmed by the fact she still remained determined though to get to the bottom of his unexpected appearance in Winston.

'I like him a lot Claire. He's funny and not bad looking. It's just...' She sighed. 'I want to know a little bit more about him.'

145

'Sam, why don't you simply ask the bloke?' Claire sounded a little peeved with Sam.

'Claire, you're right, I shouldn't have phoned.'

'You're so defensive Sam. We're friends remember. And you're obviously worried about Jason Cameron. Nor do I blame you if you feel the need to get to know him better. Leave it with me, I'll ask around, see if anyone knows anything.'

Chapter 22

Paul Jacobs agreed to see Sam at five the next day, Tuesday.

She arrived at his office on Winston High Street with five minutes to spare, and parked on the cobbles. After checking herself in the mirror, she popped the glove compartment and gave herself the luxury of a little lip-gloss. She hated make up and refrained from using any, reliant on natural good looks inherited from her mother. Using the rear view mirror, she noticed a green jeep park behind her some hundred yards away; the same one she'd noticed earlier parked at the side of the road as she entered Haughton village; impossible to miss it with its faded green paint and chunky tyres.

Difficult to make out the driver, she put it down to coincidence. Her Golf locked, Sam went into the Yorkshire Gateway's office.

From behind a bushy black beard Paul Jacobs, a fat, middle-aged little man who reminded Sam of an ugly Toby jug, shot her an encouraging smile. After her dad Nigel had died he'd attempted to court Heather without much success.

Paul Jacobs, after giving Sam a peck on the cheek – she tried not to shudder – showed her into a cluttered office that reeked of pipe tobacco and cheap aftershave. Walls displayed framed awards and certificates in haphazard fashion, each confirming his success as a writer.

For a fat man, he had unusually small hands, like a girl.

'Please.' He offered her a chair before his cluttered desk, Sam sat. 'Heather was a prolific writer you know. I once asked her to join the magazine permanently. She refused of course, citing her independence as the reason.' He reflected awhile eventually adding, 'I think

147

she thought I was flirting with her.'

'I'm sure she had her reasons Paul.'

He drifted in thought for a couple of seconds before asking, 'So what brings you to my modest domain?' He waved his hand round the office, smiling broadly.

Acting like a professional reporter, Sam plucked her notebook from her handbag. Resting it on her knee, she began; her enthusiasm obvious.

'I'm interested in finding out about Heather's articles.' Sam licked her finger, flicked the pages of her notebook. 'Specifically articles about dog fighting and the sightings of a strange creature stalking the forest.'

'Ah the creature,' he said, blowing air through fat lips.

'Was it a dog as reported or something else?' Noticing his face change, she quickly added, 'Heather told friends she believed the stalker was a man in scruffy clothes.'

Jacobs rubbed at his left eye that had suddenly developed a twitch. 'It could have been anything or indeed nothing. One witness described a dog like animal, then another a man on all fours. We'll probably never know for sure.'

Sam nonplussed said loudly, 'There's a big difference between a dog and a man creeping about.'

Paul Jacobs's smile evaporated. 'No one *said* it was a man, it just looked like a man. Poppycock if you ask me.'

Sam offered Jacobs her sincerest smile.

'Surely it's in the best interests of the town to establish the truth about what exactly is going in on the forest.'

Jacobs plucked his pipe from its resting place on the desk and chewed on it.

'Sam, you should know Heather was very single minded about the forest, convinced it was being used to stage illegal dog fighting, so it's possible she may have gilded the lily.' Realising he may have offended Sam, he hurriedly said, 'Not intentional you realise, writers' prerogative and all that. Oh, and I'm sure she had someone on the inside feeding her information.'

'Who?' asked Heather, her winning smile false yet necessary.

Jacobs poked a finger in his ear, examined the result of his efforts, and then sucked loudly on his unlit pipe.

'She didn't say.' He prodded the pipe toward her. 'Wait a minute. I heard her talking on the phone once.' He scratched his balding head. 'I asked her who was giving her information and she said his name was. . .' He paused, closed his eyes, thinking. 'No, sorry, it won't come. Don't believe she ever met him though.'

'I don't understand?'

'Sorry Sam, I mean she was going to meet him a couple of weeks before she was killed.' He saw her look of horror dawn. 'Oh, I'm sure it had nothing to do with how she was, you know assaulted.' He leaned across and patted her hand. Sam wished he wouldn't do that. 'It was just a contact, someone who could give her insight.'

Jacobs didn't sound convincing

Sam gathered her thoughts. 'Did you mention this to the police Paul, after Heather was killed?'

'I mentioned it to DCI LaSalle.'

She prickled.

'What did DCI LaSalle say?'

'He said he would bear it in mind.'

Bear it in mind? Sam was no police officer, but had the sense to know what constituted important information.

'Did Heather keep any of her stuff here, paperwork, anything like that?

Jacobs looked uncomfortable, eased his suddenly

tight collar.

'I don't think so.' He rocked gently in his chair. 'I'm sure I gave everything she kept here to the police.' His smile was benevolent.

Sam flicked through her notebook again. 'Heather wrote about these sightings of unusual animals roaming about in the forest. Did she...?'

'Heather had the oddest notion that some mythical creature was stalking the forest. Silly notion if you ask me; did make a good story though.'

'Who started the rumours about the creature?'

Jacobs stood and waved his arm toward the door. 'I'm sure the police have all the information you need. I'm truly sorry but I have another appointment.'

Sam was getting nowhere. 'Oh I see,' surprised at Jacobs sudden change in attitude. 'Well thanks for your help Paul.' Unsettled, she folded her notebook, stood and glanced out of the window.

'Bloody hell Paul, what's he up to?'

Outside, Lukas Meek watched the office of the Yorkshire Gatekeeper. The bitch had been in there at least ten minutes, no doubt poking around just like her stepmother. He knew she would gain nothing from the visit. Paul would keep his mouth shut. Why didn't these people get it into their thick skulls dog fighting and badger baiting were part of country life? Outsiders should keep their noses out otherwise... His thoughts were interrupted; the Jeep began rocking violently from side to side.

Lukas scrambled out of the driver's door, to be confronted by a man with a pasty complexion, spiky blond hair wearing thick black sunglasses. His brown leather overcoat, hung loose from his thin frame. The weirdo smiled, gently tapping his index fingers together, drumming to a beat inside his head.

150

**

Sam saw a man in a brown overcoat violently rocking the green jeep. The driver got out and began remonstrating with the man. A flash of movement, and the blond man pirouetted, moved back a yard and lashed out with his foot, smashing it into the driver's face.

'Call the police Paul,' Sam ordered. Without thinking, she fled the office and ran towards the jeep. The man, still there, head tilting from side to side, towered over his victim. The driver of the jeep rolled about on the floor, blood oozing from his nostrils.

Ignoring the attacker, Sam dropped on one knee and examined the face of the injured man.

'How bad is it?' Lukas Meek pulled his face away. Sam said,' Stay still your nose might be broken.'

Meek edged further away, sliding on damp cobbles. 'Piss off you silly cow, I don't need your help.'

Meek's attacker spoke, his voice flat, monotone. 'Wild animals do that.'

Sam looked up at him, shielding her eyes from the sun. 'Wild animals do what?'

'You know, snarl and snap when you try to help them.'

The man must be deranged. Sam protested, 'He's not a wild animal you moron.'

The stranger adjusted his dark glasses, smoothed his hair. 'I'm merely chastising him like one would a dog. Unfortunately sometimes it's all you can do; either that or put the animal out of its misery.'

Meek sobbed; his face a bloody mess. Sam believed his nose was broken.

'I don't know who you are, the police are coming and you'll be arrested. What you did was disgusting.'

The sun glared in her eyes, preventing her properly seeing his features.

151

Buttoning his overcoat, the man said, 'Samantha my dear, Lukas Meek is pond life, a thing of low moral standing, certainly not worthy of your attention.'

Sam's stomach churned.

'Who are you?'

Blake cackled. 'Samantha dear I am merely a man who dislikes dog people.'

Striding elegantly backwards a couple of paces, Blake turned and walked away.

Five minutes later police sirens cut a swathe through the noise of the traffic.

Chapter 23

After spending three hours at the police station looking through mug shots, Sam badly needed a drink.

Opening the back door of Gatekeeper Cottage she found Cameron, hair wet, a towel wrapped around his neck, much like women do after they dye their hair. He sat at the kitchen table looking forlorn, several photos before him.

Sam dropped her keys on the table. 'Something weird happened, when I went to see Jacobs.'

Cameron didn't look up, intent on the photographs spread evenly on the table.

'You were there when Blake attacked Lukas Meek in the street.'

Sam couldn't believe her ears. 'That . . . thing is Blake, your friend?'

Cameron bunched photos showing the severed paw together and tapped them with his index finger.

'I think these are photographs of Heather's Lakeland terrier, rather a piece of it. Someone thought it might be a good idea to send me its severed paw; a warning, something like that.'

Angrily, she scattered the small pile across the table. 'Are you listening? That thing you call a friend just broke an innocent man's nose.'

Cameron, lacking any compassion, sighed. 'I thought Blake might visit Meek.'

Sam looked aghast. 'You knew this might happen?'

Cameron shuffled the photos together. 'I didn't know for sure, I just thought he might.'

Sam fumed. 'Are you an idiot? Blake just committed a serious assault on an innocent man; no doubt the police will arrest him. Then where will you be?'

Cameron leaned back, faced her and smiled thinly.

153

'Describe the man you saw?'

At first she resisted replying; then thought what the heck. 'The attacker had blond spiky hair, dark glasses wearing an ill-fitting coat.'

Cameron turned in the chair and shouted, 'Blake come in here will you?'

Sam's face contorted into a mask of disgust and disbelief. Cameron actually had that man in her home. How dare he?

Cameron shouted again, 'Get in here Blake, and don't be shy.' He then eased himself from the kitchen chair. 'I'll go and get him.'

She could hear muttering. Cameron seemed to be placating his friend, reassuring him everything was fine. About five minutes later the kitchen door opened. From the living room emerged a young man wearing a tee shirt and baggy jeans. Dazzling deep blue eyes penetrated hers, his smile the kind a guy might offer when wanting to get to know you, sort of radiant in a masculine way. Fashionable jet-black hair contradicted a face reminiscent of a young Brad Pitt. Good-looking, yes but what struck Sam as the man turned and the light caught him, was his more than startling resemblance to Cameron.

Although not identical, they could have been brothers. Each had the same angular facial features and similar hair colouring. Sam stared in disbelief unable to accept that this was the same person who had attacked Lukas Meek. For heaven's sake it had only happened four hours ago.

'What happened to your blond hair?' She asked, astonished.

Blake flopped onto a kitchen chair and tilted his head. 'I decided to alter my appearance, can't have the police chasing me.'

Sam felt nauseous. Now she had two strange men in

154

her home. For the first time since her dad died, she felt vulnerable, and very frightened. She tried to control her voice. 'Why did you attack that man?'

Blake glanced toward the living room, apparently requiring Cameron's approval to continue.

'Lukas had it coming. He is, as I explained earlier, a low life. I hit him to send a message to his cohorts who are the key to solving Heather's murder.'

'This is bizarre. Yesterday Cameron was convinced Heather's murder had connections to dog fighting. Now what are you saying?' Sam's head was spinning. She felt uneasy seeing the two of them in same house. They were like a pair of maniacal twins, older versions of Wyndham's creations in *Village of the Damned*.

'With Cameron's help, I've been doing a lot of digging, Sam.' Blake plucked a biscuit from a plate. 'Heather was murdered because she uncovered something distasteful about the underbelly of the town, I'm sure of it.'

Sam wanted to leave, run and call the police. Something forced her to stay, more than keen to find out the truth about Heather's murder.

'This is weird.' She paced, came back. 'I mean Cameron is back in Winston and begins poking around, meeting with long lost relatives; making weird suggestions about dog fighting in the forest.' She ran her hand through her hair, flicking her head back, determined at least get to the bottom of this unusual little man.

Blake placated her, palms pushed forward. He asked her to try and remain calm, which she did. Sam flopped onto a chair begging an explanation. Her pulse slowed, she was in control again.

The silence in the kitchen was palpable. Blake told her Cameron could better explain.

'Cameron is more adept at explanations; I am more

155

a man of action. Talking is a pastime for the bored. Also, I have an appointment. I should be getting ready.' He twitched a horrible smile, pirouetted theatrically, entered the lounge and disappeared upstairs.

Sam could hear talking in the bedroom. Five minutes later Cameron returned wearing his customary bow tie and continued with the story. Sam listened without interrupting.

Cameron told her everything about his theory. Aware he had upset her he did decide he should reveal more about Blake. After all, Blake was the key.

'The Chief Constable has been lying.'

Sam waited, silently assessing him.

Blake whispered in Cameron's head. *It isn't the right time to disclose the truth about me, Cameron. Don't do it, not yet.*

The strain on Sam's face bothered him. He desperately wanted to keep her on side. 'I was persuaded to transfer to Winston by Christine Krill. She told me I could help her clear out corruption, particularly relating to Victor LaSalle. My role would be passive; bearing in mind my nervous breakdown and the fact I was pending medical retirement. I was surprised she could wangle it.' Then again, nothing surprised him anymore.

'In return for a couple of months light duties for her in Winston, I could have a look at the murder file. It's not true of course, Victor isn't the reason I'm here.'

Cameron watched her, agonising whether to keep going, give her the full story. Sam straightened, the way she did when she was about to launch a verbal attack on him.

Sam's eyes flashed. 'What possible reason could the Chief Constable have for lying to a sergeant with mental problems?'

156

Her words hit him like a fiery lance piercing his heart. And they hurt like hell. Yes, he had an illness; his whole life imbued with trauma. He managed by using coping mechanisms, nurtured from the days he'd been lost in the forest. Such mechanisms had later transformed him into a chameleon within the murky world of undercover policing. Right now they were proving to be a hurdle in his efforts to win over Sam.

He so desperately wanted her to accept him. After all he was a product of his past and not some horrible chimera.

He swallowed his pride. 'My transfer is an elaborate hoax; a trap to ensnare Blake who Christine believes is responsible for the murder of Martin Pope, a disgusting paedophile I arrested eighteen months ago.'

He buried his face in his hands and like a small child afraid of the dark, peered through his fingers. 'She knew I would bring Blake to Winston, I'm sure of it, that's why the police are watching the cottage.'

Quickly sitting upright she asked, 'And is he, is Blake a murderer?'

For a fraction of a second, Cameron hesitated.

'Blake killed a man called Martin Pope.'

Sam threw her arms in the air. 'And he's in my house.'

'You don't understand Sam. It was an accident. Pope abducted a small boy for sexual gratification. When the police arrested Pope, he refused to admit he had the boy. With no evidence, they were forced to release him. They made the decision to follow him to the boy. Pope realised he was being watched and gave them the run around.' He paused, seeking subtle yet give away ticks on Sam's face; ones that would indicate how she was coping. He did notice how she intertwined her fingers, the restless way she moved in her chair.

'I asked Blake to help me find the boy. Together we

157

took Pope from the police to a secluded place and began questioning him. Unfortunately during Blake's interrogation Pope died of a heart attack.'

Sam's face twitched, tears erupted. Cameron tried to place an arm about her; she shrugged him off.

'I know what we did was wrong, but before Pope died he told Blake what we wanted to know.' He tried again to place his arm around her shoulders. Again she knocked his arm away. Cameron, undeterred, said: 'Pope buried the boy alive in a wooden box in a pit. We found him in Epping Forest.' He added, 'The boy survived.'

Suddenly she got to her feet, knocking the chair over which landed with a clatter on the sandstone floor. 'So you're saying the ends justify the means?'

'That's not the case.'

'Isn't it?'

'Pope was a disgusting thing, inhuman, depraved. We didn't mean to kill him; he just didn't survive the ordeal.'

His sombre tone was devoid of his usual sarcasm. 'Blake can find out who killed Heather and he wants your help, I personally don't. Why? Because, Samantha Moon, you see things in black and white. Forget your middle class conventions, some nut job murdered your stepmother and we'll find him. All you have to do is trust us.'

Cameron, desperate to convince Sam both he and Blake were genuinely concerned about catching Heather's killer, wondered why in hell, at this moment, she appeared interested only in Blake. Maybe she didn't trust him to vouch for Blake.

'Tell me,' she said, 'these people in the forest watching the cottage, you honestly believe they're the police?'

At last, Cameron had her full attention; Sam wiped

158

her eyes. A wave of hope surged. 'Damn right they are. I have spent long hours hiding in bushes, watching, and waiting. They are the police, no doubt about it, and they're waiting for Blake.'

Blake whispered: '*It wasn't the police you saw in the trees. It was someone else.*'

Sam poked a crack in the kitchen curtain. 'Are they out there, now, watching?'

Cameron placed his arms around her slender shoulders; no rebuff this time he guided her back to the chair. 'Bet on it. I suspect they're using a covert rural operative nicknamed *Uncle Sam*. He's the best in the business, except for Blake of course' He added, 'it's fine, he has no idea what Blake looks like, and he'll doubtless have been given the description given by Lukas Meek after the attack.'

'Why would the Chief Constable go to such lengths?'

A fair question and one easily answered. 'She has orchestrated a clever plot to trap Blake. Ever since I arrived I've been suspicious. Everything has been too clinical, too predictable.' He paused, glancing at the antique wall clock. He had the time.

'Christine was in line to become the first woman Commissioner of the Metropolitan Police. Blake put pay to that when Martin Pope died. They blamed her for the cock up and now she has to settle for North Yorkshire.'

He gave her a determined stare. 'It's all about revenge for what happened.'

Sam nodded. 'So: the dog fights, you believe Heather was threatening to expose the ring leaders?'

Cameron gnawed his lip. Would she believe him?

'Sam, you already know Heather was passionate about the local countryside, as others are passionate about dog fighting . . . and what goes with it.'

159

On a breath she said, 'Jason, I need time to think about what you've told me.'

Cameron understood. He would give her some space.

Chapter 24

Claire Cousins rang later that evening, eager to tell Sam what she had discovered about Jason Cameron. Claire insisted they meet in person.

What she'd been told should come direct from the source. This would mean Sam travelling to London to meet with Claire and a man named Arnold who had information about Cameron. How he came by it was a mystery, although Claire insisted he was genuine.

'There's a slight catch though,' Claire told Sam. 'Arnold owes money. He's asked for five hundred quid to share his info' on Cameron. I did at least barter that down to two hundred.'

Without hesitation Sam had agreed to pay.

Cameron, (and presumably Blake; although she'd never actually noticed him leave) had left her alone to consider the proposal. Claire had actually telephoned twice whilst Cameron had been in the cottage, forcing Sam to be evasive. Claire guessed why. Sam had excused herself and went for a lie down on the bed. Fifteen minutes on she heard the front door open and close and Cameron's car drive off. Once they'd been gone about an hour, Claire rang back and arrangements to meet Arnold were finalised for the next day.

Before departing for London, Sam decided to track down Victor LaSalle. Sam found the number for police headquarters, contacted LaSalle and they arranged to meet at the cemetery; private enough, and it also closed at one on Wednesday, giving her ample time to drive to London to meet Claire around seven.

It would be a slog, but Sam intended driving back the same night; ten hours of driving a long time when you're tired and scared. Think positive, she told herself and trust it will reap benefits; give you time to think

161

through everything.

First though she needed information and Victor LaSalle would have it, fingers crossed!

At midday on Wednesday, whilst Cameron was at work, she left a brief note saying she would give a lot of thought to his revelations. She explained briefly about visiting a friend in London and wouldn't be home until late. "Blake can sleep on the couch." She smirked at this final touch.

Sam stopped dead, her mind on overtime.

Cameron was out of the cottage, and could be gone for some time. It forced her to realize she had never ventured inside his bedroom since he arrived. Why not? It's her home.

She darted upstairs and hesitated outside his room door. Tentatively pushing it Sam ventured inside.

The bedroom as she expected, still untouched, lacking tangible evidence Cameron actually used it. She rummaged through the drawers and cupboards finding only a few of Cameron's clothes, nothing remotely incriminating or useful to her in understanding her lodger.

Sam opened the bathroom door and noticed the sink was in a bit of a mess; the bowl stained with black hair die where presumably Blake had been altering his appearance to fool the police. What was that? Moving closer to the bathroom cabinet she breathed on the cabinet's mirrored surface. Someone had used their finger to write the words, "I DON'T TRUST HER."

Sam's heart skipped a beat. She needed to get out of here for a while.

Pre-empting a stay, with an overnight bag packed, she used the landing telephone to contact the vet's practice and make an excuse about a sick relative in London. Hunger pangs encouraged her to make a cheese sandwich. Munching it, she left the cottage and

162

drove the five miles to the cemetery parking at the ornate gates. A black Jaguar waited in the car park. Victor LaSalle sat on a bench about twenty yards from the entrance. He stood as she approached and gestured for her to sit down.

The spot overlooked Heather's grave.

'Thank you for agreeing to see me at such short notice.'

LaSalle, reflective and solemn, said, 'I'm guessing it's about Heather?'

Sam twisted to face him. 'You came to Heather's funeral, why was that?'

'She was a friend'

This surprised her. Heather had never mentioned being friendly with LaSalle. In fact she hadn't mentioned him at all.

'I didn't know you knew her before she was...'

LaSalle stood, buried his thick hands deep in his pockets. 'Heather was concerned about strange things going on in the forest.' Sam felt his edginess, his reluctance to talk. 'We found we had things in common.'

'What things?'

'Both of us were passionate about exposing the truth, no matter the consequences.'

Sam in a hurry asked, 'What's going on with Jason Cameron?'

This startled LaSalle. 'I don't follow.'

Sick and tired of being given the run around, first by Cameron, then Paul Jacobs and now Victor LaSalle, Sam didn't hide her displeasure, 'It's a simple question Chief Inspector.'

LaSalle regarded her with raised eyebrows. 'Nothing is simple when it comes to DS Cameron.' A crow landed on the perimeter fence, and for some insane reason she felt it was eyeing her. She considered what she'd been told by Cameron.

'I know Cameron is here for a reason and it has little to do with Heather's death.'

LaSalle, his voice barely a whisper, said, 'What do you think you know Sam?'

She paced the path, arms folded. 'First, Cameron has a stress related illness; in fact he shouldn't even be at work.' She watched LaSalle's face.

'Second, Heather was investigating dog fighting in the forest; you knew about it and probably knew she was in danger. Third.' She jabbed a finger at him, 'Your nephew Lonnie Slack is up to his armpits in this and I think you know what's going on!' Sam could feel her anger boiling, her heart pounding like a massive hammer.

LaSalle, visibly uncomfortable, perspiration dampening his forehead brought her to one conclusion: he was a drinker. She could smell it oozing from his pores.

'Well, I'm waiting, Chief Inspector.'

LaSalle sighed. 'I was in love with Heather.'

Sam stepped back. 'You were in love with Heather? What on earth do you mean, in love with my step mother?'

He pulled his hands from his overcoat; he stared across gravestones, his gaze coming to rest on Heather's grave.

'She came to see me about a year ago, worried, scared and concerned about her safety.'

The penny dropped. 'Paul Jacobs from the magazine told me about a contact she had; it was you. You were giving her information about the dog fighting.'

'I thought it would stop her poking around, keep her safe.' He glanced at his watch. 'One determined woman.'

A young couple pushing a baby in a pram ambled

164

by, carrying a bunch of flowers; they smiled, Sam returned it. Grief is a strange thing, almost cathartic. It shouldn't last forever though, LaSalle should be over Heather's death and then it tumbled. 'You never told her, about your feelings, I would have known.'

LaSalle's eyes were moist with the onset of tears.

'I feel partly responsible for her death; I should have listened to her concerns instead of dismissing them.'

'What the hell did she tell you?'

He looked at the couple with the pram and then whispered, 'She told me Cameron was responsible for the death of your father. Heather believed Cameron had been watching the cottage and for some reason, perhaps jealousy, knowing Nigel had a heart condition, Cameron somehow scared your dad to death.'

'Alpha one is still with Samantha Moon; no sign of the target, over.'

The young woman spoke into the covert microphone attached to the handle of the pram.

Christine Krill, sitting in HQ control room, recognised the tension in the policewoman's voice. She knew how the two police officers felt; adrenaline heightened their awareness, their skin prickling in anticipation.

'Should we hang around or leave eyeball to alpha three?'

Christine hesitated for a second, pressed the transmit button. 'Pick a suitable spot nearby and keep your eyes peeled.'

She saw the monitor flicker as the camera followed the two police officers pushing their pram to the nearest grave.

Christine rubbed her hands together. Come on Cameron, she mused, let's expose you for what you are, a complete and utter sham.

165

Blake watched from the safety of the bushes on the perimeter of the cemetery confident they couldn't see him. When LaSalle and Sam left the cemetery he waited for the young couple to follow, gave it a while and then emerged from his hiding place.

Blake walked casually to the grave were the young couple had left their flowers and read the inscription.

"Brian Mullen, aged eight, beloved son of Harry and Janice."

Chapter 25

Christine Krill fancied a cigarette. It had been two years since her last one. The strain of the operation was gradually undermining her resilience, her nerves were raw, her features ragged.

The operations room buzzed. A hive of activity with eighteen cameras strategically placed in Winston to monitor the town, the forest and hopefully Jason Cameron. This elaborate surveillance paid for by a man referred to in operational police speak as the *Operational Sponsor a.k.a. Walter Slack*.

When it came down to it though, there was no substitute for a human presence and Trevor Mason was the best in the business. He could infiltrate the most difficult terrain.

The meeting in the cemetery worried Christine. Samantha Moon was no fool and Victor looked awkward in his role. Victor was now drinking so heavily that it could be dangerous, his role in the "honey trap" integral to the success of the operation.

She examined the surveillance notes of Trevor Mason. He'd seen Cameron with Meek. Afterwards Mason had requested an urgent meeting with the Chief Constable. Under normal circumstances she would not remove him from the "plot".

Fortuitously, Sam was being followed from Winston on her way down the A1. The surveillance team were instructed to watch her until she was a safe distance from North Yorkshire and then stand down. Christine knew from the telephone tap that she was on her way to London to see her friend Clair Cousins. The Met surveillance team would pick her up in *McGowan's* pub. It was probably best. She would be safe.

Christine thanked the camera operators for their continued hard work and left the control room in the capable hands of the Operations Inspector, Sandy Dalton – a sour faced man who spent too much time in police control rooms making him an ideal operational commander of surveillance operations.

When she got to her office she found DS Mason sipping coffee from a paper cup. A filthy man, worn out; stinking of sweat and urine, the guy never washed for at least two weeks prior to an operation, ever the consummate professional.

'How's it going Chief?' Trevor asked casually, using a pseudo American drawl.

She closed the door softly, holding her breath until she placed distance between them and took refuge behind her desk.

'Better than you Trevor, you smell disgusting.' Christine didn't mince words.

He sniggered. 'Should smell me in two weeks' time; bet you I smell worse than the arse end of a cow.'

Christine had known Trevor twenty years; she regarded him as the best in the business. If anyone could expose Cameron, it was "Uncle Sam", as he was known in police circles. His pseudo American accent though was a little tedious, but then he had a penchant for all things American. Unfortunately Trevor had never been to the States. In fact, apart from his operational deployments, he rarely left London.

'It must be urgent otherwise you wouldn't have left the plot.'

Christine winced as Trevor placed the paper cup on the polished table meaning another visit from the French polisher.

Trevor tugged his expensive looking Nikon digital camera from its leather case and handed it to the Chief.

'Look at the photos, scroll down, that's it, six in all.'

He picked up his coffee and slurped, watching Christine's facial expressions as she scrolled through

168

the images.

'What the hell is it?'

Trevor shrugged his shoulders. 'I'm only guessing, but I'd say it was a wolf; to be exact an American timber wolf.'

Christine looked hard at the images. No doubt about it, they were photographs of a very large wolf, being held in check by a very large man.

'Where were these taken?'

'I shot those in the forest about two miles from Gatekeeper Cottage.'

'Who is the man? I can't quite make him out.'

'I took the first three shots when the wolf was being allowed to wander free,' he said. 'The last three were taken when Lukas Meek confronted Cameron in the forest.' He leaned over, fiddled with the camera. 'Now look at these three.'

Christine recognised the same animal. The handler though was different.

'What the hell is Sergeant Ron Stark doing with a bloody wolf?'

Christine Krill had been Cameron's mentor, now the opposite. She was using him, manipulating him. The thought of Blake – alter-ego and other self – in police custody terrified Cameron. Could this be that simple- a massive honey trap to ensnare Blake? A slippery thought wriggled at the back of his brain, attempting to pop out into the light. No good, he couldn't quite break it free; something to do with Blake. It threatened to jump into his consciousness before sliding like a ghost into a corner.

He had a strange sensation; was Blake holding out on him?

And what about Sam? He suspected her excuse about visiting a friend in London could be just a ruse. It

169

had to be Blake she was after, courting a misguided belief she would find answers about him in London. Unfortunately Sam would be disappointed. Nothing in London to find that would assist her understanding the concept of Blake. Her concerns about him were superfluous, her fear too, unfounded.

Had she contacted the police and informed them about Blake? He didn't think so; by now they would have arrived at the cottage.

Anyway, Blake had gone, for now. He did that sometimes; disappeared deep into his mind. Out of reach. Since Sam had left that afternoon, Cameron found Blake difficult and sullen mainly because Blake was upset that Sam mistrusted him. He had disappeared deep inside Cameron's sub-conscious without reason. It was after ten and Cameron was unable to wait any longer: time then to visit the compound in the forest.

Heather once told him she suspected they were holding all kinds of illegal activity in a compound yet couldn't place the location, only that it was in the forest somewhere. Cameron knew exactly where to look. The compound was the key; had always been the key.

The back door of the cottage opened with a creak and closed gently. Cameron, puzzled, eased open the door leading to the kitchen. He clicked the light on, a little surprised that Victor LaSalle sat at the kitchen table, head bowed, his hair wet and windswept and dressed in a dark green anorak. He clutched a metal-shafted hammer in his right hand, wrapped in a plastic evidence bag.

Cameron looked from the hammer to LaSalle and back to the hammer.

Chapter 26

'Relax, I'm here as a friend.'

LaSalle sucked air through his teeth. 'About eight weeks ago someone attempted to abduct a small boy from the gates of the local primary school.' LaSalle gently placed the hammer onto the wooden kitchen table and sat down.

He saw cold fear etched on Cameron's features. The terms of the operation, as far as LaSalle was concerned, could go whistle. LaSalle knew he should grab his opportunity; poke Cameron, prod him, force him into a corner.

'The boy's mother told the police her son was being stalked. We took three days before we visited her. Sound familiar?'

Christine Krill and Doctor Kumar had convinced LaSalle that Cameron held the secret to the murder of Heather Moon and the abduction of Brian Mullen. LaSalle, convinced himself he possessed the necessary skills to bring about a swift conclusion to the honey trap, decided to get down to it; demand Cameron to show him Blake.

On the defensive, Cameron sat opposite LaSalle. Sweat trickled down his back, his heart managed a few somersaults. Blake would come soon, of that Cameron was sure, and he was terrified of what might happen.

LaSalle stank of drink. His hands shook.

'Do you know why we took three days?'

Cameron shook his head, gaze locked on LaSalle's bloodshot eyes.

'Three months ago Christine sold Winston police station to Walter Slack. Staff were relocated, priorities changed.

'They opened it again for you Jason, part of an

171

elaborate plan to find out who abducted Brian Mullen twenty years ago.' He gave Cameron an icy stare. 'History repeats itself. Walter Slack spent ten years in gaol for abducting you.' He paused before emphasising: 'And it nearly happens again?'

Cameron hadn't a clue about Slack's time in custody. Why should he know; how could he know?

'They never found Brian Mullen; he's still out there somewhere.' LaSalle shook his head violently, trying to divert the effects of drink. 'Walter was released early because of ill health and successfully filed an appeal against his conviction. Now the old fool is determined to unearth the truth.' He paused, fingered the hammer.

Calmly, lowering his voice a couple of octaves Cameron asked, 'Why am I here in Winston?'

LaSalle picked up the hammer and smashed it onto the table with a loud thud. Cameron sat up, startled, brain loaded with unwanted electricity. He clung to the thick wooden tabletop, pressed hard, trying to anchor thoughts, his head fuzzy; messages banging around haphazardly.

He sensed Blake coming.

LaSalle excited now. 'Walter approached Christine with a suggestion. He believes you're the key to finding the truth about the abduction. He could be right. Think about it. You were abducted when you were eight. Your mother asked the police for help because you were being stalked. Six months ago you arrive here for your mother's funeral. And bugger me . . .' He paused, grinned and raised the question, 'Ever experience deja vu?'

Cameron astonished, his voice raised said, 'I was lost, not abducted.'

LaSalle grasped the hammer, raised it threateningly above his head, changed his mind, and lowered it, gradually overcoming his internal turmoil.

Cameron sensed Blake edging closer.

Not now Blake, not now. Wait until LaSalle ventilates some more.

Tears dampened LaSalle's eyes; he positively oozed rage, what he said next contradictory to his own condition. He said: 'You're one sick man Jason. God knows how you managed to enter the service in the first place. It's amazing you fooled them for so long, but you didn't fool me.' He jabbed the hammer towards Cameron. 'I know about you. You were abducted and you escaped. It was you put the final nail in Walter's coffin and he hates you for it. When your mother was murdered and you came back, he knew something would happen. Then Walter came up with a plan.'

Cameron's mouth dried, adrenaline pumped, dopamine flooding his brain. Was he about to lose control?

'What plan?' He managed to ask

'You are just a catalyst Cameron, you and that other person you conceal.' LaSalle waved the hammer more threateningly.

Cameron looked out into the night; Blake sat at the forefront of his subconscious, uneasy, wanting to take over. Cameron blurted, 'I know Christine lied to me about why I was posted here.'

LaSalle rubbed his eyes with his free hand, the other keeping a tight grip on the hammer.

'I failed her Cameron. I failed Heather; Victor LaSalle the ultimate professional. I couldn't see the woods for the trees.' He laughed, a dull, almost manic sound. 'Woods for the trees, now there's a conundrum.'

'Why did you fail her Victor?' Cameron said determined to keep his cool.

LaSalle gently placed the hammer in front of Cameron, slid it gently toward him. 'Take it Jason; it's what you came here for, the truth.' LaSalle pushed it

173

nearer.

'I've given you what you want; now it's time for me to meet Blake. '

Cameron arched his neck, tilted his head backwards, eyes lolling in his head.

LaSalle sat back, shocked, intrigued, and unable to take his eyes off Cameron.

Cameron, scowled, laughed. Slammed the palms of his hands down hard on the table. Blake said gutturally, 'Victor, this isn't what I was promised by Doctor Kumar.'

Victor didn't have a clue what to say. He'd come to the cottage to convince himself that Blake was a ruse, the concoction of a warped mind.

Victor looked into a pair of eyes resembling bottomless icy blue pools.

Cameron had altered. Damn it he looked different, to the extreme. He appeared darker, his facial features usually smooth, boyish almost, and yet here, seated opposite Victor, the face had developed sharper lines, it looked older, harder.

Victor swallowed, and managed to stutter 'Hello Blake. Thought it was time we met . . . face to face.'

Blake suddenly lashed out with his hand, slapping Victor hard in the face.

Victor reeled, dumbfounded. *Damn you, I'm a police officer*. He raised his hand to retaliate.

Grinning, Blake expertly caught Victor's hand and savagely twisted it. Victor was a strong man, big and burly yet failed to break free, Blake's vice-like grip immovable.

'Do you believe in me Victor?'

Victor, disturbed by the transition, attempted a jerky yet sincere approach, 'Yes Blake, I can see you most definitely exist.'

174

Blake said between gritted teeth, 'Cameron asked me to watch the cottage, look out for his mother. I saw the man who killed her. I will identify him. You do trust me on this don't you Victor?'

'Yes, yes, I trust you, now please let go of my arm'.

Cameron did. He then slumped forward, head whacking the table.

Victor, relieved, knew Blake had gone, for now.

Bile forced its way up from his stomach, stinging the back of Cameron's throat.

LaSalle gently held Cameron's head. With his free hand he tilted a glass of water towards Cameron's mouth.

'Drink, it will make you feel better.'

Cameron's throat felt like hot coals. The trauma of Blake appearing so suddenly and with such virulence left his body weak and unable to manage the simplest of tasks like holding a glass. Quivering he sipped the water gratefully, droplets dribbling down his chin, dampening his shirt collar. 'What happened?'

LaSalle helped Cameron to sit properly on the chair.

'Blake introduced himself.'

'I see, don't worry Victor, he's gone for now.'

LaSalle breathed through his nostrils, let out a sigh. Calmer he said, 'Yes, he's gone.'

He left it hanging.

'What did he say?'

'Enough for me to realise he exists.'

'You didn't believe in him did you?'

LaSalle tapped the hammer. 'You know who killed your mother, don't you Cameron?'

'I guessed, but couldn't be sure.'

Cameron felt unusually comfortable in LaSalle's company. Gone now was the drunken, dishevelled LaSalle, replaced by a thoughtful, passive man; a man

175

in control.

The electricity surges in Cameron's head were subsiding. He wanted to sleep, to absolve some of it. His face screwed up, he tried hard to concentrate.

LaSalle gently slapped his face. Cameron sat bolt upright. 'It's all right, Victor, I'm just weary. Blake does that to me.'

'I understand, but you need to tell me what you've uncovered, it's important if we are to work together.'

Work together. Cameron welcomed the thought, especially with someone other than Blake. Working with Blake sapped his energy.

Thoughts battled to the surface; Cameron looked at LaSalle. 'Two sets of prints were on the stem of the hammer, Frank's for sure, the others belonging to a child or a woman with small hands.' Organising his thoughts into a coherent stream, he thought about Martin Pope. He had tiny hands, like those of a young girl.

LaSalle didn't interrupt, didn't try to be smart or acerbic, just listened.

'The only person who had motive and access to the evidence room was Janice Mullen. She was therefore a suspect and yet never suspected. I guess because she was beyond reproach and her husband was the SIO. It shouldn't matter unless of course he was involved in the cover up?'

LaSalle's face remained impassive, like a priest listening to a confession. Not judging, simply letting it penetrate. Cameron had seen it before with suspects who accepted truth because the evidence was strong and they wanted to hear it from someone else. It was cathartic.

Cameron continued. 'Nigel was worried about Heather. Last year she became distracted, melancholic. He suspected she was having an affair. He knew the

176

symptoms because of his own affair with my mother, he recognised the signs.'

Pulse slowed, heart no longer banging like a worn oil pump, Blake's appearance here seeming a long time ago, he managed to say, 'For some bizarre reason, probably because I was policeman, Nigel asked me to help. In turn I asked Blake to watch the cottage; he's good at surveillance, very patient. He saw you visit Heather on several occasions when Nigel was at work.'

LaSalle raised his eyebrows. 'Blake followed me from Gatekeeper Cottage, saw me arguing with Janice?'

'Yes he did. When the hammer went missing, Blake and I put two and two together. Blake wanted to dive in. How could we until we knew for sure? For heaven's sake, Heather had been having an affair with the case adviser. The case had collapsed once and I wasn't going let it happen again. I knew cracks would appear; they always do, especially when I'm around. I seem to ignite the flames of guilt.'

LaSalle looked hard at the hammer. 'It's my fault, Janice was jealous'

'It's not your fault. Blake believes someone told Janice about your affair with Heather. You must understand Victor, Janice didn't kill Heather.'

'What do you mean?'

'Blake watched the cottage for weeks. It was his thing, his talent – watching.' Cameron sensed a change in LaSalle; almost certain LaSalle was genuinely shocked.

'Someone else was watching the cottage Victor, the day Janice came to see Heather. That someone, a heavy-set man, went into the cottage after Janice left and finished the job. Heather's injuries were brutal, vicious not the work of a slightly built woman. Janice hit Heather with the hammer I have no doubt, but didn't

177

deliver the fatal blows.'

'Did Blake see the man?'

Cameron felt awkward; disappointed he would have to show Blake in a poor light. He had no choice. Victor needed to know the truth. Then they could work together.

'Blake liked Heather,' Cameron said. 'When she was fatally wounded he didn't react quickly enough, he was traumatised. By the time I arrived, the assailant had gone and Blake became distressed, sullen, disappointed in himself. For a long time he didn't return, no matter how hard I tried to encourage him. The only sure fire way of getting Blake to come back to me was when I landed in trouble. He reacted to my need for assistance. With the assistance of Kumar, Blake now finds it easier to manifest. I truly believe Blake holds the key to unlock this case.'

LaSalle gawped. Cameron continued. 'It was Harry Mullen who removed the hammer from the evidence room. He knew it wasn't Frank Slack who killed Heather. Lonnie's alibi statement was too strong. Harry thought he could cover for Janice, who has no idea of course.'

'You've examined the post mortem report?'

'Yes. No one, not even the pathologist could figure out the marks on Heather's neck. They were inconsistent with the facial injuries.'

LaSalle pointed a finger at Cameron. 'You know what the marks represent?'

'Yes Victor, I believe I do. It was Blake who figured it out.' Cameron stood, felt dizzy and sat down again. 'Someone went into the cottage after Janice, that person careful not to leave fingerprints. He used the plastic bag your team found in the forest, wrapped it around the hammer and hit her. Presumably the bag was meant to prevent blood splatters contaminating the attacker.'

178

These thoughts made Cameron nauseous, yet determined enough to follow through with Blake's theory.

'To ensure she was finally dead, he used a chunky metal dog chain and choked her to death.'

LaSalle stood up, paced the kitchen. 'I could never work out the dog hairs embedded in her wounds; it's why we initially made assumptions the murderer had something to do with the dog fighting racket. It never crossed my mind the attacker used a chain. The pathologist put forward the assumption such marks could have been made with a knotted rope.

'The plastic bag we found was covered in Heather's blood. I should have realised then it had been wrapped around the hammer.'

'Don't blame yourself Victor.'

'What happens next, Jason?'

Cameron felt vindicated and pleased with himself . Victor LaSalle asking him for direction. Blake would be chuffed.

Cameron said confidently, 'Blake will infiltrate the dog fights and find the truth.'

The back door opened. It was Christine Krill.

'Cosy are we?'

She wore full uniform. Her face contorted with displeasure; Cameron confused and bewildered, looked from one to the other. What now?

The Chief Constable removed her hat, sat down at the table. Addressing LaSalle she said, 'Not exactly what Doctor Kumar ordered Victor?'

LaSalle stared straight at her. 'Though you must agree it was much quicker my way, Chief.'

179

Chapter 27

The windscreen wipers worked overtime. The traffic queue was typical of the North Circular. Sam's meeting with Clair and the mysterious Arnold in ten minutes and she reckoned she was at least half an hour away. Bugger it! Sam slapped the steering wheel.

She thought about LaSalle, his disclosures hard to believe. Why would Heather think Cameron had deliberately stalked her dad and then scared him to death? What on earth would be his motive? Yet LaSalle had been insistent in his theory. Heather had told him that Nigel had seen Cameron hanging around the cottage, spying on them. If LaSalle was genuine in his feelings for Heather then he could be delusional with grief, confused. The truth was she didn't care anymore. It was all too much. She regretted driving to London. God, what did she hope to find?

At half past eight she pulled into the back of *McGowan's* pub, its car park pretty full. Claire's yellow Volkswagen, easy to spot, was parked haphazardly occupying two bays.

They had agreed to meet in the lounge bar with its high backed booths scattered around its periphery, oversized bar menus nestling centrally on tables. Sam entered through the main door to find Claire alone in a booth nursing a pint of lager.

Sam twitched a smile and shuffled into the booth opposite her friend. Claire had changed her hairstyle.

'Suits you tightly cropped,' Sam commented. 'Red tints look great, complimenting your olive skin and high cheekbones.'

'Okay, quit with the fashion review, I know it looks ridiculous.'

Sam half expected Claire to be frosty, after all she'd involved her in a clandestine meeting with a strange man. Not so, Claire's quip was in keeping with her own attempted light heartedness.

'Sorry I'm late,' Sam apologised. 'North Circular was hectic.'

Claire winked conspiratorially and whispered, 'Keep your voice down Agent 99, the enemy could be watching.'

Sam lowered her voice. 'Not lost your sense of humour I see.'

Claire leaned over and grabbed her friend's face in both hands and gave her a kiss on each cheek. 'Girl, I haven't had this much fun in ages. What can I get you to drink, and then we'll catch up.'

'I thought Arnold would be here?'

'He phoned me. He'll be here soon don't worry. Being a regular no one will think anything. Relax Sam. Now what do you want? Lager? G and T perhaps?'

'It would make me feel better if you told me how you met Arnold?'

Claire twirled her hair and bit her lip. Sam knew immediately how her friend had come to know Arnold. She shook her head and feigned horror. 'Don't tell me, I can guess – you're still shovelling it up your nose.'

Claire blushed. 'You make it sound like I'm weird, like a pervert or something. Everyone does it for Christ's sake. There are only a few non-believers like you who can't see the benefits.' She looked around and said sheepishly. 'It's only a sprinkle every week for crying out loud.'

'Yeah, I know.' Then Sam thought: I'm so bloody perfect. There are worse things in life than casual drug use. *Get real.* Claire was a social animal, an imp, and a risk taker yet somehow loveable. Sam's tension dissolved like liver salts in water. Claire had that effect on her. Anyhow, good friends were always true and never judgemental. Claire had said that once.

Sam plonked her handbag on the table; starving, she examined the menu. 'Order me a coke, the fizzy drink kind and...' She paused glancing at the pub grub on offer. 'I haven't eaten much today, so a beef burger would be welcome *without* the usual lecture please.'

Claire a vegetarian wrinkled her nose. 'I cannot understand how you manage to stay stick thin. I eat only the best food, and look at me, tubby.'

Claire shuffled from the booth and headed for the bar. Customers moved aside, allowing her through as they might royalty, some nodding, others affectionately pecking her cheek. Sam glanced around the lounge bar. It reminded her of university. Did she miss the excitement of drinking and clubbing? She wasn't sure. She was certain of one thing; she hoped her visit would produce something positive about Jason Cameron. Liking the bloke didn't prevent her uneasiness concerning him.

Strange her mixed bag of feelings.

Claire returned with drinks and they chatted. Sam avoided the subject of Cameron, preferring to keep her friend in the dark. In truth, Sam was worried. To Claire, this was just a game. Sam on the other hand felt she was a player in a game, albeit a dangerous one. She tried to analyse the visit from Christine Krill, the Chief Constable, two weeks before Cameron arrived. It had been formal, under the guise of letting her know progress on the murder investigation and to apologise for the case collapsing.

Christine Krill told Sam she might receive a visit from Cameron who was considering transferring to North Yorkshire. Only now did Sam realise the significance of the Chief Constable's parting words:

'*Remember Sam, Cameron is suffering with post-traumatic stress. He needs careful handling. Cameron feels responsible for his mother's death, even though he*

182

had no control over what happened.'

Claire broke into her thoughts. 'Sam are you listening girl?'

Sam apologised and glanced at her watch. Arnold wasn't going to show. In a way, she was glad. It was becoming a little too involved and immensely strange.

Suddenly, from nowhere, a scruffy man stinking of stale sweat pushed himself into the booth next to Sam. Around thirty years old and wearing a tatty green fleece, he reminded her of what she generalised a sex pest would look like; bespectacled and plump with greasy hair.

'Not in here, outside, and just you, not her . . .' he pointed at Claire, 'she stays here.'

He looked over his shoulder, got up and walked to the exit; looking back once, encouraging her to follow him with a flick of his head.

Strangely, Sam didn't feel threatened. She sensed he was scared, genuinely afraid to talk in the pub.

'I suppose I'm going outside.' Sam patted her coat pocket and the envelope containing the money. 'Look after my bag. If I'm not back in ten minutes,' a clever remark evaded her. 'Just come and get me, OK.'

Claire pulled the handbag close and nodded, smiling. 'You'll be fine.'

Sam changed her mind and grabbed her handbag away from Claire. 'On second thought, I'll take that with me, it weighs a ton and if he gets tetchy I can whack him with it.' Sam laughed nervously.

Outside the air smelled of exhaust fumes from the Edgware Road. Traffic whizzed past in both directions. Greasy Arnold chaperoned her toward a small saloon car parked on the periphery of the car park. After a quick glance around the car park, she hesitantly fell in step beside him.

Chapter 28

From the darkest corner of the car park, two scruffy men strode briskly toward Sam. They took her by the arms and lifted her off her feet. Dumfounded and shocked, she didn't at first react. The car park was empty of people, the traffic noise horrendous. She eventually managed to scream. Ignoring her shrieks, they bundled her into the back of a black saloon car. One of them squeezed in beside her. He slammed the door. His mate climbed into the front.

A small blue light on the dashboard began flashing intermittently. The driver of the car wore police uniform. *Thank God—they're police.*

The three men in the car didn't speak. Sam hadn't a clue what to say. Had Claire set her up? She doubted it. Claire was a loyal and trusted friend. So: what the hell was going on?

The officer next to her, a man with hairy hands, plucked the brown envelope from her coat pocket. Sam about to protest thought, to hell with it; at least it's the police mugging me.

The detective opened the window and handed the envelope to Arnold. 'Piss off Arnold,' he rattled in a Scottish brogue.

Turning to Sam he said, 'Sam, you're a naughty girl.'

'Why am I being arrested?' Sam believed it to be a reasonable question, under the circumstances.

'Sit quiet now. All will be revealed.' He chuckled, slapping his mate on the back.

His colleague in the front passenger seat unclipped a microphone from the dash. 'Charlie one five we have the target, repeat we have the target.'

Sam was a bloody target!

'Where are you taking me?' She protested.

The front passenger twisted around. 'You're being taken to Hendon Police College to meet the man who will enlighten you as to why you have been detained. Sit quiet Miss, there's a good girl.'

What a predicament. She thought about Cameron, about the consequences of attempting to buy information from a criminal. Would they charge her? She hadn't a clue. Best shut up, wait and see. At least Hendon was a college not a police station.

'Who's Arnold? Is he an undercover policeman or something?' Sam managed to ask, her mouth dry.

They laughed. The Scottish detective muttered something under his breath. The other detective shouted from the front. 'Arnold is a police informant. One who's been handsomely paid, thanks to your generous gift.'

'My friend in the pub, she'll be worried.'

'It's taken care of.'

'My car is—'

'In the car park, you can get it later.'

After ten minutes driving in silence they pulled up outside the security gates of Hendon Police College. A uniformed guard glanced at the identification of the driver and raised the red and white barrier.

Sam craned her neck, saw tower blocks and a sports field. She had no idea what was happening and yet she felt important, somehow pleased with herself. After all, she had travelled to London, managed to meet with a police informant and was now being chaperoned by three police officers to meet another high ranking officer. It could mean only one thing: Sam Moon had stumbled into something. And whatever it was appeared important enough for her to be snatched from a pub car park.

They stopped at the rear of a two-storey red brick

building. The sign at the entrance read "Detective Training School." It was after nine; Sam doubted there would be trainee detectives still taking lessons.

The two detectives accompanied her up a flight of concrete stairs and on to a first floor corridor with four classrooms either side, all in darkness apart from the last one on the left, Classroom 8. The Scottish detective gently tapped on the door. After a couple of seconds a male voice, obviously Indian called, 'Bring her in please.'

Shown into the room, the detective closed the door behind her. Presumably, they then went back to doing whatever it was they normally do.

There were at least thirty wooden desks of the type seen in secondary schools; many had writing scratched into their surface. A television monitor flickered in the far corner of the room. A little Asian man with long black hair and a beard, and dressed in jeans and casual shirt, sat cross-legged by the television, a smirk slashing his olive face.

Sam felt awkward; wanting to shout and demand answers, but couldn't think of anything to say.

'I hope you have an open mind, Samantha?'

Sam dropped her bag onto the nearest desk and sat down on a wooden chair. She'd decided to keep her distance, which at least gave her a degree of control.

'Are you the man I'm here to see?'

'I am indeed. Sorry about the clandestine nature of your visit. It was both necessary and expedient.'

'Are you allowed to do this; abduct people in pub car parks?'

He uncrossed his legs, leaned forward. 'Let's start again shall we?'

He raised his right hand. 'Hi, my name is Doctor Ashram Kumar. I'm privileged to be an employee of the Metropolitan Police Detective Training School and

186

also adviser to the National Crime Faculty. Now, let me ask, if you understand the meaning of the word *covert*, Samantha? Of course you do.'

Sam gave him her best pissed off smile.

'Unfortunately Samantha, you are now under the umbrella of the Officials Secrets Act. To that end you must sign this piece of paper. Once you have accepted the terms described in the document, you and I can chat away until the small hours.'

Reluctantly, Sam pulled herself off the chair. She snatched the one sided document, scan read it and then signed on the dotted line. Kumar took it back and slotted it into his briefcase.

'Why am I here, Doctor Kumar?'

Kumar patted a wooden chair close to the TV monitor, indicating for Sam to sit, which she did with a thump and a huff.

Kumar pointed the remote and the television came to life.

On it Jason Cameron was being interviewed in a small room by Christine Krill. The date in the left hand corner of the screen indicated the recording was eighteen months old.

The pair sat opposite each other, a metal table separating them, Christine in uniform, her hat on the table making it more officious. Sam had an idea this was a follow-up interview, probably an interaction to substantiate something.

Christine, pen in hand, hovering over some notes, asked Cameron, 'What happened to Martin Pope?'

'It was an accident.' He looked solemn, periodically examining his hands. 'Blake didn't mean to kill him'

'Who is Blake?'

Cameron laughed nervously and shuffled uncomfortably. 'Blake helps me occasionally.'

'I need to speak to him about Martin Pope. Can you

187

arrange it?'

'It will be difficult, Commander. Blake is suspicious, distrusting of authority.'

'DS Cameron, you know the procedure; you're a serving police officer. Your friend Blake killed a man. He should therefore be brought into custody and questioned.'

'It isn't feasible at the moment; he's reluctant to show himself.'

Christine persisted. 'Can you contact him, let me speak to him?'

'I can try, Christine, if he's in the mood, he may come forward.'

Sam inched closer to the screen; interest peeked to a level she'd last encountered during her student years.

Cameron twisted in his chair, arms and hands appearing to fiddle with unseen bondage that surrounded his body. Slowly, his facial features began subtly morphing, melding, each movement accompanied by nervous ticks, twitches, yet much, much slower and more pronounced.

Christine Krill, confused, glanced back at the camera, shrugged her shoulders. Cameron went very still, head back, eyes lolling like golf balls in a water barrel, white, lifeless.

Snap! Cameron's head shot forward. Christine startled, slid backwards, the chair scraping loudly.

Cameron's head flicked from side to side, physical features hardened, the lines around his eyes much harsher. He'd transformed before her eyes. Neither Krill on screen, nor Sam herself could recognise the granite-featured man now occupying the chair where Cameron had sat moments ago.

'Hello Christine, Jason tells me you wish to speak with me?'

Christine Krill hesitated, still not wanting to believe

what she was seeing. She glanced at the camera, then beyond, seeking guidance.

Eventually she asked, 'Who are you?'

'My name is Blake.'

'Where's Jason Cameron?'

'Jason is still here, safe inside the confines of his mind.'

'Did Cameron kill Martin Pope?'

Blake laughed like a hyena. Christine Krill visibly shook. She inched her chair backwards, climbed to her feet, about to exit the room when Blake spoke in a chiselled voice that grated like a road drill on Sam's senses.

'Jason wouldn't hurt a fly. It was me, I accidentally killed Martin Pope. He was a disgusting little pervert and deserved to die.'

Christine couldn't mask the fear in her voice. 'I don't understand. Cameron's still here. Can he hear what I'm saying to you?'

Blake twitched his nose like he smelled something disgusting. 'When I want him to hear you, otherwise, no he cannot hear what's transpiring between our good selves.'

'Would you mind if I bring a doctor in to examine you Mr Blake?'

'I'm not insane Christine,' adding with a wave of his hand, 'If you must, then go ahead. I must say though, you're becoming very tedious.'

Christine indicated toward the camera she was leaving the room. Seconds later Doctor Kumar entered the room. Gave an imperceptible nod to the camera and took the seat vacated by Christine Krill.

'Hello Blake, my name is Dr Ashram Kumar. Do you mind if I ask you a few questions about your relationship with DS Jason Cameron?'

Blake smirked. 'Aha, the head doctor comes to poke

189

about in the cavernous world of Jason Cameron's psychosis.'

Without preamble Kumar asked, 'Why did you kill Martin Pope?'

Blake answered in the same manner, 'Although an accident, the process of interrogational torture was necessary in my effort to find the missing boy.'

'I see.' Kumar consulted his notes. 'When did you first *meet* Jason Cameron?'

Blake counted on his fingers like a child. 'In the forest, twenty years ago give or take.'

'Have you always been with him since the forest?'

Blake shook his head in dismay. 'Don't be stupid Doctor Kumar -of course not- some of the time I was elsewhere.'

'Please explain Mr Blake'

Blake made himself more comfortable, relishing the moment.

'I went to sleep for a while and then decided to come back and help Jason.'

'Would you accept it was you who murdered Martin Pope and not Jason Cameron?'

'Murder? Not murder my friend, an accident pure and simple.'

Kumar raised his hands in deference. 'Okay Mr Blake, an accident then.' Kumar wrote something on the notes before he continued, his tone soft, without any edge.

'You told the detectives who interviewed Cameron that you had some important information about an abduction occurring when Cameron was lost in the forest twenty years ago. What is that information?'

Blake licked his lips. 'I can identify the abductors of the missing Mullen boy. They are still there in Winston, escaping justice.'

'Who are they?'

Blake shook his head aggressively. 'I don't know who they are, but I do know what they look like.'

'Then how do you propose to identify them?'

'Arrange for Jason and myself to return to Winston. I need you to convince Jason that he is being transferred there as a recuperative gesture. It will raise his confidence and at the same time protect me.'

Kumar looked back at the camera, puzzled.

Blake slapped the tabletop, the sharp abrupt sound startling Kumar, who stood up, wondering whether he should vacate the room.

Voice lowered several octaves Blake said, 'Stay put doctor, I won't hurt you- promise.' Blake glanced beyond Kumar and into the camera, the corners of his mouth twitching in a smile.

'I need to go to Winston and infiltrate the low lives that exist there, the dog people.'

A little less anxious Kumar asked, 'And then, Mr Blake? What happens then?'

'Jason has been seeing a psychiatrist who forces him to suppress me with medication. Each day I am pushed further back. Let me out in Winston and I will help get the men responsible for the abduction of Brian Mullen and identify the murderer of Heather Moon, Cameron's mother.'

'How do I know you're genuine in your offer?'

Blake's response was quick, terse. 'You don't.'

Kumar scribbled more notes. 'You said you've been asleep because the doctors suppressed you?'

Blake snarled like an angry dog. 'Psychiatrists are fools; I'm here to help Jason not harm him. What purpose would that serve?'

'Are you suggesting we deceive Jason Cameron and allow you to dominate?'

Blake hissed. 'Not dominate, just allow me the freedom to come and go without Jason knowing why

191

otherwise he will alert the dog people.'

'And how do you propose I do that?'

Blake sat back, arrogant. 'Doctors manage to suppress me. Do the same to him.'

Chapter 29

Kumar paused the tape, licked his fat lips.

'What do you make of it? '

Talk about off the bloody wall. Sam didn't reply straightaway, thinking of something far simpler: having a cigarette.

Kumar interrupted. 'I realise it's difficult to comprehend that a man you know and trust could somehow be possessed by an alter ego.' He smiled, he hoped in a reassuring way. 'The interview lasts over two hours. Cameron eventually returns with no memory of what's taken place,' he told her. 'Unless of course he's acting.'

'Do you believe he's faking it?'

Kumar scowled. 'Certain colleagues believe that *Dissociated Identity Disorder* is a culture based myth rather than a true medical disorder.' He said it as if he disliked being contradicted in his findings.

Sam felt like screaming, *Are you bloody mad, away with the fairies or is this just a joke?* Instead, maintaining politeness, she asked, 'What do you believe, Doctor? Do you think Cameron is a fraud, trying to deflect his actions onto a split personality?'

Kumar could retaliate, remind her of what she'd seen on screen; tell her it was not camera trickery, a special effect manufactured for her benefit. Why, why didn't people accept this for what it obviously was?

He'd winced when she said *split*. He cleared his throat, rechecked his notes then said, 'What this does is proffer an ideal excuse to commit a crime and since Cameron has been accused of the most serious of crimes, in my opinion it may be the right course of action to ascertain the truth. At least we can try'

'That didn't answer my question Doctor Kumar.' Sam inched closer to Kumar, invading his personal space. 'Do you believe Cameron is genuine?'

Kumar looked a tad put out; he stood and paced the room, absently chewing his pencil.

'I've gone to an awful lot of trouble to prove he is indeed harbouring a malevolent ego; an *alter* sleeping inside him, waiting to emerge into the world.'

Sam shivered a little, a mental picture of a malevolent embryo easing into a world she was trying to come to terms with and finding it difficult.

Kumar stopped by her chair. 'I do have a slight reservation, what you might term a spanner in the works.' He tapped the pencil in his palm. 'The most powerful *alter* serves as a gatekeeper and controls when and where other personalities can reveal themselves. In this case, Blake is dominant because he has all the memory traces, Cameron of course oblivious to what has occurred when he becomes Blake.'

Sam's heart plummeted like a coin falling into a well, in her case the well her saddest, most fearful thought. 'What do you mean?'

Kumar sat. 'When an individual has multiple personalities, at least one of the personalities must possess a memory trace; in other words someone who knows everything. That is commonly the most dominant personality, the gatekeeper. In this case it's Blake who knows everything, so what I'm asking, is it possible Blake is the reality and Cameron the alter ego?'

Sam stared at Kumar. 'I need a bloody drink.'

**

Not the kind of drink she had in mind.

The training school canteen quiet, devoid of customers, two staff on duty busy cleaning tables, stacking dishes. They didn't give Sam or Kumar a second glance. Most of the lights were turned off and the pair occupied a middle table, half in the light and half in the dark.

Canteen coffee usually tasted like muck, Sam surprised this was good; the bacon sandwich a real surprise.

Kumar grinned as she tucked into her food. 'You seem to be taking this in your stride Samantha?'

Sam wiped her mouth with a paper napkin, sipped her coffee.

'With what you've just hit me with, I'm surprised you said that. In hindsight though, I suppose I am sort of relieved in a way.' Sam paused. 'You see, I believe Jason Cameron is genuine.' She uttered a small laugh. 'Albeit a little bizarre.'

Kumar brushed a hand through his long black hair and deftly tied it at the back with a rubber band, the action making his face appear tighter and younger. Sam put him in his fifties and quite handsome in a gentle, unassuming way.

She finished eating, and professed satisfaction. Now for some questions, Sam wanted to clarify what exactly she'd been told.

'Is Cameron aware he has a split personality?'

Kumar shook his head. 'I prefer the term *dissociated identity disorder*. When Cameron came out of the forest he brought Blake out with him. Since then Blake has been an integral part of what we might term the host's being.'

Sam remained unconvinced. 'Cameron talks to him for Christ's sake, he must know Blake is his...'

'His alter ego? His split-personality? It perhaps amounts to the same thing.'

'Whatever.'

'Samantha . . . may I call you Sam?' She nodded. 'Sam, Blake and Cameron are two distinct persona's

195

co-existing together. Cameron relies on Blake when he's disturbed or feels threatened. But both are very different in nature; two distinct identities, different blood pressure, posture, set of gestures, even hairstyle. Each has its own relatively lasting pattern of sensing, except, as I said earlier, Blake has the memory trace.'

Interest piqued she said, 'Will Blake always be there, inside Cameron?'

Kumar smiled broadly. 'When Cameron was in the forest he was faced with an overwhelming trauma. There was no physical escape. His captors had him trapped and under their control. Cameron saw no alternative. He simply disappeared inside his own head. By using this dissociated defence mechanism his thoughts, feelings and memories of what happened became Blake's, not his.'

Sam, highly confused asked, 'I thought Cameron got lost in the forest?'

Kumar said, 'He believes he did. Unfortunately Blake knows different.'

Sam thought about Blake's attack on Lukas Meek.

'Blake seems to be violent, narcissistic, cunning, and nothing like Cameron.' Desperate to understand, she ached for clarity in a situation which played out like a nightmare.

Kumar plucked a worn paperback book from his briefcase, flicked through the pages, and stopping halfway through he read aloud, 'He is not easy to describe. There is something wrong with his appearance, something displeasing, and something downright detestable. I never saw a man I so disliked, and yet I scarce know why.'

Kumar put the book on the table. 'Sound familiar?'
Sam nodded.
Kumar said, 'It's a passage from, "The Strange Case of Dr Jeckyl and Mr Hyde." It fits Blake perfectly.'

Sam said, 'You're very eloquent in your explanation. This is obviously your field of speciality.'

Kumar grinned. 'It wasn't my speciality until I met Jason Cameron. It was a case of having to re-educate myself. I'm a trained psychologist but this type of psychosis is not within my remit. We have psychiatrists for that. When the investigating detectives interrogated Cameron about the death of Martin Pope and out popped Blake, I for one thought it was a con. Since then, well when you hear my audacious plan you might become a believer.' He returned the paperback to his briefcase. 'My nagging doubt concerns his ability to switch from Cameron to Blake so quickly without triggers.'

'I saw him switch.' She recalled the cottage incident. 'Initially I thought I had them both in the cottage and now when I look back, it's abundantly obvious that Jason was swapping from his true self to Blake.'

He interjected. 'Switching can take seconds or hours but don't be fooled into believing it's that simple.'

'Honestly,' she said excited, 'it was like they were both there in the same room. It wasn't until I saw your tape recording that I realised he was leaving me alone and then returning like a quick change artist.'

Kumar looked like a scholar about to chastise his star pupil for getting calculus wrong.

'That might not have been Cameron.'

'I don't understand?'

Kumar whispered. 'It might well have been Blake pretending to be Cameron. Complicated isn't it?'

Feeling foolish she repeated how baffled she was.

'Imagine yourself as Blake; hidden, emerging when Cameron is vulnerable. You would be defensive, suspicious, most of all you would be careful. Blake is all these things and more. Until he trusts his

197

environment he will use his knowledge of Cameron's personality to delve deeper until he knows you're no longer a threat to him; and Cameron of course.'

'You make it sound like Blake is dominant. That he rules the roost.'

'He did until Cameron began taking medication to control his affliction.'

Sam's heart fluttered. The mirror!

'I think Blake wrote a message on the bathroom mirror telling Cameron to be wary of me. Let me tell you that scared me fucking shitless.' Sam blushed, her flippant use of bad language unusual, at least since her university days.

Kumar ignored it; he looked pensive, concerned. 'Blake might see you as a threat to his existence, particularly if he dislikes you.'

Sam said, 'You're getting close to letting me know why I'm here. I realise it must be difficult because of the weirdness of Cameron's condition.' Sam tidied up the cutlery she hadn't used and gave Kumar an earnest stare, her fears placed to the back of her mind, dealing with the situation. 'It isn't a coincidence that he turned up at my place is it Dr Kumar?'

The twitch in Kumar's left eye and the ringing of his hands told her she'd struck a nerve, her own or Kumar's? Probably both.

'When Heather Moon was murdered,' Kumar told her, 'we chanced upon something which could hold the key to an abduction occurring twenty years ago.'

He took a five pound note from a tatty leather wallet and left it on the table. 'It's time I showed you the full extent of our little operation.'

Chapter 30

Whilst Kumar entertained Sam in London, Victor and Christine Krill decided to return to Winston police station to engage in some much needed dialogue with Cameron.

Victor decided to use DI Mullen's office, telling Christine he would prefer to speak with Cameron alone. Cameron didn't argue since he now trusted the brusque detective, believing Victor LaSalle to be a friend.

For her part, Christine didn't argue, professing to be more interested in what was going on in the police control room at Headquarters.

During the short drive from Gatekeeper cottage, Cameron felt reflective, quietly pondering his position, not quite pulling all the pieces of this intricate puzzle together. Victor hadn't pushed him for more information on Blake, for which Cameron was grateful; time to recharge.

They now sat comfortably side by side in Mullen's office like two mates planning a holiday.

Victor placed a photograph on Cameron's lap. 'Do you recognise this man?'

'No, should I?' said Cameron.

Victor placed the photograph back in a manila folder.

'Blake insists this is the man who abducted you. You should know the Met allowed Blake to trawl through thousands of photographs of criminals known to have been arrested in North Yorkshire for sexual related activity. Blake patiently waded through them; he eventually picked out this man. He allegedly recognised him about two years ago when you attended a dogfight in North London. Since then the guy's changed his appearance, grown a beard and is now here, back in Winston.'

Cameron was confident Blake would be correct with his identification.

'I trust Blake,' he said. 'By the way did he say when he would be back?'

Victor said, 'According to Blake, when he returns is entirely up to you.'

The jaded LaSalle of yesterday had gone; in his place was a sharp, confident individual with an honest interest in Cameron's well-being. Was it an act or had something occurred that had snapped him back to his old self?

'Who is the man in the photograph?'

LaSalle looked at Cameron like a nurse giving a patient the once over before allowing him to get out of bed.

'It's Lukas Meek. 'Victor said. 'On his visits to Haughton to watch over the cottage, Blake saw Meek and followed him. We only put two and two together in the last couple of days as a result of his vehicle which Blake recognised. Blake trailed Sam to the offices of the Yorkshire Gateway and in doing it found she was being followed by Meek in his jeep. After he attacked Meek he rang the police control room to get the message to Christine Krill. Apparently Blake is keeping his end of the bargain.'

Meek's unpleasantness came back to haunt Cameron. 'How come I don't recognise Meek?' he demanded.

'According to Dr. Kumar, because of what occurred in the forest twenty years ago; you have suppressed the memory. Blake is the only hope we have of recreating the memory and getting the evidence we need to put Meek away.'

Cameron thought about the implication here.

'Victor, you and I both know Blake would not make a plausible witness in court.'

200

Victor chuckled. 'It would still be a sight to behold my young friend.' Victor went to the window that overlooked DI Mullen's garden. Out there the day was bright, a far cry from the thoughts in his mind.

'Jason do you remember much about when you were initially interviewed here in this police station after Walter Slack found you in the woods?'

Cameron scratched his stubble. God he needed a shower. 'Bits and pieces, not the whole event; I passed out at one stage, probably exhausted.'

He looked at Victor deciding Victor wanted to get on with the interrogation. He knew though that these things required delicate handling.

Victor said, quietly, placing a fatherly hand on Cameron's shoulder, 'Why do you think Walter was found guilty of abducting you and Brian Mullen when it was Walter who found you in the forest?'

Cameron didn't know and shrugged.

'Jason, the trial hinged on your testimony. It was you who gave evidence on video link that Walter had been in the compound, had interfered with you. Do you remember this?'

Cameron groaned, placed his head in his hands.

'Victor, if what you're saying is correct then how did he win his appeal?'

'They never actually got you to repeat the allegations, either in open court or on video link. After Victor's release lawyers argued there was insufficient evidence- that the prosecution had been unsafe. Walter got a boat load of money as a result.'

'No wonder he's interested in Blake and me. He's probably intent on clearing his name for absolute certainty.' It was Cameron's turn to walk the room, banging his head with a clenched fist.

'WHY? Why can't I remember?' He stopped, light dawning. 'Jesus Victor, it was Blake, Blake gave the

201

initial evidence. No wonder I don't remember.'

'Exactly. Walter needs to believe Blake exists otherwise you condemned him to ten years in gaol.'

Yes, Cameron thought, and Walter may also harbour a deep hatred of Blake, therefore me.

Cameron realised Victor was scrutinizing his every reaction to the questions.

'What's the plan with Blake, Victor?'

'If we can find Brian Mullen's body out there we'll hopefully, using forensics, tie Lukas Meek to Brian's abduction and murder. Blake's convinced he can do this if you let him get close to Meek.'

A peculiar thing to say since Blake takes little notice of Cameron unless it somehow threatens his own position.

Cameron, only too aware Blake was growing in strength; the temptation to let him loose for good overwhelming, was growing scared: scared for himself and what he knew Blake was capable of doing.

Was this the initial plan? Why couldn't he remember?

The proposition by Victor, he knew beyond a doubt would be acceptable for Blake.

'I agreed to come to Winston with the understanding it would help find Heather's killer.'

Victor sat beside him again. 'When I spoke to Blake at the cottage he told me he saw Heather's killer. He also said you asked him to watch over her. I got the impression Blake believes he let you down, that he's determined to make amends. Jason, I'm confident Blake will identify the killer.'

Yes, he had asked Blake to watch the cottage and despite his, Cameron's, close tie to Blake, the quid pro quo of information sharing was loaded in favour of Blake. It hadn't always been like this. Time had conspired to steer it that way, and thus it had coincided with Blake appearing more frequently and, God forbid, with greater depth.

What if Blake was taking over? This concerned Cameron. He would ask Dr Kumar to hypnotise him again, enable him to have a conversation without Blake's knowledge. This way he was fairly sure of not upsetting Blake. Fairly sure? Why only fairly sure? Did he doubt his own abilities to confine Blake?

For sure the hypnotherapy detached him from his alter ego with outstanding effectiveness.

As if reading Cameron's thoughts, Victor said, 'It must be a burden, having Blake inside you, on the verge of reawakening.'

Until now Cameron hadn't discussed his affliction with anyone except Kumar and his psychiatrist; it would therefore be difficult for Victor to understand.

'When Kumar showed me the videotapes I was astounded. Of course I knew about Blake but hadn't realised the extent of his influence over me. I had only fleeting recollection of being Blake. It's weird because Blake can hear my voice, feel my emotions, experience my thoughts and memories; unlike me because I have little recollection of Blake unless he allows it.' He paused then added thoughtfully,

'After the taped interview we, that's Blake and me, began to argue, regularly.'

He sought Victor's reaction. Victor nodded thoughtfully.

Cameron wondered if Victor understood or was he humouring him?

Victor said, 'Christine told me it was you who decided what triggers would effectively encourage Blake to come out.'

Cameron went back to his first meeting with Kumar after the tapes. He echoed Kumar's words, saying, 'The correct term is "switching". And yes I agreed on their use. Of course, it's preferable and more effective if I have no conscious knowledge of the chosen triggers, otherwise Blake would be on his guard. Believe me he knows about triggers; he prefers the word "hotspots."

Victor chuckled, evidently relaxed in Cameron's company. A long time since Cameron had experienced the joy of another's company without limitations of thought and action.

Cameron had, perhaps unwittingly, allowed them to control Blake's appearance and it worked. Blake had agreed to assist the police, unreservedly, accepting the use of the triggers because it was orchestrated for his benefit or so it would seem.

'Did using the wheelchair annoy Walter?' Cameron wanted to know if Christine was being disingenuous, knowing that the Martin Pope affair was still unresolved and simmering in the background. He also concluded that when the operation to snare Brian Mullen's abductors was complete it would be impossible for him to continue as a serving police officer.

'No, Walter accepts it,' Victor told him. 'He had no choice, being so fragile.'

Cameron fought against the sparking in his head. 'You realise why these things, like wheelchairs bring Blake out?'

Victor reflecting said, 'I know everything about Martin Pope. Also, Kumar told me about your father.' He grasped Cameron's forearm. 'I was reluctant at first, pretending to be alcohol dependent, depressed. It seemed cruel.' He looked at Cameron apologetically. 'I'm no actor, Jason.'

'I respond to those memories.' Cameron patted Victor's big hands, 'you must understand Victor, Blake has helped me, he's not the enemy.'

'I know that now, remember, I've met him; I have

204

the bruises to prove it.'

Cameron had a strange sensation. His brain suddenly felt spongy, an intense feeling of anguish settled in his mind's eye. *Blake it's all right, Victor is a friend.*

Cameron bit his lip, banishing these sensations to a subliminal level. 'It's very bizarre though Victor, when the only witness to an abduction is the alter ego of a policeman.'

They both laughed.

After a short while of contemplative chuckling Victor said, 'Why did Blake attack Lukas Meek?'

Blake murmured something; somehow listening in to their conversation. *How could that be?* Blake didn't normally interfere in Cameron's conscious self, only when they were alone.

'I don't know for sure,' Cameron said. 'Probably did it as a precursor to him getting on the inside, you know infiltrating the dog fighting. If Lukas Meek is the man who abducted me, then Blake would be angry. Tell me Victor, what is Ron Stark's connection to the case?'

Victor answered matter-of-factly, 'He was the original investigating officer when Brian Mullen was abducted. Kumar thought he might trigger some memories. At least it was the original intention but it would seem Sergeant Stark has much to hide.

'A Detective Inspector, Sandy Dalton, was later appointed to lead the enquiry into yours and Brian's abduction. It was Dalton who debriefed you when you were found. At the time it was felt that Ron Stark wasn't up to the job.'

'I've heard that name before Victor. What happened to DI Dalton?

Victor sighed, 'Unfortunately, when the case against Walter collapsed, they blamed Sandy who found himself relegated to a life in Control Room for the remainder of his service. Walter made some extremely damaging complaints about the handling of the enquiry.'

Victor slid a blue coloured file across the seat. Cameron turned it around.

'It's the covering report of the original investigation into the abduction of Brian Mullen.' Victor indicated the name on the report. 'Original investigating officer- DS Ron Stark.'

Cameron felt Victor watching him. Suddenly, Blake said something, this time he heard it; *'Stark was there in the forest, with that cunt Meek.'* Blake's profanity startled Cameron.

Victor, failing to notice Cameron's anxiety said: 'Also, Stark had a brother who disappeared shortly after the abduction. The brother changed his name from Luke Stark to Lukas Meek, doubtless to avoid having a criminal record; Meek being somewhat bizarre in his sexual preferences.'

Chapter 31

Victor noted the concentration on Cameron's face as Cameron read the file. Like a man fighting inner turmoil, which of course he was.

Doctor Kumar had explained about Cameron's condition in some detail, Kumar marvelling at how Victor had so easily grasped the context. So much so that Victor congratulated himself in the ability to disguise his true intellect. He agreed it had many useful advantages, particularly when it came to self-preservation.

'I have a question, Jason,' he said, and carried straight on with, 'Is there any time without the use of hypnotherapy or drugs that you can escape Blake's influence.'

Cameron visibly stiffened, slight agitation evident.

'Blake's influence only comes to bear when I need it. He isn't such a burden. Have to say hypnotherapy works.'

Victor had no skill in the practice and so pressed on in his own way believing he should persuade Cameron to stifle Blake for a while otherwise he wouldn't be able illicit the information he required.

'Don't get me wrong Jason, I'm just curious.'

Cameron relaxed. 'Let me explain it this way, Victor. In Italy for example, it's not unusual for two football teams to play in the same stadium. Each team has its own colours, fan base and players. Both teams are different yet they inhabit the same space, but not at the same time.'

'I accept that, but Kumar told me there is a way that you can slide Blake into a coma, just to enable you to speak privately, *with me*?'

Victor winked, produced a litre bottle of single malt from his drawer and beckoned Cameron to follow him

207

as he led them to the deserted cell area.

'Are you comfortable in a locked cell drinking whiskey?'

Truthfully, Cameron looked dreadful; the colour had drained from his face. He flopped onto the single bunk and sighed.

He managed, his voice cracking, 'The one thing Blake fears is confined spaces. It diminishes him, buries him deep inside my subconscious. Just like when they arrested me for killing Martin Pope. Blake disappeared when I was in the cells. He only came back when the interviewing detectives put me under immense pressure. Confinement forces Blake to hibernate, it's that bad.'

'I know,' Victor said. 'Kumar told me.'

Victor took out two plastic containers from his jacket pocket, unscrewed the whiskey top, and poured two healthy measures. 'Here, drink. You'll feel better.'

They raised the glasses in silent toast, Victor thinking let there be an end to it soon.

'Done for a reason, Jason, the drink I mean. Kumar let it slip that alcohol, more specifically drunkenness diminishes Blake's ability to remember; like any intelligent entity, the booze dampens his recollection of events. Drink up my friend we have a lot to talk about.'

The cell smelled of stale urine. Various etchings had once adorned its cream walls depicting a variety of sexually explicit drawings and the odd crude poem, mostly denigrating the police. They had been glossed over. All that remained were indentations like cave drawings on rock.

'This cell hasn't been used operationally for some time. Apparently it's capable of withstanding a terrorist attack.' Victor attempted to change the subject, put Cameron at ease.

He swirled the contents of his glass, avoiding full

208

eye contact with Cameron; ashamed he would be caught out for attempting to con him into revealing secrets about his condition. Then again, did the situation demand such extreme measures as a full blown orchestrated operation designed to eek out a subdued alter ego? Victor wasn't convinced. For heavens sake, if the media ever cottoned on to the ramifications of Operation Bifurcate, they would have a field day.

Cameron drained his first glass of malt. Admittedly he felt a little better. 'Victor, I know you're sceptical about my illness; it's not unusual. You're a pragmatic man and therefore uneasy with the concept. I understand, and so does Blake.'

Victor undid his tie; relaxed he dipped his index finger into the dregs of the malt, licked it thinking: Fine, but I need more answers from you my young friend.

'Tell me, Jason, is Blake listening to our conversation?'

Without hesitation, Cameron answered, 'I don't think so.'

Victor thought how he could manage to slide his thoughts on Blake into their conversation without alarming Cameron, or bringing Blake into the room.

In the past couple of weeks he'd deliberated calling a halt to the operation, maybe confronting Christine with an alternative plan involving a raid on the compound followed by an old fashioned line up of suspects. One problem: if Cameron was genuine he wouldn't pick anyone out because he would be unable to identify them. Only Blake could manage that feat.

Sod it. Victor threw caution aside and asked, 'Have you considered the possibility that Blake scared Nigel Moon to death?'

Victor sat back, expecting Cameron to be affronted.

Instead, Cameron answered calmly, 'Yes I have and it's a possibility. We both know from Frank that just before Nigel collapsed someone shouted out a name, Bull or Blake or something similar.' Cameron sipped more malt and said, 'If Blake, and in essence myself, was there watching over the cottage, then it could have been me who shouted something, Blake's name perhaps, warning him that Nigel had collapsed. I just don't know for sure.'

Surprised at such a candid reply, Victor pursued his interrogation.

'Could it be possible also that Blake, out of fear or jealousy killed Heather?'

Victor decided not to elaborate, the question succinct and pertinent without explanation, extra cautious of Blake's tendency for violent behaviour.

Cameron hesitated, took the whiskey bottle, poured himself a top up, took a slug and said, 'Blake has always protected me from harm. I have no indication he was jealous of Heather, and besides, he will identify her killer, I'm sure of it.'

Victor nodded towards Cameron's glass and Cameron necked the contents in one swift gulp. Victor refilled it and his own and they followed the same ritual until the bottle was empty.

Victor watched Cameron's features soften as the drink took effect.

'I suspect Blake killed your mother.'

Slurring his words, Cameron said, 'No, not possible, I would know; intrinsically I mean, deep down, I'm sure I would know. Yes, I'm positive he didn't kill Heather.'

'Has Blake been involved in fighting, you know for money, bare-knuckle stuff?

Cameron visibly agitated, groped for the right words.

'Funny that Victor, I've often found injuries to my face and hands which cannot be accounted for, so it is possible, yes. On occasions I fall into a fugue state, a time when Blake is his most comfortable. Days go by when I can't remember where I've been. Not a very good aspect of my life with Blake, particularly when I went undercover.'

Victor, recognising Cameron could be near collapse perhaps realised he'd overdone it with the booze and cursed himself for the oversight. Sink or swim, he pressed Cameron with, 'Why did Blake torture Martin Pope? I read the file; Pope was a lightweight, a man of jelly. Surely, once threatened he would have led you to the missing boy no problem.'

Cameron's eyes were glassy, his nostrils flared; he was finding it difficult to stay awake. Victor had overdone it.

'Pope recognised me . . . me from the forest, years ago.' Cameron belched, whisky turned to acid in his gut. 'He . . . he was there when they put me in the pit with the dog.' Cameron licked his lips, Victor's shape hazy. 'Blake found out from Pope who did it to me. This little scheme to infiltrate Winston was his idea not . . . Kumar's.' On the verge of passing out, Cameron said quite clearly: 'Blake wants revenge.'

211

Chapter 32

Cameron regained awareness, time immaterial. Where had he been? Ah yes, the cell, bomb proof and Blake proof. He managed a wry grin. He thanked Victor for getting a driver to bring him home.

With the help of fruit juice and aspirin his hangover eased. The small chiming clock convinced him he was alive. Gone eleven, he thought what the hell, two mugs of coffee and a couple of toast slices later he'd improved. After a quick wash in the bathroom sink, he pulled on jeans and a lumberjack shirt and a warm coat. Gathered a few things together – a torch, a flick knife, a water bottle, Sam's digital camera and binoculars, and wrapped up, he aimed for the track behind the cottage that led into the forest far more confident and definitely less tense.

His time spent with Victor LaSalle had reassured him that the big man was indeed on his side. Yeah, a friend, Cameron agreed accepting the questioning as necessary and understandable.

Now I must face my demons.

Leaving by the back door, he ventured toward the tree line, hesitant at first, gaining confidence with each step.

Blake stirred when Cameron entered the undergrowth.

Good, he thought. It's time Blake came to the forefront. He would doubtless need his skills tonight.

Finding the compound wouldn't be easy. Cameron's best efforts may well go unrewarded despite knowing he had to give it a go. No sense waiting for Blake to venture in without a precursory reconnoitre. Certainly Blake would know the terrain better after tonight's incursion.

Eyes flicking right to left, Cameron mapped his

212

route as he went along. He welcomed the darkness like an old friend, a man no longer afraid of the forest, rather enjoying its spiritual comfort and eerie sounds.

Roughly an hour on he stopped at an intersection and swigged from his water bottle. Darker now, towering trees a distraction, undergrowth likewise; Cameron didn't see it at first. Blake sensed it, putting Cameron's sensory mode into overdrive. He was being stalked, Blake convinced whatever it was had been following for some minutes. It's presence given away by the odd crack of twigs.

Cameron gently eased Blake back. *It's not your time Blake; I can handle this.*

Scanning the foliage, Cameron sought the unusual. Nothing appeared out of place, just the odd twitch of a branch. Moonlight helped, the light here better by the second, light pollution yes, but he was still able to see reasonably well. How long it would last, Cameron didn't know. Quarter of an hour for the moon to roll by, or clouds to block it, *did it matter?* Cameron and Blake were accomplished covert surveillance operatives; the two knew how to handle darkness.

What the hell was that?

A shape scuttled across Cameron's line of sight.

Quickly putting his binoculars to his eyes, he peered along the track. There! About two hundred yards away stood the strangest creature he had ever set eyes upon. Magnificently tall, the size of a Great Dane with a striding gate and thick black woolly hair, it galloped onto the track and flicked it's huge canine head, offering Cameron a brief glance before it plodded nonchalantly into the undergrowth.

Cameron jogged to the spot were the creature had stood. On his haunches he found several large paw prints. Whatever the creature was, it had to be related to either a wolf or dog. Of that he was confident.

Taking a couple of shots of the prints, Cameron failed to notice the creature had fooled him. Now it stood thirty yards behind him. It watched him, motionless, unwavering in its vigil.

Blake warned him not to overreact; the creature may simply be curious.

Without any sudden movement that might well alert the beast, Cameron reached for the flick knife in his coat pocket, and let his hand fall slowly to his side; with a soft click he flicked open the blade.

The creature moved toward him, every so often pausing to sniff the air, assessing any potential threat from Cameron.

Keep calm Cameron, murmured Blake. *Listen to your body's rhythms; if it attacks aim the blade for its neck.*

Stopping twenty yards from Cameron, hackles rising, it howled, its gums ruby red reflecting teeth sharp and white.

The beast bore a striking resemblance to the dog he'd seen with Lukas Meek, yet seemed larger, leastways as much as he could assess in the gloom. He remained still, mesmerised by the dog's weird shape and immaculate icy black woollen mane. Unbelievable!

Shit! Suddenly, the brute charged. Heart rate racing, Cameron took a defensive stance, holding the knife tight; both arms stretched out rigid like a spear.

Two yards away and bizarrely the creature fell at his feet in a heap, misty breath pumping from its nostrils like a snorting bull. Eyes glazed, its breathing slowed. What the hell just happened?

From the bushes, Victor appeared dressed in a camouflage jacket and trousers, and carrying a rather unusual looking gun. Like a handgun except its barrel length made it as long as a rifle. It reminded Cameron of a glue gun.

'Now that's one weird dog,' said Victor, grinning from ear to ear, definitely pleased with his marksmanship.

Cameron, relieved and delighted to see his friend asked, 'Is it dead?'

'I don't think so.' Victor waved the gun at Cameron. 'This is a C02 gas powered dart gun. Since the sightings in the forest; we've kept them on hand at the nick. Samantha helped out with the dosage.' He gave the dog a gentle kick. 'Worked a bloody treat though. Funny thing is my second shot missed, I fired the first about ten minutes ago. It took that long to work.'

'Don't tell me; it was you following that, following me?'

Victor cocked his head and winked. 'Before she left Sam asked me to keep an eye on you, said you were a bit headstrong sometimes.'

Chapter 33

A map of Winston dominated the wall of the small conference room, the detail spectacular. Sam noticed a red cross in the middle of the forest.

'What's that?

Kumar said, 'We believe it's the location of a compound.'

'Cameron spoke of a compound.' She moved closer. 'He stumbled onto it when he got lost as child.'

Kumar sat down in a chair positioned about ten feet from the map and regarded Sam with a concerned expression. 'The police, well to be exact Victor LaSalle, believed Heather blundered into the compound and guessed its use.'

'Is that why she was murdered?'

'Possibly. And the fact she wrote several articles about dog fighting and unusual creatures stalking the forest.'

Sam examined the map. 'I don't see any access road to the compound.'

Kumar nodded appreciatively and smiled. 'There isn't one, at least not one easily navigable. The police believe it's accessed using an underground tunnel somewhere near here.' He indicated Gatekeeper Cottage.

Sam gawked at the spot, aghast. 'I've lived there a long time Dr Kumar, believe me if there was a tunnel near the cottage I would know about it.'

From a nearby table, Kumar picked up a pencil and twirled it in his fingers, a habit from his student days: it helped him concentrate.

'You know Sam, the forest wasn't always here.' He wafted the pencil over the map. 'Fifty years ago the hills around Winston were riddled with mine shafts. The forest now conifers, trees not indigenous to this area, planted as fuel for the many power stations. Unfortunately, they've also provided an excellent hiding place for unlawful practices, including dog fights.'

This implied evil men heading into the forest in the dead of night with wild and dangerous dogs, Sam remembering as a child hearing strange noises emanating from the dense forest, particularly at night when the noises awoke her. She'd run into her father's bedroom, Nigel Moon absent, only Heather there to comfort her. Where had Dad gone in the middle of the night? She didn't ask but Heather said:

'It's all right sweetie, Daddy's working away, he will be back in the morning.'

A weird and unsettling thought crossed her mind right then: Had Dad been involved in dog fighting? She knew he spent many nights away, often smelling funny when he came back. That smell she now recognised as dog lanolin.

'Dr Kumar,' she asked, 'The strange creature seen by witnesses roaming the woodland, is it connected to the compound?'

Kumar stood and moved towards the map, turned towards her, hands clasped, Sam thinking his lecture mode was kicking in. He enjoyed it, she could tell.

'The police believe the men who run the compound have been experimenting with hybrids. Highly possible one of their chimera's escaped.'

Sam's eyes widened. She's thinking, alter egos and now hybrids. There was a difference, but somehow in her mind one felt like the other.

'Probably German Shepherd dogs interbred with wolves.'

Sam felt nauseous. Here she was a vet and dedicated to the preservation and humane treatment of all animals, the brutal practice of actually breeding dogs to

217

fight for the pleasure of humans extremely abhorrent.

'Why on earth would anyone wish to breed wolf dogs?'

Kumar said, 'I suspect because the wolf hybrid is a genetic mixture. Presumably because their physical characterises cannot be predicted with certainty, they may have experimented until they got what they desired – a particularly vicious fighting dog.'

'I understand why the police would want to stop dogfights and see the logic in utilising police resources in an imaginative way, although I have to admit this scheme...' she waved a hand at the map, 'seems extremely elaborate and bloody way-out weird.'

'It isn't really. Imagine living in a small community where two boys are abducted and one never seen again. Imagine you're a suspect in those abductions and no matter how hard you try you can't convince anyone of your innocence.' Kumar tapped his pencil on his teeth. 'Of course, you could relocate; try to live your life again elsewhere. That is unless your roots are so firmly entrenched you cannot tear them free.'

He gazed steadily at her. Sam nodded thoughtfully, gradually beginning to comprehend the inspirational audacity of both Walter Slack and Kumar.

'Sam,' Kumar said quietly, 'You have doubts I can tell. Let me put it another way. Walter Slack owns a lot of land in Winston; he has many dependants and accepts he is very poorly. Winston is his pride and joy and yet it should be vibrant, alive with new developments, after all it is in the heart of the North Yorkshire. Very few new developments have been built since the abduction, rumours remain rife; investors reluctant to take risks. And then your mother is murdered.'

Kumar took off his glasses, wiped them with his handkerchief. 'Following his successful appeal Walter

Slack sued the authorities. He acquired a substantial sum of money and later took it upon himself to buy land for housing development. Not long afterwards Heather wrote about strange creatures in the forest; real or imagined, it didn't matter. The take up of houses slowed, the town's economy became comatose. Then Heather died.'

He paused, climbed to his feet and opened a window; he breathed deep, the fresh air reviving him from his closeted situation.

'When Jason Cameron introduced us to Blake it became probable that Blake had witnessed the murder of Heather and would be in a position to identify Brian Mullen's abductors. I took it upon myself to visit Winston to further develop the Blake theory; became captivated by its implausibility, yet drawn to investigate it like a moth to a flame.

'In my work I came across Victor LaSalle, who introduced me to Walter Slack who immediately recognised the potential of allowing Blake to come back to Winston to hopefully identify the original abductors and your mother's murderer.'

Sam's thoughts spun; a nagging throb at her temples, everything Kumar had said making some way out, yet logical sense. Trouble was it bothered her, like an itch she couldn't scratch. In fact a dozen or so itches!

'How on earth did you manage to pull this together?'

Kumar chuckled. 'Initially with great difficulty until Christine Krill was appointed Chief Constable of North Yorkshire. But it was LaSalle who became the key to the operation. He agreed to play his part with great aplomb as it happens. Also, he persuaded Lonnie and Frank Slack to assist, the only real hurdle being Harry Mullen mainly because of his connections to the

219

original abduction. He was given a cock and bull story by Christine Krill. To be fair on Harry, he nearly messed it up by dobbing Victor in the mire over his informant handling.'

Sam whistled.

'In essence, you've been using us all in an elaborate plan designed to get Blake to come out and help trace the abductors.' Sam searched for appropriate words to describe her feelings on the subject settling for, 'Is everything about the operation fabrication, illusion and deceit?'

Kumar patted her hand. 'No my dear, it isn't. When I chanced upon Walter Slack and he told me about Cameron's family history, I thought it was an ideal way of luring Blake out. You must understand Sam, since the Martin Pope affair, Blake has been buried deep inside Cameron's subconscious, held there by drugs, and the lack of anxiety in Cameron's life.'

Kumar went back to the window wondering if he was overburdening Sam. Too late to stop now, he knew. 'Cameron has been subdued, stress free. Following his subsequent trial and acquittal, Blake disappeared. The only definitive way to bring him back, and remember it was Blake's idea originally, was to create a world of anxiety for Cameron using emotional triggers.

'Understand that our friend Blake responds to Cameron's emotional well-being or importantly the lack of it. Jealousy, rage, anger, fear, a bunch of ingredients carefully filtered into him thanks to LaSalle and Walter Slack. Clever isn't it?'

Sam was not entirely convinced the operation to be clever or indeed necessary, and in some ways she felt saddened by what man will resort to in order to gain closure. She didn't say this, only: 'Why didn't you simply stick Cameron in a room then place him under

220

duress?' Something to say that indicated her appreciation of catching a killer, and disguising her true feelings about Jason Cameron.

'Because, Sam, that wouldn't have had the scientific benefits of a controlled environment wherein Cameron's welfare would be protected.'

Sam wanted desperately to believe in Kumar.

'I still don't get it.' She needed to stretch her legs and walked to the door; she swivelled around. "Doctor, if Blake can speak to Cameron, can't he simply indicate to Cameron at such time he comes across the men responsible?' She moved closer. 'You know what I mean, just simply say *that's him*?'

'Cameron isn't strong like Blake. Again, try to understand that Blake must delve into their world on our behalf, and confront them, it's the only sure way.'

She wasn't convinced. 'It appears to me that you intend keeping up the pressure on Cameron in order to literally force Blake to . . .to come out, and presumably stay out for long periods to enable him to complete, for want of a better phrase, "his mission"?'

Kumar, about to speak, found himself interrupted, 'What if Blake decides he doesn't want to fade into the background when it's all over, Doctor. Any thoughts on that?'

The look on Kumar's face reiterated an unspoken truth: They didn't care about Jason Cameron. Further reasoning on her part assured her that Kumar had become infatuated with the Blake character. That was all.

Kumar realising her anxiety, changed the subject. 'It gets better.'

Sam played along, allowed him to place an arm about her slender shoulders.

'Sam,' he said, 'LaSalle has found a dog to act as a capable prop to assist Blake with his undercover

221

adventure.' Kumar's grin looked deceitful. 'Blake wants your help to train the brute.'

Chapter 34

Christine Krill could hear Harry Mullen pacing and mumbling incoherently through her closed door.

What should she say to him since it was obvious that Brian Mullen might be buried somewhere in the forest. Was it time for her to come clean? Now there's a strange concept, truth in police work! If the government ever got hold of that little beauty, there would be an avalanche of paperwork.

In the maelstrom, which had evolved since initiating the operation, Christine accepted that the rules of the game had become fuzzy around the edges, initial stimulus forgotten, goalposts definitely moved.

Christine's excitement hadn't waned, the operation still having merits, capable of coming together, Cameron still proving to be a worthwhile asset, again. Would he guess that once the operation had been finalised to everyone's satisfaction that his career would be well and truly over? Kaput! Down the tubes. If they succeeded in identifying Heather's killer, then the poor sod would finally be forced to medically retire. Christ, it had taken all her stealth and guile to allow the operation to go ahead in the first place. Strictly speaking, in Christine's opinion, Jason Cameron was mentally unsound.

And poor Harry, still pacing, had no idea why history unravelled around him. Presumably he'd have one objective in sight – to find his missing son. Yes, Christine Krill would tell the truth, after all, none of it had been her idea, not directly anyway.

She buzzed her secretary and told her to show Harry into her office. Only the third time she had met Harry Mullen, the first was three months ago when she'd briefed him about Jason Cameron's posting to Winston. He hadn't believed her. No matter.

Harry the tired old sod, didn't amount to much.

Harry shuffled into the capacious room, suit crumpled to the extent he might have slept in it, his hair wild.

'Make yourself at home Harry. Tea or coffee?'

Harry flopped into the nearest chair. He had yet to look at Christine, preferring to stare at his hands clasped together, prayer-like.

'No thank you, Chief.' Christine heard him murmur something else but couldn't make it out.

'Sorry Harry, didn't quite catch that?'

He stated more loudly, 'What the hell is going on?'

Yes, the truth would hopefully placate him. That was her plan anyway.

'How much has Victor told you, Harry?'

'Only that Jason Cameron might help to find Brian's abductors.'

She had to be careful. Harry sat on the edge of an abyss.

'Harry, Victor knew Janice had visited Heather Moon. He came to the wrong conclusion thinking Janice had murdered Heather. He was wrong.'

A look of dread washed over Mullen's features, he paled, his eyes bobbed like golf balls in a water bucket.

Immense stress was a mere half of it, Christine concluded. What on earth had Harry Mullen been up to? Forget the gently, gently approach; Christine headed straight or the jugular. She wanted the truth: his version.

'Something you want to get off your chest Harry?'

Mullen whimpered like a whipped puppy. Did Christine care? Come off it, she wanted, needed to know what was swilling around in his addled brain.

Christ, he should have retired last year. Why on earth did LaSalle pick him to be the lead investigator for the Heather Moon case? Has Harry finally lost his marbles? No more than her, she reasoned, having brought him back to Winston and involved him in this charade?

She shoved a coffee at him; he refused. She plonked it on the edge of her desk. 'There if you change your mind. So come on Harry, out with it man, get it off your chest. Make you feel better, just spit it out.'

Mullen swiped his nose with a hanky that obviously needed a wash.

He looked like a man at the end of his tether, echoed when he said, 'LaSalle has been having it off with my Janice, the bastard.'

The penny dropped. LaSalle you dirty bugger, keeping Harry busy so you can service his missus.

An even bigger penny landed with an almighty clang. 'Jesus Christ, Harry you made it all up.' Christine slapped her forehead. 'LaSalle's as pure as the driven snow.'

Christine rubbed her tired, drawn face, trying to concentrate, hoping there would be damage limitation. Not another bloody detective suspended. What will the media make of it?

Mullen sobs gave him away; he baulked as she gave him a blow torch stare.

There has to be more. What else had the old bugger done?

'Tell me everything, or so help me I will drag your putrid balls through a ringer.'

Harry told her about the hammer.

Following his chat with Cameron, LaSalle told Christine he found the hammer in Harry's drawer. She simply hadn't found the time to confront Mullen. 'Harry, why on earth did you take the bloody hammer? You were the SIO for God's sake.' She banged the desk. Coffee from his cup splashed the surface. 'And why in heaven's name admit it?'

225

Christine turned her back on him, made a sign of the cross and quietly asked God for his forgiveness; her use of profanities so much a daily ritual lately.

Harry mumbled incoherently; she thought he said *Cameron*.

'What about Cameron?'

Harry was desperately trying to communicate his thoughts to her. 'Cameron knows I'm sure of it. He's been poking around in the property office, pestering Janice. He knows. He has this awful way of getting inside your head with his weird innuendo's and self righteous questions.'

'Let's go to the canteen Harry, their coffee is better.' Christine nearly had to help him to his feet. 'You look like you need a proper caffeine hit.'

Having paid for the coffees, which raised a few eyebrows with the kitchen staff, cheeky buggers, Christine picked a table in the corner, less busy there. A delicate wicker screen enclosed them, a brief reminder of holidays in Spain. Too right, she'd be ready for one after his little caper.

Harry sipped his coffee. Christine felt sorry for him; he looked ancient like one of the characters in *Last of the Summer Wine*. Why couldn't she remember the character's name?

'I presume it was just a foolish fling, between Janice and Victor?'

Mullen nodded, avoiding eye contact.

'You thought it was Janice who murdered Heather Moon because of jealousy, Victor having had an affair with Heather?'

Harry nodded imperceptibly.

Christine clapped her hands, the resounding crack causing Harry to jump spilling his coffee.

'You're not in a bloody coma Harry. I want more

226

than flickering eyelashes and raised pinkie fingers. Let's hear it man.'

Shocked at the Chief's outburst, Harry spoke, and perhaps a little too loudly, Christine indicating he tone it down with a wave of her hands.

'Victor was having an affair with Janice; he ended it and Janice grew morose, went all quiet, sort of monosyllabic. We used to talk but now…' A shrug closed that statement. 'She followed Victor to Gatekeeper Cottage, actually saw them together. She told me she'd struggled with Heather, insisted she only hit her once. I made it look like Frank Slack did it. Then I realised if she ever came into the frame, her fingerprints and DNA would be on the hammer, as well as Franks so I bloody well took it— all right.'

Christine tossed Harry a packet of tissues.

'Tell no one about this Harry. LaSalle's returned the hammer to the evidence room.' Harry looked bewildered. 'You hid it in you're bloody drawer Harry. LaSalle is no genius but he isn't a fool.'

Harry fumbled for words, finally saying: 'What happens now?'

'Simple enough. You retire. LaSalle solves the murder and we let sleeping dogs lie. Happy? You bloody well should be.'

'Is Cameron here to help find Brian?'

The question caught her off guard. She thought bugger it. Truth shall set us free. 'Yes, Cameron and a man named Blake will help us find Brian.'

Christine Krill arranged for an urgent briefing to take place at police headquarters. Both Kumar and Sam were contacted, not a request, but a summons.

Due to Christine's impatience, the operation had been upgraded, moved into a higher gear, which meant a complex organisational task for Victor and his team.

227

The complication of Ron Stark's apparent involvement had underlined Christine's insistence that measures should be implemented forthwith to force their weird prodigy Blake into the open. This resulted in everyone gathering at short notice and a costly exercise in shuttling a very important couple to North Yorkshire. (Walter Slack agreed to meet the additional costs).

The couple were the parents of the boy found by Cameron following Blake's interrogation of Martin Pope. Victor's idea and a ploy he felt confident would enhance the chances of Blake manifesting himself before the chosen audience.

Following her briefing in London, Kumar asked Sam if he could hitch a lift back to Winston. On the long drive from Hendon, Sam enjoyed Kumar's company. After much persuasion by Sam, Kumar agreed to stay in the spare bedroom of the cottage: having Kumar there gave her a sense of being safe, more so because of her insecurity concerning the emergence of Blake.

It was late Saturday morning when they reached Haughton. The cottage looked empty. A note from Cameron said he had gone for a walk in the forest and wouldn't be home until late. Sam was tired. At Hendon she'd agreed to stay the night in one of the bedrooms normally allocated to trainee detectives. The bed had been rock hard and the room claustrophobic and sleep hard come by.

She groaned when Kumar effervesced about the folly in the cottage's rear garden.

Like an excited child, he demanded, 'Show me the folly, please. Show me now.'

Sam, ready for something to eat and then an hour or two's kip, humoured him.

The garden, she noticed required attention, the lawn

cutting for starters. Embarrassed she said, 'It's a little untidy but to be fair, I have been a trifle preoccupied.' She uttered a nervous laugh.

Kumar ignored her and trotted off toward a folly resembling a miniature summerhouse.

'How long has it been here?'

Sam tried to remember exactly what she'd been told.

'Heather said it was here before they built the cottage. No one appears to know why it was built or by whom. I thought it was a bandstand for kids. Like small.'

Kumar dropped onto his knees and began scraping soil from the bottom rim of a keystone. He said, '*Lacuna via cavernum.*' The words had been engraved into the stone.

'Did you ever think about establishing its origins or having the writing translated?'

Sam shook her head. 'Doctor Kumar, I didn't even notice the writing.' Ashamed of being assessed a philistine she added, 'It's the first time I've actually took much notice of it.'

Kumar huffed and walked inside the ten feet of space beyond the rusting metal gate. He pirouetted round and round, examining its interior.

Sam keen to impress offered, 'The inscriptions Latin isn't it?'

Kumar snapped from his examining mode and said like he had just this second noticed her presence: 'Yes Sam, it means, *to the pit via the cave.*'

Chapter 35

Saturday evening. Cameron paced outside the dark oak of the briefing room doors at North Yorkshire Police Headquarters; alone and somehow more vulnerable. He considered his future.

Already he'd accepted he'd be medically retired; they had little choice really. He wouldn't be allowed to continue it being contrary to medical advice. Worse, what if the media latched onto it?

He tried to forget about the future and concentrated on the present.

Confident he could help with the search for those responsible for Heather's murder, he was not sure how Blake would react when asked to pay a visit in front of an audience, small as it might be.

Cameron thought about the developing relationship with Blake and wondered if he would be forced to slip into the background – he hoped briefly – to allow Blake the opportunity to use his skills. It was the only sure fire way of finding the truth about what happened to Brian Mullen and to positively identify the men responsible for the illegal dog fighting. In a perfect world this would then enable him to solve Heather's murder.

The lengths gone to by Doctor Kumar to allow Blake to emerge in plain sight he found difficult to comprehend. The convoluted plan could only have emanated from the mind of a man with a massive ego, one with his own agenda.

Kumar certainly had a fascination with Blake, yet what the good doctor and the others seemed to forget about was the pain and discomfort Blake's presence caused Cameron. It had been Cameron who had to tolerate Blake 24-7.

A bonus though: Victor had been considerate and

very understanding of Cameron's position. What a wonderful performance he'd delivered to encapsulate the type of stress required to wrench Blake from his hiding place deep within Cameron's subconscious. Victor had played the part with verve and aplomb. Was he acting all of the time, some of the time, or perhaps not at all?

The conference room door opened, Victor came out and quietly closed it behind him. He placed his thick arm around Cameron's narrow shoulders.

'Nervous, Jason?'

Quietly, and a touch embarrassed, Cameron replied, 'Only about Blake. What if he refuses to come out, they'll think I'm a liar and a fool.'

Victor slapped Cameron's shoulder; a good old 'don't-worry-we'll sort-it slap.

'You leave Blake to me. You seem to forget, I'm Blake's friend now.'

This didn't reassure Cameron. He knew fine well Blake was a manipulator, his only true friend being Cameron, when it suited him.

Doctor Kumar's shrill voice penetrated the doors. 'Whenever you're ready Detective Sergeant Cameron.'

Cameron pushed the door open. Others were seated in a horseshoe, their backs to him. Christine Krill stood on the small stage like the President of America, leaning against a lectern with the North Yorkshire logo emblazoned behind her. On her right sat Doctor Kumar, beaming like a Cheshire cat; to the left of the lectern a vacant chair. Christine smiled benevolently and ushered Cameron forward.

Excited chattering stuttered into silence. Cameron faltered, gripped the door handle, closed it behind him and began his lonely walk to the stage, noticing what few chairs were in use by the meagre audience, the

231

remainder stacked neatly around the walls.

Cameron reflected upon his decision to allow Kumar to invite comparative strangers to witness his transformation into Blake. *If it happened*.

In an instant, sensations of fear and anxiety melted. He could smell Sam's perfume. After all, what could anyone do to him with Sam here to protect him?

Climbing the three stairs to the stage, Cameron's sideways glance caught a slender pair of olive legs. He recognised them *immediately*. Yes, there seated at the end of the front row, wearing a serious look yet Sam's eyes were smiling. More elated, he approached Christine and thought of the Oscars ceremony.

Probably right: the whole game read like a movie script. Then, who was the star, himself or Blake. No contest today, Cameron reasoned.

Christine indicated the spare chair. Cameron sat and surveyed his audience. Sam offered a gentle wave.

Harry and Janice Mullen sat in the middle holding hands, eagerness and anticipation etched on their faces, despite Henry's paleness.

Victor LaSalle took his seat at the front. He winked at Cameron.

Bollocks, who should be in the seat next to LaSalle, none other than DS Trevor Mason. The last time he'd seen Mason was in Epping Forest the day he took Pope to the scout hut. Trevor was involved in the botched surveillance of Martin Pope, Cameron vitriolic in his condemnation of the poorly run operation.

Cameron's heart pumped with adrenalin. He saw the pair of them, sitting like they were about to watch a hanging. Eleanor and David Brock, the parents of Alistair Brock, the boy he found alive buried in a shallow pit in Epping Forest.

Cameron glanced at Victor who winked again: as

232

good as giving a thumbs-up.

Clever. Cameron had to hand it to him. Victor had done it again. The Brocks had thanked Cameron from the bottom of their heart. They knew, or suspected what had happened to Martin Pope and didn't care. Cameron was a hero, plain and simple. If anyone could convince Blake to appear it was this couple.

Next to them, in full uniform sat Inspector Sandy Dalton, the original abduction investigator twenty years ago. His contribution as Operational Ground commander for Operation Bifurcate had been professional if somewhat disbelieving. His scepticism would soon melt like ice cream on a hot day when Blake took the floor.

Last but by no means least; sitting in the middle of the row was Walter Slack, the banker behind Operation Bifurcate. Slack wore a neat blue suit and polished black brogues, a steely look disguising his eagerness to continue and somehow reach the finale, not least his eventual goal of establishing the true perpetrators of the abduction and winning final forgiveness for the false accusations levied against him twenty years ago.

Cameron looked toward the rear of the room, for the first time noticing the two police officers in uniform standing either side of the door. The officers acknowledged a signal from Christine and left the room, presumably taking up a sentry position on the other side of the door.

Christine Krill began the briefing by introducing the police officers present and thanking them for their patience during the first phase of Operation Bifurcate.

The first phase; he wondered what phase two looked like? Cameron would wait and see.

'First, I would like to express my sincere gratitude for the financial assistance given by Walter Slack.

'This operation has been designed to enable a

233

witness to identify the perpetrators of wicked crimes occurring twenty years ago and also hopefully assist in the identification of the suspect in the recent murder of Heather Moon.' Nodding sympathetically toward Cameron and Sam.

With less emphasis Christine said, 'It may also have the added benefit in allowing us to solve the riddle of the strange creature seen wandering the forests surrounding Winston.'

Christine regarded her audience, her gaze passing over each individual.

She continued, louder this time, 'Our distinguished guest Doctor Kumar from the National Crime Faculty will now explain the history behind Operation Bifurcate and the reason I have gathered you here today.' Christine moved back from the lectern. 'Doctor Kumar, if you would be so kind.'

Kumar's eyes narrowed. Ringing his hands like a moneylender, black hair shining in the lights, he moved to the lectern.

In a blink, behind Kumar, the North Yorkshire Police motif disappeared, transformed into a map of Winston. Cameron turned his head when he noticed the audience flick their eyes to the screen.

Not a recent map; the date on the bottom read 1863. No forest, just the town and numerous mine locations with unusual names like, *Betty's Baby* and *Son of Odin*.

Kumar stated: 'I first came to Winston four months ago to research an unusual phenomena.'

Cameron cringed, hating his condition being described in such clinical terms. *Get use to it, Jason Cameron, it's going to be a long night.*

'Before I illuminate you all with my findings I would ask you to scrutinize the map behind me and think about what the nomenclature on the mineshafts represents.'

234

Sam, the shy girl who never asked questions in lectures at university, suddenly stuck her hand in the air. A flashback to her student days popped into her head and sheepishly, she lowered her hand.

Kumar indicated for Sam to stand. 'Deliver your verdict on the names of the mines, Sam.' His knowledgeable gaze scrutinized her.

Sam felt like he was burrowing into her subconscious.

'Come, come.' Kumar encouraged, 'don't be shy.'

Sam rattled out words like a machine gun, hoping the audience wouldn't laugh. 'They sound like the names of racehorses,' she said attempting humour and sat down quickly, blushing, her body boiling, perspiration soaking her silk blouse. Did she smell? Self-consciously she tucked her arms into her sides.

Kumar clapped. 'Excellent!' he shouted. 'Sam, you're very close with your guess. They are actually the names of dogs used by the miners for fighting, a distraction from their laborious life down the pits. Champions were immortalised in the naming of the shafts.'

Kumar waited a while until a smattering of chatter subsided.

'As you know, I advise the Metropolitan police on aspects of unusual cases. About a year ago I chanced upon this young man.' Kumar placed his ebony hand on Cameron's shoulder.

'Everyone in this room is aware of Jason Cameron's unusual dilemma. Some of you believe in him, as I do, others are sceptical. Regardless of your individual viewpoint, we should accept that Jason is here to help us or indeed...' Kumar nodded toward the Brocks. 'Or indeed has already done so.'

Sam, proud of Cameron and sympathetic with his

235

predicament, gave him her warmest smile. In turn, Cameron embarrassed, looked at the floor before returning her gesture with a nervous, twitching grin.

Kumar continued, occasionally glancing over his spectacles at his notes on the lectern.

'Twenty years ago, a boy named Brian Mullen was abducted from Winston. He has never been found. The police strongly suspect there was a link with Brian's abductors and the world of illegal dog fighting'

Kumar let his words penetrate the audience, his tone sombre, adding a respectful nod to Janice and Harry.

Sam, confidence raised asked, 'Why do they suspect the link to dog fighting?

Kumar said, 'After Brian Mullen was abducted, his friend Jason Cameron, found himself alone in the forest. The police believed someone came across him lost, confused, hungry and tired. By pure fluke that someone took him to the compound were his friend was being held captive. Cameron attempted to escape.'

Sam's brow furrowed. Cameron flicked a self-conscious glance in her direction.

Kumar explained why he had gathered them all together, the appearance of Blake, his information about the abductors, Walter Slack's involvement and the carefully executed scenario to enable Blake to confidently appear without reservation.

Christine Krill nodded earnestly, offering Cameron an occasional benevolent glance.

'Unfortunately,' Kumar said, 'this whole affair also involves the murder of Heather Moon and her pledge to uncover those responsible for subjecting canines to the brutal fights put on to entertain. I should add that the police have now established, again with thanks to Jason, that the weapon used by Heather Moon's attacker, a hammer, may have been a precursor to her being strangled with a metal dog chain.'

Kumar tapped Cameron on the shoulder. 'Jason would you be so kind?'

Blake, eager to appear, began chattering in Cameron's mind, insistent, persistent, indicative that no amount of placating would subdue him.

Let go Cameron.

And Cameron let go.

'Cameron,' said Kumar 'is willing to allow Blake to venture into the murky world of illegal dog fighting. He believes that Blake can identify the abductors and also help us apprehend Heather Moon's murderer.'

I've already identified the abductors you idiots.

Kumar stepped away from the podium.

My turn Cameron, step aside now, let-me-out-of-here. For Christ's sake, I feel like the genie in the lamp.

Chapter 36

Blake is in the room! Sam saw it, although she doubted anyone else had.

During Kumar's address, Cameron had removed his bow tie, uncrossed his legs and leaned forward. When their eyes met, she saw Blake glaring at her; the tiny twitch in the corner of his mouth, his annoying grimace another giveaway.

Everyone, including Kumar none the wiser; all awaited the dramatic entrance, the unbelievable Jekyll and Hyde routine. *Not this time.*

Kumar offered the lectern to Cameron.

Blake said, teeth bared like some restive animal, 'My name is Anthony Edward Blake and I'm here to help.'

Anthony *Edward*! A significant use of the forename Edward! Sam detested the baleful Blake having found Stevenson's Edward Hyde character extremely malevolent.

'I've been here in Winston before, initially with Cameron as a boy and lately, watching, waiting, assessing. There is evil in your little town folks, and I can help eradicate it.'

Kumar said loudly, 'Ah, ah.' He sat down with a thump, smiling broadly, enjoying every minute.

'Cameron asked me to keep an eye on Heather,' Blake announced. 'She knew she was being watched. I saw the man who killed her; unfortunately I was unable to come to her aid until it was too late. I regret not being there in time and intend rectifying that.' Like a boxer before a bout, Blake looked to the ceiling, cracking his neck.

Sam desperately wanted to believe Jason Cameron had an illness.

Here goes nothing.

Sam asked, 'Are you a threat to your host, Jason Cameron?'

Blake's nostrils flared like a racehorse after a run, Sam could only imagine his annoyance.

'Novel expression, *host*,' he spat.

Sam stole an anxious glance at Kumar and repeated her question, raising her voice. 'Are you a threat to him?'

The tiny audience shuffled in their seats, the atmosphere switching from palpable curiosity to heightened unease. Sam looked left and right for support; strangely enough Victor came to her aid.

'It's a fair question Blake,' Victor said with a wan smile.

Blake leaned back. 'Jason Cameron is my friend; we share the same body; we experience the same emotions; I have his memories.'

Sam remembered her meeting with Kumar in London and said, 'Does he share your emotions, your memories?'

Blake banged the lectern; Sam startled, did not back down, no way. She fired him her most indignant stare, held his look for a few seconds.

Blake said, 'you're concerned because you have feelings for Jason Cameron: understandable. Cameron is a thoughtful, genuine man and you view me as his nemesis. Think about this Miss Samantha Moon, do you believe your father was an honest, trustworthy human being? Remember each of us has skeletons in the cupboard.'

This isn't right, Sam thought: Why isn't Kumar interrupting, protecting me from Blake's outburst? She guessed it was because Kumar had handpicked this audience, including Sam. Its part of the game, she told herself; keep Blake rattled, force him to become defensive, angry, enabling him to remain in the

239

conscious world, and so protect Cameron.

All the while, Kumar sat impassive, simply the observer. He'd set the ball rolling and just stepped out of the game for a while.

Sam settled down, confident her father had been a kind, honest man.

'Spit it out Blake,' she prompted.

Blake used his fingers to elaborate his counting.

'Fact one: Nigel Moon wanted to buy Gatekeeper Cottage because of its strategic location as a hidden entrance to the forest and the compound where his friends organised dog fighting for cash. Two: Nigel owned a terrier, the favoured dog for mauling badgers, also a pastime of disreputable characters in Winston. Three: Nigel dabbled in the local housing market; therefore he had a vested interest in the town. Five—'

Victor jumped to his feet waving hands in the air. 'That's enough Blake; it's all circumstantial, hardly relevant to finding the abductors.'

Blake crossed his legs, placed his hands on his knees. *Had Cameron come back?* Sam wasn't sure; it certainly looked that way. Wasn't anyone else keeping track of this so-called *switching*?

Following Victor's intervention, and the ensuing silence, Walter Slack broke the deadlock.

'It's difficult to comprehend your predicament, Mr Blake. You are indeed a strange individual and this affair is bizarre to say the least.' Slack inclined his head toward Sam.

'Samantha my dear, Blake's assertions about Nigel are correct. Nigel was indeed involved in the old ways and did dabble in the local housing market. Although I have little regard for enhancing his profile, rest assured your father sincerely had nothing to do with anything we're investigating. Blake is attacking when he should be assisting.'

240

Walter Slack turned his attention to Blake.

'Jealousy, contempt and resentment,' Slack said, 'are wicked concepts. They will rot you from the inside Mr Blake. Please focus your attention on the task at hand.'

Sam said incredulously, 'I'm sorry, but here we are pandering to this *thing*, when we should be out there discovering what happened to Heather.' She shook her head, tears evident.

Emotionally, Sam was a car wreck and Blake's performance made the butterflies in her stomach flutter like bats. Oh to scream out, grab Cameron back from wherever he was and just get out, leave them all to it. Everything she heard was preposterous, difficult to comprehend and she believed, totally unhelpful.

'Sam,' Blake said, 'I know I disgust you and that's understandable. You hate me because of Martin Pope. I accidentally killed Pope to save a small boy. Interrogational torture is sometimes the only way to wrench information from a suspect when time is of the essence.' Blake's smile had the look of a gorgon. 'It will be easier if you think of me as a necessary evil, someone to condone because I can help identify the man who killed Heather.'

Deep in Winston Forest, Ron Stark stood motionless at the edge of the killing pit and contemplated his predicament. Ron would protect his halfwit brother even if it meant sacrificing his career in the police. *Lukas you are an embarrassment and a liability.*

When their parents died from cancer within months of each other, Ron took his younger brother into his family home. When Lukas abducted Brian Mullen, Ron Stark should have done the right thing. Instead, he covered it up.

Hindsight being a wonderful thing, and wishes ten a

241

penny, he stupidly hadn't heeded his conscience and would be forced to live with the consequences of his failure to act for the rest of his life. There had been benefits though; the dog fighting had earned him a small fortune.

Without Brian Mullen's body, Ron knew his colleagues had no chance, nothing to hang a hook on, just a disappearing boy and Walter Slack in the wrong place at the right time. That had been unfortunate, Stark aware he would eventually pay for Slack's incarceration, when Walter eventually got round to it.

On the death of his parents, Stark had tried to deal with his brother's illness using counselling and psychiatric help. In the end he failed. With no other option available, he'd sent Lukas to live with their aunt in Grimsby. She raised the boy and gave him her name, thus protecting him from his previous criminal history. In the beginning it worked, until that fateful two weeks when Ron agreed to look after his sixteen-year brother whilst Aunt Mary went into hospital. Those two weeks twenty years ago had changed Ron's life forever. And Harry Mullen's.

Staring into the pit the memory rampaged: the killing pit built originally as an inspection pit for wagons used by the miners. When the mine buildings were demolished, the pit survived. The day Lukas arrived at the compound with the boy sent shivers down Ron's spine.

'What have you done you bloody idiot?' Ron slapped his younger brother hard in the face. Lukas cried out.

'I couldn't help myself Ron, it just happened.'

Ron had to think and act fast. They would be looking for the lad and because of his brother's penchant for perversion he would be a prime suspect.

The boy wriggled inside the potato sack, obviously

gagged, his muffled cries desperate and horrible to the ear. Ron felt sick.

'Untie him; let me have a look, see if he's hurt.'

His brother wiped snot from his nose and began undoing the string on the sack. 'Keep still you little bastard.'

Ron, impatient, pushed his brother aside, 'Who is he, the boy? Who is he?' Ron screamed to hide his fear, and how sick he really felt.

'They call him Jason, his mother's that weirdo who lives in Gatekeeper Cottage.'

Ron was flabbergasted. 'Are you crazy Lukas? His dad's a bloody prison officer; do you think they won't look for him? Maybe searching already!'

Lukas, eyes soulful and pleading, said, 'It just happened Ron, what should I do?'

Ron ignored his brother. He tried to calm the stricken boy, 'Easy lad, let's have a look at you.'

The boy's eyes were wide with fear, his ear was cut, his nose bleeding.

It wasn't his injuries, which startled Ron. 'Jesus Lukas this is Harry Mullen's boy.'

Ron should have immediately returned the boy to his father. Instead he locked the boy inside the compound shed and went to see Harry in person. When he told Harry about the snatch his reaction wasn't what Ron expected and this changed Ron's life *forever*.

His police career just a hobby anyway, a safe pension pot. Revelling in the money he made from selling off the family farm to developers, arranging the dog fights, annoying the likes of Nigel Moon and Walter Slack who wanted to monopolise the growing popularity of Winston as a commuter town and holiday retreat. Walter Slack intent on banishing the old ways of dog fighting into oblivion, migrating it into a new form of pursuit.

Nigel Moon's untimely death had come at such a vital stage in his bid to control the gate through the escarpment and into the compound. If only his stupid wife hadn't become infatuated with the compound. Nigel should have controlled her, the silly bitch.

Ron thought the abduction had vanished into the background, just another unsolved case. And then Aunt Mary died a year ago and Lukas came back to Winston. Ron arranged the volunteer position for Lukas with the Forestry Commission to keep Lukas out of trouble, letting him live in the compound, look after the dogs.

Why Jason Cameron had failed to recognise Lukas, he had no idea. Ron had discovered Cameron near to the compound and locked him away with Brian Mullen. During a failed escape attempt, Cameron had fallen into the killing pit and somehow one of the dogs got free and attacked him, Cameron, in his fight to survive, managed to chew through the dog' throat. What a hellish sight that had been, blood gushing like a geyser. Martin Pope and Ron enjoyed the spectacle like Romans during the infamous Coliseum games, when thousands screamed delight as gladiators fought tigers to the death.

Somehow, Cameron managed to escape, running off into the forest pursued by Lukas. Walter Slack found Cameron before Lukas caught up with him and right then events had taken a terrible turn.

Lukas enjoyed the spectacle of watching Cameron in the pit so much, he threw Brian Mullen in! The dogs tore at the lad, yet the little bugger survived the ordeal! Fortunately, with the only witness being Pope, a man who'd kept his word and the secret of the killing pit, the boy had remained hidden in the forest.

So why doesn't Cameron recognise Lukas? He hadn't changed significantly, beard, yes and long hair. Still, Cameron should know him, shouldn't he?

244

Stark had hesitated when Lukas suggested hosting another fight. After all, no one would blame them if they declined. Something was going on and Stark suspected Cameron was involved.

What if they knew or strongly suspected who had killed Heather Moon? They could be close to an arrest. If so then it might be time to deal with the person who killed her, *discreetly*.

Chapter 37

Victor drove them in his black Jaguar, Cameron sitting in the front with Victor, both chatting about police work. Two old buddies having a reunion. Sam was so annoyed with Cameron. She thought he should be giving her attention not Victor La Salle.

Sam clenched her fingers together. Come on remember the university lecture: The evolution of the wolf has been reconstructed through a combination of fossil records and the analysis of genetic material. That's it, that's it. The history of a wolf's lineage can be traced back to an ancient species called creodonts.

Sam, trying desperately to remember her training, scanned her brain for the correct terminology to help describe the subtle differences in present day domestic dogs *and the wolf*, a very special and social animal that hunts in packs. Yet the specimen they were about to see was presumably alone in the forest when LaSalle shot it. If it is a wolf, then where is the pack?

Cameron returned to the conscious world after an hour of Blake, seemingly none the worse for Blake's appearance. Sam, now calmer, in control again, wanting to distance herself from Blake. How could she though? Her feelings for Cameron had intensified; Blake viewed as a stumbling block to her affections for Cameron.

Cameron's alter ego appeared to be taking over, gaining respect from Victor and Christine Krill, and now what? They were on their way to Walter Slack's property, Sam agreeing to examine the beast Victor and Cameron found in the forest.

Walter had arranged for Lonnie and Frank Slack to meet them; apparently they had the knowledge of badger baiting, which would assist in their plans for the beast. What plans exactly, they declined to disclose.

Sam remembered Kumar's suggestion for Blake's mission into the world of dog fighting. If they think she would assist in training one beast to attack another, they are stupid.

A macho bond had been forged between the men; the symptoms amounted to whispering in corners and avoiding eye contact with Sam. If they thought for one second she would roll over, they had her all wrong. Sam Moon was determined, forthright and not a woman to be ignored nor ostracised.

Slack's house stood in its own grounds about half a mile from Winston, between the forest and the new housing development. Two vehicles were parked on the blue gravel driveway; a black Toyota pick up with blacked out windows and a rusted Ford Fiesta, the type popular in the eighties. A large double garage sat at the side of the house and Sam presumed Walter's favoured mode of transport languished behind big metal concertina doors.

Parked up, Victor led them round the back of the ramshackle house. He had no problem with the dodgy bolt securing the wooden garden gate. Sam followed in silence hoping she would soon become the centre of attention again when she vocalised her knowledge about wolves.

Rounding the corner of the house, Sam heard one of the most beautiful and haunting forms of communication; the howl of a wolf. Then she saw the creature, secured safely in a metal cage the size of a squash court. When it saw her it flung itself at the wire mesh, bouncing off with a resounding thump, the cage vibrating and rattling with the impact.

'Feisty bugger, isn't he?' said Frank Slack.

Lonnie and Frank sat on a wooden bench drinking tea. They gave the arriving party a grimace of recognition and remained where they were. Lonnie's hand, Sam noticed, had a bloodstained bandage wrapped around it. Both eyed the creature with disdain.

Sam walked cautiously toward the cage, stopping about a yard away. The animal raised its hackles and growled showing vicious, stained teeth and stark red gums.

'What do you make of it Sam?' Cameron had moved to stand by her. 'I'm presuming it is a wolf, of sorts.'

Sam knew what Cameron meant. Bigger than a wolf, about the size of a large German shepherd dog except for its coat being woolly and very black.

Sam said, 'A wolf may have been interbred with a compatible breed of dog to produce...' She pointed her finger at the cage. 'Well that thing in there.'

Victor asked, 'How did they manage to acquire a wolf for crying out loud?'

Sam grimaced, shot Victor a funny look. 'At the practice we often receive circulars about exotic animals being stolen from zoos and the like. A few years ago I remember Pickering Zoo reported two grey wolves had been stolen.

Walter, quickly interrupting said, 'I think the mystery of what's been stalking the forest has been solved, don't you Victor?'

Victor nodded imperceptibly and joined Lonnie and Frank on the bench.

Walter Slack said he would make some tea for his guests and disappeared into the house.

'What on earth is that?'

Sam pointed to the wooden treadmill; a large dog collar fastened to a wooden arm hovered above the contraption.

Lonnie answered without taking his eyes of the wolf. 'It's a treadmill for dogs; you know to get them match fit.' He added nonchalantly, 'Borrowed it off a

248

mate of mine, just in case.'

Sam shook her head in disgust. 'In case of what exactly'

Cameron said to Sam quietly, 'Blake wants to go inside the cage.'

**

'I took a phone call while you were out.'

Lukas buttered a slice of brown bread, watching his brother take off his uniform. Envious little shit, thought Ron Stark.

'Who telephoned?' asked Stark

Lukas shoved bread into his mouth, butter congealing in his beard.

'You are a sloppy pig Lukas.'

Between mouthfuls Lukas said, 'That weird bloke who attacked me in Winston high street. He says he's got a fighting dog, says, it can beat all comers.'

Ron Stark asked 'What did you tell him?'

'Said it's up to you, said I would ring him back. What's even weirder, he's at Walter's.'

At this moment in time, Stark didn't trust Walter. The old bastard was definitely up to something. Why on earth let the weird bloke visit his place? When Lukas described the bloke who hit him, he insisted he strongly resembled the copper, Jason Cameron. Were they related? There were far too many questions and too many loose ends.

The arrangements for the dogfights had been sweet until Nigel Moon began demanding more money for access to the tunnel leading to the compound. Lukas insisted he could navigate his way through the forest without using the tunnel. One problem though. It took ages whereas the tunnel gave access within thirty minutes since it literally cut through the escarpment.

249

On Nigel's death Ron got used to accessing the compound via Gatekeeper Cottage whilst Samantha Moon was working. Since Cameron had moved in, things had gotten awkward. Nor did the punters appreciate a long ride in the back of a filthy land rover.

'Have there been any more sightings of the lost hybrid?

'Hasn't been seen for months,' Lukas said. 'I reckon its dead.'

'Doesn't matter anyway, the damn beast can't be trained, vicious bastard.'

Lukas eyed his brother. 'What should I do?'

'We could do with the cash, ring the weirdo back, and tell him yes.'

Lukas shovelled the last of the bread into his mouth.

'How much are we charging for entry?'

Ron Stark pondered a while. 'Tell him the stakes are very high with some important punters. Tell him it will cost him a hundred quid to enter. And then ring Walter, give him an update.'

Lukas absently said, 'Give him a what?

'Tell him about the bloody arrangements, you moron.'

Chapter 38

Victor saw the switch, subtle and extremely smooth. Cameron's eyes flickered, lolled, his head snapped forward, face becoming sterner, lines under his eyes pronounced, chin jutting, arrogance etched on his forehead like a badge of honour.

'Hello Blake, nice of you to join us.'

Blake grinned. Jesus, the change evident and yet Cameron still there in Walter Slack's garden, in the background like a grainy photograph hanging on a wall.

Keeping his eyes on the creature, Blake said, 'Sam, I need you to tell me about wolves, anything which might help me befriend it.'

Victor saw disgust on Sam's face.

'If you believe I'm going to help you train it to fight you're sadly mistaken Blake. It's barbaric and against my code of ethics.'

Victor now accepted that the only definite way of getting into the heart of this murky affair would involve Blake entering the dogfight. He knew all the suspects would be there, unable to resist the invitation thus enabling Blake to identify Heather's killer and the abductors of Brian Mullen twenty years ago.

Also, the police desperately needed to find the body of Brian Mullen, a move to hopefully tie down the murderers using DNA matching.

Victor took hold of Sam's hand and led her away from Blake, stopping when he thought Blake could no longer hear them.

Victor said, 'It's difficult for you I know. If by helping Blake it would mean arresting those responsible for killing Heather, then surely you must put aside your dislike of him, if only for a few hours.'

Victor desperately wanted to hug Sam, to reassure her. He resisted, suspecting she might view his

251

advances as inappropriate.

Sam turned and confronted Victor.

'I believe you Victor when you say you were in love with Heather, but *please* do not underestimate my loathing for Blake. To me he is an abomination, a leech hiding inside Cameron. We should be exorcising him, not feeding him blood. I can't do it. Sorry.'

Victor knew he could convince her. 'It's the only way. Do this and I promise I will deal with those responsible for Heather's death.' Victor leaned close to her ear and whispered. 'Also, I know a way of getting rid of Blake once this is over.' Victor winked. 'Trust me like Blake trusts me and I will bury him forever.'

'How will you get rid of Blake?'

'The tranquillisers used to subdue animals, could you mix a dosage suitable to subdue a man, without actually harming him?'

Sam's eyes twinkled. She nodded yes.

Walking briskly back to Blake Sam said, 'Okay Blake, what do you want to know.'

'Anything and everything you can tell me.'

She folded her arms, regarded the wolf, Sam's eyes narrowing to slits.

'I think this is some form of hybrid, yet leans more towards a wolf. Wolves are extremely social and live in a pack or family. My guess is this is the result of bringing together a large German shepherd dog and a grey wolf. Without its pack it may respond to bonding with another alpha male.' Sam hesitated, shot Blake a quick glance and said, 'The pack follows a strict hierarchy, if you can convince it you are the alpha male it might just be happy to be the beta male and follow your lead.'

Blake scowled. Then suddenly he howled, a teeth tingling mighty howl, which took everyone by surprise including the wolf.

The creature growled, crouched down and waited.

Blake whispered to Sam, 'What else?'

'If you can be very confident and make it your subordinate, then who knows, it may succumb.'

As Blake went to unlock the cage Sam said, 'Wolves enjoy playing and pretend fighting, although this one appears to be beyond that.'

Blake smiled, unlocked the bolted cage door, slid inside and closed it.

The wolf didn't move.

Blake wiped perspiration from his forehead with the back of his hand. Victor watched, fascinated, unable to take his eyes of the cage. Everyone else had moved back a couple of yards, distancing themselves physically and psychologically from what they knew was about to happen, namely that the wolf would tear Blake apart.

Somehow, Victor didn't think so.

Blake leaned with his back against the cage door, eying the beast, every so often twisting his head this way and that, mentally sparring.

Suddenly the creature lunged at Blake, aiming for his throat. Blake twisted and caught the animal a glancing blow to its head with his fist, sidestepped and allowed the wolf's body weight to propel it sideways into mesh which rattled like gunfire.

Quickly the wolf regained its composure and scampered to the other end of the cage. Baring its teeth it skulked toward Blake again. This time it went for Blake's ankles, snapping and biting.

Blake kicked it heavily in the head, once, twice, three times. Each time the wolf shrieked in pain until once again it scampered back to the opposite end of the cage.

This time Blake edged forward. Victor noticed he held a white bone handled knife. The dog attacked

253

again. Blake sidestepped expertly and with a swish of his arm he swiped the blade toward the animal's ear. Blood spurted from the wound, the wolf cried in pain, and once more scampered away from Blake to skulk in the corner, confused.

Blake tentatively approached the beast, bent down, whispering in hushed tones, reassuring it, stroking its inky black fur, soothing its agony.

After only three minute's the wolf had relented. It licked Blake's hand. Blake was now the dominant alpha male. Impressive, thought Victor, bloody impressive.

In the morning, when things settle down, Victor will be just as impressive. Victor will do what he does best. Victor will bend the rules.

Chapter 39

Victor was a shrewd man. Cleverer than many people thought; smart enough to know when to smell a rat and when to dig around, check things out, check people out. Kumar's insistence he be personally involved in operational police matters ruffled Victor's feathers. Victor failed to understand why they all listened to this fat lump of a man. Something just didn't add up. And so he had checked out Kumar. Why not? There had to be something fishy about a man who offered his initial services free of charge.

On the surface, everything about Kumar appeared kosher, except for one thing; doctors are motivated to help people recover. Kumar's plan would do the opposite to Jason Cameron and to Victor's reasoning that didn't fit.

A foregone conclusion Jason Cameron's condition wouldn't improve because of Operation Bifurcate. In fact he would probably get worse. And who would benefit from that scenario? Doctor Kumar would.

This morning the doctor's ego would take a dent. Kumar sat by the side of the rusty iron waste pipe, tied to a chair with a dirty coal sack covering his head.

Like faithful servants, Lonnie and Frank, had followed Victor's instructions to the letter. Priorities. From the crack of dawn the two had waited outside Gatekeeper Cottage until Sam Moon had left leaving Kumar alone.

Prying open a small bathroom window, Frank quietly eased himself inside and opened the back door for Lonnie. Not wasting time, they surprised Kumar, barely awake, dragged him from his bed, blindfolded him and then taken him by car to the drainage pipe located on the edge of the new housing development.

The terrified doctor, tied to a plastic chair, balanced

precariously on the edge of the bank some fifteen foot above the rocky stream below, breath erupting in sharp, short gasps, the cloth bag wheezing like bellows. Frank gripped the chair back, every couple of seconds tilting the chair forwards, making Kumar wriggle like a maggot on a fishhook.

'What do you want?' bleated the very frightened Kumar.

Victor, who had looked on as the others did the business, thought about the question. What he wanted didn't seem important anymore. The kid Cameron had gotten into his head. He liked him and wanted to ensure Cameron got a fair deal even though he didn't fully believe in the existence of Blake. And he wanted to know if Christine Krill, devious bitch as she was, had set Cameron up.

'What I want Doctor is your co-operation.'

Kumar twisted his head, trying to focus on the direction of the voice.

Victor strolled casually around his captive, marvelling at how easy it was to break the rules when you knew for sure you would never be caught.

'It's *you* LaSalle! Why are you doing this?'

Victor nodded at Lonnie who snatched the bag away. Kumar squinted into the sunlight, eyes caked with sleep, and finding it difficult seeing without his specs.

Victor said, 'Look at the drainage pipe spewing its guts out and tell me what you see, Doc.'

Frank, glad things were getting back to normal, laughed like a little kid. He enjoyed adventures with Victor and hated the way things had been over the past couple of months. Victor knew this and wanted his two cohorts to be happy, so what better way to make them happy then a smidgen of abduction and blackmail.

Victor repeated: 'Tell me what you see, Doctor.'

Kumar spluttered, 'Dirty water, I see dirty water.'

'I'm talking about what the dirty water represents.'

Kumar twisted in the chair, looking from one man to the other. But not too much because every movement caused the chair to creak and lean, Kumar hating the thought of what might happen.

Victor said theatrically, 'Detritus, muck, slime draining away into the stream. The designers of the pipe got it wrong. Pollution isn't good for the environment; it contaminates the clean water in the stream.' Victor had his attention now, Kumar settled down, a flicker of relief glimmered in his eyes.

'Let me go please, I won't say anything, honest.'

Victor winked at Lonnie who giggled.

Victor shouted, 'You're like a contaminant doctor, a polluter of people. You are like the dirty water.' Victor slapped Kumar's head, hard.

Kumar's face tightened, he grimaced in pain, his features underpinned with sheer disbelief. 'Have you gone mad?' Do you know the consequences of kidnap and torture do you?'

'I am au fait with them, yes. But it really is of no consequence.' Victor was enjoying this. 'Of no consequence because you're real name is Roger Khan. You are a disgraced medical man, a phoney, a mad doctor.' He chuckled, tacking on for good measure and to amuse his helpers, 'And you stole your new name from a packet of curry paste.'

Frank and Lonnie giggled.

Kumar nodded his head, vigorously. 'Okay, okay, very funny so what do you want?'

'It wasn't difficult finding the truth about you, Doctor. I knew from the outset you were a phoney. No one works for nothing, not even on first consultancy, it just doesn't happen.' Victor kicked some dirt into the stream. 'After our second meeting I decided to make

257

some enquiries. First though I needed your fingerprints. Not difficult, I just confiscated your drinking glass.' Victor smirked at his two friends.

'After that it was easy. Using a doctor friend to check medical scandal sheets I discovered a story about a disgraced psychologist who had conducted unauthorised experiments on patients before supplying said doctor with the necessary research, enabling him to write a successful book on the benefits of allowing dangerous mental patients access to the outside world. In other words, this enabled them to ventilate their weird fantasies. This gave the doctor the opportunity to analyse their behaviour and submit unbelievably accurate accounts of their motivational factors; the driving forces behind their afflictions. Unfortunately, innocent people got hurt, didn't they Kumar?

Victor slapped Kumar hard across the face, careful not to inflict any visual damage. His handprint would fade eventually.

Kumar eased back, the chair creaked; his bonds bit.

Victor said, 'The photographs of the disgraced doctor were extremely similar to you Kumar and the fingerprint analysis confirmed your true identity as Doctor Roger Khan, Indian by birth, trained and qualified at the National Institution of Mental Health and Neuroscience in Bangalore.

'Khan disappeared off the radar six years ago, reappearing in London three years later with a bogus identity. It wasn't difficult to understand why the Met latched onto you especially when you provide your initial advice free of charge, as long as you can write about your exploits and secure further work.

'Calling yourself Doctor didn't sit right. Psychologists are not the type of medical practitioner you purport to be DOCTOR Kumar.'

Kumar's eyes widened.

258

Victor squeezed Kumar's face, tight. 'You are going to help me get rid of the abomination named Blake. Together we are going to rid Jason of his affliction. You will do this because if you don't your world will crumble around you.'

Kumar, despite his pain, laughed. 'Blake might just be a figment of Cameron's imagination.'

Victor clicked his tongue; he nodded at Frank who obligingly tilted the chair. Loose soil gave way, tumbling to splatter in the stream, dissolving like coffee granules in hot water.

'If you're so sure Blake is merely...' Victor searched for the right phrase, settling for, 'an invention, a clever ruse enabling Cameron to escape justice, then how come you are proposing to use this little adventure to further your somewhat bogus reputation?'

Kumar said through gritted teeth, 'I'm not here for that, you imbecile. Christine paid me to expose Cameron as a fraud. She wants him to fall, enabling her to clear her name from the mess that was Martin Pope. She may then be able to rescue her faltering career.'

Victor suspected as much although he still didn't know for sure if Cameron was indeed possessed by the Blake thing; neither was Kumar exactly reliable in his assumptions about Cameron. After all, Victor had witnessed Cameron changing at first hand and suffered bruises because of it. And he'd done his research. If Cameron wasn't genuine, then he must be a bloody good actor. Time to close the deal.

'You once told me we all have a sleeping beast inside us, waiting for an opportunity to come out. Do you still believe that Kumar?'

Kumar winced. 'Yes, yes, off course I do. Despite what you may think of me Detective Chief Inspector, I am not a charlatan, my qualifications aren't bogus, just my title and identity.'

259

Victor knew Kumar liked to be thought of as an eminent expert.

'I have a sleeping beast inside me, just like Jason Cameron, except mine is motivated by a force known as *doing the right thing* even it means bending the rules. I want to get evidence on Lukas Meek for abducting Brian Mullen. And I want to know who killed Heather Moon. And while we're at it, I want Blake out of the picture. You will agree to help me on all three counts otherwise ...'

Victor paused, bent down in front of Kumar and whispered: 'What are you more afraid of Kumar, me or Christine Krill?'

Kumar shook his head. 'You bloody fool, LaSalle. Christine is psychotic, teetering on the edge of a breakdown. I didn't come here to support her bizarre ambitions. After the Martin Pope affair, she went downhill rapidly, came to see me for advice, I put her onto a psychiatrist colleague of mine. My friend told me that Christine is desperate for revenge on Cameron and harbours deep disturbing anger toward him. I'm completing research on the psychological effects of senior leadership in the police. When Christine blows I want to be there.'

Victor knew Christine had been hiding the truth. 'Answer me this then, Doctor: If Cameron goes back to where his nightmare began ergo the compound in the forest, is it possible that he could be cured of his affliction?'

Kumar smiled thinly. 'Yes it might well do, *if* Blake exists.'

Victor sensed Kumar might be settling down, aware that realisation might have dawned and that Victor meant him no harm, not really.

He began untying Kumar.

'Is there anything else that could happen Doctor, say

for example if Jason Cameron were to be exposed to some unexpected trauma?'

Kumar rubbed his wrists. 'Possibly.' He eased himself from the chair and kicked it into the stream, the action emphasis enough that he didn't intend being bound to it again.

Straightening his clothes he said, 'If Cameron has been conning everyone in an effort to escape justice, it could well be he believes in his own ruse. Put more succinctly, he could be deceiving himself. If he is, and if subjected to an immense flashback to the original incident which caused his dilemma, then Blake might not be there. This means Cameron may have to accept it was all own terrible concoction, a mere coping mechanism. In other words it would kill off the section of his mind occupied by Blake.'

Victor said, 'What if I convince Blake that Jason Cameron is about to die, would Blake die also?'

Kumar said, 'It's a possibility.'

Chapter 40

The plan couldn't be simpler.

Blake agreed to enter the dogfight and accompany Ron Stark and Lukas Meek to the compound using the forest tracks to get there in the back of Meek's stinking jeep.

LaSalle and Trevor would use the gateway, thus enabling them to suss out the compound ahead of Blake, and back him up if required. Christine had been primed to await their radio message giving the exact co-ordinates; once achieved the snatch squad would move in and arrest everyone at the compound. Blake would identify the abductors and Heather's murderer.

Job done!

Sam didn't like it, mainly because she wasn't involved and secondly because Blake appeared to be controlling everything. Why wait for Blake, why not simply go to the compound and arrest everyone?

The small group sat in the back garden of Gatekeeper Cottage like they were about to have a tea party, question being, certainly to Sam's way of thinking: Who amongst them was the Mad Hatter?

Kumar pensively walked around and around the folly, the entrance through to the escarpment eluding even his magnificent brain. Sam chewed a troublesome nail and Christine hummed some way out tune to herself as she too tried in vain to find the entrance.

Victor sat on a wooden bench, sifting through the contents of his haversack. He'd prepared well, Sam amazed at the amount of equipment he possessed, including a large torch, a long bladed knife in a sheath, a two way radio, a coil of rope and an assortment of drinks and chocolate bars. His clothes now functional; instead of his customary suit and overcoat, he wore camouflage gear similar to Trevor Mason.

262

Earlier, Sam had noticed Victor having what she'd decided as "a sinister chat" with Cameron who'd left five minutes earlier for a rendezvous with Lukas Meek, and promising to prevent Blake from taking any form of aggressive behaviour.

Suddenly, Trevor broke into her thoughts.

'How windy is it today?'

Victor spoke for the first time in over half an hour. 'Fairly, the trees are rustling and swaying about, why?' He treated the question in blasé fashion until Trevor pointed toward the weather vein on top of the folly.

'That's not moving.'

Sam said, 'It's probably riddled with rust.'

Trevor wasn't convinced. 'No, look at where it's pointing, up there below that ridge. Is that a cave or something?'

Sam squinted. 'Yes it is, but how on earth can we get up there, it's a sheer rock face?'

Victor said, 'Sam do you have a ladder?'

She shook her head unable to accept what they were thinking. 'Yes, there's a ladder at the side of the cottage, but it will never reach.'

Victor stepped backwards a few paces, making it easier to check the escarpment. Satisfied, he fetched the ladder. Haversack over his shoulder he positioned the ladder against the rock face and began climbing. Instinctively Heather held the ladder in place.

Victor climbed the full length of the ladder and disappeared into thick gorse bushes hugging the rocks like clinging children. Minutes later he reappeared.

'There's a set of wooden steps leading straight to a cave. They start on this ledge then carry on upward. Amazingly they are in good state of repair; obviously well used.'

Trevor said, 'That's it then, let's get on with it.'

Sam grabbed her haversack, which she'd earlier

filled with bandages, sedatives and several medical bits and pieces. 'I'm coming with you.' Victor, about to argue, was interrupted by Sam's raised hand. 'No arguments, you'll need a vet if it's what we think is happening.'

Victor shrugged. He waved her up the ladder, Trevor close behind.

Not a cave, a tunnel, Victor astounded at its design and workmanship. Strong wooden handcrafted beams were spaced evenly along its length. Tiny metal oil lamps had been expertly fixed to the beams at regular intervals. The floor had been carved from solid rock. The surface pitted every foot or so with one-inch diagonal ruts to avoid slipping.

Walking in the dimly lit passage, Victor tried to imagine what it had been like for the miners. If this tunnel indeed led to a pit used for fighting dogs, the miners must have endured a turgid existence if dog fighting was their excuse for entertainment.

Next came thoughts about his discussions with Frank regarding the true nature of the modern dogfights. If Frank's suspicions were correct, then what would befall Jason Cameron when he entered the compound in the guise of Blake? Could this be an elaborate trap? Victor wasn't too sure. His detective's brain did allow him the luxury of disbelieving Cameron, forcing him to delve into his background, digging, excavating Cameron's past and ultimately Blake's actual existence.

Ten minutes of walking in the dark, lit only by flashlights, Trevor interrupted Victor's thoughts. 'How long is this bloody tunnel?'

Victor read Trevor's mind. He too experienced an awkward feeling akin to a rush of adrenalin. The pit of his stomach churned like a butter machine, his chest growing tighter with each step. He had to keep up his resolve. Difficult to do when he had the strangest sensation they were being followed.

Victor shone his torch on Sam's gaunt face. She looked ghastly.

'Are you alright Sam?' His voice boomed off the tunnel walls.

'Not really, I feel a bit weird and my chest is tight.'

Victor quickened the pace. 'We all have it, the fear of being enclosed, trapped.'

Suddenly Victor remembered something Blake had said, something about being trapped inside Cameron then seeing a light and escaping.

Trevor shouted, 'I can see a spot of light ahead.' Victor sighed with relief. They'd been in the tunnel thirty minutes, a long time. The ball of light grew. Five minutes later they emerged into the daylight.

What they encountered ensured they all stopped in their tracks, issuing a cumulative gasp of amazement.

Victor had lived in Winston his entire life, yet parts of the forest remained a mystery. This was no exception. What Victor saw humbled him, made him feel small. He guessed the crater to be about two miles wide, round, carpeted with trees, mainly of the tall, magnificent green conifer-type. Almost as if he'd emerged on the other side of the world, not just five miles from Winston. Of course he knew about the forest, everyone hereabouts did.

As children they had been discouraged from entering too far into its dark canopy. Walter Slack had recounted stories to Victor about lost children, indeed there were rumours that small aircraft had crashed into the forest with no survivors. Walter had many anecdotes about dangerous disused mineshafts. It all made sense: keep the forest untouched, leave it alone and it becomes out of bounds, preserved by the escarpment and the trees, no one to venture here unless invited.

Victor had an idea his compatriots felt the same. Sam, eyes shaded some from the piercing sun, looked out in astonishment. Trevor, the consummate professional scanned the trees with his binoculars, taking his time, taking it all in.

Victor said, to no one in particular, 'Have we any idea where the compound is located?'

Trevor answered without dropping his binoculars from his eyes. 'Rumour has it; it's well disguised, in a gully somewhere in the middle of the crater.'

Victor thought about what Walter had told him. 'Walter found it once, a long time ago; he reckons it's in the middle somewhere near a stream. Do you see a stream Trevor?'

Trevor lowered the binoculars. 'Down there, by those rocks, see, it runs parallel with those beech trees.'

Victor guessed the beech trees were indigenous to the crater and therefore would be near the water supply, a good indicator for anyone heading legitimately for the compound. After all, the miners didn't have the luxury of all these conifers to hide their little secret from the rich mine owners and their prying spies.

Victor made his pack comfortable on his back and said with determination, 'Let's go then.'

Chapter 41

Some thirty or so minutes later the trio, having scrambled down the rocky escarpment, emerged into the tiny valley carved out by the perpetual running of the stream – a stream pure like a commercial for natural spring water; crystal clear, sparking in the sunlight like a zillion diamonds. Sam thought about soaking her feet; lying down on the mossy bank and dreaming about an affair with Jason Cameron. No time to dwell, for time was important, fear for Cameron's safety mounting by the second.

Without seeking each other's consent they stopped on the mossy embankment and took stock of their surroundings. Victor was distant, examining the forest for the umpteenth time, Sam aware he was worried, concerned for Cameron's well-being.

For certain Victor had fallen for Cameron's charms, in a fatherly way; in fact quite a natural progression for Victor LaSalle. She'd noticed how Lonnie and Frank idolised him, admired him and would be lost without him. His paternal nature ensured they stuck to him like lichen to a rock. In the same interminable manner, Sam had seen Cameron bonding with Victor. A jealous rat nibbled her insides, preventing her from fully liking Victor. Appreciating him yes, anything more, then no, not yet.

Trevor Mason cupped his hands, dunked them into the stream, dribbling water onto his rugged face.

'You have a soft spot for Cameron, don't you Sam?'

It felt like Trevor had been reading her thoughts.

She said quietly, 'I think he's vulnerable. Blame that Blake thing, if he exists.'

Victor plonked himself on a large rock, head cocked to one side, listening to the forest.

Trevor said, 'I've seen Blake in action Sam, he

267

exists, don't worry about that. The only person who is reticent about Cameron's condition is Christine Krill.'

Victor latched onto the comment. 'What did you just say Trevor?'

'I said Christine is a non-believer. She believes Jason Cameron is a phoney.

Sam sensed a sudden change in Victor's demeanour.

Victor asked, 'Has she discussed our operational objective with you Trevor?'

For the first time, Trevor appeared nervous, evidently reluctant to divulge his private discussions with the Chief Constable.

'Christine believes Cameron is somehow involved in the death of his mother. She won't accept this personality disorder thing. She thinks it's a distraction from the truth.'

Victor said, 'And the truth is?'

Trevor Mason grabbed his rucksack and heaved it onto his chunky frame. 'She's convinced Cameron is a psycho, a mad copper. This operation will enhance that belief, so she hopes.'

Sam disliked Christine Krill almost to distraction. She hoped Cameron would prove her wrong and identify the people responsible for Heather's death, and the ones who abducted Brian Mullen twenty years ago.

About to ask Trevor a question, Victor suddenly asked it for her.

'Trevor, have you been watching Gatekeeper Cottage from the adjacent trees?'

Trevor mused, before answering, 'No, my brief was to remain near to the housing development, keep an eye on the meeting with Walter Slack and follow Jason. Why do you ask?'

Victor said, 'Jason told me he'd seen a figure in the trees overlooking the cottage, watching it.'

Trevor swatted a mosquito with the palm of his

hand, squashed it into his cheek, leaving a pea sized stain of blood. 'Wasn't me.'

**

Victor heard it; stopped dead in his tracks, a finger to his lips.

He whispered. 'Sounded like a dog barking, up ahead about a hundred yards.'

They'd been walking for twenty minutes; sufficient enough time for them to realise that neither the Forestry Commission nor casual back packers visited this part of Winston Forest. One fire road meandered round the valley edge, the remaining forest a zigzag of tracks barely two feet wide, presumably made by a combination of animals, perhaps the odd ranger; and of course visitors to the compound.

Trevor unfolded the ordinance survey map, had Victor stand still and placed it on Victor's back, tapping the stream. 'I reckon we're about here.'

Victor felt adrenalin rich blood pumping through him. His legs trembled, his heart pounded.

Definitely his trepidation wasn't the result of failings in his past; in fact, he had a reputation for bravery, an admiring entourage of younger officers all wishing to emulate the bold big man.

What Victor felt today was hardly the fear of impending violence or the dread of failure – fears that usually plagued police officers. Today Victor felt the fear of the incomprehensible: civilised men fighting animals in a pit for a cash reward.

He considered Cameron again. Would Blake keep his word and identify the killer of Heather Moon? Had Kumar blabbed to Christine Krill? There was comfort in knowing that Walter, Lonnie and Frank were out there somewhere, watching his back. Walter, the old bugger knew the forest and Victor sensed Walter had a

269

score to settle, that he'd be there when needed.

They kept moving along the rocky path, Sam slipping and sliding on small boulders. Victor grabbed her arm, steadied her; he smiled and Sam returned it. She blew hair from her face.

Victor admired her pluck. And certainly he would honour his promise to Cameron and watch out for her, whatever the cost.

Trevor, in the lead, threw up an arm. The trio stopped. Trevor squatted. Victor and Sam took up similar positions alongside him.

'Can you smell it?'

'The stink of fire,' said Victor. 'Means we're getting close; let's fan out. Sam, stick with me.'

Chapter 42

Bull watched from the grub hut as they arrived at the compound. Ron Stark sat in the front passenger seat, Lukas was driving and the visitor sat in the back. The Lupine thrashed about in the cage in the jeep's rear compartment.

So that's where you went.

And didn't it all seem to be coming together nicely? Once inside the compound Bull would change the rules and the fight he'd waited for so long would become a reality- a fight promised to him by the man who had expertly manipulated the whole thing. Bull's true mentor.

Ron would whinge. Did it matter? Not one bit. Bull always got his own way when it came to the bouts. After all, he was the star attraction not some bloody furry hybrid.

Bull thought Nigel's death would have brought Cameron to him, no such luck. He'd scared Nigel Moon to death, knowing fine well about his weak heart. The fool thought he was the main man, the Gatekeeper of the tunnel. Up to a point, maybe, but he was never the true gatekeeper. They are all so blind. Bull knew who the true gatekeeper was, the one who manipulated everything.

If Nigel's Moon's snobby wife Heather had known about his addiction to the dogfights, she would have left him. Martin Pope had told the Gatekeeper about Nigel's dodgy ticker after one of the bouts a couple of years ago. The Gatekeeper bided his time, picked his moment and arranged for Bull to scare Nigel Moon shitless.

Soon afterwards his bitch of a wife had begun poking around, sticking her journalistic nose in, spoiling their fun, the silly cow. Hadn't he sorted her

271

out good and proper? And surely enough, just as the Gatekeeper had predicted, her son had come home. Not only had Cameron left Bull in the forest twenty years ago at the mercy of Lukas Meek, he'd also murdered Martin Pope, his best friend in the world. Poor Martin, the one who'd become Bull's soul mate, all thanks to the Gatekeeper. They liked the same things, preferred the same tastes in young boys.

And now here he was, Jason Cameron, pretending to be some weird psycho calling himself Blake. It was Cameron though, no doubt about it. Jason Cameron had come back to the killing pit, where Bull would mete out his revenge, as the Gatekeeper promised.

Victor scanned the compound with his binoculars.

Oblong, about seventy yards long and thirty wide, it couldn't be accessed from the sides, only at its far apex by a small track. Victor saw what looked like a tunnel entrance on this side of the compound. Jesus, the place was so well hidden, even from the air it would be difficult to find; a perfect location for illegal activity.

Two four-wheel drive cars stood at the far end of the compound, the killing pit clearly visible in the middle- a long narrow crevice with brick built walls and wooden steps leading down to the floor, like a garage inspection pit only three times bigger.

A green jeep arrived via the far track and three people got out; Cameron, Lukas Meek and Ron Stark.

Who the hell is that?

A bald headed man the size of a small mountain clambered from the wooden hut at the compound's centre. *Huge* barely did him justice. Dressed in blue dungarees, he reminded Victor of the giant Lenny in the movie, *Of Mice and Men.*

A small revolver appeared in Ron Stark's hand. Stark pointed it at Cameron's head. Lukas forced

Cameron down to the ground, kicking him hard in the stomach. Cameron doubled up and the big man with the shaven head clapped his hands together. Was he dancing?

In that moment Victor glimpsed the bald man's face.

Sam whispered, 'What's going on down there, can you see? Is Jason alright?'

'Shush Sam.'

The face Victor saw startled him, the rounded features mainly. Had it not been for the man's age and bulk, it could be Harry Mullen down there in the compound.

Victor lowered his binoculars.

'I didn't think it possible, but things just got more complicated.'

Sam's eyes wide with fear, she asked, 'what did you see Victor?'

Pennies dropped in Victor's brain, dead circuits became live wires, jigsaw pieces locked together forming a picture that scared him to death.

'When I read the original abduction file I remember Brian Mullen had a nickname. At school they called him Bull, because he was so strong.'

Sam looked frantic. Victor held her by the arms, keeping his voice calm, making her look directly into his eyes.

'Who in the world had the motive to kill Heather and want to harm Cameron?'

Sam startled, her eyes searched Victor's, her own unsure, demanding explanations. 'I don't know what you mean Victor?'

Victor spoke his thoughts aloud, realising he had been taken for a sucker.

'The Mullen's blame Cameron for the police failing to react quickly enough when Brian was abducted, so

273

just imagine how Brian Mullen must feel.'

Sam said, 'Brian Mullen is dead Victor.' Statement cut and dried.

'Sam, I think I've just seen him down there in the compound.' Victor ground his teeth, gums aching with the effort. '*Bull* is Brian Mullen, alive and well and seeking revenge on the man who abandoned him in the forest.'

Sam's features had fear mixing unpleasantly with anger. Her top lip quivered then the tears welled. She sniffled, wiped her face with her hand, composed herself and said, 'Daft question, what will this Brian Mullen do to Jason?'

Victor didn't answer. One thing for sure though, he was scared for Cameron's safety.

Grabbing the radio from his pack he contacted Trevor Mason and put him in the picture. Trevor said he would move in, try and get a closer look.

'Bear in mind,' he told Victor, 'the troops are not scheduled to arrive for another half hour.'

'Contact Christine, 'Victor said, 'let her know the situation and insist that backup move their arses.'

Sam waited patiently, listening to Victor's instructions to Trevor Mason. She admired Victor's cool manner, always choosing his words carefully, not raising his voice an octave. Sam had warmed to Victor; and now understood why Heather would have fallen for his charms. She also believed Victor had as much at stake as she did, particularly when it came to Jason Cameron.

Victor sat on his haunches, scanned the compound, weighing up his options.

Sam said, 'Jason is important to you isn't he Victor?'

Victor let the binoculars fall to dangle around his thick neck; he paused for a couple of seconds, finally

274

saying, 'We have a lot in common.'

Yes, so many similarities. Sam could see his point of view.

'Both of you believe you were abandoned by your parents, Jason by Heather and you by both yours. You also share a common peculiarity- you both deliver your policing in unconventional ways.'

Victor stifled a laugh. 'I feel like Cameron and I have had similar experiences in the police which have left us, let us say, tainted to a degree.'

Sam nodded her agreement.

Victor checked the compound again. He scowled, muttered something Sam didn't catch.

The screw inside Sam tightened. 'What can you see now? Are they hurting Jason?'

Victor spoke without taking his eyes from the binoculars. 'No, Cameron is being held in the wooden hut next to the pit. Everyone else seems to be outside in a huddle. Funny but every so often they look up here, like they know we're watching.' Victor again whispered something; then more loudly, 'Someone else is down there; I know him but can't put a name to him. Bloody annoying.'

Sam tapped his shoulder, 'Let me have a look.'

Reluctantly Victor handed the binoculars to Sam. A minute passed before she looked up and said, 'Describe the man you want to identify.'

Victor said, 'Tubby, small and bald, you can't miss him.'

Sam recognised him immediately, 'It's Paul Jacobs, the Editor of Yorkshire Gateway.'

Victor stroked his stubble. 'And so the rats gather together.'

'What do you mean?

The final piece of the jigsaw fell into place. 'Who did Heather discuss her sightings with; you know the

275

strange creature in the forest, who we now know is Brian Mullen?'

Sam said, 'Her editor.'

Chapter 43

Outrageous. Shocking. Unbelievable. Words she knew the press would use when they got hold of the story. Christine Krill didn't care. Her career had nosed dived since Martin Pope; the one thing she desired was to make Jason Cameron pay.

After taking the post as Chief Constable of North Yorkshire Christine had spun her web, luring Cameron back to Winston and conning Walter Slack into believing the operation would benefit both his reputation and the welfare of the town. Kumar had played his part wonderfully. Did Kumar fancy her? She hoped so; because her admiration for his wit and charismatic charm had begun to rekindle feelings in her she thought had vanished long ago. *I must lose weight,* one thought that haunted her.

Christine had her retirement plan in place. It didn't matter about the end result of Operation Bifurcate. Kumar had promised the position of Special Crimes Adviser at the National Crime Faculty would be hers. After all, they had asked Kumar to chair the interview panel.

Christine let her mind drift. Wondered what it would be like to go on holiday with Kumar, somewhere exotic, India perhaps? Suddenly the cackle of the radio interrupted such audacious thoughts. The fully equipped incident van was parked in the Forestry Commission car park, three miles from the compound. It had become claustrophobic, sweat and deodorant mixing like deadly gas.

She heard Trevor Mason asking for the back-up teams to be in place quickly. Apparently Blake, well Cameron, might need urgent help.

Christine placed her hand on the shoulder of the civilian radio operator.

'Tell DS Mason not to worry, the troops are on the way.'

The radio operator obliged.

'Now tell the back up teams to await my specific command before setting off into the forest.' Christine noticed the look of astonishment on the face of the operator. 'Do as you are told my dear, there's a good girl.'

The operator reluctantly did as she was told. Maybe later she might report her misgivings.

Now where was she? Oh yes, holidays in India.

**

The jungle formula mosquito repellent Sam had given to Victor hadn't worked. Victor's head had become a permanent itch. The little buggers had had a feast on his face, evidenced by purple spots.

Victor said 'She's holding the support back. I knew she would. Bitch.'

Sam smacked her bare leg, exterminating a blood filled fly.

'Can she do that?'

Victor thought about his Chief Constable. Christine Krill didn't know about Kumar's false credentials, since she wasn't, for all her strutting pretensions, a detective. Christine's rationale for her weird plan now based on unreliable information. Victor would deal with her later. The priority now was Cameron and arresting the murderer of Heather Moon.

'She can do what she likes; she's the Chief Constable,' Victor said with a grimace. 'I'm going down there, Sam. You stay here and keep the binoculars. Let me know if you notice anything which could put me in danger.'

'What about Jason?'

278

Victor winked. 'Jason will be fine.'

Sam pulled him back. 'What do *you* think happened to Brian Mullen?'

Before setting off down the grassy embankment and into the trees below, Victor thought why not give her his views?

'I believe Lukas Meek abducted Brian Mullen for his sexual pleasure. Bizarrely, his brother Ron Stark covered it up. This left everyone thinking Brian Mullen was dead, so his abductors kept him in the forest compound as their plaything and later...' Victor searched for an appropriate description, 'Brian became their *warrior*, a man with little morality, someone who had endured abuse most of his life, and knew no other existence until he was old enough and trusted enough to venture to the outskirts of town. I believe Heather may have seen him, followed him perhaps, we'll probably never know. I'm guessing Heather must have stumbled onto the compound and they needed to get rid of her otherwise they would be rumbled.'

Sam said, 'I still don't understand why Brian Mullen didn't simply leave, go home?'

Victor said, 'Brian probably "*Stockholmed*" with his abductors, bonded with them to such an extent he couldn't physically bring himself to leave. He probably blames Cameron for leaving him in the forest and wants revenge. Simple really, wished I'd figured it out sooner then we wouldn't have to go through this.'

Victor took Sam's hand, squeezed it, but failed to ease her worry. 'I like Jason and believe he's genuine,' he said. 'Cheer up; I'll get him back to you in one piece.'

Sam conjured a smile and gave Victor a gentle peck on the cheek. Victor flushed. He then took off down the embankment, taking care not to make too much noise.

Chapter 44

Gently, Cameron eased Blake to the back of his mind. Gradually he clawed his way to consciousness. *God how I wish I could remember what Blake's been doing.*

The compound appeared much smaller than he remembered. The wooden hut still in the middle to the right, the wire cages for the dogs rusted but still intact.

It had been a shock at first, seeing Brian Mullen standing there like a bloated wrestler. Cameron didn't understand why Brian hadn't simply escaped, gone home to his parents. Did they know he was alive? Cameron thought not, otherwise they would be here destroying the compound.

Blake had fulfilled his promise and brought Cameron back to the compound. Following the murder of his mother, Cameron had willed Blake to the forefront, knowing he would be better equipped to flush out the rats of Winston. It had worked, beautifully. Blake came when Cameron experienced stressful situations because Blake had been born from stress. Now he could take a back seat. Cameron didn't feel worried, in fear of his safety. On the contrary, he felt elated, relieved to be able to return to the compound and confront his demons.

When he'd found out about the existence of Blake, he felt violated, invaded almost. Blake had been there most of his adult life, Cameron refusing to accept him at first until a time when Blake began to emerge as a friend, someone else to rely upon in times of need. However, it worried him that his recollections of his time as Blake were sketchy. When Blake emerged in full view of the interview team after the Pope affair, Cameron had been relieved. Then came the suggestion from Christine to use Blake to identify the killer of Heather and the original abductors, the whole idea too good to be true, Cameron seeing it as a chance to finally put his childhood bogey man to bed, and arrest the one who'd deprived him of his mother.

And he needed to do it his way, which meant reducing his medication, letting Blake out without his own conscious knowledge. The triggers were the key and thankfully Victor had done a wonderful job of prising Blake out into the open. Of course, complications had entered the equation.

Cameron had fallen for Samantha Moon, and accepted it would be extremely difficulty for her to understand his predicament; his love for her insufficient on its own to warrant any commitment on her behalf. Did she truly love him? In truth he didn't know, only time would tell.

From being lonely, Cameron now found himself with friends, family. His relationship with Victor one of kinship, two like-minded individuals, confident Victor would be at his side when the sparks flew. In the meantime, he would get those involved in the compound to ventilate; after all, they had no idea why he'd returned.

After shackling him with plastic washing line, they tied him onto a wooden chair and locked the hut door. Brian Mullen hadn't said a word, at least not whilst Cameron had control. He may have spoken to Blake, Cameron unsure.

A shiver shot down his spine. He gawped at a wheelchair parked in the corner of the hut. And, God almighty, they'd removed his shoes and socks.

This isn't the type of bloody police work I joined for, thought Victor quickly scanning the trees. Nothing to worry about, only the birds singing, leaves rustling in the wind like thousands of green ticker tapes. The dogs had stopped barking and he could still smell burning

281

wood wafting along the track.

Only then did he become aware of a presence behind him. Slowly he turned to again scan the trees, or what might be edging through them. It was nothing, just his imagination. Not so. The foliage moved slightly. Like a ghost Walter Slack emerged dressed in combat fatigues, and looking sharper than his seventy plus years.

'Jesus Walter, you scared the shit out of me. Aren't you a little bit old for this cloak and dagger stuff?'

Walter regarded his friend, grinned, cocked his head to one side and winked. 'Never felt better Victor; told you I could find the compound again. It's four hundred yards ahead so keep the noise down.'

Victor accepted that Walter had peaks and troughs with his Parkinson's decease. He also knew that placing Walter in a wheelchair to meet Cameron had been Kumar's idea. Still, rather unusual to find Walter hopping about in the forest like a forty-year old.

'Are you sure you're up to this Walter?'

'Trust me Victor, my medication has been improved lately thanks to the intervention of Doctor Kumar. I'm fine, honest.'

Victor, relieved to see his mentor, relaxed a little.

'Are you there, Sam,' Victor whispered into the radio.

Her voice floated over the static, angelic despite detected worry, yet soothing, making him proud to be her friend. 'I'm here. Jason is still in the hut.'

Victor said, 'Okay, remember stay on the hill, no matter what you see happen down there.'

Victor turned to Walter and saw he held a lightweight crossbow in his hand.

Victor impressed said, 'I like the look of that does it work?'

Walter twisted the weapon around with his two

beefy hands, the shakes absent as he admired the weapon. 'Trust me Victor. This little beauty will deliver with pin prick precision.'

Shocked Victor said, 'I didn't realise you knew how to handle a crossbow?'

'I don't, not really. Lonnie gave it to me. I think he wanted to impress me.'

He handed the crossbow to Victor. 'Here you have it.' Walter fumbled in his pocket, producing three small crossbow bolts. 'I only have three, so don't miss.'

'I won't, don't worry'

Walter smiled nervously and scuttled off into the undergrowth and out of sight.

Strange behaviour, thought Victor. Before he had the chance to reflect on Walter's sudden improvement Victor's radio cackled to life. 'Are you there Victor?'

'Go ahead Sam.'

'You're not going to believe this,' she said. 'Detective Inspector Mullen has turned up.'

Chapter 45

The windows of the hut were covered with black plastic bin liners, preventing any daylight penetration.

The door to the hut was flung open, Brian Mullen there in the doorway; backlit he resembled the enormous silhouette of a bloated angel.

'Hello Cameron.' Brian's voice was squeaky, like a girl.

Cameron could sense Blake attempting to return; *no, stay back Blake, this is my moment. I'll handle Brian Mullen.*

Before Blake receded he flashed words into Cameron's brain: *This bastard strangled Heather with a dog chain.*

Cameron slowed his breathing, cracked his neck like Blake.

'Probably do me no good reasoning with you Brian. It's obvious you're angry as hell.' Cameron pushed Blake back, wouldn't let him cloud his concentration.

Brian said with a sneer, 'This isn't about revenge for abandoning me, leaving me to the mercy of Lukas twenty years ago. This is about Martin Pope, my only friend in the world. And you murdered him you bastard.'

Cameron noticed the hammer in Brian's hand. His heart sank. Tied up, what the hell could he do? Be strong, deal with this and come out of the mist, it's the only way forward. Blake nibbled at his subconscious, desperate to emerge. Cameron focused, concentrated on the task of persuading Brian Mullen to relinquish his control, ventilate his feelings, answer questions burning inside Cameron's head about the death of his mother.

He gave it a go. 'Why did you stay in the forest for so long, hiding?' This appeared to surprise Brian who flicked his head back, then shot it forward craning his neck, pretending to be disinterested. Cameron added, 'Indulge me, presumably we have the time?'

Brian slapped the hammer into his shovel like palm.

'I haven't been hiding you idiot. I live in Whitby; Martin fixed it up, paid money for me, let me move in with his mum, told folk I was his cousin, got me a job on the trawlers. I come her for fun, you know to relax, we all do.'

Cameron couldn't believe that Brian had been allowed to blend in, find a life so near to his parents. People were still looking for him for Christ's sake.

'Why haven't you been in touch with your parents or the police?'

Brian laughed, slapped his thigh.

'Everything has to be so black and white with you cops. You've no idea about the real world, a world of pleasures, devoid of morals. Parents aren't that important when you have like-minded friends who enjoy perversion, violence even.'

Cameron listened carefully, trying to identify a weak chink in Brian's armour. He wasn't ranting; he possessed an intelligent grasp of the English language and his demeanour, although strikingly threatening, didn't emit an immediate threat of danger, not yet any way. Somebody had taken the time to teach Brian about the world, who, he had no idea, unless...

Cameron decided to poke and prod a little bit more. 'For God's sake, Lukas Meek kidnapped you, took you away from your family, locked you away for years. Don't you feel hatred for him, and his brother?'

Brian pressed his back against the wall of the hut, slid down and settled on the floor, crossing his legs. At least Cameron had bought himself some time.

'I got used to being here, didn't want to go home. They should have found me, didn't look very hard did they, especially that bitch who calls herself my mother.

285

'When I met Martin at a dogfight here in the compound, we bonded like brothers, didn't need my mum no more. Martin got me educated by a schoolteacher friend who liked the dogfights.'

Brian closed his eyes, tilted his head back like he had just taken a hit of some powerful drug. Cameron noticed the sandy mud on Brian's boots; lighter in shade than the housing development mud, much like the mud ever present on Harry Mullen's shoes.

'Your dad knows you're alive, doesn't he Brian?'

Brian stood up. He whacked the hammer onto the concrete floor; the impact causing tiny sparks to fly like flint striking rock.

'Like all coppers you're so predictable, trying to confuse me, make me lose control, give you an opportunity to escape.' Brian whacked the hammer onto the floor again. 'You seem to forget, I survived my ordeal, learned how to fight, earn money. What did you do? You got yourself a mental disease.'

The door to the hut opened. Harry Mullen walked in, smiling malevolently.

You just couldn't help yourself could you?' Harry sounded weird, edgy, rattled; indicative of his total lack of hold on reality perhaps? Janice a philanderer, Harry's career reaching its end, his son a monster; Harry must be totally delusional.

Cameron said, incredulously, 'You knew Brian was alive and yet you didn't even tell his mother? What sort of a man are you Harry?'

Harry Mullen looked disapprovingly at his son, his complexion waxy, face muscles taught.

'Janice changed when Brian was born. She began to hate me, always trying to humiliate me in front of the boy, ranting on about my lack of ambition, wishing she were somewhere else other than Winston. She gave him all her attention, all her love. When Brian went missing

286

she changed, became dependant on me again.' Harry banged his chest. '*Loved me*, not him.'

Harry gently removed the hammer from the grasp of his son.

'Then along came a posh builder named Nigel Moon, followed by Victor. She couldn't control herself.'

Cameron shook his head in disbelief,

'You found out about Nigel's dodgy ticker and got this brute to scare the living daylights out of him?'

Harry giggled, placed his hand across his mouth, like an altar boy laughing inappropriately during Communion.

'Didn't realise it would work. Hilarious really; they even had me investigating it.'

Cameron had the strangest feeling he had missed something important, something more to do with the Brian's disappearance. Yes, something in the original abduction file about Harry requesting the investigating officer to be a local who had knowledge of the area and understood the terrain – someone like Ron Stark perhaps?

Then it hit Cameron like a speeding train.

'You dealt with my mother's complaint about the man stalking me. You arranged for the observations on the school and made her look an idiot. You knew it was Meek all along, right Harry? Ron must have confided in you about his brother's problems. When he abducted Brian you decided to do nothing. Christ Harry!'

Without warning, Harry Mullen arched the hammer into the air and smashed it hard into his son's forehead. The sound it made on contact, sickeningly lethal. Brian dropped to the floor like a felled conifer, hitting the concrete with a dull thud.

Harry gazed at the twitching body of his son, blood leaking onto the floor, all the while humming to himself.

Cameron, sickened by what he'd witnessed, managed: 'This is getting out of hand Harry. Think, man, you are a Detective Inspector. Call an ambulance; it's your son down there bleeding to death.'

Harry spoke, though his gaze remained on his stricken son. 'You know something, after a while he got used to it here at the compound. Eventually after a year I came to see him, explained why it had to be this way. And do you know what is weird? He accepted it, began to feel more at home here than in Winston. Everything was going smoothly until your mother saw him in the forest, wanted to write about it. Because of her interest, Brian grew infatuated with Heather; he watched the cottage from the trees. If Heather had recognised him and told the police well . . .' Harry shrugged his shoulders.

'So I told Brian about how you killed Martin Pope. His anger erupted like a volcano; he wanted to hurt you . . . badly. When Janice went to Gatekeeper Cottage to confront Heather about her fling with Victor, Brian watched the argument, saw Janice hit Heather with a hammer.' Harry studied the hammer in his hand. 'By the time he got to Heather she was dying. He finished her off with a dog chain; to him it was like putting an animal out of its misery.'

Cameron couldn't help it; he shook violently, face twitching with anger. Blake desperate to be unleashed, Cameron forcing him back, as he did the bile in his throat.

Harry said quietly, 'Funny thing was, when he told me about it he said he thought he saw you in the bushes watching, unable to move like a rabbit trapped in headlights. I couldn't figure out why you never came forward.'

No wonder Blake felt guilty; he hadn't done enough

288

to save Heather. Cameron realised Blake had probably gone into a fugue state, which sometimes happened during times of stress or reaction to extreme trauma. Like a switch activating, effectively preventing an overload, making Blake stutter like a computer switching itself off because it recognised it had a problem.

Harry walked toward Cameron, towered over him, 'Now it's time for you to take over from Brian and entertain us.'

The hammer arched in Harry's hand, falling rapidly, hitting Cameron's left foot with an awful thwack. An excruciating pain shot up his leg.

Harry ignored Cameron's pleas and cut the bonds fastening him to the chair. He dragged Cameron from the hut by his hair, Cameron's hands still bound behind his back, dirt and gravel in the compound stinging and scratching the exposed flesh on his feet.

Harry barked at Ron Stark standing near the dog cages. 'Get the dog into the pit.' Ron didn't move; stood there dumbfounded, mouth open, catching flies.

Harry shouted again, 'Ron, get a grip, the Gatekeeper will be here shortly, let's give him a show he won't forget.'

Cameron fairly sure Brian Mullen had perished, considered his situation, pain knifing through his shattered foot. Christ, why did this nightmare ever begin? Strangely though, he suddenly realised he needed to experience it again in order to hang on to his sanity.

Harry's admission had shocked Cameron to his soul. Cameron accepted he had gone as far as he could. Blake should deal with this from here on in. Cameron didn't have the guile, or fighting skill to cope with what lay ahead. Additionally, Blake had bonded with the lupine. That could be an ace card.

Harry cut the plastic rope and freed Cameron's hands before he shoved him down the wooden stepladder and into the killing pit.

Cameron landed in a heap on concrete, hurting his knee, the pain in his foot making his pulses race, and increase stress levels. Harry pulled the ladder up.

Cameron gagged, smelled the gore from countless bloodthirsty bouts that had taken place in this godforsaken hellhole. Childhood memories hurtled back filling his mind with images of dogs mauling flesh, men cheering, the oil slick of blood underfoot causing him to slip and slide unable to control his legs. Horrible memories could be good. Blake would come soon and Cameron would not remember the ordeal about to engulf him.

On his feet, using the brick wall to steady himself, his foot one bloody mess. Cameron glanced around the pit's perimeter; rusty metal chairs were positioned close to the edge affording maximum viewing potential. No chance of escape. The pit at least nine feet deep, its walls wet and slimy, a milky mist slowly engulfed him; sliding down the wall of the pit he allowed the mist to slip him into unconsciousness.

**

Victor eased himself from the drainage ditch surrounding the compound, took a peek. He saw Ron Stark busy unlocking a substantial cage door. Harry gesticulated wildly, shouting orders at Ron. Had Harry gone mad? Clear to Victor that Harry was somehow involved in this circus.

At the edge of the pit, Lukas Meek held a long wooden pole, which he poked at someone or something in the pit, smiling all the while like a demented child.

Jesus, he thought he saw Cameron is in the pit.

290

Victor knew he could no longer rely on Christine to send reinforcements in time to halt the carnage soon to occur.

Walter would want to be there when Victor confronted Ron Stark about the original allegations surrounding the disappearance of Brian Mullen and Jason Cameron. In the meantime Victor would use the crossbow on the lupine, hopefully hitting his target.

A rustling of bushes behind him made the hairs on his neck bristle.

Victor rolled over.

'Nice crossbow, Uncle Vic.'

Lonnie, dressed in combat fatigues, slid his slim frame down onto the grass and took a peek at the compound. Victor wondered if everyone in Winston owned combat gear. There must be an army surplus store doing a roaring trade.

Victor grabbed Lonnie's shirt, dragged him back into the ditch.

'I thought I told you to wait at the police station.'

Lonnie pulled Victor's hand away, indignantly. 'You need me.'

Victor knew Frank would not be far away.

'Where's Frank?'

Lonnie twitched a smile, pointed to a tall conifer overlooking the compound.

Frank halfway up, clinging to a thick branch, his face covered in green paint, gave them a little wave: the child waving to his dad from a tree in the park.

Lonnie said, 'Paints great eh? Frank nicked it from the paintball place near Whitby.'

Victor shook his head in dismay.

'Stay here Lonnie, I'm moving closer.'

Victor stole another peek at the compound.

Jesus, Joseph and Mary- what the hell is *that?*

From the cages at the back of the compound, Ron

Stark emerged looking like a smug gladiator. Yanking on a chunky metal chain, he struggled to keep a massive wolf-like beast in check. Even from this distance Victor realised this wasn't the dog Blake had brought to the compound. This beast looked horrible.

The dog's coat glistened wet like sea coal; it's neck sleek, overly long making it peculiar looking. What had these idiots created?

Snarling, shaking its enormous head from side to side, the beast resembled a mythical monster designed by maniacs. Victor's heart sank. He slid back into the ditch. Carefully he loaded the crossbow.

Chapter 46

Rain clouds edged closer to the forest. A distant clap of thunder echoed like a whip cracking. The rain began slowly at first, increasing to a deluge that emptied into the killing pit.

Cameron flicked his eyes open. Did it ever stop raining in Winston? What sounded like a generator, or similar hummed, the noise emanating from the dank walls of the pit, bricks vibrating like a living thing.

Above a massive dog snarled at him from the lip of the pit. And worse, Blake wasn't here with him, Cameron definitely alone, unable to rely on his alter ego.

He thought: This is where it began: this is where it will end.

Images of that awful day in his childhood continually flashed into his brain. The blood of countless dogs, the salty taste forever returning each time he dreamed.

Today the dog looked nothing like the beast that had attacked him in this exact spot all those years ago. Here was a thing enormous, evil, and cunning.

Police training kicked in. He took stock, began planning his defence, searched for any type of weapon.

In one corner of the pit he noticed a small ditch containing a floating pump mechanism. The water table! Of course!

Cameron dragged himself to his feet, the cold water numbing his damaged foot. He limped purposefully toward the water pump, sat down. Praying he could do this, he kicked and heaved at the pump. He sweated, it hurt, his shoulders and arms screamed with the effort, not least his good foot. It moved, then again, finally detaching itself from its metal housing; the result instantaneous.

Water leaked into the pit from every possible avenue. One inch, then two. A fair bet the pump had been keeping the underground streams at bay, all now desperate to invade the pit, purge it of the horrible stains of an evil past.

Ron Stark didn't appear to notice, Ron some yards away and too busy screaming at Harry Mullen: 'HELP ME GET THE DOG INTO THE PIT.'

Cameron pulled frantically at the metal clasp securing the fat round pump. Strength from somewhere proved rewarding- it snapped! Gratefully Cameron examined his weapon, turning it over in his hand. It resembled a six-inch spatula, with a hole at one end where the retaining screw had sat, its opposite end square. Like a madman he began scraping the makeshift metal dagger against the brickwork, sharpening it, making it fit for purpose.

A round face appeared at the edge of the pit, smiled at Cameron. It was that bastard Paul Jacobs. Cameron grimaced, stabbed his weapon toward Jacob's bloated face.

'YOU'RE NEXT, FAT BOY,' Cameron shouted.

Jacobs did a little jig, enjoying the spectacle of Cameron thrashing about in the cold water.

Without warning Cameron launched himself at the brick wall of the pit, his good foot, though painful, placed on the pit's wall. All it took was one good push; he catapulted upwards, his momentum allowing him to reach the lip of the pit. Momentarily airborne, he arched his arm and brought the homemade dagger down hard onto the editor's exposed foot, yanking it out as he tumbled backwards into the water.

Jacobs screamed like a banshee, stumbled, dislodged a metal chair enough for it to slide and tip and simply hang there. Jacobs didn't, he followed Cameron head first into the pit. He landed in two feet

294

of water. Disorientated, damaged foot spilling blood, he floundered.

Cameron dragged Jacobs to his feet, held the weapon to his throat.

'Don't hurt me anymore, please, I beg you,' Jacobs pleaded in a tone high pitched and frightened.

Ron Stark appeared at the edge of the pit. He laughed like a hyena.

'Do you think for one second we give a damn about the fat man?' Ron said. 'Cut his throat, we don't give a shit.'

Suddenly a dark shadow loomed above Cameron. The lupine dived into the pit landing with a loud splash.

Cameron had no alternative. He released his grip on Paul Jacobs, pushed him hard in his back and into the path of the dog.

Jacobs screamed, thrashing about in the water desperately trying to escape wildly snapping jaws.

The dog pounced, locking its jaws around Jacob's neck. The icy water turned pink, then deep red, the dog tossing its massive head from side to side, shaking the editor like a rag doll, a bloody abstract painting the walls.

At least a minute and half passed before the animal finally released its grip leaving Jacobs face down in the water, lifeless. Then the beast weighed up Cameron like a lion about to take down an unsuspecting antelope at a water hole.

No water hole but a brick pit filling rapidly, the animal up to its belly in water, finding it difficult to manoeuvre.

The longer he delayed the dog from attacking, the better chance Cameron would have of survival. Slowly he eased away from the snarling monster, water pushing hard against his calves.

How could he gain an advantage?

Cameron looked round, then up at the pit top. *The metal chair!* It still balanced on the edge! Cameron inched toward the chair, his eyes on the dog, which in turn tracked his every movement, keeping its distance for now, waiting for the moment to strike.

Closer, closer, keep away you big bastard, just for a teensy weensy second.

Cameron stretched to his full height, shot out his arm and grabbed the rusty chair leg. The chair teetered and tumbled. HA! Now, like a true Roman gladiator, he had a sword and shield.

He shouted, 'Come on you bastard, I'm ready for you.'

Chapter 47

Victor had no choice. It didn't take an idiot to realise the situation had escalated into a scenario that could only end in severe bloodshed, immediate action the only solution.

Victor grabbed the radio from his backpack.

'Trevor are you there?'

The radio cackled to life. Victor turned down the volume.

'About thirty yards to your right, in the bushes.'

Victor pressed the transmit button again, hand trembling.

'Me, Lonnie and Frank will meet you at the trees near the entrance to the compound. We're going in Trevor, can't wait any longer.'

A moment's silence, then a brief reply.

'You're in charge DCI LaSalle. Meet you there in two minutes.'

Victor motioned for Lonnie and Frank to follow him, as he blatantly stepped from the undergrowth. It didn't matter anymore, let them see him.

His immediate concern was to assist Jason Cameron, the operation now fragmented, pointless. He understood the ramifications of the webs, which had been woven by the men in the compound. Decades of violence involving dogs, manipulation of human beings for their own gratification. All that remained was to end it, destroy the compound, save Cameron and bring to justice to those involved.

Victor strode purposefully toward the gate of the compound; Lonnie, Frank and then Trevor Mason falling in step alongside him. He loved that film Gunfight at the OK Coral.

Walter Slack should be here by now. Where the hell was he? Surely he would have witnessed the scenario unfolding within the compound? A strange thought overwhelmed Victor. He came to an abrupt halt, some distance away from the compound's gate; the others cast him quizzical looks. An electrical circuit in his brain made a live contact with some vital information he'd gathered when preparing for the operation.

'*Walter has his own agenda*?' He dismissed such misgivings and carried on, the others falling in step again.

Birdsong made it difficult to imagine what lay ahead; what they were about to do.

He stopped again, a mere two hundred yards from the gate.

'Trevor, can I ask you a question? And don't worry about its importance, I'm just curious.'

Trevor nervously examined the compound, eager to continue, get it done. He sweated, scoured his face, decidedly uncomfortable.

'What is it, sir?'

Victor worded his question carefully, in as few words as possible, he too eager to get going.

'When Martin Pope was incarcerated for sexually assaulting a little boy in Hammersmith in 1990, can you remember which prison he served his sentence?'

'Durham,' Trevor came back, 'presumably for security reasons and his own safety.'

A gunshot rang out.

**

The water filled the pit at an incredible speed, Cameron knee deep, watching the awkwardly moving beast.

Evidently realising its own situation, survival instinct kicked in. The dog searched for a way out of the pit, its attention directed away from Cameron who felt less threatened.

Ron Stark appeared at the lip of the pit, glowering at his creation, disappointment etched on his skeletal face. He muttered something under his breath and disappeared from view.

Cameron heard a loud crack, like a gun going off. Things were happing above over which he had no control. He hoped Sam was safe.

Desperate to get out of the pit, Cameron considered his options. He could tread water until the level rose sufficiently to enable him to reach up and haul himself out. He realised the water level had became reasonably constant. The water table had been reached, so any further flooding would take a while.

Shit! The lupine had also realised this. It growled, edged closer, its hackles raised, creating a more horrendous illusion.

If the thing attacked now its immense size alone could overwhelm him. One option left.

Sliding the makeshift dagger into his leather belt, he grabbed the metal chair with both hands. Charging at the dog, screaming at the top of his voice, the beast startled, failed to react quickly enough; the chair legs whacked into its upper torso, flinging it onto the brick wall, effectively wedging it in the corner. Cameron, fumbling for the dagger, felt a whoosh of air pass his ear, saw the crossbow bolt thump hard into the dog's exposed belly.

The dog's howling intensified bouncing off the pit's walls. A contained, chilling echo. Suddenly the creature went limp, its own weight dragging it beneath the water.

Cameron relieved, let go of the chair and looked up to see Victor grinning at him, the empty crossbow still aimed at the dog.

'Took your time Victor,' he called up.

Victor lowered the crossbow. 'Had an idea you

could look after yourself Jason.' A pause then: 'It is you isn't it?

Cameron held up his arm, which Victor grabbed and hauled him out of the pit.

'Yes, it's me Victor, alive and kicking. Just. What happened to Ron Stark and the others?'

Victor squatted on his haunches, casting a gaze around the compound.

'We heard a gunshot. Trevor, Lonnie, Frank and me came in through the gate expecting to be confronted by an armed rabble. When we entered, the place looked deserted except for the cages.'

Cameron glanced into the pit. The dog, now like an immense woolly rug, floated head down. Glad to be out of the pit, past events seemed incredibly distant.

'What's in the cages, no more weird creatures, I hope?'

Victor beckoned Cameron to follow him. Cameron waved a grateful hand at Lonnie, Frank and Trevor who relaxed beneath a tree like a conquering army, glad of the rest.

Cameron asked, 'What's with the crossbow?'

Victor turned the weapon over in his hands. 'Walter gave it to me.'

Cameron detected disappointment in Victor's demeanour. He said, 'I have a funny idea you have something to tell me.'

The pair stopped short of the metal animal cages in the far corner of the compound. Both men realising the worst of it was over, they exchanged stories. Cameron told of his experience in the cabin, Victor wincing occasionally.

Cameron then learned of Victor's concerns regarding Walter Slack.

'Walter has some questions to answer, Victor. After all it was him behind my returning here to Winston. I

300

hope his motivations aren't for personal revenge.'

Metal cages rattled; there was no wind. Both men turned toward the corner of the compound.

Running now, ever more alert, they reached the cages at the same time. From inside the cages Harry Mullen and Ron Stark stared back. Both men were *naked*.

Making sure they were locked inside, they headed for the cabin.

Chapter 48

Gingerly, Victor eased the cabin door open with his foot.

Janice Mullen sat in the far corner; her son's bloodied head balanced gently on her knee. Tear tracks stained her face, her eyes wet, bloodshot, showing grief, pain and love; a terrible mixture of emotions. A revolver lay at her side.

The dog shot by Victor in the woods languished in the corner, whimpering.

Victor gently kicked the revolver sideways, picked it up and sniffed the breach.

'What happened here Janice?'

Janice looked up for a second, ignored the question and began to stroke her son's head. Eventually when she did speak, her voice cracked with emotion:

'I often suspected Harry was hiding something from me about Brian's disappearance. Long ago I sensed things hadn't been right.'

Cameron, about to say something shut up as Victor squeezed his arm, eyes stating *let her speak*.

Janice wiped her face with the back of her hand.

'I volunteered to run the property office; including looking after evidence, case papers et cetera. Something bugged me, kept coming back to me all the time. Something about you, Jason Cameron, the day you were found by Walter.'

Cameron felt unusually calm, the memories returning without intensity, occupying rather than flooding his mind. He had an inkling Janice had the key to unlock his trauma, and to banish the bad memories for good.

Janice sniffed, blew her nose. Both men leaned on the hut's walls listening intently.

'Harry always kept the files locked away in his

office. No way could I get at them. The only thing in the property office was your clothing, the day you were found wandering in the forest. Something about the clothes didn't seem right. Then it dawned on me. They were cleaner than they should be.' She laughed, 'For heaven's sake, I had a little boy, I knew about washing dirty clothes.' Janice looked at her son, a wan smile twitching the corner of her mouth.

'After a day in the forest, I could smell Brian a mile away- if you'd been in the woods for three days, your clothes would have been sweaty, filthy, covered in dirt. Yes they were soiled, not that bad though, mainly your shoes and socks covered in sandy mud. When I questioned Harry about it, he was evasive almost angry with me for interfering.'

Cameron had to speak, couldn't stifle mounting anger any longer.

'The bastards had me here in this compound. I was never wandering about in the forest. I must have told myself that to repress what actually happened to me.'

Janice stopped stroking Brian's head, and gently eased it onto the floor. She straightened her skirt, sniffled again, long and hard.

'When you arrived here for your mother's funeral, Harry became tetchy, unbearably anxious. You were the fly in the ointment, a reminder of what happened here twenty years ago. Harry and Walter would have clandestine meetings in our house, always whispering, plotting.' She huffed. 'I knew we couldn't afford the new house. Walter bought Harry off a long time ago. Of course I suspected but...' Janice tailed off, the hurt there for them to see, and peppered with guilt no doubt.

'Janice, Walter did find me and realised I couldn't remember anything about my time in the compound. He took me to the police, gambling I would be his ace card, a diversion from Brian's abduction. Thing was, he hadn't realised about Blake.

'I never picked Walter out of the line-up; it was Blake who identified Walter. No wonder I couldn't remember. They even videoed my evidence, yet all the while it was Blake who relived the trauma. They couldn't know Blake even existed. And it's the reason Walter orchestrated this whole scenario. When Kumar told Walter about Blake, he wanted Blake to appear, to exact his revenge. My mother's death acted as the catalyst to get me back here.' Cameron stopped there and searched Janice Mullen's face.

'Walter told you about Victor's affair with Heather didn't he?'

Janice nodded. 'He knew I would be unhinged, capable of aggression, probably expected me to give her a thumping, never expected ...' Their eyes met, a world of denial in hers. 'I didn't kill her Cameron.'

'I know Janice.'

Cameron looked imploringly at Victor, desperately wanting him to fill in the gaps. Hell fire, Victor had been close to Walter so surely he must have known what had been happening in the compound: perverse, disgusting, controlling. Things like that couldn't be suppressed and likely had been visible to Victor LaSalle, otherwise...

Janice, sensing Cameron's frustration said quietly, 'Victor is in the dark Cameron, like most honest folk in Winston. He's been misled, manipulated by Walter Slack his whole life.' She clasped her hands in prayer. 'Victor, listen to me please.' Janice hugged herself, rocked back and forth, speaking to the floor. 'Lonnie and Frank adore you because they respect you.' She looked directly at Victor. 'They knew you would protect them from Walter, if he made advances again...'

The realisation hit Victor hard. He shouted, 'BASTARD . . . THE BLOODY BASTARD.' He slid

304

down the wall to land on the dusty floor, hands either side of his head, squeezing hard, forcing the pain to go away.

Cameron wanted answers. Janice held the key which would finally unlock the mystery of Winston.

'How did you get here Janice?'

Janice puzzled, answered matter-of-factly, 'I followed the markers in the forest, the yellow dots painted on the trees.'

Cameron didn't understand. 'How did you know to follow the yellow dots Janice?'

'Harry came home one day with yellow paint on his clothes. When I asked him about the paint he told me he had been helping Walter paint his house. A lie; Walter's house is falling to bits. One day I tried to follow Harry into the forest. Then it dawned on me, there was yellow paint on your clothes, the day you were found.' Janice paused sensing they disbelieved her, quickly adding 'Oh come on, how else could I have found this place?'

Cameron remembered the yellow markers, their significance when he escaped from the compound leaving Brian behind to suffer at the hands of Lukas Meek. The guilt in the cabin was almost palpable.

Victor said sombrely, yet meaningfully, 'Janice did you take a pot shot at Walter?'

Janice laughed, tossed her head, black hair flying; white spittle formed at the edges of her mouth.

'I spotted the revolver on the ground, knew Cameron was struggling with that thing in the pit, thought I could shoot the damn thing. I was hiding in the trees, watching Walter take charge, ordering Harry about, shouting instructions. I just couldn't stand it any longer, the deceit; I knew they were up to their necks in perversion. Whilst they were distracted I snuck in to the compound, found the gun, aimed it at Walter, fired, hit

305

a tree.' She looked down at Brian's limp torso.

'Walter saw you lot coming along the path; he even smiled at me, the sick bastard. He made off into the forest with that leech Lukas Meek. I ordered Stark and Harry to strip; wanting them feeling as helpless as I have for the past twenty years, locked them in the cage, waited for you to arrive. Then I saw the cabin door open...'

Police sirens interrupted Cameron.

Cameron and Victor moved toward the door.

'I won't be long Janice.' Cameron cocked her a smile.

The dog stood and slowly moved towards Cameron, head bowed.

'Come on boy, let's get you some water.'

Janice warned: 'Take care Jason, Walter has a rifle.'

Chapter 49

Victor ran from the cabin. He fully anticipated seeing Christine Krill, his Chief Constable. She wasn't there; instead he saw three silver grey Range Rovers arrive, screeching into the compound, mud flying everywhere. Each vehicle carried four officers who disembarked like storm troopers, heavily armed with Heckler and Koch machine pistols.

They jumped from the vehicles, barked orders at Victor, insisting he kneel down, hands on his head. Victor ignored the instructions, went to greet them, holding his warrant card in the air, stating his name and rank. They ignored his pleas, pointed pistols at his head, forced him to the ground, cuffed him and ordered Cameron and the others to do the same.

After carefully studying his identification, a burly sergeant lifted Victor off the ground, asked him what the hell was going on. Victor did his best to explain.

'I thought the Chief Constable would be with you,' Victor said as the sergeant released the cuffs.

'The Chief has been ordered to take sick leave, sir. The Deputy Chief Constable is now in charge. Apparently the Chief has cracked up in a manner of speaking, as in nervous breakdown. She kept muttering about going to India, amongst other strange stuff.

'We were despatched by Inspector Sandy Dalton. He heard your earlier request for assistance, realised there'd been an almighty cock up and gave me the job of getting to you.'

Sandy Dalton, the only senior officer who firmly believed Walter Slack had been involved in the original abductions.

The sergeant removed his cap, scratched his head. 'To be honest boss it was a bugger of a place to find. We wouldn't have done it so quick if DI Mullen's wife hadn't telephoned us with the information about the yellow markers.'

In itself, the remark installed confidence in LaSalle. He would later thank her for having the forethought to raise the alarm.

Victor said, 'Sergeant . . .' He realised he didn't know the sergeant's name.

'Sergeant David Dalton boss, my Dad is Sandy Dalton.'

'Well Sergeant Dalton, please arrest Inspector Harry Mullen over there for the murder of his son Brian. The body is in the cabin. This compound is now a full blown crime scene and should be treated as such.' He gestured to the metal cages and pointed at the pile of clothes. 'Arrange for those two to be given paper boiler suits; have someone bag and tag their clothes. The other man in there is Ron Stark, also a serving police officer. Arrest him for assisting in the abduction of Brian Mullen twenty years ago.'

Cameron saw Dalton's mouth open and close like a goldfish. 'Bloody hell boss, what a mess.'

Victor wanted to laugh but couldn't. 'It doesn't get any better son. Inside with the body of Brian Mullen you'll find Mrs Janice Mullen, his mother. Please bear in mind she'll be heavily traumatised. She is to be taken into custody for the assault on Mrs Heather Moon six months ago at Gatekeeper Cottage.'

'What about those three under the tree?'

Victor stifled a laugh.

'The man struggling with your officers is Sergeant Trevor Mason of the Metropolitan police. The other two are with me.'

Victor mentally began to prepare a plan to capture Walter Slack, once a friend, mentor and confidant. Jesus, Walter had manipulated him from the beginning, the realisation hurting him immensely. He felt used, disgusted and disappointed. The man who controlled Winston, who'd invested in its future, now a known paedophile, a man who corrupted, poisoned and tainted everything he touched. Thank God he didn't touch me. Or did he? The very thought made Victor shiver.

'Sergeant Dalton, ask your dad to organise a comprehensive search of the forest for a suspect named Walter Slack, wanted for the abduction of Brian Mullen and of child molestation going back several years.'

Sergeant Dalton, well over the shock of mounting revelations, and about to comply, paused to answer his radio. 'It's my dad boss, he wants a word.'

Victor leaned into the radio. Sergeant Dalton said, 'Go ahead with your transmission Control, DCI LaSalle is listening.'

The voice of Sandy Dalton calm, deliberate said, 'I don't know whether this helps boss, but when we examined Slack's clothing twenty years ago, we found quarry dust. If you are a searching for Walter Slack he might be headed toward the quarry on the edge of Winston forest. Oh by the way, he owns the place.'

More secrets. Knowing Walter most of his life, Victor had no idea he owned the quarry.

Hang on a minute: the quarry, something about the quarry, when he was younger, much younger.

Sandy Dalton added, 'Air support cannot get to you boss because of the weather front, but there is a track leading to the north of the compound. The track is about ten miles long and won't take a vehicle. Sorry, but it's probably the only route he could have taken, bearing in mind I have officers controlling the only other two tracks leading back to Winston- unless of course he's gone through the forest and over the escarpment which I very much doubt. In any event I will despatch officers to the quarry by the main road but it will take at least forty five minutes.'

Victor knew they didn't have that long. Walter Slack had access to a private helicopter and pilot and what better place to land than a quarry bottom. Also, Walter knew every inch of the forest. Victor was convinced there would be a short cut. No, no, Victor knew about a short cut, didn't he? Dark thoughts began clouding his brain, his pulse raced.

Pressing Dalton's transmission button, his hand shaking, just a little, Victor said, 'Thanks Inspector- for everything.'

A moment later Sam appeared at the compound gate, shouting.

Cameron's heart missed a beat. In all the excitement he'd forgotten about his precious Samantha.

He ran toward her like a demented lover. She looked anxious, animated. 'What's wrong Sam?'

'I know where they went, Walter Slack and Lukas Meek, I saw them leave through these...' She waved the binoculars in the air, excited.

She fell quiet and frowned. 'Cameron, you seem . . . different.'

Cameron let go of her shoulders, looked into her eyes. Sam's face glowed; she smiled from ear to ear. Suddenly she grabbed his face with her hands, and planted a very long and extremely luscious kiss on his lips. This shocked him, though not for long and he hugged her like crazy.

Someone tapped his shoulder. It was Sergeant Dalton looking serious. 'I think you need to see this DS Cameron.'

Cameron holding Sam's hand, walked behind Dalton toward the tree in the centre of the compound. Lonnie and Frank, without their shackles stooped over Victor, sitting cross-legged looking confused.

Lonnie shrugged. Frank muttered an obscenity and

310

walked away from the group.

'You alright Victor?' asked a concerned Cameron.

Victor looked up, head lopsided, eyes narrow slits. Confused, he rocked back and forth on his haunches.

Cameron reacted to the bloodshot eyes, at the tears flowing down Vic tor's face.

In a tone an octave higher, Victor said, 'He did it to me Jason. In the quarry, many times, I remember it all, God help me. *And forgive me.*'

He stopped rocking, his look more than startled. 'Shit Jason, I changed my name, tried to alter my identity, brushed aside the trauma. So many years with the bastard.' He begged Cameron for an answer. 'How is that possible?'

Cameron heard a familiar voice. 'It's possible, yes, and probably the only way you could have realistically coped.' Kumar raised a finger, placed it across his lips. 'It's a hallmark symptom of post traumatic stress disorder, ergo the subject actively represses intrusive thoughts of some past traumatic event, until something causes the dam in the mind to breach and then *whoosh*, it all comes flooding back.'

'Kumar!' Cameron shouted.

'Before you over-react DS Cameron, I'm here because I've unfinished business, I've also been the subject of an almighty scam.'

Kumar pushed past Cameron and sat cross-legged in front of Victor.

'Let me help you Victor.'

Victor nodded without protest, acquiescing to the request of this strange man.

Kumar patted Victor on the head like a little boy. To Cameron he said: 'We must get Victor to hospital.'

'Just hold it one minute Kumar, I want some answers. How the hell did you get here?'

The question appeared to irritate Kumar.

311

'If it's of use to you, I followed Victor through the tunnel of course, how else? I hated every minute, bloody awful place full of spiders. I couldn't resist witnessing this little scenario unfolding.'

Kumar helped Victor to his feet, the great man resembling a deflated doll who found it difficult to stand.

Kumar said, 'We must accept that the concept of Walter's charade was one of revenge, further to create an opportunity to dispose of any witnesses to his years of abuse.' Kumar scanned the wire fence and shuddered at what had happened here. 'If we accept that everyone here is somehow connected to that scenario, then their disappearance would leave only one witness; i.e. Lukas Meek, correct?'

'Looking around, I agree with your assumption,' Cameron said.

Kumar, taking his time, began to walk Victor to the gate. Passing Cameron he said, 'DS Cameron, you are an excellent detective but sadly even you fail to see the obvious.'

'Please enlighten me, good doctor.' Cameron walked with them, as another police officer assisted Kumar with Victor.

Kumar had a slight reprieve. 'Get the DCI to a car, I'll join you directly.

'In the early days, DS Cameron, when the mines were the main source of employment here in Winston, Walter Slack followed in his father's footsteps and became a blaster and therefore would be very learned in the use of explosives. Everyone in here ...'

Cameron yelled: 'EVERYONE OUT OF THE COMPOUND ... NOW!'

Chapter 50

The explosion disintegrated the cabin in a ball of yellow-red flame. Deadly wooden needles sliced the air like Norman arrows.

By some miracle everyone managed to escape the compound except Janice Mullen. She refused to heed Cameron's warning and remained in the cabin with her son.

A couple of minutes later a second explosion blew the cages apart, white hot metal searing surrounding woodland, snapping off branches with frightening ease.

The killing pit erupted in a ball of flame, blitz-like, a ton or so of bricks and mortar flew upwards and outwards, to thump on the sandy mud.

All had dived for cover, and apart from a few cuts and grazes everyone stuck up a hand and indicated they were alright.

An eerie silence descended on the woodland; not a bird twittered nor leaf rustled, everything subservient to the unequivocal quiet.

The escapees, a few partially deafened by the shock waves, emerged from beneath the conifers, bewildered, and more than a little scared in respect of further booby traps. Some ten minutes on they began to venture back toward the compound, police officers taking charge, holding them back. The three police Range Rovers had broken windows, otherwise they were intact.

Sergeant Dalton said to Cameron, 'What now? Do we go after them, bearing in mind Slack may have set more explosive surprises?'

Victor suddenly appeared at Cameron's side, tugged his sleeve- held him in check.

'No hospital for me, Jason.' Victor looked resolute, straight backed.

'Sergeant Dalton, take some of your officers to the

quarry the long way round. Make sure Harry and Ron are booked in at the police station *first;* I want this affair to be evidenced and recorded properly, no slip-ups. Cameron and me will follow Walter Slack; I know a way through the escarpment.'

He hesitated, looked dotingly at Sam.

'Sam, please go with Lonnie and Frank to the police station and make written statements about everything that has occurred today.'

Victor searched for Trevor Mason, and found him under a tree smoking a fat cigar.

As Victor approached Trevor said, 'Always keep one handy in times of stress.' His silly American drawl irritated Victor.

'Trevor, ensure they all return to the station. Imperative all events are documented and I do mean accurately. Understood?'

Trevor nodded, slightly surprised as to this revived character standing before him.

Time now for Victor to exorcise his demons: only Cameron could help him.

Sam was about to argue when an adamant Victor interrupted. 'Sam, I will look after Jason, don't worry. I'm clear in my mind what has to be done and I need him with me.'

Frank shifted his feet. He was sulking. Victor decided he needed a little praise. 'Frank you've done a good job. Now look after Sam and Lonnie, *please.*'

Kumar appeared from the tree line, his face grimy with soil.

'Are you sure you're up to this challenge DCI LaSalle?'

Victor wrapped an arm around Kumar's shoulder, ushered him out of earshot of the others.

'Listen carefully Kumar, I require your expert opinion.'

314

Victor checked over his shoulder, ensuring no one could hear them, or notice how tight he bound his forearm around Kumar's neck.

'Kumar, if Walter has Parkinson's disease, is it possible for him to suddenly become extremely agile, almost completely mobile again?

Kumar, uncomfortable with Victor's arm around him shrugged off the big detective, and stepped away, unease noticeable. 'No it isn't possible. Such a disease is controllable with medication, but does not prevent it becoming increasingly worse. Walter is in the advanced stages of the affliction. Why do you ask?'

Victor fell silent, weighed his options, and kept an eye on Kumar. Did he trust him?

He had little choice. 'Doctor Kumar, you will say nothing about my breakdown. I'm fine and dandy now.' Victor gave Kumar a wide-eyed stare, deep brown eyes like lasers, penetrating and hypnotic.

Kumar nodded emphatically; he'd got the message.

Victor, his tone hushed but unequivocal, said: 'For my part I will say nothing about your identity. All I ask is for you to return to Winston and submit a written report about Christine Krill's involvement in this charade. Also you will agree that on the evidence seen over the last couple of days, Jason Cameron is certainly suffering from a personality disorder.'

Kumar said childlike, 'I liked it better when you called it a split personality. At least I knew you were taking me seriously.'

Victor felt like slapping the man in the face but Kumar, quick to notice the intent, and having felt LaSalle's power earlier, added quickly, 'Alright, alright, I'll do it, calm down.' The voice didn't disguise his fear.

Victor asked, 'Could Walter pretend he has Parkinson's disease?'

315

Kumar didn't reply immediately. He paced away and came back. 'If Walter has been pretending, then it must be in order to divert attention from something more sinister than Parkinson's disease. Chief Inspector, every illusion is designed to divert attention from something else.'

'Like early release from prison perhaps?'

Kumar looked at the floor. 'Perhaps'

'Don't look so worried, Doctor,' Victor said. He squeezed Kumar's face between his massive hands. 'Rest assured, I merely wish to put things right and that doesn't include exposing you, providing of course you keep your end of the bargain. Otherwise...?'

Had he been slapped in the face or had a bucket of cold water been thrown over him? Within the past half hour Victor LaSalle was in command again, his demeanour rapidly altering from a quivering jelly to the hard line, confident investigator of old.

Sam looked on while Victor had had his private chat with Kumar. She took the opportunity to usher Cameron to one side. 'Sit on that log for a moment; I need to talk to you.'

Cameron, wearing a silly grin, complied. Sam knelt in front of him. She removed her haversack, laid it on the ground, taking out several bandages, creams and a needle pack. She eased up his trouser leg and proceeded delicately to clean his injured foot with an antiseptic wipe, every so often glancing at his face. Cameron winced a few times, otherwise he remained silent. Gradually, after an injection, the pain eased.

Sam wanted to use the opportunity to make contact with Blake.

'Jason I want Blake to come out before you confront Walter Slack. You will need his skills in the next couple of hours. Can Blake hear me?'

316

A sudden glare in Cameron's eyes convinced her that Blake had heard her plea.

Sergeant Dalton walked forward holding a pair of boots.

'I think these are your size.' The sergeant nodded toward an officer in stocking feet. 'He'll manage until we get back to the station.'

Chapter 51

'What's the plan, Victor?'

Victor didn't have a plan. Walter would try and evade capture, of that he was certain. No way would that man wish to be incarcerated a second time. It left one viable option, flee the area and use his wealth to hide.

He was certain that Walter had manipulated him for some time. The abuse he'd suffered as a child remembered as weird games involving Walter and his friends. The quarry held greater significance in Victor's mind, a sense of loss of those formative years meaning he couldn't quite iron out the horrible images.

'We follow him to the quarry,' he said, 'through the escarpment using the access tunnel hidden over there.' Victor pointed to a rocky outcrop, its small gate barely visible through bramble and bracken. How he knew about the hidden gate was the real question. He just did.

'You OK, Victor?'

Victor was far from alright. He suffered with immense feelings of dread and anxiety from which he could find no escape. He was not like Jason Cameron, damaged goods, blighted by suppressed memories of maltreatment and cruelty. Victor's one desire was to rid the world of the sick shit who he had come to trust, a man who betrayed his own soul for the sake of wanton desires.

How could he deal with it? Arrest Walter Slack and comply with his lawful duty as a serving police officer . . . or kill the bastard?

Such were Victor's thoughts; what he said was: 'I'm fine Jason. Let's go and find Walter Slack and put an end to his dreadful legacy.'

They said their goodbyes without fuss; Victor reiterated his instructions to Sergeant Dalton. He then

318

shook the officer's hand.

'My father has instructed me to tell you he will give you forty five minutes and then the troops will arrive at the quarry.' Dalton saluted. He'd no need to do so, it was an antiquated tradition; he simply felt he wanted to.

'Thank you Sergeant Dalton.'

Sam stood motionless, fear etched on her face like a badge.

Cameron gave her a peck on the cheek. She grabbed him, pulled him close, and for the second time today kissed him full on the lips. 'Be careful, be safe,' she said, glancing awkwardly at Victor.

Victor and Cameron headed for the gate. 'Wait a second, Jason.' Victor trotted back to Sam.

'Did you bring tranquilliser darts?'

Without speaking she fumbled in her haversack and fetched out a couple neatly packed in plastic. Like a hypodermic needle, its tiny red flight was the only indication of its use.

She told him, 'It needs to be delivered with some force to activate the syringe.'

A grateful Victor said, 'Remember my plan to get rid of Blake.'

Victor winked and joined Cameron, carefully concealing the syringes in his pocket.

They reached the escarpment in five minutes, the track from here straightforward.

When they arrived at the gate it opened easily enough despite rusted metal bars. The tunnel itself was much the same as the one running through the escarpment from Haughton village except it lacked the lights on its walls. Victor's torch was a bonus. The intrepid duo set off in silence each with personal thoughts concerning any outcome.

Five minutes later Victor glanced at Cameron. He said, 'Have I been blind Jason?'

'I don't believe so, not entirely.'

'You and Blake, you're in this together. There's no light between you both. You're one and the same person.' The statement held clout, proving it a final realisation on Victor's part.

The tunnel remained silent apart from their heavy breathing. Cameron, not about to get involved in what might turn out an overblown conversation said: 'We have more pressing things to worry about Victor.'

Victor unabated said, 'I want honesty. You and Blake cooked this thing up between you. It is revenge plain and simple.'

It was Blake not Jason Cameron who shone his torch onto Victor's face. 'We are symbiotic and therefore have no need of a Gatekeeper. We are twins in the same body.' Blake paused, his hand on Victor's shoulder. 'You still harbour immense disbelief of my existence, right Victor?'

Victor grimaced. Or was it a grin? 'Doesn't everyone?'

Blake touched a temple with his free hand. 'In here I exist, make decisions, and alter my destiny.'

Victor quoted: "I think therefore I am?"

'Exactly Victor. Exactly.' Blake smiled. 'Let me just say this dish is definitely being served cold. Now shall we continue?'

Victor didn't know whether Blake's disclosures were helpful or not. He decided it wasn't the time for analysis.

It took another twenty minutes to reach the quarry, abandoned apart from a ramshackle shed and an ancient bulldozer sitting near the entrance like a rusting dinosaur.

Not massive, perhaps two hundred yards by ninety

yards, a fringe of grass tumbling over its edges, the place was flat on one side, towering to around sixty feet on the other three. Remnants of large rocks from its once thriving sandstone industry lay scattered about its bottom giving an impression of a lunar landscape.

'He may well have flown the coup,' offered Blake.

'I don't think so, unless he planned the escape meticulously. I'm guessing what happened today hasn't gone according to plan.'

More to it, thought Victor. Something niggled: a strange irritating doubt, a warning he'd missed a vital segment of information.

'He's still here, I sense it.'

Victor kept his eyes peeled; scanning the quarry, looking for anything unusual which might indicate Slack was still in the vicinity.

Victor felt a strand of information unravelling in his head.

'Before your posting to Winston . . . I'm speaking to Cameron. Did Kumar hypnotise you or administer any medication?'

Blake, still there, said nonchalantly 'Yes I believe he did. Before that Cameron was unaware of the full ramifications of returning here.'

Victor tugged at the thread of memory, elusive for so long. It had begun to unravel the moment he'd spoken to Kumar about the operation to identify the original abductor twenty years ago, also to identify Heather's murderer.

Discussing Jason Cameron and his apparent failure to recollect his time when occupied by Blake, they'd been standing in the corridor at Hendon detective training school awaiting Christine Krill's arrival for the final briefing before they embarked on the operation. Victor had been curious about hypnosis, asking questions, passing the time until Christine arrived, late as usual.

'Will the hypnosis manage to keep Blake in the background until we need him to come out?' Victor had asked.

Kumar placed his briefcase on the corridor floor, folded his arms, chin on chest thinking about it. He eventually said, 'Hypnosis in itself is not a panacea for Cameron's condition. It will only create a state of calm and suggestibility allowing me to implant certain instructions into his subconscious, which will hopefully blank out Blake until we need him. It will be the emotional triggers we choose which will then successfully tease Blake into the open.'

Victor asked: 'Can hypnosis be used for anything else, say in the treatment of extreme trauma, for example on abused kids?'

Kumar answered quickly, evidently an expert in his field, 'Hypnosis can sometimes produce a deep-rooted contact with one's emotional life resulting in some insight into buried fears and conflict. This, if faced head on by an individual could result in some of easing of the initial trauma.' Kumar had grinned. 'Rather like looking into the mouth of the dragon.'

'Like that eh? Tell me, has it been used to conceal unsavoury or disturbing memories, like for example war veterans suffering from post traumatic stress?'

'On occasions yes, it has been utilised to ease such burdens.'

'Can anyone develop the skills to hypnotise?'

Kumar chuckled. 'DCI LaSalle, the answer is yes. There are many courses available out there which can supply the fundamentals. However, my bear like friend, you do not seem the type to be the perfect operator of such skills.'

Could it be that simple?

'Blake, I'm of the opinion Walter has been using hypnosis on his victims, effectively burying the memory.' Reflecting he added almost *sotto voce*, 'including his exploitation of me, Lonnie and Lord only knows how many more.'

Before Blake could reply, Victor noticed movement behind the shed. He put a finger to his lips.

Chapter 52

Meek strode out from behind the shed carrying a huge, ugly looking knife. He waved it provocatively in their direction.

Victor examined the terrain, saw the flash of sunlight glinting upon metal and realised Walter Slack had been waiting and watching for their arrival.

Slack emerged from a grassy knoll about twenty feet up the far side of the quarry, a long rifle with telescopic sights aimed right at them.

Victor sighed. 'I think he wants us to go down to the quarry bottom. If we don't I fear he may have the drop on us, that rifle is more than capable of hitting both of us.'

Blake agreed.

Together they scrambled down the lowest side of the quarry and stopped some little distance from Meek, who smiled malevolently.

'Welcome boys, glad you could join us.'

Victor wanted nothing better than to tackle the brute head on; confident he could avoid the knife. Meek looked drunk, his eyes glazed as he rocked slightly from side to side. Victor decided he'd wait before trying anything until Walter moved closer and afford him a better opportunity of disarming him.

Blake shook his head imperceptibly and whispered, 'Wait, bide your time, it will happen.'

Walter Slack ambled confidently down the rocky path snaking the quarry, the rifle hanging loosely at his side.

Walter stopped alongside Meek, the rifle now carried at waist height, its deadly barrel pointing at Victor's midriff. 'It could have been so different Victor.'

Victor didn't try to hide the hatred, words tumbling

324

in short rasps, his mouth dry; tongue like rubber.

'You have a lot to answer for Walter. You know it won't end by killing us. The police are on the way; there's no way back for you except total and utter recrimination for your sins.'

Walter laughed. 'You sound like a preacher, Victor.'

Meek said, 'Let me have Cameron, I have a score to settle.'

Blake arched his back, cracked his neck and said, 'I should have killed you a long time ago Lukas. You're simply the lowest form of pond life I have ever encountered.' Blake then whistled, nonchalantly.

Blake's every syllable accentuated his tone confident, cool almost.

He couldn't help himself, Victor felt relieved Blake was alongside him.

Victor said, 'How do you propose to escape Walter? They will hunt you down and send you back to prison where you belong . . . with all the other filthy perverts.'

Walter scowled. 'Describing what I enjoy as a perversion is one dimensional.' Sensing Victor's tension, Walter took a couple of steps backwards, still aiming the rifle.

Victor said, 'How would you describe it Walter, fun, enjoyment?'

Walter sounded angry, reproachful. 'Don't you get it Victor, you're one of us; it's inside you like a beast waiting to come out. Stop fighting it; let it into the light where it belongs.'

Victor swallowed, forcing bile back down his gullet.

'It took me a while to figure you out,' Victor said, 'this place, the days I spent here as a boy. Hypnosis is a powerful tool in the wrong hands; Lonnie and Frank's mistreatment by you and your sick friends, satisfying your whims, all of it here at the quarry, away from prying eyes. The police didn't find Brian Mullen in the

325

forest because he wasn't there. You brought him here after the fights, locked him up in that cabin. Cameron escaped, managed to find his way through the tunnel back to the compound. You quickly realised he couldn't remember anything and brought him to the police. You weren't trying to blow us up back there, you were destroying evidence.'

Blake suddenly spoke. 'Are you the Gatekeeper Mr Slack?'

Walter regarded Blake with suspicion.

'You're well informed DS Cameron,' he said. 'During the days of the mines, until they closed in fifty-three, dogfights were a distraction for the miners. After a while the fights began attracting outsiders from the towns with money to gamble; lots of money. The miners decided to form a syndicate, to control it, regulate it. Each fight took place inside a metal cage where the dogs could be controlled and watched in safety. One very powerful man organised the bets, decided which dog would be entered into the cage and at what price. The role evolved, the power became more profound. That man was known as the Gatekeeper, a privilege that has been passed down from generation to generation. My grandfather was a gatekeeper, my father also. I simply modernised the concept.'

Blake said, 'You owned Gatekeeper Cottage didn't you Mr Slack?'

Slack replied, smiling, 'It had been in my family for generations until Nigel Moon offered me an extraordinary amount to rent it, all to impress your mother. What could I do but accept on the understanding we would be allowed to utilise the gateway through to the compound. I have to say Moon's lust for the dogfights was insatiable.' Slack kicked at the sandy brown mud with his boots. 'When I

326

was arrested I was forced to sell the cottage to him for a fraction of its true value to pay for my defence. Upon my release I explained to your mother how I wanted it back, offered her a fair price. She of course refused to sell.'

'And so you had her killed,' Blake said.

Walter replied quickly, 'you know it didn't happen that way, you were there watching it unfold; you saw Janice Mullen hit your mother with the hammer, witnessed Bull finish her off. You could have stepped in at any time and you chose to let it happen didn't you DS Cameron?'

Blake said in a tight, controlled manner: 'I am not Cameron you fucking moron.'

With lightening speed, Blake shoved Victor sideways. With his other hand he whipped a small bladed knife from his pocket. In one swift movement Blake slashed Meek's throat, the blood gushing out in torrents, splattering on the ground. Meek clutched his gullet, face a white mask of pain and disbelief. In the same instant, the rifle went off with a loud crack, the bullet somehow missing both Blake and Victor, the stink of cordite stinging Victor's nose.

Victor scrambled to his feet. Realising Walter was about to fire again.

Victor fumbled for the dart in his pocket. Clutching it tightly and with all his might he launched himself at Walter and stabbed the dart into Walter's neck, easier to do than risk clothing diverting it.

Walter dropped the rifle. He tried to grab the dart. Too late, by then a massive hit of tranquilliser flowed towards his heart. Walter fell forward, dead before he hit the ground.

Chapter 53

With two men lying dead at his feet, Victor switched off, stuttered, blanked out. The turmoil inside created an emotional dam, threatening to rupture at any minute. Victor had killed a man, albeit in self-defence.

And then Victor erupted. Vomit cascaded into the mud, retch after retch until his stomach was purged. He wiped his mouth on his sleeve, glanced at his cohort who looked on, now wearing his customary sunglasses, his transformation into Blake full and complete. A wry smile that stated *job done*, slashed his face.

Blake said, 'The dart? It was meant for me, yes?'

Victor nodded, expecting Blake to come at him. He had no will to fight, his energies drained. He managed to say, 'I have another, but I won't be using it. I never intended to kill Jason, just get rid of you.' He stared at Blake. 'What happens next?'

Blake wiped the knife on his thigh, and carefully closed the blade.

'That depends, Victor.' Blake made a clicking sound with his tongue. 'If I go back they will arrest me, probably commit me to some institution or other.' Fierce, threatening eyes bored at Victor, *into* Victor. A statement followed, it didn't require underlining. Blake said: 'I will not be incarcerated. *Ever.*'

'I cannot pretend I understand any of this,' Victor said meekly. He needed time to think. What came next tumbled out. 'Why you didn't save Heather Moon I will never know. You were there in the forest, watching like a voyeur?'

Blake, hands in pockets, a statement he posed no threat, told Victor: 'In simple terms my brain, and therefore Cameron's brain, went into overload. I've lived with the guilt since. Believe me, I really have'

Blake removed his shades and shot Victor a fiery

glance.

Victor didn't believe that for one minute. Guilt was a concept alien to Blake.

Victor climbed to his feet, his heart heavy.

Blake took a defensive stance, voice determined, filled with menace. 'Be careful Victor, I have no specific desire to harm you.'

Victor freely admitted he was no match for Blake. The man was a killing machine, devoid of conscience.

'Then I say again, what happens now Blake?'

Blake back paced slowly, his eyes on Victor.

'Cameron has disappeared into my subconscious. For now I am out of my cage and enjoying the freedom.' Blake raised a hand, waved slightly. 'Do not search for me Victor; otherwise you will be placing Samantha in immense danger. Remember, I can *pretend* to be Cameron.'

Victor said, unconvincingly. 'I might still come after you. I have my reputation to think of. Remember this, I am a police officer.'

'If you did come after me it would be extremely hazardous to your health. You might be a stubborn ox Victor, but you're no fool.'

Blake continued to edge closer to the tree line at the quarry's entrance. And then, as if remembering something important, Blake stopped in his tracks.

'On second thoughts, I know you Victor; you will not rest until you rid the world of me.' Again his eyes probed Victor. 'I am right? Hmm, I am. I see it in your eyes.'

Purposefully Blake began walking toward Victor, the knife clearly visible in his hand.

Victor's heart sank like a stone. He knew Blake would get the better of him and he didn't want to die, not today, not in this awful place.

'Move any closer weirdo, and I'll drop you like a

deer.'

Victor looked to his left. Lonnie stood on a large boulder, a very mean looking crossbow held steadily in his hand, and levelled directly at Blake.

Blake stopped, began to laugh. 'Hello faithful hound, nice of you to join us.'

Frank appeared from the direction of the tunnel, carrying a similar weapon.

'We were always rubbish at obeying orders Vic,' Frank said, smiling.

Victor couldn't believe it. He wanted to hug them both but realised the danger wasn't over.

Blake said, 'Whatever happened to brotherly love, Frank?'

Without hesitation Frank shouted, 'I'm Jason's brother not yours, weirdo.'

Victor said to Lonnie, 'Keep that thing aimed at his heart Lonnie.'

Lonnie nodded his head, grinning, proud.

Blake said, 'Let me go Victor. Blame this whole thing on me, they'll believe you, after all I'm the psycho.'

'I'm going to let you go Blake, on one condition.'

Blake said, 'Pray tell me?'

'I want to speak with Jason.'

Blake crouched down on his haunches, looked up at Victor and grinned. His head fell forward and remained in that position for perhaps a minute. No one spoke, they simply watched, mouths agape.

Slowly, Cameron lifted his head.

'I wouldn't allow Blake to hurt you, Victor.'

Is it really you?

Victor said, 'It's been a difficult time for me Jason. This charade has become clouded with deceit, buried in complications. Before you go, because I know you must, answer me this.' He waited, eying up the man before him. 'Who has been controlling this game of cat and mouse? Kumar, Walter, Christine or..?

Cameron grinned. 'I am not as good an actor as you, Victor. For our game to succeed it was necessary for me to be kept in the dark.' Cameron saw the look on Victor's face. 'Ignore Blake's macho bullshit about dominance and being caged. He likes to be dramatic.'

Victor cracked a wan smile.

Cameron carried on. 'Walter truly believed by bringing me back he would be in a position to exact revenge with the added plus of finding out exactly what I remembered. He used Doctor Kumar to assist in the deception. Christine was his legitimisation. Unfortunately, I don't think Walter quite grasped the concept of Blake.'

Victor nodded, although still not convinced.

Cameron said, sincerely, 'Victor my friend, my demons have been destroyed, a murder solved and Christine has blown her chances of furthering her career. And no doubt you will be promoted. All in all it worked a treat.'

Victor felt used. He remained quiet.

'I must go now. Blake and me have plans and they don't include being sectioned in a psychiatric hospital. Tell Samantha it wouldn't work out for us, not at this moment in time. Perhaps in the future; let her know I love her and if fate plays her hand we will be together, sooner than she thinks.'

Cameron's features hardened. He had vanished into his own subconscious.

Blake theatrically folded the knife, slipped it into his pocket.

'I must admit Victor, you certainly do surprise me with your deviation from standard police procedures; perhaps we could work together in the future. You never know, one day you may need my unconventional

331

skills?'

Victor spat on the ground. 'I doubt that very much.'

The barking took them by surprise. Blake raised a hand in the air and the beast from the compound quietened and lay down near the tunnel entrance.

'My faithful hound has arrived,' said Blake, a sardonic grin slashing his face.

Chuckling, Blake ambled casually toward the forest, making a gun of his hand, pointing it momentarily at Frank then at Lonnie. In a flash, he disappeared, the dog following close behind.

Lonnie inspected the bodies. 'Sweet Jesus, Uncle Vic, what a bloody mess.'

Victor couldn't help it, he sniggered.

'Lonnie, you are indeed the master of the understatement.'

Victor contemplated his next move, knowing his actions in the quarry could finish his career. Sitting down on a large boulder, he looked at Lonnie and Frank, both waiting patiently for him to take charge, make a decision. But right then Victor wanted to cry, not because he'd killed another human being; more than that Victor felt humiliated.

Fine, he'd become a great man in the eyes of Lonnie and Frank and now he couldn't muster a single positive thought. Most certainly he had become a victim, just like Lonnie and Frank.

Frank placed a hand on Victor's shoulder, patted it gently, that broad shoulder not now broad enough to carry the weight of being victimised. Sure there's been closure, of a sort, but hey, what of the life that still remained, haunting him?

'The cops will be here soon Vic.'

Suddenly, Lonnie clapped his hands together like he'd discovered gold. 'Find a shovel Frank,' he shouted. 'Uncle Vic get off your lazy arse, we've work to do.'

Victor nonplussed, eyes moist with the onset of tears, said quietly, 'What have you got in mind Lonnie?'

An excited Lonnie began dragging Lukas Meek by his hair toward a sandy hillock.

'You get Granddad Frank. The old bastard is dead, he can't hurt you anymore. Come on, jump to it before the cops come.'

Victor stood, pushed Frank away from Walter Slack. 'Leave him be Frank, Lonnie have you gone nuts?'

Lonnie shouted, 'Think about it, Uncle Vic. No one knows what happened here except us and that crazed loony Cameron. For all any of them know we never got here in time, these two have gone to ground, disappeared, vanished.'

Victor stood aghast. 'Are you crazy Lonnie? They'll organise a search and this is the first place they'll look.'

'Not straight away, Uncle Vic. Bury them in shallow graves for now and we'll move the bodies later.' Lonnie shook his head in disappointment. 'Uncle Vic, think about it. Who'll be in charge of the search?'

Victor looked at Lonnie, marvelling at the boy's sudden attempt at logic. 'Me. I'll be in charge.'

Lonnie beamed, 'Exactly, Detective Chief Inspector-bloody- LaSalle.'

Edinburgh, Two years later

The conference had been sufficiently informative if not a little boring. Sam didn't care; she loved Edinburgh, adored the place, and dearly wished she could stay a little longer.

The taxi stopped at a set of traffic lights not far from Waverley station just beyond Rose Street. Absently Sam gazed out of the window, admiring the fancy shops and the variety of pubs and restaurants.

The young man with the very short blonde hair glanced at her for half a second before going back to reading his newspaper, relaxing in the sunshine, enjoying a late afternoon latte.

Sam held her breath. *CAMERON!* It's you in the flesh.

She recognised him immediately. He looked older, although it was definitely Jason Cameron. The traffic lights changed and the taxi set off. She screamed for the driver to stop; he did abruptly and pulled over, horns blaring from angry motorists. Sam fumbled in her purse, handed over a twenty-pound note through the plastic divider and scrambled from the cab, dragging her case with her.

Dodging the traffic she headed for the small café.

Cameron had gone, the only evidence of his presence being the empty coffee cup and a five-pound note slipped under the saucer.

An attractive Asian waitress began cleaning the table, pocketing the five found note.

'The young man reading the newspaper, sitting here, do you know him?'

Samantha realised she sounded distressed, urgent.

The young waitress twitched a smile.

'Yes, kind of, he comes here once or twice a week.'

Samantha asked, 'Do you know where he lives?'

'Not really, he doesn't say much.'

Samantha calmed her breathing, tried to sound rational.

'He reminded me of a friend, someone I met couple of years ago. You wouldn't know his name would you?'

The waitress picked up the coffee cup, gave the table a wipe.

Suddenly she stopped wiping, folded her arms and said, 'Are you Samantha?'

Flabbergasted, Samantha nodded her head.

'Wait here a minute.'

Samantha sat down, dumfounded, yet exhilarated.

'The young man said I was to give you this if you ever enquired about him.'

The waitress gave Sam an embossed business card. It read "Cameron Blake- Private Investigator"

The moniker offered hope.

Epilogue

The Brown Trout Public House, Caithness, Scotland.
One year later.

At seven thirty the door of the bar opened. A nondescript couple entered the pub; that is nondescript, except for a very large woolly dog, which the man held in check with a chunky metal chain. Victor immediately recognised the brute.

The man's partner, a petite woman in a loose fitting summer dress, wore her hair short in a bob. Upon seeing Victor, she smiled broadly.

Her blonde companion looked relaxed, at ease. He'd aged a little, the lines around his eyes the result of over-frowning. They looked like tourists.

Victor stood up, held out his hand. Samantha took it gently, leaned in close and pecked Victor affectionately on his cheek. 'Congratulations on your promotion Detective Superintendent,' Sam said.

Victor smiled warmly.

Cameron shuffled his position, leaned around his wife. He gave Victor a firm handshake.

Cameron took a couple of steps backwards. He released the dog from its shackle and clicked his fingers. Laying its massive head on its lion like paws, the brute flopped down with a groan.

Victor, extremely uncomfortable, ignored the beast. He waved for the couple to join him at the small wooden table. They were the only customers. The trout fishing season didn't begin for a couple of weeks. Until then the Caithness pub trade would rely on locals and the odd tourist.

'What can I get you to drink?'

Sam blushed awkwardly. Cameron said 'A pint of beer for me and just a soft drink for Sam.' Cameron gave his wife a wink. 'She's expecting twins.'

Victor congratulated them both, went to the bar and came back with the drinks. He sipped his single malt, enjoying its warmth, clasping the chunky glass in both hands, using it as a comforter, the spectre of Blake uppermost in his thoughts.

Victor eventually broke the awkward silence. 'Why choose to live here, of all places?'

Glancing reassuringly at Sam, Cameron answered.

'It's difficult to trust people Victor, after what happened. It's remote here. Only single-track roads and the farmers are grateful for Sam's expertise. Generally people don't ask questions, including the police.'

Victor blushed.

'I kept my word Jason. I came alone.'

Cameron grimaced. 'I believe there are no police around Victor. Just don't expect me to believe Lonnie and Frank aren't here, somewhere.'

Victor smiled. 'Parked up about a mile away.'

Cameron smirked. He hadn't underestimated Victor.

'Why are you here Victor?'

Victor didn't know where to begin. It felt very awkward, bearing in mind their last encounter.

'When Frank got your letter,' he said eventually. 'He made me swear an oath never to reveal your whereabouts.'

Cameron waved a consolatory hand, 'Tell Frank not to worry, I'm cool with it. I trust him, he's my brother.'

Victor adjusted his seat, leaned in conspiratorially.

'I came because I need Blake's help.'

Cameron cracked his neck, widened his eyes.

Blake said, 'Victor it would be my pleasure.'

The End

338

Lightning Source UK Ltd.
Milton Keynes UK
UKOW050451130712

195921UK00001B/1/P